Anotech Chronicles Book 2:
Reshner's Royal Threat

By Julie C. Gilbert

Aletheia Pyralis Publishers

For information about special discounts available for bulk purchases, sales promotions, fund-raising and educational needs, please email: devyaschildren@gmail.com

http://www.juliecgilbert.com/
https://sites.google.com/view/juliecgilbert-writer/

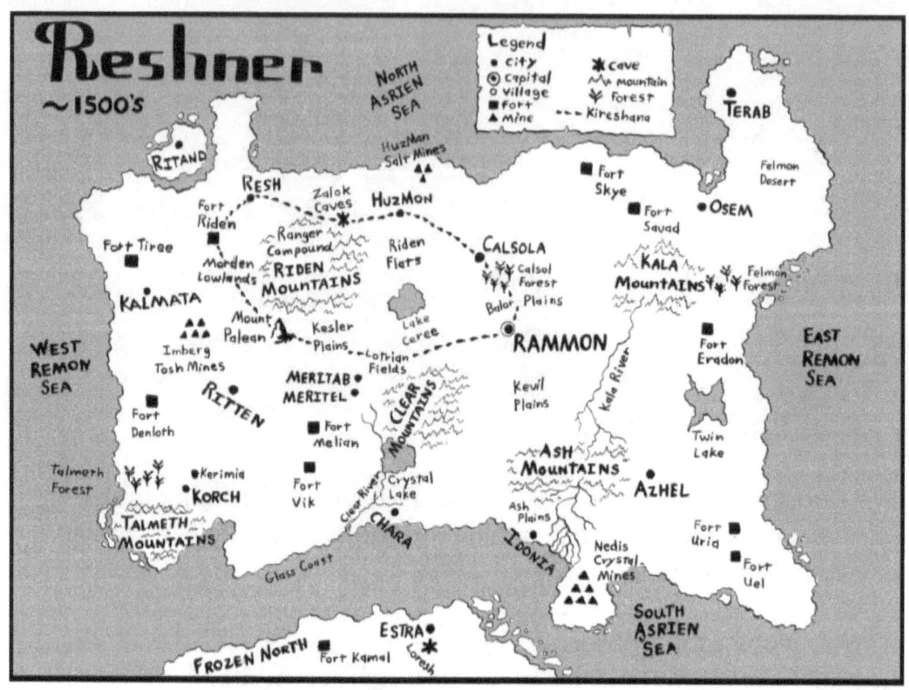

Visit: **http://www.juliecgilbert.com/**
to request a full-sized map.

Acknowledgements:

Special thanks to:
Lucas Dalenberg, Chewie, J. LaRocco, Timothy Sparvero,
and Alan Pinck for helpful suggestions

Note: this book may be read on its own,
but it might help to start with *Reshner's Royal Ranger.*

Table of Contents:

Cast of Characters:

(Spoiler Alert)

Royals:
King Terosh Minstel – ruler of Reshner
Queen Reia Minstel – wife of Terosh, former Ranger
Lady Mavis Altran – Terosh's aunt, mother of Lord Kezem
Lord Eldon Altran – Governor Lord of Idonia, eldest son of Mavis
Lord Mitrek Altran – Governor Judge of Idonia, second son of Mavis
Lord Kezem Altran – Governor General of Idonia, third son of Mavis
King Padric Creston – ruler of Gardan, Terosh's grandfather

Rangers:
Kiata Antellio Wellum – Nareth Talis Ranger, Reia's sister
Todd Wellum – Nareth Talis Ranger, Kiata's husband
Master Niklos McGreven – substitute father for Reia and Kiata

Restler-Tarpon Alliance:
Vera Tarpon – mother of Brook, Alden, and Merisia
Tyko Tarpon – father of Brook, Alden, and Merisia
Brook Tarpon – eldest son of Vera and Tyko, Nera's husband
Alden Tarpon – son of Vera and Tyko
Nera Tarpon – wife of Brook, recruited by Lady Mavis
Gareth Restler – eldest son of Arista, Merisia's husband
Ariman Keldor – RT agent, Taly's father

Other:
Ectosh Laocer – Royal Guard captain
Merisia Restler – daughter of Vera and Tyko, Gareth's wife
Niktrod Keldor – Taly's grandfather, assassinated the former queen
Talyon Keldor – former RT agent, Ariman's son, Merisia's friend

Villains:
Kolknir – Kezem's agent, mercenary, former Ranger master
Lucas Telon – Ranger master, Kezem's undercover RT alliance agent
Maledek – alias for Lord Kezem

Chapter 1:
Enemies and Emissaries

Pirua (September) 20, 1538
Maledek's Private Retreat, City of Idonia

Lord Kezem Altran adjusted the voice modulator to the settings for Maledek, a personal favorite he'd not had the pleasure of using for a week. At the same time, he eyed the young man featured in the hologram display. Gareth Restler looked distinctly uncomfortable. Kezem already knew the essence of the man's request, but he waited for him to articulate it.

As Maledek, Kezem had dealt with the Restler-Tarpon Alliance many times, but this was his first direct contact with the Restler heir. Gareth's light brown hair stuck out at several odd angles, telling Kezem he had probably agonized about making this call. His brown eyes flickered between anger and worry, but his posture remained stiff.

Gareth tipped his head down in a bow.

"Greetings, Lord Maledek, it is a pleasure to finally speak with you. Your support of our great alliance is much appreciated."

"I trust you have more than greetings and thanks in mind," said Kezem. He left out the obvious part that contact of any sort was risky. Kezem had the latest in anti-spying equipment, but he doubted that would stand up to the technology his mother could access. Thankfully, her sources usually outstripped anything the Royal House could come up with as well, but Kezem liked to avoid unnecessary risks.

"I do, my Lord. My wife has gone … missing," Gareth said.

"I assume you seek my aid?" Kezem's inflection inserted the hint of a question into the words.

"Yes, my Lord." Gareth said it stiffly but a slight shift in his jaw betrayed his nervous energy.

"It has been more than a month since your wife left, has it not?" asked Lord Kezem.

Gareth flinched as Kezem expected he would.

"Why do you care now?" Kezem wondered, enjoying the rich tone the voice modulator added to his Maledek voice.

"I have always cared!" Gareth declared. "The Alliance has done everything it can to track them to no avail, but I cannot accept that. I'm told you have resources beyond us and an interest in keeping this alliance viable."

"What makes you believe the Alliance itself is threatened?" asked Kezem.

"This … misunderstanding has strained the trust holding the Alliance together," Gareth admitted. "I have word that measures will be taken against a similar situation happening within the new Tarpon household. I do not wish it to come to that."

Kezem took a moment to absorb Gareth's concern before voicing his next question.

"Has Lady Nera Tarpon indicated she might leave as well?"

"No, but that does not mean the Tarpons believe my sister is loyal to the Alliance," Gareth answered. "I fear they may do something ill-advised. Getting Merisia back is the easiest solution to setting everybody's mind at ease."

"Assuming my contacts can locate your wife, what will you do?" Kezem asked, genuinely curious.

"I do not know, my Lord. I suppose that will be decided once my wife is recovered and the full story comes out," said Gareth. "The best scenario would hold that the boy forced her to leave with him, we catch them, he dies, and my wife sees the error of her ways."

Kezem laughed. "Your wife left of her own accord, Master Restler, all the evidence points to such."

"How do you know?" Gareth challenged.

"I like to protect my interests, so I keep agents in every city, including Meritab. That's why the Alliance came to me in the first place, and as you said, it is why you come to me now."

"I see," said Gareth. His tone turned sour. "Will you help?"

Kezem let a few moments pass to see how the young man would react. Gaining nothing more than a solemn stare, he finally said, "I will do what I can to see that the Alliance remains strong. To that end, you have my aid in the search for your wife, Master Restler."

"Thank you, my Lord," said Gareth with another stiff bow. His hologram disappeared abruptly.

Lord Kezem turned off the hologram display and went to his desk to read a few reports from his agents.

***

Pirua (September) 20, 1538
Same Day
The Lady's Estate, Kala Mountains

Lady Mavis Altran replayed the conversation between Gareth Restler and her youngest son.

Kezem received many requests every day, and she certainly didn't have time to review every one of them. Still, she made a point to at least know each person with whom her three sons spoke each day. Kezem happened to speak with more interesting people than Eldon or Mitrek. His ambition had always impressed her.

This particular conversation told her nothing new except that Kezem failed to identify the implications of Merisia Restler's defection. Lady Mavis paused to ponder whether Merisia's actions could be qualified as a true defection. The word usually implied a change of allegiance to something else. Mavis decided it qualified anyway, even though Lady Merisia's allegiance seemed only to herself.

Next, Mavis debated with herself over whether she should help her son, or not. Her agents already knew where to look for Lady Merisia and her young escort, Talyon Keldor. She also knew whom to send after them: Talyon's father. Ariman Keldor was the only one who would hope both Merisia and Talyon lived through the encounter. She didn't know why she felt compelled to save Talyon, but her instincts said he was worth saving. He possessed the sort of incorruptible good nature that would doom him in time, but that also made him easy to manipulate. The more she thought about it, the more certain Mavis grew in her conviction that Talyon could be used against her nephew.

Terosh was regent now, but he would soon be Reshner's official king. Mavis indulged in a sweet, heady rush of anger that made her feel more alive. Terosh and his new wife both possessed a delightfully predictable good nature, same as Talyon Keldor, but Terosh also had a healthy fear of Mavis, one that made him almost untouchable.

If reports could be trusted—and she paid dearly to ensure such—Talyon had once been saved by a Ranger. Thus, the Ranger,

Kiata Antellio Wellum, was connected to Talyon. However vague that connection might be, it could probably be exploited at some point. By extension, Ranger Wellum reportedly doted on her younger sister, the only Ranger in decades to break the code prohibiting marriage into the royal family. Lack of shared blood between the sisters meant nothing in this case. Having lost their parents early in life, they'd grown very close indeed.

Part of Mavis admitted to stretching things, but many a fine plan had started as series of convoluted connections. Her nephew had already proven he would take stupid risks for someone he loved. By all accounts, his wife would do the same.

Concluding Talyon Keldor's life hinged on helping her son see things her way, Lady Mavis weighed various options of how to best make contact. Nearly any contact would remind Kezem that her resources were far superior to his. She did not wish to needlessly provoke him, as he was likely her best chance to gain the throne.

Eldon, her eldest son, also had the hardest and hottest head. Mitrek, her middle and most moderate son, lacked ambition. Both fell far short of Kezem's discipline and deviousness.

Mavis had been officially stripped of her royal rank by her own dearly-dead father, Salen Minstel, but he had loved her sons almost as much as his other grandsons. Mavis and her recently deceased little brother, Teorn, had never been terribly close, but he had never felt threatened enough to remove her sons from the royal records. Thus, they maintained their positions in the succession. Kezem could be king. It would be a long and not entirely pleasant road, but it was possible.

After following her thoughts down familiar, fruitless paths, Lady Mavis settled on the direct approach and activated her hologram projector. The machine blinked four times as it tried to establish the connection. Finally, Kezem's unsmiling face materialized. She had the projector set so that only his face and shoulders showed. Over the years, she had learned that facial expressions divulged the most information. She recorded calls for later reference if she needed to see the whole speaker, but the face usually told her enough.

"What do you want?" Kezem asked. His tone lacked strong emotion. He spoke unhurriedly, but his dark blue eyes had telltale yellow flecks indicating irritation.

Mavis silently thanked her long-dead husband for his Bornovan genes that made their sons so easy to read. She chuckled, as her mind flashed back to her brother asking that very question. It had ultimately led to his downfall. She fervently hoped the same would not hold true for her son.

"It is customary to exchange pleasantries before conducting business," she said.

"As you wish," Kezem said with a nod. "How are you, Mother?"

"Oh, you know me," Lady Mavis said. "I am still a little disappointed the Rangers didn't crumble quite as expected, but I am hopeful that our other endeavors will prove more successful."

"Other endeavors? I wasn't aware we had any other endeavors," Kezem said.

She laughed outright.

"Perhaps *we* do not, but I do. If I raised you right, you do as well."

"I have a lot of problems to deal with at the moment. I don't really have time for word games."

"Then I shall make my point," Mavis said graciously. "You were recently contacted about recovering Lady Merisia Restler. Help her husband find her, but I want her escort to live through the confrontation."

Kezem stayed silent a moment, trying to work through the same thought process she had moments before.

"How is the young Keldor useful to you?" he asked at last.

Locking her disappointment inside, Lady Mavis tried to console herself with the knowledge that he didn't have as much information as she did, but it didn't completely exonerate his ignorance.

"What do you know about him?" she asked, instead of answering his question.

"I don't keep files on—"

"Maybe you should," Mavis interrupted, not bothering to sweeten her tone. "Every scrap of information could be useful. I shall have Dennel send you what I know about Talyon Keldor. It should be there momentarily." She keyed in the order to Dennel, and he complied. She waited for her son to read the file.

It wasn't a big file. At sixteen, Talyon Keldor was barely a man. He had not lived long enough to generate a large file.

Lady Mavis watched in growing anticipation as her son absorbed the pertinent facts. She consciously contained her comments, wanting him to draw his own conclusions.

Kezem returned his attention to her and nodded slowly.

"I see."

"What do you see?" asked Mavis.

"You want to spare the boy to get to the queen's sister, which might be a way to get to the queen and king," Kezem summed. "It is a valid point, but I don't think it's necessary."

"Why not?" Mavis didn't argue about the royal titles. It would be official soon enough.

"They have both recently proven themselves idealistic fools taken captive by threats to complete strangers," said Kezem. "I don't think an elaborate plan will be necessary."

"Power changes people," Mavis replied. "At the time you're referring to, Terosh was merely Dulad Prince, the spare, and Reia was a Ranger. Your cousin needed to take risks to prove himself. Most Rangers are fools, but the mantle of rule does not come without direction. Sedir and Colander are sure to imprint their stuffy selves on our young monarchs."

Kezem chuckled. Then, he closed his eyes and bowed his head in a gesture of respect. When his head came up again, he said, "I still do not completely agree with your assessment, but since it is very hard to bring people back from the dead, I will heed your advice concerning the young man. Good day, Mother." With that, he cut the connection.

You will come to agree with me in time, my son.

***

Pirua (September) 29, 1538
Ashatan Council Chamber, Riden Mountains

Once again finding herself in the meeting chamber of the Ashatan Council, Ranger Knight Kiata Antellio Wellum willed her emotions to remain in check, wrestling with resentment. Most of the members arrayed before her were the same ones who had banished her sister three weeks before.

Of the Council members, only Master Hiram Alikron had perished in the attack on the compound, but the Osem masters had promptly fled home. Master Niklos McGreven had accepted a temporary position until a permanent replacement could be found or the Riden Mountains Council officially agreed to exist with only three members.

No big loss, Kiata thought bitterly of Alikron. She felt guilty for thinking ill of the dead, but Alikron had called for the trial that led to Reia's banishment.

"Do you understand the situation, Ranger Wellum?" asked

Master Niklos, gently breaking into her thoughts. She couldn't think of him as Master McGreven. It sounded so impersonal.

Kiata briefly wondered why her husband wasn't here with her. There had been a lot of "situations" of late.

"What are your thoughts, Kiata?" prompted Master Jolinda Ekris.

"I'm sorry, masters. I'm not sure which situation you're refer to," Kiata admitted. "I don't know why I was summoned."

Master Liam Deliad frowned.

"Have you not heard—"

"Please, Master Deliad, these are trying times for everybody," said Master Kale Corida. "Kiata, we were discussing the situation with the royals."

How much did I miss?

Kiata commanded herself to focus. She felt like a first-year apprentice caught napping.

"What do you want me to say?" Kiata snapped, trying to keep her tone civil.

"Relations with House Minstel are understandably strained right now," Master Niklos said. "We want your honest opinion on how your sister will react."

You of all people should know how she'd react, Master Niklos.

"React?" repeated Kiata, genuinely stunned. Their implication started to sink in.

"Will she ask for our resignations?" asked Master Deliad. "Will she disband the—"

Kiata's sharp laugh cut off Master Deliad's second question.

"They are valid concerns, Ranger Wellum," said Master Ekris. "The Order's first mandate has always been the protection of the Royal House. Should the queen wish for new leadership, we would be compelled to resign."

Kiata made eye contact with each master before speaking.

"Your positions are safe," she assured them.

"How do you know?" challenged Deliad.

Feeling her jaw tighten, Kiata used one of Master Niklos's calming techniques to hold her temper.

"I know my sister, Master Deliad," said Kiata. "She is not stupid, petty, or vengeful. She knows very well what the Rangers stand for, and I doubt she even knows she possesses the power to demand change within the Order."

"I agree with your assessment of her character, but as to her knowledge, she will soon learn the extent of her power. We should mend this relationship quickly," Master Ekris said. She looked meaningfully at Kiata.

Holding Master Ekris's gaze, Kiata bit the inside of her lower lip to keep from speaking. If they wanted her help, they would have to ask for it. She refused to offer.

Master Niklos sighed as if in her mind.

"We want you and Todd to move to Rammon."

"You want us to move?" Kiata had expected to be sent to Rammon with profound regrets, copious apologies, and solemn promises to aid the new king and queen. She had not expected the assignment to be long term.

"You would still be part of the Nareth Talis," said Master Niklos.

"We would issue you orders via comm," Master Corida added.

"The political climate has changed much in the last few years," said Master Ekris. "We have been discussing the need for more of a presence in Rammon for quite some time. We feel this is the right time and that you and Todd are the right people. Will you accept the position?"

"I will need to speak with Todd," said Kiata, hoping to put off further conversation.

"We already spoke to your husband," Master Deliad said. "He is for it."

"I would like to speak to him anyway," said Kiata.

"Of course. How much time will you require?" Master Niklos's eyes silently asked for a quick decision.

"How much time do I have?" asked Kiata.

"Can you reach a decision by tomorrow morning?" asked Master Ekris.

"I will do my best." Kiata nodded farewell and took her leave of the Ashatan Council.

***

Pirua (September) 29, 1538
Same Day
Wellum Home, Riden Mountains

Hearing the front door open, Todd Wellum stopped cleaning his kerlak pistol. Some traditionalist Rangers refused to use any weapon besides a shootav or a banistick, but Todd was practical enough to familiarize himself with any weapon he might have to face.

"What did you tell the Council?" Kiata demanded, appearing across the table from him.

Todd clamped down on a response that would rile his wife. She seemed agitated enough.

"They asked if I would be willing to move to Rammon. I told them to ask you," he said.

"Why?" she asked, almost breathless. She dodged the table and stood beside him.

Todd put the gun pieces down and wiped his hands on a rag. He avoided her gaze, but felt it burning through him anyway.

"Because I know what it would mean for *our* plans," he said as gently as possible. He finally met her eyes and emphasized the "our" so she would know that his wishes aligned with hers. He pushed his chair away from the table and held out his arms.

"We can't wait forever," said Kiata, settling herself sideways on his lap. She reached up, traced the faint scruff lining his jaw, and cupped his chin.

He turned his head and planted a kiss in her palm.

"I know," said Todd. "It's just that now doesn't seem to be the best time to ask for a break."

Kiata let her hand fall to his shoulder.

"There will never be a 'best time,' my love."

"Well, I'm sure there will be a better time than now," Todd offered.

He didn't have to list the problems the Rangers currently faced. The Restler-Tarpon Alliance had shown a considerable increase in boldness. Their attack on the Riden Mountain compound, though largely a failure, was troublesome to say the least. Reia's trial had highlighted some of the fundamental rifts in the Order, rifts that threatened to undermine crucial cohesion. The government transition provided enough of a gap for bolder criminals to expand their spheres of influence. Rangers tried to avoid politics and private affairs, but the lines blurred when those endangered members of the Royal House.

Kiata leaned forward to kiss him lightly and leaned her forehead against his.

"I'm not sure things will ever get better now that Reia is queen," said Kiata.

"Your faith in your sister is overwhelming," Todd teased.

She pulled back and shot him a dirty look.

"You know what I mean," said Kiata.

He did. Ever since the day he'd met her, Todd knew Kiata's private mission consisted of safeguarding her little sister. He couldn't blame her. He would probably feel the same way if his parents had been murdered when he was a small child. His parents were dead, but they had passed away from separate incidents of disease years apart from each other. They had given him to the Rangers as a small boy because his mother was too ill to watch over him. His father and older brother, Terik, had to work the farm. When given the choice to return home or stay, Todd had chosen a life with the Rangers.

Kiata paced, confirming Todd's suspicion that her agitation had not diminished.

"I thought things would get better when she chose the healer path. This is all Lucas's fault."

"How so?" Todd struggled to follow her logic.

"He pushed the Council to accept Reia as Prince Terosh's Kireshana guardian," Kiata said.

"I thought you were happy for her," said Todd.

"I *was* happy for her. Right up until she married the man with the biggest target on his forehead." Kiata's tone added: *How could she be so stupid?*

Todd laughed.

"He seems like a nice man."

"Tell that to the people who are going to try to kill him," Kiata muttered.

"When did you get so cynical?" asked Todd.

"When did you get so naïve?" she returned.

Todd held his hands up in mock surrender.

"Cease fire. I come in peace," he said, standing to equalize the verbal battlefield. "We have a lot of packing to do."

"You'll go?" Kiata asked. "But we haven't even discussed it yet."

He shot her a long-suffering look.

"What's to discuss?" Todd asked, spreading his arms wide. "There's trouble here," he said, waving his left hand as if presenting the problem. "There's trouble in Rammon," he said, holding out his right hand. He raised a finger like an idea had just struck him. "But the capital has the added attraction of your baby sister and her new husband. Both of whom tend to get shot at a lot. You don't particularly like that part and wish to go crack the heads of the would-be shooters.

I'm going to go because someone needs to keep you out of trouble. There, wasn't that a great discussion?"

Kiata marched over to their couch, snatched up the nearest pillow, and launched it at his head. He caught it easily and fired it back.

Chapter 2:
Fugitives

Pirua (September) 29, 1538
Same Day
Tarpon Estate, City of Kalmata

"I'll wear it," said Lady Nera Tarpon. She gently eased the distasteful band from her husband's clenched fists.

"You shouldn't *have* to wear it," Brook Tarpon declared. "You've done nothing wrong." He looked like he wanted to punch his brother.

"Please calm down. This isn't going to help us," Nera said, adjusting her position so she stood between the brothers. She slipped her right hand through the metal loop she had taken from her husband and flinched when it snapped snugly into place midway up her forearm. An unnatural coolness from the band caused her heartbeats to quicken. Two small dots of light blinked yellow, transmitting her reaction to the Target Tracker-65 unit linked to her band.

"It won't be for long," Alden Tarpon offered. He sounded guilty, but his fingers were sure as they tapped commands into the TT-65. The yellow lights stopped their frantic flashing.

Nera turned and nodded to her husband's younger brother, smiling to ease his discomfort with the assignment. She could easily imagine how awkward he must feel guarding her while men hunted his sister.

Oh, Gareth, be gentle when you find them, Nera silently begged her brother.

"It's already too long," Brook complained.

Nera turned back to her husband, reached out, and patted his right arm.

"I'm all right," she assured him. She let her hand rest on his arm briefly before sliding it down to his clenched fist.

"Nothing's right. Nothing's *been* right since Merisia left. Why would she leave?" Brook's words rushed out. "She knew what this alliance means for our families."

"We don't know the whole story. My brother isn't always the easiest man to get along with." Nera curled her hand around Brook's fist.

"What do you mean? Would he hurt her?" A protective glare lit up Brook's green eyes.

"I don't know," Nera answered honestly. "I don't think so. Gareth is volatile sometimes, but he's fiercely loyal." She left off that her brother was loyal to those he loved. She honestly didn't know where he stood with his wife.

Why would Merisia leave him?

***

Pirua (September) 29, 1538
Same Day
Gareth's and Ariman's Camp, Felmon Desert

"You're going to break your gun if you keep holding it that tightly," said Ariman Keldor to his companion.

The younger man, Gareth Restler, stared through the sniper's scope and pulled the trigger several times. Each pull produced an empty click.

"What would her face look like if I killed him?" Gareth said, clicking the trigger twice more.

The question brought up a mental image of Merisia Restler. Ariman had been the first to spot their camp and gaze upon the fugitives. The young man's wife retained her beauty despite the strain of fear. Her black hair possessed a gray tint thanks to the desert dust, but her purple eyes still had a determined glint to them. Ariman had purposefully unloaded the gun so they would never have to find out Merisia's reaction to Taly's death. Gareth seemed like a level-headed man, but Ariman didn't want to take the chance with his son's life.

"Keldor, I'm going to beat your son until he breaks," Gareth promised.

"I doubt he has useful information, but Lord … Maledek wants him alive," Keldor reminded. "I'm half-inclined to beat him myself.

This is killing his mother."

"It's quite simple," Gareth said, his voice tight with anger. "Your son ran away with my wife. Tomorrow we're going to catch them. I will beat him to my satisfaction before handing him over to Maledek's agents."

Ariman listened without comment to Gareth's threats. Things didn't look good for Taly and Lady Restler. He rubbed a hand down his face, trying to focus. He had almost let Gareth know Maledek's real name. Such a mistake would have been unforgivable. The slip would have forced him to kill Gareth, and Lord Kezem and the Lady still needed the Restler-Tarpon Alliance.

"We should rest now," Keldor suggested. "Everything's set in Terab." He stifled a yawn. "I'll take the first watch."

Gareth had shown remarkable restraint so far, but Keldor did not wish to test him too much. It took about ten minutes to convince Gareth to cease his morbid vigil and sleep.

Twenty minutes into his watch, Keldor picked up the sniper rifle and sighted on his son and Lady Restler. They were too far away to hear, but they seemed to be arguing. Drawing on many years' experience, Keldor read their body language.

Several minutes later, he finally learned something useful.

He considered waking Gareth but decided against it. There was no telling how the man would react to such news.

***

Pirua (September) 29, 1538
Same Day
Merisia's and Taly's Camp, Felmon Desert

"What's wrong, Merisia?" asked Talyon Keldor. He hated having to ask, especially since he knew it would have been easier to list the few things favoring them.

Tomorrow morning, they would reach Terab and the safe anonymity of its masses. Their food and water supplies, though tight, would carry them through. They even had a friend willing to hide them for a few days. Everything else fell under the "wrong" category.

Merisia Restler pierced Taly with a long, mournful look that spoke volumes, but she said nothing.

Taly despised that look. She had leveled it at him more than once during their six-week journey, but its frequency seemed to be increasing. This was the fourth time today. The look combined apology, guilt, and heart-wrenching sadness. Taly knew she didn't mean to hurt him, but he caught her sentiments anyway.

I'm sorry I got you into this mess, very sorry. The corner of Taly's lips twitched in a weak smile. *Great, just great, now I'm even thinking like Merisia.*

"We're almost there. We'll be safe once we reach Terab," Taly encouraged.

"Thank you, Taly. Thank you for staying."

"Where else would I go? I'm a wanted man." He meant it in jest but saw that his words wounded Merisia. "It's not your fault," he added quickly.

"It is my fault," Merisia said. "It most definitely is but thank you all the same. I can always count on you to be there. I know I can, which is why I have a favor to ask you, a big favor."

"Anything," Taly said instantly. The look on Merisia's face gave him a sudden chill. He mentally cringed at the hasty promise. "You know I'm with you until the end of this."

She nodded and smiled weakly.

"I know, Taly, I know. You're not going to like my request, not one bit, but please hear me out."

Taly braced as best he could, but Merisia's next words still ripped through him.

"If—when they catch us … I want you to kill me." Tears sprang to Merisia's eyes and flowed down her cheeks. "Please, promise to kill me."

Taly scrambled off his bedroll, rushed to Merisia, and hugged her.

"I can't do that," Taly whispered.

Merisia allowed the embrace but stiffened at his refusal. Several awkward beats passed before she relaxed in his arms. Then, she pulled away and gripped his upper arms with desperate strength.

"It's got to be this way, my friend, got to," said Merisia. "I won't go back, I won't! They can't use my child against me or my husband, never the child."

"They won't," Taly promised. "Once we reach Terab, the crowds alone will—"

A bitter laugh cut off Taly's protest. Merisia squeezed his arms once more before releasing him. Another tear worked its way down her left cheek.

"You're not blind, but you can be stubbornly stupid when you want to be. I know you saw the pursuers we picked up two hours before the moons rose."

"I saw them," Taly admitted. "But what makes you think they're after us?"

"We're not exactly the desert's swiftest travelers. We're not swift at all. They stopped when we did with an hour of good travel time left in the sun. Anybody else would have passed us."

Taly silently cursed. He had hoped to avoid worrying her with those observations. He adjusted his position on her bedroll, content to offer her physical comfort instead of the promise she sought.

***

Pirua (September) 30, 1538
Deegan Estate, City of Terab

Dread opened a chasm in Talyon Keldor's stomach a split-second before a pair of blue stun beams flew at him. Without thinking, he shoved Merisia to the ground and dropped to his knees beside her, trying to shield her. His kerlak pistol, set to high stun, dropped their hostess before she could utter a sound.

Merisia screamed and tucked her knees to her chest, trying to protect her abdomen.

Anger and fear fueled Taly. He scrambled in front of Merisia and unleashed a sheet of blue beams at their attackers. Most of his shots slammed harmlessly into the walls and ceiling but one connected with a kerlak rifle. The resulting yelp brought a smile to Taly's face as he basked in his blind luck. His knees burned, but he ignored them. His kerlak pistol emitted a buzzing whine that said the battery pack was almost depleted. He squeezed off one more shot then fumbled to grab a spare pack from his belt.

"Duck, Taly, duck!" shouted Merisia. From the sound of it, she had managed to crawl to the only meager protection in the room.

Trusting her, Taly flattened himself on the ground, landing awkwardly on his pistol. It dug painfully into his chest. A blue energy beam flew over his right shoulder and blackened a spot in front of him. He blinked, forgetting the chest pain. Part of him understood the beam had come from behind. He doubted the shot had come from Merisia. Despite his best efforts, she remained the lousiest shot—besides his mother—with twice the hatred for all weapons.

Taly rolled onto his back. More beams crisscrossed over his head, but he ignored them. He suddenly understood why his father had demanded he practice loading and unloading serlak and kerlak guns repeatedly. Putting those skills to good use, Taly snatched a new battery pack off his belt, ejected the old pack, and clipped the new one in place. Then, he adjusted the gun to semi-automatic fire so he wouldn't immediately drain the new pack.

Rolling twice then scrambling ungracefully brought him to the lone couch in the room. Unintelligible curses crowded his head at their lousy position. He had one entrance in front of him, one next to him, and one behind him. The ambush had been perfectly planned. Even if Merisia was a crack shot, they would have been hard-pressed to cover three entrances.

Sound crashed over Taly's senses. Merisia's weeping provided an odd counterpoint to the men's shouts and the sound of heavy boots pounding the ground.

Taly threw the pistol to his left hand and reached for Merisia with his right. She clutched his hand unable to speak, but her eyes pleaded her case again. Taly locked eyes with her for the briefest second. Her desperation struck him like a physical blow. He shook his head once.

The shouts and boots were closer now. Dark forms rushed toward them.

Merisia dropped his hand.

Taly shot the first three RT Alliance soldiers to enter the room before a stun beam struck his left hand. Another beam hit the back of his right shoulder as he spun with the first blow. A third slammed into the space between his shoulder blades, driving him forward and relieving him of consciousness.

Chapter 3: The Gift

Pirua (September) 30, 1538
One Day after the Coronation
Royal Gardens, City of Rammon

Queen Reia Minstel lifted her face toward the sun, closed her eyes, and tried to dispel the sadness clinging to her like a cloak. Part of her felt she had no right to be sad.

Things were finally settling down. The isolated protests in Azhel and Idonia had ended peacefully. The previous day's coronation and Terosh's first address had gone wonderfully well. The Senate and Governors Council had finally finished wording the appropriate pieces of legislation confirming her husband as Reshner's undisputed king.

Everything was right, yet she still felt lost and lonely.

She could handle isolation. Much of her Ranger training had her trekking through the Riden Mountains in search of healing herbs. But she had a husband now and wished to see him more than once or twice a week. His duties often pulled them away from each other, but she took the pain in stride.

She could handle danger. The last year of traveling the Kireshana trail with Terosh had proven quite the learning experience. Together, they had weathered windstorms, graveground, and korvers. Surely those were comparable to wild senators and stormy governors.

Unknown expectations scared her beyond speech.

What is my role as queen?

Terosh had mentioned something about training with his former tutors, but the last few weeks had passed too quickly to spare thought for educating her in royal matters. She had suffered through one fitting and hair styling session after another, so the seamstresses and tailors could create a wardrobe fit for a queen.

Now that Reia could think, the full meaning of recent events started to coalesce in her mind. Terosh had told the people she was a Ranger and a healer, but the former title no longer fit. It had defined her for so long, yet the Ranger High Council had stripped her rank and cast her out of the Order because she defied them by marrying a royal.

Lost in thought, Reia failed to sense the breach in her solitude.

***

King Terosh Minstel studied his wife from afar and felt his heart constrict with the sense of loss he saw in her.

Guilt flooded him. What kind of thoughtless, reckless wretch would knowingly chain an innocent woman to a family such as his? What made him think he would escape his family's curse? So many of his ancestors had perished before their time, he marveled that the family name had ever survived. His mother had been poisoned, his father and brother assassinated on Mitra, and his brother's secret family had perished here on Reshner.

When guilt faded, love replaced it full force. He felt its warmth sweep through him. As he watched, Reia's expression cleared, becoming less sad and more accepting. He remembered why he loved everything about her.

Suddenly, Terosh didn't know what to say. He wanted to make everything right for her. The gift held behind his back suddenly felt inadequate. The anotechs assured him of the gift's appropriateness, but he argued with himself anyway. Most women would want jewelry or flowers or sweets.

Not this woman.

Gathering his courage, Terosh straightened his shoulders and moved down the path with sure strides until he was two meters from his wife. Then, he slowed, stopped, and waited for her to notice him.

Reia stood with her face tipped toward the sun. The garden spread around her in a riot of resplendent colors and delicate shapes. Terosh had never appreciated the garden's beauty quite like this, enhanced as it was by his wife's presence. A gentle breeze rustled the flowers and played with the folds of Reia's dress and the flowing tresses of her hair. Her sad expression somehow simultaneously enhanced and marred the scene's perfection.

"If I could take away your pain, I would," Terosh whispered.

The sound of his voice startled him, for he had not meant to interrupt her solitude. He rather liked observing her this way.

Reia's eyes flew open and joy replaced sorrow.

Suddenly, Terosh found his arms wrapped firmly around her. The gift clattered to the ground behind him. He didn't care. Life would be perfect if he could stop it here forever. He grunted at the force of her return embrace.

"Was I gone so long?" he asked.

For a time, Reia stayed tucked in his arms, content to prolong the moment. Finally, she pulled away with a sigh and slid her hands down his arms until she caught his hands.

"Every moment apart is forever," she said. "I never was much good at sharing."

"How good are you at accepting gifts?" asked Terosh. Before she could answer, he pulled her close and kissed her.

When the kiss finally ended, Reia smiled.

"I thought kisses were supposed to follow gift-giving."

"You're avoiding the question," Terosh said, leaning his forehead against hers.

"I'm out of practice, but I usually accept gifts graciously," said Reia.

"I want to give you lots of practice. Anything you want, it's yours," he promised.

It was the wrong thing to say.

She stiffened and stumbled back a step, looking ready to cry. Her expression flickered between anger and sorrow. Her eyes said that the thing she wanted most was beyond his power to give. He should have seen as much.

"I'm sorry," Terosh said, frantically casting about for something profound to say. "I—please don't cry. I'm no good at this. I want to fix it, make it better, but I can't. I don't know how. I'm sorry I ever—" He cut himself off. His mind went into a blind panic for several agonizing seconds.

He watched in horror as his words cut through his beloved wife.

***

—married you, Reia's mind finished. She felt her world collapsing. Her head felt light and unattached, ready to tumble from her shoulders.

"That's not to say that I—" Terosh babbled, stopping himself again.

Reia wanted to flee but could not pry herself away from his painful words.

Terosh took a few deep breaths before attempting to speak again.

"What I mean to say is that I'm sorry about what happened with the Rangers. They were your family, and I'm sorry they withdrew from you—from us." He closed the gap between them again and tenderly reclaimed her hands. "I love you, and I meant what I said before. If I could take away your pain, I would. I … hope the gift helps you heal. Please don't ever doubt my love."

Terosh released her hands and walked back to where the gift had crashed to the ground. In seconds, he stood before her cradling a sheathed sword. Three metal clips on the hilt folded down and locked around the sheath to hold the sword in place. The markings running up and down both the sheath and the hilt were identical to those on her banistick, the weapon the Ashatan Council had wanted to destroy. Kiata had saved the weapon but nothing could change the fact that Reia could never use it again.

Breath hitching and cheeks flushing, Reia couldn't speak. After all they had been through, she had let herself doubt his love.

Uncertainty and vulnerability shone from his striking blue eyes.

"Do you like it?" asked Terosh.

For an answer, Reia gently pushed the sword aside, stood on her tiptoes, cupped his face, and kissed him.

When Terosh finally drew back so they could both draw a breath, he said, "I'll take that as an affirmative answer."

"Thank you," Reia whispered. She accepted the sword with two hands and studied the design.

"You're welcome. I … it's a symbol and a promise," Terosh said, suddenly shy.

Reia stopped looking at the sword and instead studied her husband. His outfit had a military flavor to it. A three-centimeter-wide stripe filled with silver and gold threads in alternating sections ran up each side of the black pants. The shirt was black with silver threads weaving back and forth in a tight, regular pattern. A series of three black buttons sat near the right side of his collar ready to secure his formal cape. Knowing how much he despised the cumbersome thing, she was not surprised to see him without it. His next words did surprise her.

"I want you to come to the next Governors Council meeting

tomorrow morning," said Terosh. "It's smaller than the Senate, but it should give you a good introduction to our planetary politics."

"What could I possibly do?" Reia wondered. "I haven't even met with Master Sedir yet."

"Masters Sedir, Cadrish, and Colander are all eager to meet you and impart their knowledge. They have quarters here in the palace. Whenever you're ready, you can summon them."

The casual way he said it gave Reia pause.

"What if they don't want to come?" Reia asked.

"Why would they not want to come?" Terosh shot her a puzzled look.

"I will see Master Sedir this afternoon then," Reia said, dropping the subject. Terosh had been a prince his whole life. People naturally obeyed his every whim.

Terosh shook his head.

"Can't. I've scheduled a sword lesson for you with Master Colander this afternoon." He paused and cocked his head to the side as if a new thought had struck him. "You can change it, of course, but the gift is useless until you learn to use it."

Reia nodded. Everything he said made sense, but part of her felt confined by the sheer amount of order in her new life.

Not sensing her disquiet, Terosh continued, "I'm afraid you might need it."

"What happened?" Reia asked, sharpening her senses.

"Nothing yet, but Reia, we've talked about this. My family has a long history of premature deaths. More than anything in the universe, I want you to be safe." Terosh smiled that gentle, teasing smile that always lightened her mood. "And I'm well-aware that you would resent being locked in the palace for the rest of your life. The sword is my compromise."

Reia responded with a wry smile.

"If anyone gets close enough for a sword to matter, we're in serious trouble, my dear."

"Master Onro will teach you how to handle a kerlak pistol as well," Terosh said, nodding to acknowledge her point, "but hopefully, you won't have to use either of them. I've been training with weapons since childhood, but I never really used the skills until the Kireshana."

"Let's hope ruling the planet proves less *eventful* than that," said Reia.

Chapter 4:
Miscommunication

Pirua (September) 30, 1538
Same Day
Deegan Estate, City of Terab

Tears streamed down Merisia's face as she watched her dear friend fall. Taly's kerlak pistol dropped from his left hand and clattered to the ground. His body collapsed atop the weapon. Needing that gun and the end it offered, Merisia crawled to Taly and tried to reach around him.

Two stun beams struck her back and she fell forward onto Taly. An anguished cry tried to rip itself from her paralyzed body but came out as a mournful whimper. As her tears soaked Taly's back, she prayed more energy beams would finish her. Blood pounded through her skull, making her head throb. She tasted something bitter. Her breaths came in little raspy fits. She wished she had the will to stop drawing them.

Hands hauled her upright and held her while stuncuffs were applied. The minor shocks from the cuffs brought feeling back into her arms. She wanted to protest. Merisia knew there was a reason shocks would be bad, but her mind went blank with dread. The hands pulled, tugged, pushed, and prodded until her uncooperative legs carried her two steps back to the couch. She felt herself falling backwards, but the hands caught her and eased her onto the couch. Then Gareth was before her, shouting. His words made no sense, but they fell upon Merisia in waves, battering her worn nerves.

Mother appeared and argued with Gareth.

They shouted at each other.

Mother won the argument.

Gareth stormed out, taking his minions with him.

Mother knelt before Merisia. Love, concern, and anger played with Mother's expression.

Merisia wept some more.

***

Vera Tarpon wanted to nurse her anger. She needed the strength of it, but it leeched away as she gazed up at her broken daughter.

Hands resting on Merisia's knees, Vera fought the urge to embrace her. This was her youngest child and only daughter, her baby. She knew the story behind each scar. She had prayed for and rejoiced in the beautiful changes as Merisia eventually stopped chasing frogs with Taly and took up more genteel pastimes. She had waged—and lost—the battle against this arranged marriage. Now, she wondered why she failed to fight harder.

With tremendous effort, Vera wrenched her thoughts out of the past. Merisia's bleak expression spoke of much more than physical exhaustion. The hundreds of unanswered questions seemed trivial now, but Vera needed answers before Gareth took Merisia away.

Gently squeezing her daughter's right knee, Vera said, "Meri, I'm here now. Tell me what's wrong. I want to help you."

The vacant glint in Merisia's eyes told Vera her words were bouncing away harmlessly.

"Meri, focus!" said Vera, gripping Merisia's knee harder. "We haven't much time. Your husband wishes to leave soon, and he will have his way unless you give me a reason to hold you."

The silent sobs slowly abated, and Merisia's breath evened out.

"Why did you leave him?" Vera asked, fighting to keep her voice steady. "Was he rough with you? Did he hurt you?"

The second and third questions provoked stiff negative twitches from Merisia.

"Then what is wrong? Why all the tears? Why run so far for so long?" Vera bit her lip to stem the tide of questions.

Give me answers, Meri!

The silence stretched Vera's nerves near to the breaking point. Being so close to answers and meeting such resistance was worse than knowing nothing. Her eyes searched her daughter's face, hoping to see answers etched amidst the tear streaks.

Merisia sniffled, wiped at her eyes, and finally held Vera's gaze. Longing, loss, confusion, and pain radiated from her haunted eyes.

Then her hands clamped down on Vera's right hand and crushed the bones together painfully.

Feeling her throat closing, Vera swallowed hard several times and tried not to wince at the discomfort of her daughter's desperate grip. Strong shocks from the stuncuffs flowed through Merisia's hands into Vera.

"You lost something," she said in a hoarse whisper.

"I lost something," Merisia repeated mechanically. She squeezed Vera's hand hard again then let go. Merisia leaned back against the couch. The movement drew more shocks from the stuncuffs.

Vera waited for her to continue, but the three words hung between them for more than a minute.

"What did you lose? Why did it drive you—" Vera cut herself off.

She knew.

Merisia nodded slowly.

"It's not what you think; not all of it anyway." She sounded weary.

"Help me understand, Meri," Vera said.

"I'm so tired of running, so very tired," said Merisia. "I wish I were brave like Taly, brave enough to face this."

Vera tapped Merisia's knee urgently.

"Do *not* mention that name to your husband. Do you hear me? Taly is dead to you!"

"Dead? No, not Taly, not dead." Merisia's words poured out with childlike conviction.

"He is to you," Vera said slowly, willing the words to sink in. "Meri, regardless of Gareth's retribution you must accept the fact that Talyon Keldor does not exist in your world anymore."

More tears escaped Merisia, but she nodded.

"Tell me he's not dead, tell me. I need to know that much, need to."

"He was alive when I last saw him," Vera said.

"Please look after him, Mother, please."

"I will do what I can, Meri," Vera promised, "but this is very important. If you value his life, do not let yourself think of him. Now, tell me what you lost." Vera let an edge sharpen her request.

Merisia's face contorted as she struggled for words.

"A child, Mother, I lost a child."

***

Pirua (September) 30, 1538
Same Day
Deegan Estate, City of Terab

They've talked long enough.

As the thought crystallized in Gareth Restler's head, he motioned his two hand-picked men to follow him. He had as much of a right to speak with Merisia as that meddlesome Tarpon woman. At least Ariman Keldor had agreed to wait with Talyon. He almost wished the man would do something stupid like try to escape with his son.

Gareth marched into the room where he had left his wife with her mother. He paused in the doorway. Merisia looked awful. Her eyes were puffy from crying and her dark hair was a mess. His anger slipped. Narrowing his eyes, Gareth looked to his men and nodded curtly.

Adrik Bentanner and Einer Akurin immediately moved to carry out his silent orders. Adrik moved to Vera Tarpon's left side, and Einer took a position to her right side. Each man grasped an arm and gently but firmly pulled her up, so they could escort her out.

She protested loudly, but Gareth ignored her.

He was too busy trying to figure out what to say to Merisia. His entire planned speech escaped him. Despite their marriage being arranged and the massive trouble this merry chase had caused him, he still loved her. Her odd way of phrasing things could be annoying, but he often found it charming.

Not knowing what else to do, Gareth knelt in front of Merisia, taking the space her mother had occupied.

While he was still searching for words, she asked, "Where's Taly? Where is he?"

Gareth's sympathy vanished.

"Dead," he answered coldly. "I figured it was personal since he ran off with my wife, so I stuck a dagger in him." The lie came easily, but the pain filling Merisia's face struck him as well. He twisted the pain back into anger.

She wept, and he hated her for it.

"He lives," Gareth spat, pouring his contempt into the two words. "How long he lives depends on how you answer my next question. How long did it go on, Merisia?"

She looked startled then offended.

"You're jealous."

It took much willpower to not reach out and shake her.

Merisia blinked back tears and laughed bitterly.

"I don't believe it; I just don't. Gareth, this has nothing to do with Taly, nothing."

"How can you say that?" Gareth demanded. "Merisia, you ran away with that boy."

"No, Gareth, no. He helped *me* run away!" Merisia raised her bound hands. "Can't you see the difference, the big difference?"

Gareth got to his feet, forcing her to sit back and look up at him.

"No, I don't see the difference. Why would you want to leave me?" Gareth tried to hide his hurt but didn't quite manage it.

Merisia's gaze hardened.

"Kia Meetcher."

The name sounded familiar, but it took a moment for Gareth's mind to locate the image of a small, angry child brought to his house.

"What does the Meetcher kid have to do with—"

"They took her away, Gareth, away from her family." Merisia sounded close to tears again.

Gareth hoped she held them in. The tears tugged at his spirits. His glare demanded she explain.

"Don't you see? I didn't want that to happen to our baby. They would do it; you know they would," said Merisia.

Gareth's mind vainly tried processing the news. Shock and unbridled joy threatened to make him mute. He fought the feelings.

"Who would dare interfere with our child?"

"The Alliance," Merisia spat.

Her vehemence slapped Gareth.

"But it doesn't matter now, doesn't matter," she added in a dreamy tone.

"What doesn't matter?" asked Gareth.

"Nothing matters, nothing. The child is dead." The words seemed to suck the life out of her.

"What do you mean? How?"

"Nothing matters now," Merisia repeated.

Try as he might, Gareth could not coax another word from her.

***

Pirua (September) 30, 1538
Same Day
Guest Quarters, Deegan Estate, City of Terab

Angela Deegan moved gingerly, still stiff from Talyon Keldor's stun beam. She dipped the soft cloth in the warm water basin and wiped more blood from the boy's face.

"Will he live?" inquired Lady Vera Tarpon. She stood at the threshold flanked by two RT Alliance men.

Angela couldn't tell whether the men were there to protect Lady Tarpon or prevent her from interfering.

"He'll be fine," said Angela.

Having finally removed the blood from the young man's face, she lifted his shirt and started on the blue-black, sometimes red masses of abused flesh on his chest and stomach.

The patient moaned.

How did this happen?

Angela meant more by the question than merely how the boy had come by his injuries. She knew that part very well. Everything else was a mess in her head. At first, she had been thrilled to hear from her childhood friend, but Merisia's call had been immediately followed by representatives of the RT Alliance under Gareth Restler's orders. Lacking time to prepare a proper lie, the Alliance people had quickly gotten the truth from her. She hated the cowardice that drove her to betray her friend, and she hated the Alliance for their poorly veiled threats against her family.

Anger made her absently clean harder, drawing a louder groan from the boy. His pain suddenly reached out and seized her. She dropped the cloth and burst into tears. She cried for him, herself, Merisia, and because she was tired of holding the fear inside. More than a few tears were shed in relief that she had sent Ronnie and Rachelle to her sister's house for the week. A gentle hand landed on her shoulder. Instinctively, she turned and embraced the woman offering comfort.

***

Vera Tarpon let the younger woman cry, wishing it was Merisia. When the sobs subsided, she gently extricated herself from Angela's grasp and looked at Taly. Gareth and his men had been very thorough in administering their own brand of justice. Picking up the cloth Angela had abandoned, Vera continued the cleaning process, aware of her two shadows.

"I need some fresh water," Vera said, directing the comment to Adrik and Einer.

"That can wait," said Gareth Restler.

Vera leveled a contemptuous gaze at her daughter's husband.

"He needs care now, not questions," she insisted.

"He needs to record a message now. This cannot wait," said Gareth. "You can leave peacefully, or my men will escort you out. They will fetch you back when we're finish with him."

Vera stood reluctantly.

"May I see my daughter?" asked Vera.

"Yes, but I need you to deliver a message for me," Gareth said.

Vera inclined her head in acknowledgement.

"Tell her he died."

Chapter 5:
Urgent Request

Pirua (September) 30, 1538
Same Day
East Weapons Training Room, Royal Palace, City of Rammon

Terosh Minstel stretched his neck, trying to work out Senate-induced stiffness. As far as he knew, they had accomplished nothing in the three-hour morning session. He had begged off the afternoon session, leaving Miles Cadrish behind to take notes. His former speech and language tutor, recently promoted to advisor, had been less than enthusiastic, but Terosh knew he would acquit himself well.

Part of him felt like a stalker. Once again, he found himself standing out of the way simply watching his wife. Drenched in sweat and clad only in a plain exercise outfit, she looked perfect. Despite a slightly finer cut, the brown pants and white shirt reminded him of her Ranger attire. Reia had worn a similar ensemble practically every day for as long as he had known her. It surprised him to realize the days of their acquaintance numbered less than a year. The fierce concentration in her eyes and the determined set to her jaw reminded Terosh of their first meeting.

A sense of peace came over him, followed closely by a longing to participate in the sword lessons. During the Kireshana, he had taught Reia how to handle a kerlinblade, and she in turn taught him how to fight with a banistick. Though he had given her what skills he could, Terosh accepted his limits as an instructor. It helped to know she would be in capable hands.

The weapons master, Victor Colander, alternately encouraged

and corrected Reia, skillfully pushing his new student to her perceived limits and then slightly beyond. He fought with a blue kerlinblade set wide and flat.

For an irrational moment, Terosh worried his gift would be destroyed by the kerlinblade. Then he remembered the craftsman's claim that it would handle almost any substance created. The man had refused to reveal his secret formula, but Terosh guessed it was an alloy of tosh, iron, and compressed carbon.

The kerlinblade and sword met several times in quick succession. Each time they met, Colander's blade changed color. From blue the blade turned indigo then to violet. Terosh squinted against the glare of the rapidly changing colors, a force of habit more than a necessity. The anotechs automatically adjusted to the glare for him.

Colander spun away, giving Reia a brief respite, and touched the control panel on the bottom of the kerlinblade. The blade blazed with blinding white fury. He attacked with renewed fervor, slashing high and low, left and right, seemingly everywhere at once.

Reia worked frantically to deflect the strikes, but twice she had to leap back, slowly surrendering ground.

Colander drew another kerlinblade from his belt and activated it to a short setting. The green blade extended to a length slightly longer than a dagger. While the full kerlinblade kept Reia's sword busy, Colander took a few probing stabs at her undefended side.

Terosh could tell Reia didn't know how to adjust to the new threat. She ducked and dodged more and more of Colander's strikes, giving up more ground but being careful to avoid corners. Terosh watched the duel with interest, knowing that Colander could win whenever he wished.

"I'm sorry to disturb you, Highness," said a female messenger. "There is an urgent communication for you in the Comm Chamber. It's from off-planet."

Resenting the intrusion but determined to be civil, Terosh frowned at the messenger.

"I thought the interplanetary communications array was being repaired," he said.

"That is correct, my Lord. This is a new array," explained the woman. She spoke clearly and quickly. Her accent and light brown skin hinted at a Terabian background. "It arrived with the cargo ship, *Dicey*, last night. Security scanned it carefully and cleared it, so the tech crew installed the basic elements this morning. It's not complete, but it can accept the call. Captain Darrow tried your personal comm but failed to reach you. He sent me to deliver a request for your presence."

With one last look toward Reia and Colander, Terosh followed the messenger out of the training room. It bothered him that he couldn't remember the messenger's name.

Lelianna Rivers, supplied the anotechs. ***Daughter of Governor*** **Edeline Pallav** ***and her consort Brendan Calik, wife of Simon Rivers, a native of Terab. Would you like a more thorough background?***

Terosh declined, still a little unnerved at sharing thoughts with the anotechs. He considered asking who the message was from but settled for following the messenger. Lelianna set a brisk pace, faster than a normal walk but not quite undignified. Terosh knew exactly where they were going. He could have made it there on his own. He spared a wistful thought for the bygone days of unsupervised leisure. As king, he would have to get used to escorts.

Captain Ivan Darrow stood at attention just outside the door to the Central Communications Chamber. He greeted Terosh with a low bow.

"Thank you for coming so quickly, Highness," said Captain Darrow. "I hesitated to interrupt you, but the caller would not be deflected. She awaits you in pod three."

"It's fine, Captain," Terosh said, acknowledging the man with a nod. He entered the main chamber and walked toward pod three.

Before he reached it, a new male voice said, "Highness, I must protest. There could still be unknown danger from the array."

Terosh stopped and faced Aster Captain Surd Antar of the Royal Guard.

"Your concerns are noted, Captain Antar, but your men already cleared it. I'm sure it's perfectly safe." Despite his words, Terosh sent anotechs into pod three to verify that the new equipment was free of traps. "It would be ill-mannered to not use such an expensive gift."

Antar bowed, but his expression remained querulous.

"As you wish, my Lord, but expensive gifts always have their price."

The anotechs returned with a clean report for the equipment.

Suddenly nervous, Terosh keyed in a code to unlock pod three and stepped into the cool, sterile air inside the pod. A brand-new interplanetary communications array lay before him. It was surprisingly small for such a powerful piece of equipment. The sleek, silver box sported a dozen or so buttons, a few knobs, and a standard keyboard. The anotechs regarded it with disdain, but Terosh ignored them. They were snobbish when it came to other technology.

The holoprojector and receiver display took up most of the small room. Terosh moved to a position where the vidrecorder could capture his image and activated the projector.

The woman who appeared made appropriate gestures acknowledging his rank. Her skin possessed a slightly blue tint and her forehead bore an intricate tattoo. The pattern seemed to change with every movement of her head. Her posture and bearing said she had formal training as both a fighter and a diplomat.

"Greetings. I am told you have an urgent request for me," said Terosh.

"It is so. I am Ashel Privim, Voice for King Padric of House Creston, ruler of Gardan and its two moon colonies. Please confirm your lineage. My master has a private matter for the remnants of House Minstel." The woman's voice flowed like an unhurried stream.

Terosh paused to consider the request, wondering how they would confirm his lineage.

Voice pattern analysis, said the anotechs.

"I am Terosh, son of Teorn and Kila Creston Minstel, brother of the late Taytron Minstel, currently the last of my bloodline." A chill ran through him at the last part. The knowledge was nothing new to him, but speaking the words aloud made them more real.

Ashel's eyes flickered away from him, presumably to check a display he could not see. When her attention came back to him, she said, "Identity accepted. Await transfer."

She disappeared before Terosh could offer his thanks.

A distinguished man with icy blue eyes appeared and leveled a penetrating gaze at Terosh. Short gray and blond hair mingled freely on the man's head. Everything from the arrogant tilt of his chin to the haughty, demanding glint in his eyes declared him a man used to immediate and complete obedience.

The few times Terosh had seen this man he had both literally and figuratively hidden behind his mother. He drew on years of rigorous diplomatic training to keep from recoiling from the display.

"Have you no greeting for family, boy?" asked King Padric Creston.

"Hello, grandfather," Terosh said awkwardly.

What does he want?

To Terosh's knowledge, Padric Creston had never made a simple social call. If he contacted Terosh's mother, it was to demand something of her. She had hated it, though she said nothing of her feelings to Terosh.

King Padric laughed harshly.

"It will have to do. I see you lack your mother's oratory skills, so I will speak plainly. I want my daughter's killer delivered to me immediately."

Terosh vaguely recalled reading a report detailing the capture of Niktrod Keldor, the assassin accused of poisoning Terosh's mother. The man was slated to be delivered to Gardan, but Terosh could not remember if the transfer had occurred. The current conversation indicated no transfer.

"I will look into it, Your Grace," said Terosh.

"I will accept nothing less than complete compliance with this request, boy," said King Padric.

Anger spiked inside Terosh, but he managed to keep his expression neutral.

"You have my word, sir. I will investigate the matter. If I find the prisoner has not yet been delivered, I will hasten to rectify the situation."

King Padric was silent a moment, but his eyes slowly swept every part of Terosh's face.

"So be it. That is the first matter I wished to discuss with you. The second matter is your wife."

Terosh blinked, again calling upon his training to resist reacting physically. His defensive instincts flared.

"I apologize, but I fail to understand what my wife has to do with our discussion."

His grandfather gave him a pitying look.

"I understand you took her before becoming king, but your sudden ascension changes things."

"How?"

"She is a commoner. You are a king," said King Padric.

"She is my wife, that makes her queen," Terosh retorted.

"I would agree with you, if Reshner were just another Edge Planet with no political potential, but its fate is tied to Gardan and it holds secrets that could compromise the balance."

"What are you talking about?" Terosh asked.

"If I knew the secrets, I would conquer Reshner myself," King

Padric said, sounding amused. "I do not know them, but I am adequately convinced of their importance. Long ago, I promised to do what I could to safeguard Reshner. The planet should not even be habitable. The Galactic Alliance of Populated Planets will not take you seriously as king until you ally with your betters. You may not think it, boy, but I say this for your own good."

"My own good?" Terosh echoed. "How do you suggest I fix this terrible situation I've gotten myself into, grandfather?"

Ignoring the sarcasm, King Padric answered, "The simplest solution would be to annul the marriage, but since I doubt you would consider such simplicity, I will offer a second solution. Bring her to me."

"What?" Terosh wished he had something more intelligent to say, but it captured the essence of his confusion.

"Your wife is an orphan, according to my reports. If she became part of my family, it would reinforce the alliance between Gardan and Reshner," King Padric explained. "I'm sure I have a child willing to take her."

"Why should we care about this alliance?" Terosh asked, knowing it was a stupid question.

King Padric gave Terosh a feral smile.

"You should care because it is one of the only things keeping both our planets off GAPP's list of ripe targets. Our own alliance has suffered for several years now. One of your people killed my daughter on your soil. In GAPP's eyes, the alliance no longer exists. My insistence on bringing your mother's killer to Gardan for justice is to re-establish our alliance."

Terosh despised the fact that his grandfather actually had a point.

"Why would my wife have to come to you?"

Assuming she'll even agree to this madness.

"Adoptions can be started across planets, but to make it official, she will need to spend a year here."

The news hit Terosh hard, leaving him dazed. He said hasty farewells and turned the machine off. Then, he sank down onto the chair to think.

Every option seemed terrible.

Chapter 6: New Opportunities

Pirua (September) 30, 1538
Same Day
The Lady's Estate, Kala Mountains

Slapping the vidscreen controls, Lady Mavis Altran froze the image at a split view of her nephew and the hologram of Gardan's infamous king. It had cost her dearly to arrange vidrecorders for each communication pod in the Royal Palace, but her foresight finally paid off. The two faces, though strikingly alike around the eyes and mouth, showed such a difference in disposition that Mavis could only chuckle.

Poor Terosh. The throne may cost you more than you can imagine.

The boy looked so incredibly lost that one would think he had just received news of his beloved wife's death, not a threat veiled as a favor. It was most certainly a threat, but the details and motives escaped Mavis. She let her gaze linger on Terosh a second longer then enlarged the image of King Padric Creston so that it covered the whole screen.

There is the face of power, thought Mavis, hoping her own features never showed such harsh markings. Even now, she felt her heart flutter with fear. This was the face that drove her from the palace, seeking safety in a hasty marriage.

As the third of four children, Mavis had always excelled at being unobtrusive. Her skills at judging character had almost failed her at the time. She had been drawn to the alluring power of Gardan's king. Only a series of fortunate—and unfortunate—events had spared her from becoming a pretty bauble mounted in Padric Creston's crown, officially married to one of his handsome sons yet ultimately a political game piece to be played at will.

Forcing herself to stare into his face, Mavis confronted the rising sense of unease. She soothed her mind by concentrating on the many questions the conversation raised. Why did Creston want Queen Kila's assassin? Simple revenge seemed a flimsy reason to bother with the details involved in claiming him. Why this sudden interest in renewing the treaty built through her little brother anyway? Did Creston truly want the new queen or was she merely a target of convenience?

Seemingly unrelated reports of random disappearances sprang to the forefront of Mavis's mind. Individually, they had meant nothing, but she had long ago learned to trust such instincts. The motive was so obvious as to be laughable. Creston had said it aloud to Terosh: he wanted the secret to the anotechs. He had probably already brokered a deal with GAPP, selling Reshner for Gardan's peace.

Her unique position offered several choices. Mavis could do nothing and wait for things to unfold. She could warn Terosh, risking valuable sources in the process, or she could send a subtler warning. Those were the easy options. The others required much more elaborate involvement. Higher risks also meant higher rewards. Ironically, she and Creston both sought stability for their planets.

Slowly, a plan formed. Mavis would need to earn Creston's trust. A few changes to previously laid plans should accomplish the task. After seriously weighing the consequences, she decided to embrace the new plan. Summoning her faithful servant, Dennel, Mavis dispatched him to research everything official and unofficial known about Gardan.

***

Pirua (September) 30, 1538
Same Day
Deegan Estate, City of Terab

With an odd mixture of relief and fear, Ariman Keldor watched his new orders appear on his private infopad. The Lady rarely risked such direct communication. That she did so now reinforced the sense of urgency.

This will endanger Taly.

He dismissed the thought. Leaving Taly with Gareth Restler was also hazardous. The man kept his emotions under tight control, but Keldor sensed the deadly hatred. He doubted Maledek's order to keep Taly alive would last much longer in Gareth's mind. Keldor continued reading and felt his heart seize at the blind trust he would need to place in complete strangers.

Draw the Rangers' attention and record their every move when they rescue Talyon.

Keldor wondered how the Lady could predict the movements of others so well. Could he trust Taly's life to her? Though he had never met her in person, she knew him better than his own wife. Her ability to bend him to her will made her dangerous, but in this case, their desires aligned.

Committing himself to the new orders, Keldor turned his attention to the details. The Rangers would sense a trap if he gave them too much information but withholding information could hinder their efforts.

***

Pirua (September) 30, 1538
Same Day
Maledek's Private Retreat, City of Idonia

Lord Kezem mulled over his mother's message about changing the situation in Terab. He did not delude himself into thinking he could alter her mind, but he desired clarity. Modifying plans so late could be dangerous. Something drastic must have prompted her to take the risk. Irritated at having to constantly turn to her, he indulged in some brief, murderous thoughts. Her hologram appeared almost instantly, indicating that she had expected his call.

"Trust me," said his mother without greeting.

"What changes have you ordered?" Kezem demanded.

"If I thought you needed to know, I would inform you, my dear."

Kezem narrowed his eyes.

"How am I to know what orders to issue, if I don't know what will happen?"

His mother gave him a penetrating gaze, and her next words surprised him.

"You are still my best hope for regaining the throne, my son, but Terosh is no longer our only enemy. I have been blind to another threat for longer than I care to admit. These changes are in hopes of rectifying that lapse. Whatever happens in Terab can be turned to our advantage. Let things play as they will. Your men know their parts."

"Are they still *my* men?" Kezem asked. His voice shook with suppressed rage.

"They are yours as long as you can control them," his mother replied. "Study the information I am having Dennel send you. It may ease your mind. I have a personal messenger standing by to deliver a vid if you can get one on short notice."

***

Kest (October) 1, 1538
Wellum's New Home, East Quarter, City of Rammon

Hearing a faint knock, Todd Wellum cautiously opened the door and found nothing. A split-second later he spotted the small, cylindrical comm unit lying on the ground, and his ears picked up frantic footfalls to his left. He considered whether to go for the comm or the mystery person and decided on the chase. With a quick mental apology to his wife, Todd leapt over the comm and sprinted down the street. He achieved his top speed quickly, grateful to finally be doing something besides moving boxes and furniture.

This wasn't what I meant when I said I wanted to see the city.

He was almost disappointed when he caught the fleeing boy after only two blocks.

The child screamed and dove to the ground to evade Todd for one more second.

Todd plucked him from the air midway to the ground, pinned his arms in place, and forced him to his knees so he couldn't kick.

"Calm down!" Todd ordered.

"Unhand that boy!" shouted a woman from a nearby doorway.

Todd twisted toward her, so he could watch for any new threats.

Screaming again, the boy wriggled furiously, trying to break free.

"Let him go, or I'll call the police and the Royal Guards," the lady threatened.

"Calm down," Todd again told the boy. He emphasized the order by squeezing a pressure point in the boy's upper arm. "You can go as soon as you answer a few questions."

"I didn't do anything!" the boy cried.

Todd flicked his attention back to the woman as a kerlak pistol leveled his way. Grunting his annoyance, he turned his back to the woman to protect the boy. "You don't need a gun, ma'am," Todd assured the woman. Turning his head, he kept his right eye trained on the woman. A flicker of movement caught his attention.

"Let me go," whined the boy.

"I told you the terms," Todd reminded his captive. "You go free when I get answers."

"Who gave you the comm you left on our doorway?" asked Kiata Wellum.

Todd craned his neck around and saw his wife calmly standing next to the dumbfounded, weaponless woman. The kerlak pistol was in Kiata's left hand. Her right hand held her banistick in a guarded, semi-threatening position. The question was directed at the boy, but Kiata's attention stayed on the woman.

"I don't know," said the boy, suddenly sullen.

"Who are you?" asked the woman, her voice a little awed.

Kiata returned her banistick to her belt in one smooth motion before removing the kerlak pistol's battery pack and presenting the two pieces to the woman.

"Just new neighbors," Kiata answered. "Sorry for the misunderstanding, Lady …"

"Channer," supplied the woman. "Elise Channer, cloth merchant."

"Was it a man or a woman? You must have gotten paid somehow," Todd pressed the kid. He hauled the boy to his feet and turned him around, keeping both hands on the child's shoulders to prevent escape.

The boy's dark eyes glared at Todd.

"Another messenger," he answered finally. He shrugged. "It happens all the time in the East Quarter. It's why I like working here."

"We should go," Kiata said. "He knows nothing more." She directed the words at Todd before smiling at the woman. "It was nice to meet you, Lady Channer."

***

When they got back home, Kiata set the comm on the kitchen table and checked it for traps. Finding none, she hit play and listened as Talyon Keldor's voice floated out of the tiny speaker.

"Ranger Wellum, you once saved my life, and now I want to return the favor. Meet me at moonrise on the tenth of Kest (October) where the firfe spice burned all those years ago."

"What do you think?" Todd asked.

Without answering, Kiata reviewed the short message another four times while pacing the kitchen. Still thinking, she reached up into a cabinet and retrieved two glasses. By the time she set them on the table, Todd had found the appola juice. He poured the juice as she settled into one of the chairs.

Kiata noted that they seemed to be having a lot of meetings at their lonely kitchen table.

"Taly's in trouble," she replied, finally answering Todd's question.

"Agreed." Todd slid one of the glasses over to her. "But why the sudden interest in you? It's obviously a trap."

Kiata caught the glass, nodded thanks, and lifted the drink to her lips. After taking a sip, she asked, "Did they get caught? There's no mention of Merisia. That's … troubling." She did not wish to discuss the reasons why she might suddenly draw interest from the wrong sorts of people. The obvious answer was her link to Reia, but that opened a line to many more questions. She wanted to focus on Taly.

"I hope they're safe," Todd said. His tone said he shared her doubts about that. "They seem like nice kids."

Kiata chuckled and drank more of the juice.

"They're not that much younger than us," said Kiata.

"Merisia maybe, but Taly's what? Fifteen? Sixteen?"

Kiata smiled gently at her husband.

"He's probably sixteen or seventeen. That's only five or six year's difference."

"Really? This business must age us." Todd studied his drink for a second then drank the whole thing in one shot.

"Must be all the high-speed chases involving messenger boys," Kiata teased.

"Or the disarming of little old ladies," Todd added.

"All in a day's work," said Kiata. She raised her glass toward Todd and drained the rest of the juice. Setting the glass down, she added, "Unfortunately, there's also this aspect." She picked up the comm and let the message play again.

Todd listened with his eyes closed.

"He tried to warn you," he said, when the message stopped. "His voice trails off a little when he speaks of the favor and then it starts up again strong. He sounds nervous, too."

"Either he's afraid of being caught or he's being forced to record the message against his will," said Kiata. "It doesn't really matter which. The key question is: what do we do about it?"

"Are you up for a trip to Kerimia for old time's sake?" asked Todd.

Sliding her empty glass back and forth between her hands, Kiata considered Todd's question.

It would be the simplest answer, she mused, but she knew better than most how complicated the simplest answers could be sometimes. She shook her head slowly then turned it into a sort of half-nod.

"We need to find Taly and Merisia," said Kiata.

Todd sat up straighter, his playful expression gone.

"What about your sister?" asked Todd.

"What about her? She's been safe without me these past few weeks. She should be fine for another week and a half, but I'll see her before we leave. We are technically assigned to her. At least we will be soon."

"A week and a half isn't much time. They've been gone for a long time." Todd sat back and ran both hands through his thick red hair.

"We need to think like them," said Kiata. "I don't believe Merisia's the sort to rough it too long in the wilderness. She seemed ill the last time we saw her. That narrows the search down to cities, but we don't have time to search each one."

"We should tell Master Niklos," said Todd. "Perhaps he can help us find them. And Nils, of course, we'll have to tell him."

Kiata felt the first inklings of excitement and the nervous energy that began every mission.

"We should speak with Nils first. He would have the best insights into the RT Alliance, and they have the most reasons to want Taly and Merisia."

Todd nodded agreement and flipped his empty glass up in the air.

Kiata winced as her good glass went sailing through the air end over end. Todd caught it easily, laughing at her expression. She was tempted to throw her own glass at him but knew it would be useless.

Thankfully, Nils arrived from his surveillance assignment.

Chapter 7:
Night Visitors

Kest (October) 1, 1538
Same Day
Queen Reia's Private Chambers, Royal Palace, City of Rammon

Moonlight streamed in from the large, open windows. Kiata Antellio Wellum pressed her back against one side of the window she perched on, trying to keep from blocking the light. An odd mixture of relief and irritation battled within her as she watched her sister sleep fitfully. A fine sheen of sweat glistened on Reia's brow. A breeze blew past Kiata and caused Reia's sleeping form to shiver.

Kiata leaned her head back against the window frame, sighed, and pondered her next move. Breaking into the palace, though not easy, should not have been possible. The imposing palace walls enclosing the gardens took less than a minute to scale. The expansive gardens provided nice cover the entire way to the palace itself. Kiata had narrowly avoided several Palace Security and Royal Guard patrols on her ascent to Reia's private suite of rooms. Had she been a real assassin, Reia would be dead.

She could call out to her sister, but Reia wasn't exactly the easiest—or quietest—person to wake. The nightmares usually kept a strong grip on Reia, but occasionally, they released her suddenly, waking her with a full adrenaline rush. Master Ekris had once confessed to Kiata such sleep patterns were quite unnatural and very worrisome.

As usual, Kiata settled upon the direct approach. Still conscious to stay out of the moonlight, she ducked, crept around the bed, and cautiously climbed up.

Reia tossed her head violently and rolled onto her left shoulder.

Kiata froze and waited for Reia to roll away from her. She could have made her move at any time, but she wanted to wait for the best angle. Crouching on the edge of Reia's bed, she silently willed her sister to move again.

A few minutes later, Reia finally settled onto her back again. Quick as a striking snake, Kiata slapped her left hand over Reia's mouth, used her free hand to grip Reia's upper left arm, and leaned close.

Tucking her mouth next to Reia's ear, Kiata whispered.

"Chalmd. Ceme." (Calm down. It's me.) She didn't bother speaking the Kalastan words backwards, as was her custom with her sister. Reia's sleepy brain would have enough trouble absorbing the quiet words through the trauma of waking. Kiata patiently waited out the seconds of blind panic, throwing her weight into pinning her sister down. "Neskrimda. Ehcamemastas," she said lightly, when Reia's struggles abated. (Please don't scream. It would cause me much trouble.)

When Reia stopped thrashing, Kiata cautiously released her sister's mouth so she could speak.

"Kiata," Reia whispered, sounding like she was trying to believe it.

Kiata eased her grip on Reia's arm and spoke softly.

"Tuisola. Dimesunarethdrims." (We are alone. Tell me your nightmares.)

"You were in Kerimia," Reia answered. She sat up carefully and arranged the blankets around her knees.

Kiata's lips pressed together but she said nothing right away. It was one of four dreams that haunted Reia night after night. The first dream featured their parents' murder. If one wanted to get technical, the dream featured the murder of Kiata's parents and Reia's adoptive parents, but the distinction had never made a difference to Kiata. Although practically an infant at that time, Reia remembered the event far more vividly than Kiata who had been four. The second dream forced Reia to relive the criessa training, complete with the cold terror of being abandoned by Master Kolknir in a mountain cave. The third dream consisted of endless fights against korvers, bears, lions, and other mountain creatures.

This was the fourth dream where Reia experienced everything

that had happened to Kiata on her level-seven trial in the village of Kerimia. Kiata had been captured and beaten with her own weapon until a viper had bitten Talyon Keldor. Then, the boy's father had spared her in exchange for saving his son.

"I'm sorry. You shouldn't even have those memories," Kiata said finally.

Reia shrugged, wincing with the movement.

"I'll let you know when I learn to block them. Was there something specific you wanted?"

***

Reia knew her sister meant well but talking about the nightmares only reinforced their hold on her.

Kiata touched the bottom of Reia's chin in a motherly gesture.

"What happened? You're moving like someone who wrestled a goritor."

"Just stiff from sword training," Reia admitted. "How was your day?"

Kiata tweaked Reia's chin and let her hand drop.

"All right, we'll talk about something else besides bad dreams and sword training if you want, but I'm here if you need me."

"I know."

"Contrary to that statement, Todd and I are leaving Rammon for a few days. Taly's in trouble and probably Merisia as well. We need to find them." Kiata shifted her knees to a more comfortable position.

"How do you know? Where will you look for them? Why are you telling me?" The thoughts flowed out of Reia in rapid succession.

"We received a message from Taly earlier this evening. Nils thinks there's a good chance they went to Terab. Todd is contacting Ranger Zinn now. Hopefully, he'll have something more specific by the time I get home, and I'm telling you because we've been assigned to Rammon."

Clarity crashed over Reia.

"You're asking my permission," she said, stunned.

"Precisely, Highness," said Kiata, grinning. "Nils will be around if you need to contact us. We won't be gone long. If we find nothing, the message said to meet Taly in Kerimia on the tenth of this month."

"What if I refused to let you go?" Reia knew she wouldn't, but she wanted to hear Kiata's answer.

"I'd be tempted to kidnap you myself," Kiata replied. "In actuality, I would probably just ignore you. We don't have official orders from the Council. They gave us until the seventh of this month to move, but Todd and I didn't have much to move."

Reia detected a hint of sadness in Kiata's last statement, but it disappeared before she could confirm it. A wave of tiredness swept over her as the last of the adrenaline rush disappeared. She blinked.

"Why didn't you wait until morning?"

Kiata's grin widened and she shook her head.

"You have no idea what you've gotten yourself into, do you?" she asked.

"Do you?" Reia challenged.

Chuckling, Kiata picked up Reia's right hand and began massaging it.

"Your life is no longer your own. You'll be admired by many, hated by many, and probably misunderstood by everybody."

"You make it sound so glamorous," Reia said.

Kiata stopped massaging Reia's hand and patted it affectionately.

"It will fall to Todd, me, and Rangers you'll never see to make sure you and King Terosh have a long, boring reign," said Kiata. "I chose this method of entry because I wanted to see you tonight, and I wanted to test the palace security, which could stand for some improvements."

"Terosh is not going to be pleased by that news," said Reia.

"Why isn't he here? Is everything all right?" asked Kiata.

"He needs his rest. My nightmares aren't exactly conducive to sharing a bed," Reia answered.

"That I remember vividly," Kiata commented, no doubt recalling the bruises earned through years of easing Reia's nightmares.

"Besides, this is how the royal quarters have been arranged for decades."

"Reia." Kiata said it with equal measures of gentle reproof, amusement, and pity. "You are queen."

"Yes, I know—oh." Her sister's meaning slammed into her. She drew a quick breath and tried to explain. "People here don't really like change."

"Very few people in the universe like change," said Kiata. "It's hard, but sometimes it's also right. I'm not saying your sleeping arrangements should change. I'm saying you need to choose your battles wisely."

"What battles?" Reia asked, stifling a yawn.

Her sister's wry expression asked: *how did such a sweet thing like you make it so long in this world?*

"You should try to get some sleep, but be careful," said Kiata. "People are going to want to change everything about you. They're going to redefine your looks, speech patterns, and ideals. I know you must let them mold you into a queen, but don't forget who you are deep down." A playful grin added: *you're my kid sister.*

"What am I?" asked Reia.

Kiata got up, went to the window nearest the bed, and climbed on the windowsill.

"We'll find out soon enough," she said, before vanishing out the window.

***

Kest (October) 1, 1538
Same Day
King Terosh's Private Chambers, Royal Palace, City of Rammon

Terosh knew he should be asleep, but he could not stop thinking. His grandfather's statements still bothered him. He understood the need for vengeance against Niktrod Keldor, but the part about Reia baffled him.

Growing up, Terosh had slipped into Tate's room or gone down to Master Sedir's chambers on the third floor when sleep eluded him. Kaimon Sedir always received him warmly.

With inexplicable rising fear, Terosh dressed and eased open the door leading out of his private rooms. He looked carefully left and right before realizing the ridiculousness of his caution. Nobody would scold him. He could go wherever he wanted no matter what the hour. Straightening out of sneak mode, Terosh walked down the long hallway to the East stairwell. His first few steps were tentative, but the strangeness of taking the main stairs gradually wore off.

About seven minutes later, Terosh arrived at Sedir's quarters. He reached up to knock.

Sedir swung the door open before Terosh's knuckles could brush the door.

"Enter to find the answers you seek, Your Grace," said Master Sedir.

Terosh smiled, trying to recall how long ago he had first dared to come here.

"How did you know I was coming?" he asked.

"Some old friends told me," Sedir replied easily. He motioned

Terosh inside and gestured for him to sit in one of two comfortable chairs arranged for easy conversation.

Terosh realized Sedir must be talking about the anotechs and felt stupid for not understanding that sooner. He perched on the edge of a chair.

"I knew you would seek answers eventually," said Master Sedir.

"How did you come to know about the anotechs?" asked Terosh.

"Someone told me. You have discovered some of their powers, but not all of them. Your grandfather, King Salen, was friends with my father. When my parents died in a water hov accident, the king made sure my sister and I were well cared for. Eventually, he saw I liked to teach, so he instructed me in the knowledge of the anotechs and entrusted me to teach his children."

"Did you teach my aunts and uncle?" asked Terosh. "I thought only the eldest was to know."

"I taught them all something about the anotechs, but most of my efforts were spent with the twins."

Terosh longed to know his Aunt Uria and Uncle Uel.

"How come you didn't teach me?" Terosh wondered, trying not to sound miffed.

"That was your father's decision," said Master Sedir. "King Teorn knew next to nothing about the anotechs because he had no interest in knowing. He had me instruct Prince Taytron because tradition demanded that at least one Minstel know the family legacy. Now that your brother is gone, it falls to you to learn everything you can."

"Will you teach my children?" asked Terosh. "When I have children, I mean."

"If you have more than one child, would you like them all to know the truth about the anotechs?" asked Sedir.

Terosh considered the question. The anotechs were a wonderful, beautiful, and dangerous secret as well as a heavy burden for the bearer, but they had also saved his life several times over.

"Yes. Finding out later is harder. I think my children will need every advantage they can get," said Terosh.

"Very well, but I should probably start by teaching you and your wife. I will try to schedule some daytime lessons, but I think a large part of this should be done at night."

"Why?" Terosh wondered.

"The less people who know about the anotechs, the safer you will be."

"Speaking of anotechs and secrecy, my grandfather said something about Reshner not being habitable. What did he mean by that?"

Instead of answering directly, Sedir asked, "Have you listened to every message in Loresh, Your Grace?"

"I believe so," said Terosh. "The Chamber of Enlightenment only opened for me recently, but I have always had access to the Chamber of Wisdom." He paused and added, "You don't have to use honorifics, Master. I'm still just me."

"True, but you need to be comfortable with the title," Sedir said gently. He cleared his throat to dispel the ensuing awkward moment. "You've probably forgotten my history lessons, so I shall summarize. When Jaspen Turgot crashed here centuries ago, Reshner held only a few research scientists. His arrival changed everything."

Terosh cocked his head slightly to the right, a habit present since childhood.

"Should I send for the queen?" he wondered, nearly stumbling over the last word. "She would enjoy hearing this."

"Call to her from here," said Sedir.

After a few failed attempts, Sedir coaxed Terosh into a state conducive to a strong connection between minds. When the message was delivered, received, and accepted, Terosh reported his success.

"Well, keep at it," instructed Sedir.

Terosh blinked at him.

"She will not know the way unless you guide her, Your Grace," Sedir explained. "I'll see to some refreshments while you practice."

***

Kest (October) 1, 1538
Same Day
Queen Reia's Private Chambers, Royal Palace, City of Rammon

Reia felt Terosh's call in her mind like a half-remembered whisper. She ignored it the first three times, attributing it to her troubled sleep, but the fourth time she answered aloud.

"What is it?"

King calling for you, answered the anotechs.

What does he want?

Ask him.

She did and felt the urge to follow his voice. Feeling silly and insane, Reia dressed and left her private chambers. The guards standing in the hallway asked if she wanted them to accompany her, but she politely declined. If she was destined to wander the palace halls like a lost little tretling, she would do it more comfortably alone.

After about ten minutes, Reia paused in front of a door identical to countless others she'd just passed. As she gathered the courage to knock, the door swung open and Terosh stood before her. He wore comfortable nightclothes and nothing on his feet. Relief rushed through Reia and propelled her into Terosh's awaiting arms.

A lingering kiss later, Terosh pulled away slightly.

"What took you so long? I was calling half the night." A twinkle in his eyes told her he was teasing.

"Most people use comms, my love," Reia said.

"Most people lack your unique abilities, Majesty," said a soft male voice from behind Terosh.

Reia recognized the voice as that of Master Kaimon Sedir.

Terosh sidestepped and turned, tucking her left hand in the crook of his arm. He led her to a finely threaded couch. A low table laden with cakes, pastries, and fruits lay in front of the couch.

"Please, sit. Have some refreshments. Would you like some tea?" Sedir spoke easily, but Reia knew even now he was instructing them. "His Highness said you had a fondness for mintas and wuzzle root teas. Both are available in plenty."

Graciously accepting some mintas tea, Reia waited for someone to explain why she was in Master Sedir's quarters at this unholy hour.

Sedir busied himself rearranging the pastries while Terosh picked apart an appola tart.

"You have lovely quarters, Master Sedir, but I doubt you had me roused at this hour to delight in them," said Reia. "May I inquire as to the occasion?"

Sedir smiled expansively.

"Well phrased, Your Majesty. Master Cadrish's labors are showing."

"Master Sedir was explaining some of the history of the anotechs, and I knew you would want to hear it," said Terosh.

Sedir reviewed the little they had covered without Reia, then continued, "The king's ancestor, Jaspen Turgot, brought the anotechs to Reshner in his own body. They spent three years piecing together his shattered body and carving out Loresh. What happened after that is debated, but I favor the simplest explanation."

"Records say the planet was ice around a molten core back then," said Terosh. "How did the anotechs change the entire core?"

"It has not been proven, but I believe the entire core *is* currently anotechs," said Sedir. "I do not know why they would spend so much effort, but the nearly constant weather is proof of a sort."

"Could their numbers grow so large in such a short time?" asked Terosh.

"If every anotech created could build another like itself, I believe it is likely. The question then becomes why have they not consumed the entire planet?" Sedir arched an eyebrow at Reia and Terosh, waiting for one of them to venture a guess.

"It would not serve their purposes," Terosh said at last.

Sedir nodded.

"That's as close as anyone has ever come to a reasonable explanation. The anotechs serve their makers. Turgot—presumably one of the anotech creators—landed on a relatively inhospitable planet, so they changed it to suit him. Perhaps we were too close to our primary star as scientists theorize, and the anotechs needed to move Reshner. Perhaps they merely funnel energy from the core, redirecting it as they will. I am less certain of the mechanics, but the results seem to speak for themselves. After all, we only have one truly temperate continent."

"I'm not sure I follow," Reia admitted.

"Planets caught too close to their suns burn; those too far away, freeze," explained Sedir. "The slightest degree can make a big difference. Somehow, the anotechs have established a haven suitable for humanoid life without an expensive terraforming patent. I'm sure the how of it is something GAPP scientists would kill for."

"GAPP again," said Reia, recalling Terosh's recap of his conversation with his grandfather.

He had seemed uncomfortable, like he was omitting details.

What would he hide from me?

To distract herself from the disturbing train of thought, she looked deep into her untouched tea, drank a little, and put the cup down on the table.

"They keep coming up," she murmured.

"They are one of three major powers in this galaxy," Sedir offered, sensing her unspoken question. "The other two powers are the Vambri Consortium, an alien collective largely on the other side and the Unclaimed or Independent Systems, depending on who you ask."

"We rely on a series of alliances to remain independent," Terosh said. The look he gave Reia told her he had much more to say on the subject. He reached over and squeezed her right hand.

"Perhaps we can discuss such alliances tomorrow evening. We should retire for the night. May I escort you back?"

The tender, shy way he asked the question filled Reia with a sense of peace. She quickly consented.

Chapter 8: Bold Moves

Kest (October) 1, 1538
Same Day
Deegan Estate, City of Terab

"This is absolutely going too far," Vera Tarpon declared, piercing her daughter's husband with a scornful look. The pup had just had the nerve to send her hov away.

"Have some Charan wine and hear me out, Lady Tarpon," said Gareth Restler. He held a delicate glass of blood-red liquid out to her.

Vera took the glass from him, quelling the delightful urge to upend the glass over his head.

"There is nothing to hear," she said, sitting on the edge of the room's sole couch. "You have my daughter back, and you have had your revenge against her friend. This matter is closed. I am going home."

Gareth took a sip of his wine and carefully placed the glass on the low table in front of the couch where Vera sat primly.

"I have taken the liberty of informing your husband you wish to extend your stay for a few days."

"Then I shall have to disabuse him of that foolish notion," Vera said evenly. She took out her personal comm and began keying her husband's private code.

Gareth cleared his throat.

"I apologize for taking another small liberty. Your comm will only work if I release it to do so."

Vera arched an eyebrow at him.

"That is indeed a bold move. What precisely do you hope to gain by holding me?" Vera asked.

"Merisia will need you, and I need to be elsewhere for a few days," said Gareth.

"Then let her come with me. Perhaps what she needs is some time among her childhood comforts," said Vera.

"That may be, but it would also shift the alliance balance too much. This incident has destroyed a lot of the trust between our families. I will not risk destroying the rest over so trivial a matter as where to send Merisia to convalesce. She will stay here on neutral territory."

"Yet you would risk this self-same trust to get your way, by holding me captive and lying to my husband?"

"You are free to come and go about the estate as you wish, Lady Tarpon. My men will escort you, of course, for your own safety. I simply desire that you refrain from making unnecessary calls, hence the lock on your comm. As for what I told your husband, I am fairly certain I did not lie."

Vera cast a dagger-sharp smile at Gareth.

"Of course, you simply left out all details except my concern for Merisia's health." Vera contemplated the glass of wine in her hands. Then, taking a long breath, she tipped the glass to her lips and drained it all at once. Setting the glass down carefully, she said, "This is a very dangerous game, Gareth. Choose your allies and enemies wisely."

***

Kest (October) 3, 1538

Desert Dreams Inn, City of Terab

"What is our next move?" asked Kiata Antellio Wellum. She quickly removed the confining headwrap typical to Terabian attire. Two days of hot surveillance had convinced her that the headwrap's inventor was evil. She would rather deal with the sting of sand against her face than suffer under layers of stifling cloth.

"Well, we don't have much of a choice," said Todd, stating the obvious. "We wait. They're both in there somewhere. They'll have to be moved sometime."

An idea came to Kiata, and she gave her husband a sly smile.

"There is another option." She wadded the headwrap and tossed it onto the rickety bed.

Knowing that expression usually led to trouble, Todd winced.

"I know what you're thinking and that is *not* a valid option," said Todd. "We have no jurisdiction here. Ranger Rinn—"

"Would have to help you if I got into trouble," Kiata finished.

Todd walked up to her, draped an arm over her shoulders, and led her to a seat on the bed. It creaked and popped ominously but held. Todd eyed it suspiciously and chose not to further test the bed.

"We've tried this plan before," Todd began with a let's-be-reasonable gesture.

"Yes, and it worked," Kiata said.

Removing his headwrap, Todd tossed it onto the nearest pillow and crossed his arms over his chest.

"You have a very selective memory."

"I remember you and your fancy shooting," Kiata said, lifting her chin a bit and grinning. "You were pretty impressive."

"You got shot," Todd reminded her.

"Yes, that part was less impressive," Kiata admitted. "It hurt like hungry fire beetles, too, but the point is we rescued the hostages, caught two of the perpetrators, and restored peace to the City of Korch."

"You got shot," Todd repeated, glaring at her.

"Yes, I did," Kiata said. "And Master Ekris did a lovely job of fixing me. How does that change anything here?"

Todd uncrossed his arms and held out his hands in a halting motion.

"Let's just wait and see what happens. Even if they confine Merisia to her friend's house indefinitely, they have to move Taly eventually, especially if they want to bait that trap in Kerimia."

Kiata flopped back on the bed, which squealed in protest.

"I hate waiting."

***

Kest (October) 3, 1538
Same Day
Maledek's Private Retreat, City of Idonia

"What did you do today?" asked Lady Mavis Altran. Her hologram flickered as it adjusted to the glare of her red and gold shimmersilk dress.

Lord Kezem noted the finery as he gritted his teeth against the tediousness of this exercise. He had endured this test nearly every day of his life. It was always a battle to keep secrets from his mother. Every answer he gave would be analyzed considering information she already knew.

"What is the occasion?" he asked, instead of answering.

"I was deciding what to wear for tomorrow's banquet at the palace," said his mother. "Dennel sent your people the reminder hours ago. Have they failed to notify you?"

Kezem cursed silently. He did not doubt that the message had been delivered on time, but Dennel had probably time stamped it to be given to him just after this impromptu meeting. It was yet another petty test from his mother.

"I will have to check my messages more often," he said mildly.

"Indeed. Has the Keldor boy arrived yet?" asked his mother.

Kezem shook his head.

"Gareth said there was a delay."

"Gareth is unstable," said Lady Mavis. "This business with his wife has unhinged him, but he should be able to hold together long enough to be useful. When the time comes to dissolve the alliance, you'll have a fine weapon in him."

"I believe so," Kezem agreed. "The delay is of no consequence. Whether the young Keldor is there, here, or some other place, the Rangers will track him down."

"Do you have enough people watching over him?"

Kezem nodded.

"The guard on him is adequate for the moment. I'm more concerned with how to capture and keep the Rangers."

"You don't have to keep them both," said Lady Mavis. "Besides, killing Todd Wellum should take some of the fight out of his wife. Just remember that I need Kiata alive."

"I will consider your advice, Mother," Kezem said noncommittally.

"Good. I have another matter to discuss with you."

"And that would be?"

"It would behoove you to save our young royals a time or two." Seeing his blank look, she added, "Get the common people to like you."

Kezem listened raptly while feigning disinterest, as his mother outlined her thoughts on this new matter. By the end, he was truly speechless. He knew his mother could be coldly calculating but this was a new level even for her.

***

Kest (October) 3, 1538
Same Day

Deegan Estate, City of Terab

Todd Wellum checked the charge on his kerlak pistol and gripped his banistick hard.

How does she do that?

He ran their conversation over in his mind. He thought he'd convinced her to do nothing, yet here he sat tucked under thick bushes on the Deegan Estate, waiting to enact her crazy plan.

Movement to his left caught his eyes. A dark figure—presumably Kiata—sailed over the wall and landed in a crouch. Then, tossing a mock salute in Todd's general direction, the figure raced around toward the back of the huge house.

Todd put his banistick back on his belt, scrambled out from under the bush, and climbed the wall to the fourth room from the front on the third floor. There was no convenient balcony, and the window had a dozen sensors to detect movement and prevent tampering. Todd dispatched some anotechs to deal with the window sensors and reinforced lock. When they returned a moment later, he slid the window glass left into its space in the wall and climbed through the opening.

A lone woman lay on the massive bed, surrounded by a small army of pillows and mountainous blankets. Todd regretted the fright he would cause her. A few more commands to the anotechs had the woman sitting up straight, wide awake, scared to death, and, thankfully, mute.

Todd willed the floor lights to come on dimly so Lady Deegan could see his form but not his face.

"I apologize for the intrusion, Lady Deegan. I assure you I mean you no harm. I seek Merisia Restler and Talyon Keldor. Are they still here? Please nod, if so."

Lady Deegan blinked rapidly. She nodded then shook her head, looking frustrated.

"I'm going to unlock your vocal cords. Please just answer my questions without trouble. I seek only to help them." Todd spoke like a man trying to tame a wild korver. He issued the correct commands but had the anotechs wait with the woman and react if she so much as thought about screaming.

"Merisia is gone," said Lady Deegan, sounding like she had a sore throat. "Her husband had her moved out of Terab earlier this evening." She swallowed hard and a tear worked its way down her left cheek. "Talyon is here. Three rooms down the right hallway, but you'll never reach him. There are too many guards."

"Thank you, madam," Todd said, infusing his voice with sincerity. "Would you like to leave this place?" he asked impulsively.

She shook her head.

"I am safe enough but find Merisia. She is not safe."

"I shall do my best," Todd promised. "Sleep now. I apologize in advance if you wake up with a slight headache." He gestured and the anotechs rendered Lady Deegan unconscious before returning to him.

Counting windows, Todd exited Lady Deegan's room the way he had entered. Once outside, he climbed the wall horizontally, disabling the motion sensors in each window as he reached them. When he had passed twelve windows, Todd disabled all security measures, slid the window aside, and entered. He found Talyon Keldor asleep on the bed, bound with stuncuffs secured to the headboard. Korverhide ropes held the young man's ankles together.

Three RT Alliance soldiers slept in the room, one on each side of Talyon's bed. Todd considered shooting them but rejected the idea. These men simply worked for the wrong people. Taly too had worked for the RT Alliance once upon a time. Moving swiftly from one guard to the next, Todd silently rendered each man unconscious.

After turning up the lights, Todd assessed Taly's injuries and winced. The boy had been beaten. Both eyes were multicolored and swollen. His left cheek had a jagged gash down the side like someone had been punching with more than bare knuckles. Todd imagined the rest of Taly's body probably looked the same, so moving him would hurt a lot.

The muffled whine of energy beams tore Todd from his thoughts. He snatched up his kerlak pistol, raced to the door, and swung it open. A man's limp body fell toward him. He stepped back and let the man crash to the floor. Instinctively, he crouched to feel for a pulse and was relieved to find a pathetic, erratic excuse for one.

So much for quiet, Todd lamented, casting a few anotechs to scout for his wife.

Finding her down the hall to his right, he ducked into the hallway far enough to fire four shots left in the direction Kiata was shooting. Six angry answering shots, bright red with deadly energy, sailed back at him. He pulled his head back into Taly's room in time to keep it.

Knowing it was dangerous but a better bet than wading through kerlak beams, Todd grabbed his banistick off his belt to have a focal point, sat on the floor, and sank into a trance. It took several seconds to marshal enough energy to gather the anotechs and several more seconds to properly word the orders in Kalastan.

"Seblaetdiscurtotevons," said Todd. (Find and disable all enemies.)

Anotechs flooded out of him and scurried down the hall like a silent stream of water. Todd felt strangely drained. He hoped his gambit worked because if any of those men rushed him now, he would have no hope of stopping them.

***

Kiata felt the anotech surge and knew her husband's intent.

That was not part of the plan!

She redoubled her efforts to take out the RT soldiers shooting at her. Blue and red beams lit up the hall in an impressive display of sizzling light. At any other time, Kiata would have thought the display pretty.

Suddenly, the red beams stopped coming.

Kiata sprinted down the hall to the room where she had seen her husband. Sending a few anotechs to confirm the enemies were down, Kiata knelt beside Todd and gently tapped his face with her palm.

"Wake up, Todd!" Kiata commanded. "Wake up, so I can yell at you for that stupid move."

Frowning down at him, Kiata considered a more forceful method of waking Todd. Pounding footsteps on the stairs convinced her to try. Closing her eyes, she gripped Todd's shoulders and willed anotechs to flood his body. Then, she sent a strong shock down her arms and into him. He awoke with a pained cry, which she muffled with a hand across his mouth.

"Shhhh. This is no time to sleep on the job!" Kiata scolded. She planted a quick kiss on his lips to take the sting from her words.

"You shocked me," Todd said.

"I did, and we need to go," Kiata said, hauling Todd to his feet.

"Taly won't be easy to move," Todd warned.

Kiata cast a glance at the bed where Taly lay.

Todd's kerlak gun snapped up and fired twice into the hallway. Two men toppled. Todd scrambled to his feet, slammed the door, and pushed a dresser in front of it.

Kiata sent weak stun beams into the three men surrounding Taly's bed, one of whom had staggered to his feet. The task gave her something to focus on while she thought. Moving Taly would be risky but leaving him to the tender mercies of the RT Alliance would be tantamount to murder. As she turned to offer her opinion to Todd, she found him standing before her holding a bundle of sheets that probably contained Taly.

"Out the window then," Todd said, throwing one last glance at his makeshift barricade.

"Just once, I wish you'd factor a door into your escape plan!" Kiata measured the distance to the window, sprinted forward, and launched herself out the opening.

***

Todd Wellum's heart climbed into his throat and rattled his teeth as he watched his wife jump out the window. Silently apologizing to Taly, he used anotechs to render the boy unconscious. He considered releasing the stuncuffs and untying the ankle rope but decided it would be easier to move Taly if his limbs stayed in place. Todd grunted. For such a frail-looking pile of beaten flesh, Taly still weighed a lot.

You're getting old.

Gritting his teeth and willing strength into his tired limbs, Todd hauled Taly to the window and peeked to make sure Kiata was ready.

No going back now.

Todd heaved Taly out the window, dropped him, and imagined a cushion of anotechs forming beneath him. He had done this a few times before but never with a person.

Kiata stood below with her head bent forward and her arms outstretched like a frozen swimmer.

Hoping everything would work out, Todd allowed his body to tumble forward out the window. They dropped like ungainly rocks. With huge effort, Todd twisted so he would land on his back and not on top of Taly. He hit the aircushion before the ground, but it knocked the breath from him all the same.

A siren cut through Todd's head. Two hov bikes flashed around the corner, firing streams of red energy. Before the air cushion could dissolve, Todd willed it into a stronger form and whipped it up as a shield. The red energy met the white shield and splashed it with crimson light. Todd's hands hurt from the influx of heat, but he maintained the shield anyway.

Meanwhile, Kiata leaned around the shield and fired four blue beams at their attackers. Two went wide and two caught the front attacker. He flew off the bike with a cry of dismay. His bike barreled forward without him. Kiata slapped her kerlak pistol back into its holster and leapt aboard the passing bike. Then, she drew her banistick and reversed the thrusters. The results sent her hurtling backward toward the remaining attacker.

He defiantly raised a kerlinblade but never got the chance to use it. Kiata's banistick caught him full across the chest. She reversed thrusters again at the last moment, so the force wouldn't be deadly. Still, Todd practically heard the man's ribs break with the impact.

Digging deep into energy reserves, Todd released Taly from his bonds and draped the boy across his back. Then, he hauled himself aboard the recently vacated hov bike and used anotechs to secure Taly to his back. Not burdened by their charge, Kiata ran interference against three additional pairs of hov bikes that pursued them. Todd had not had many opportunities to observe Kiata's driving, but he concluded strapping himself to a wind-launched cannafitch might be safer.

The chase took them through most of Terab, winding through residential and business streets alike. Luckily, the late hour meant little foot traffic. A police hov joined for a while, but Todd wasn't about to stop and answer a dozen questions, not with half a dozen fancy hov bikes chasing him.

At last, they lost their pursuers long enough to ditch the hov bikes and smuggle Taly back to the Desert Dreams Inn. Upon arrival, Todd tossed Taly onto the poor excuse for a bed and collapsed onto an old blanket thrown on the floor.

Chapter 9:
Royal Role

Kest (October) 4, 1538
Queen Lissa Banquet Hall, Royal Palace, City of Rammon

Queen Reia Antellio Minstel nodded graciously as each guest was introduced by the excitable Banquet Hall Master. The existence of such a position had surprised her, but she accepted that surprises would be quite normal for a while. As advised, she kept her movements slow so she would not strain her neck. Reia had thought Sedir's warning ridiculous until a painful twinge convinced her to take him seriously.

One by one, Reia met Terosh's aunt, cousins, and their families where applicable. In spite of her husband's dire warnings concerning his aunt's manipulative nature, she found Lady Mavis Altran fascinating. The older woman wore her dark hair pinned up in such a way that the gray sections looked like foamy, cresting waves. Her eyes, which matched Terosh's shade of deep blue, absorbed and measured everything with cool calculation. Reia wondered what impression she was making on the former princess.

Lady Mavis's sons each towered over her, but they also deferred to her. The eldest and most physically impressive son, Eldon, bowed deeply upon introduction then made a sweeping gesture toward his wife and sons. His two boys copied his movements and waved to their mother, drawing a warm smile from Reia. On cue, Eldon's wife, Lady Calia Altran, stepped forward and curtsied. Her blond hair was swept up and subdued by a small army of pins. The older boy, Emry, jostled the younger one, Jaedin, and Lady Calia stepped between them, parting the boys like a woman wading through a wheat field.

Mitrek Altran ushered his family forward as Master Roth announced them. Looking like Calia's twin, Lady Delia Altran held a disgruntled baby swaddled in white shimmersilk robes. Reia couldn't tell the child's gender until he was introduced as Lord Sullivan Altran. Next presented were Lady Silvia and Lady Arabeth Altran. The girls, six and two respectively, attempted curtseys. Silvia's was mostly successful. Arabeth simply plopped down on her tiny rump and screeched with delight. Lady Mavis scooped the child up and whispered in her ear. To Reia's amazement, Arabeth jammed a thumb into her mouth and rested her head on her grandmother's shoulder.

Last presented was Lord Kezem Altran, the youngest, shortest, and most serious of Mavis's brood. He bowed stiffly to Reia and Terosh in turn then stepped back almost shyly.

The Banquet Hall Master, Wesley Roth, babbled on for a few minutes about each Idonian lord and his position, but Reia only partially listened. She already knew their positions. Governor Lord Eldon was Idonia's representative to the Governors Council. Governor Judge Mitrek oversaw legal matters for the city and the surrounding villages. Governor General Kezem handled the details of running the city.

When Master Roth finally asked everybody to be seated, Reia gratefully rose from the throne, accepted Terosh's hand, descended the three steps to the ground, and walked over to the table. Then she waited for two servants to pull out her dining throne. Terosh had assured her the imposing monstrosities would be used sparingly, and she sincerely hoped he was right. Murmuring thanks, she hauled herself up as gracefully as possible, feeling silly about the formality and embarrassed by the ornate chair.

Once the ordeal of sitting down had been successfully overcome, Reia relaxed a little and tried to feel dignified with her feet hanging half a meter off the ground. The urge to imitate young Emry and Jaedin—who were bouncing up and down and kicking with abandon—almost overcame her sense of propriety.

"There's a control on the left armrest for a foot support," said Terosh, leaning over to whisper in her ear.

Reia glanced down and saw a disconcerting array of buttons tucked beneath a glass cover. She shot her husband a mildly panicked look.

"The glass slips aside," said Terosh. "Press six, eight, two, and the little green button in the lower right corner."

Following the instructions, Reia waited anxiously until the throne responded by slipping a thin metal rung beneath her feet. Before she could thank Terosh, the loud crash of Master Roth taking a mallet to a large gong made her flinch. She stopped just shy of throwing herself off the throne. Terosh's comforting hand landed on her arm, which had unconsciously moved toward where a banistick ought to have been attached to her waist. He squeezed gently and sent a few calming thoughts through the anotechs.

There's nothing to worry about. It's just the evening meal being summoned. The gong can be used as the fire alarm and the heralding of an impending invasion as well, but not tonight.

After shooting Terosh a quick questioning look, Reia cleared her expression and glanced about to see if their guests had noticed her reaction. Lady Delia and Lord Mitrek were deep in conversation. Calia whispered furiously to one of her sons, and Kezem chatted with Eldon. Only Lady Mavis appeared to be paying any attention to them. A faint smile said she noticed but sympathized with Reia's unease.

Lively music sprang from various points around the room. Willing her overactive heart to calm down, Reia watched as a line of servants entered from a side door. Each wore a white uniform with a wide, brightly colored belt cinched at his or her waist. The color corresponded to the type of food carried on heavy-looking trays. The servants' steps had a definite rhythm that matched the music perfectly. Reia admired the display of strength and coordination as the servants surrounded the table and descended on it as one.

***

Sweet and spicy aromas rose from the steaming plates. Fried wallay legs, rine bat wings, ferbel meatballs, turtle soup, plains turkey soaked in jintal juice, swordfish fillets, crab legs, and scerims appeared in generous quantities. Terosh felt conflicted but soon settled on the plains turkey in jintal juice, some buttered wheat bread, and the mixed vegetable casserole.

Conversation stayed to safe areas such as the most recent windstorm to sweep the Balor Plains, until Jaedin caught up a long, slender crab leg and whacked his brother upside the head with it. As he drew back for another blow, his mother's hand shot out and plucked the crab leg from his grasp.

"That is *not* a kerlinblade," Lady Calia scolded.

"Is too," Jaedin insisted, reaching up to reclaim his toy.

"It is food," said Lady Calia calmly. "You love crab,

remember?" She used a crab cracker to break the shell and pulled out the pink and white meat.

"Do not," said Jaedin, scowling at the meat.

"Do too," said Lady Calia, matching her son's obstinate tone. Speaking thus, she grabbed her fork, speared the strip of meat, and tapped the boy on the nose with it.

He giggled and took a bite as Calia floated it past his mouth.

Terosh observed the scene with a mixture of admiration for Lady Calia's skill and a sudden, inexplicable pang. He gazed at his wife and tried to read her expression. As usual, simple study failed him, so he gauged her emotions with anotechs. His senses flooded with her warm affection, fierce love, and an odd, stabbing fear of failure. The reason for his pang and her fear suddenly smacked him. They both wanted a child.

It's too early, Terosh thought, shaking free of the feeling. *You've only been married a month and a half. There's so much to take care of first.*

"I want a kerlinblade!" Jaedin declared.

"When you're older," said his father.

"Uncle Kezem has one," Emry declared. "He has a special Ranger weapon, too."

"Have you ever killed anybody with it, Uncle Kezem?" asked Jaedin.

"Boys! This is not polite dinner conversation," said Calia.

"I am sorely out of practice with a kerlinblade," Kezem admitted.

"He used to be quite the duelist," said Lady Mavis. She casually lifted her Nedis crystal wine glass. After taking a delicate sip, she added, "His Grace, the king, used to be quite the duelist as well." She languidly lifted her eyes to meet Terosh's curious gaze. "I wonder if he has kept up those skills."

"There is but one way to know," said Kezem, setting down a forkful of swordfish. He picked up his wine glass and raised it to Terosh. "Your Highness, would you accept a friendly challenge to a Dollan duel at the next Colored Crossblades Tournament? It is about a year off."

The boys' faces lit up with the possibility of a fight.

"It would be a pleasure to accept such a challenge," said Terosh, not wishing to disappoint the boys. Picking up his wine glass, he sealed the promise with a brief toast and took a long swallow.

The smooth wine filled his mouth with the taste of sweet

rielberries then burned a little as it slid down his throat. The slight kick brought about that familiar dread of the wine containing more than fermented rielberries. The thought released a cascade of further fears. They tossed around his head until they settled on one particularly painful thought.

What if Reia is poisoned?

He had lost his mother to poison. He would not lose his wife to it. Setting down the wine glass harder than intended, Terosh vowed to do everything in his power to protect his wife. Perhaps Dr. Dentelich would have a contact that could help him. The physician knew an awful lot about everyone in the palace.

***

Kest (October) 5, 1538
Senate Great Hall, City of Rammon

Queen Reia tried very hard to not let the size of the Senate Great Hall bother her, but the place was designed to be imposing. The meeting areas were much more manageable, but the hallway leading to them covered several city blocks. Sedir had explained the rationale for this massive waste of space, but Reia still didn't understand the need for pillars commemorating long-dead senators. She felt like a condemned person as she continued along at a steady pace. Most of her just wanted to jog to the end and be done with the grand entrance.

Conscious of the crown atop her head, Reia felt ridiculous. She had protested wearing the extravagant thing, but Master Sedir insisted first impressions were important. If she thought too long about the crown's cost, she got dizzy. It featured a sea of diamonds cradling amethysts and emeralds of varying sizes atop a gold and silver band.

The crown's weight settled evenly over her head but fears of tripping clung to her. It did not help knowing that the crown had been crafted for Terosh's great-grandmother, Queen Cora Savron Minstel. Only considerable will stilled Reia's trembling heart enough to keep her feet moving forward. When she finally reached the end, she waited to be announced. Then, she endured the stares of a few hundred people crammed into the General Assembly Chamber.

They stood as one.

Forcing a smile, Reia met as many gazes as she could while being ushered to her seat at an ornate desk marooned in the middle of the room. Once she sat down, the masses resumed their seats.

"Queen Reia, we are delighted to formally meet you," said Senator Byron Price. "Our counterparts in the Governors Council speak very highly of you. We have gathered here today to know you better and answer any questions you may have concerning this august body."

"Thank you, Senator Price," said Reia. "I look forward to joining you in service to these people and the masses they represent."

"Do you understand your true role as a royal, Majesty?" asked Senator Collie Bristol in a voice like gravel skipping down a slope.

"I am certain there are many aspects of my position that have yet to be revealed to me, Senator Bristol," Reia replied, trying to ignore her pounding heart. "Can you be more specific as to which aspect you mean?" She silently thanked Master Cadrish for his instructions on how to turn a question.

"Of course, Highness, your predecessor, Queen Kila Creston Minstel, bore the crown prince not one year after their union. Have you plans to compete with her timing?" asked Senator Bristol.

Did you seriously just ask that? Despite her resolve to not be shaken, Reia flushed. She smiled to cover the discomfort.

"It has not escaped my attention that there is an expectation to continue the royal line, Senator. However, definite plans have not been laid out." Reia couldn't believe she was even discussing this with these emotional black holes.

"How will House Minstel address the disappearances?" asked Senator Gabriel Luvak.

What disappearances?

"I apologize, Senator Luvak. I was not made aware of any disappearances. Can you please illuminate the situation for me?"

"I filed a report three days ago," said Senator Luvak. "What has been done in that time? Nothing! The Royal House is useless."

Reia endured the complaint with tolerable good grace, but she felt her serenity slipping.

"I cannot answer for what has or has not been done in the absence of my attention. Now that I am aware there is a situation, I shall have it investigated."

"That's not good enough!" declared Luvak.

"Senator Luvak, please calm down," said Senator Price. "Be reasonable. Her Majesty the Queen has just invited you to share your report. I suggest you take it."

"People are disappearing," said Luvak sullenly.

"From where?" asked Senator Bristol. Her voice boomed the question on Reia's mind.

"From everywhere!" Luvak cried. "Meritab, Azhel, Korch, farms on the Kesler and Kevil Plains. You name a populated place and look at the incident reports for the last few months and you'll see the truth."

"The truth about what?" asked Reia. "Senator, I do not doubt your report, which I shall read in its entirety as soon as possible, but the disappearances you speak of sound like a symptom, not the problem. We must work together to find—"

"What is there to find, Majesty?" Luvak challenged. "This is an invasion, an attack on our sovereignty by Gardan. If the Royal House wanted to prove itself, it would move to sever ties to that nest of—"

"That is enough, Senator Luvak," said Senator Price. "Your sentiments are well-recorded. This is not a discussion about the alliance with Gardan. If you wish to place such a conversation on a future agenda, please have an aide inform Senator Moraton."

What makes you think Gardan is responsible?

Reia wanted to question Senator Luvak, but she resisted for Senator Price's sanity.

Murmurs arose as the senators quietly consulted—or complained to—their aides. Question lights made Reia's display come alive. She chose one, hoping for an easy question.

"Can you enlighten us on the current state of the alliance with Gardan, Majesty?" asked Senator Urik Dade.

His face appeared before Reia on the vidscreen that replaced the top portion of the desk. She found the effect disorienting.

"At this time, I know little more than you do," Reia said demurely.

Actually, I know a whole lot less than you do.

Inside, she made a note to ask Terosh about the man's question. She suspected this might be the matter Terosh had been hiding from her when he had reported on his strained chat with his grandfather.

A cacophony broke out. Though Reia couldn't make out specific words, she gathered they didn't believe her and felt denied by her response.

Senator Price called for order three times before it was restored.

"Has anyone else a question for our queen?" he asked, once the senators had settled down enough.

"How was the dinner with Lady Altran and the Lords of

Idonia?" asked Senator Victoria Turrel. The vidscreen accentuated each line of the senator's face. The challenge in her eyes contradicted her neutral tone.

Reia silently thanked Sedir again for insisting she know each senator's biography. Senator Turrel of Idonia stood firmly in the camp that Lady Altran had been wrongly cut off by Terosh's grandfather, King Salen Minstel.

Reia reviewed her impressions of Terosh's aunt, cousins, and their families. Governor Lord Eldon and Governor Judge Mitrek both had fair hair and rough, chiseled features, and stood nearly a head taller than their brother. Their wives and children stayed firmly in the shadows. The youngest Idonian Lord had inherited his mother's dark hair, sharp features, and famous, icy blue Minstel eyes. Lady Mavis Altran carried herself with a cool confidence.

"Are there plans to restore the relationship with the former princess?" demanded Turrel.

"We are aware of the tensions existing between House Minstel and House Altran," Reia began, casting about wildly for something substantive to say. "Nothing formal has been made official, but I will say my husband and his cousins seemed comfortable with each other. Lord Kezem challenged my husband to a Dollan duel at the next Colored Crossblades Tournament, and the king has accepted. It seems a friendly competition is a step in the right direction."

"What is your personal opinion on the matter?" pressed Turrel.

Warnings from Cadrish, Sedir, and even Colander sounded in Reia's head. Refrain from giving official personal opinions, especially when addressing one of the councils. As Cadrish had put it: *Those vipers wait for words they can string together and hang you with.*

With this in mind, Reia said, "Lady Altran is a strong woman. I can only hope to show such strength when faced with trying times."

After that, the questions seemed easier. Reia could almost predict which type of question each senator would ask. They inquired about everything from her favorite meal to her history to her favorite colored crossblades combatant. To that question, she again admitted a lack of knowledge and made a mental note to ask Sedir about the popular game.

Chapter 10:
Uncomfortable Conversations

Kest (October) 5, 1538
Same Day
Vengal's Alehouse and Inn, City of Meritel

Above all life's burdens, Lucas Telon hated waiting the most. He almost wished to be back in the Calsol Forest stalking Kireshana derringers or even in the zalok queen's lair battling that great korver beast. He thought of Reia and their first kiss. Everything had been right in that moment. Lucas drank some of his ale and let the burning sensation clear his senses.

At midday, the place had been busy, but by now, business had slowed to a trickle. Lucas felt secure at his corner table. Tiny candles and weak glow panels provided the room's only illumination. The darkness suited his mood. Kolknir was late, but that could mean any one of a hundred things. Lucas assumed the most likely explanation was a misguided attempt at teaching patience.

After cutting ties with the Rangers in the semi-successful attack on the Riden Mountain compound, Lucas had done little more than continue his private training. His only order was to remain free to receive further instructions.

Half an ale later, Kolknir appeared in the seat across from Lucas.

"We have a job," he said without preamble.

"What is it?" Lucas asked softly. "Who needs to die? I haven't killed for weeks now. I might forget how."

"Why do you do this?" Kolknir demanded, crushing Lucas's

playful mood.

"Do what?"

"The Lady and I need to know your heart is in the right place before you learn the mission details," said Kolknir, ignoring Lucas's feigned innocence.

"Reia?" Lucas asked. His eyes widened, and he tried to keep a tremor from his voice.

"Not yet, but when that order comes, I need to know if you can handle it," said Kolknir.

Lucas searched his feelings. Lying to Kolknir would be stupid. Reaching deep for the burning anger at Reia's betrayal, Lucas said, "I have chosen my side. Those who oppose us are my enemies."

Even her.

Kolknir's gaze hardened.

"You are using anger as a fuel. It is effective to a point, but you will need to wean yourself off this crutch."

Feeling like cold water had just been dumped on his head, Lucas clenched his teeth in annoyance.

"Yes, master." He tried to keep his tone free of sarcasm.

"I have sent a list of targets to your infopad. They are marked terminate, wound, or capture accordingly," said Kolknir. "There's even a job or two demanding theatrics. I hope you have a clean black cloak."

"Have I not already proven myself?" Lucas complained.

"I do not question your ability to kill," Kolknir assured him. "I am merely honing your skills through practice."

Feeling like a third-year apprentice, Lucas abandoned the rest of his ale and stalked up to his room. If Kolknir wanted to continue these silly games, Lucas would play. He had no choice. The Lady would kill him if he failed her.

***

Kest (October) 5, 1538
Same Day
Royal Gardens, City of Rammon

I see what he meant about the governing bodies being soul-sucking leeches.

Exhausted, Reia chose a grassy spot with a full view of the bright sun. Sitting down, she tried escaping the countless questions she had just answered. The Senate session had gone on much longer than anybody anticipated. Reia couldn't decide if that was a good thing or very, very bad.

Her head felt light from lack of food, but her limbs would not obey a command to rise. Instead, she lay back, grateful that the dress's short sleeves allowed her to feel the grass. After a moment, she let her legs stretch out and rest until she lay completely prone. Her hands idly mingled with nearby blades of grass. She concentrated on breathing slowly and letting the anotechs enhance her senses. The sun's warmth relaxed her even more, and she enjoyed the pleasant scents rising around her.

Footsteps drew near then a shadow blocked out the sun. Raising a weary hand, Reia squinted up at Terosh. Her eyes adjusted almost instantly, courtesy of the anotechs, but she let her hand hover in front of her face and studied his expression. He knelt beside her, looking relieved. Reia knew if she felt his heart, she would find it racing. She lowered her hand to his chest and rested it there, enjoying the pulsing vitality.

"You had Captain Laocer frantic," said Terosh, clapping her hand to his chest.

"How did I manage that?" asked Reia, drowsy from the sun's warmth.

"He thought you'd been slain right here in the gardens," Terosh said. "You can guess how often people come to the gardens the last few years."

"It would be a pity to waste such beauty," said Reia.

"So it would," said Terosh, his voice low and serious. His left hand tightened briefly around the hand still clutched to his chest.

Reia knew his mind was far from the garden. His grip tightened even more, and a shock of panic shot from his hand down her arm before he dropped her hand.

"What's wrong?" Reia sat up to get a better look at him. She wanted to bring up the subject of the disappearances, but Terosh's worry superseded her wish.

A dozen defensive lies flitted through his eyes.

"I don't think this—"

"I'm here when you're ready to share," Reia promised. "Whatever it is, it will be easier to face together."

Terosh stalled by rearranging his legs in a more comfortable sitting position.

"I meant to ask you something before the senate hearing," said Terosh. He finally settled his right leg down and bent the left at the knee so he could clasp his hands around it and lean toward her.

Reia nodded and gave him a tight-lipped *go-on* smile.

"You probably noticed I left out some details about my conversation with Grandfather the other day."

"I did," Reia confirmed, relieved to finally get to the heart of this little mystery.

"He wants to renew the treaty between Gardan and Reshner," Terosh said slowly.

"I take it you have reservations about that. Can you tell me why?"

"The original treaty took place before I was born. It was supposed to involve two marriages, Princess Mavis Minstel to Prince Zarik Creston and Princess Kila Creston to my father."

The story fit with what Reia knew about Lady Altran.

"Your aunt disapproved?" Reia's words embodied both question and statement.

"She ran away and married Dravid Altran," Terosh confirmed. "But the Gardanian princess had already been delivered. The treaty continued on the weakened grounds of the one marriage."

"Your parents," Reia concluded.

"Yes. My mother's assassination further weakened the ties between us, and now, with my father gone as well, the treaty holds very little strength," said Terosh.

"Is it a treaty we need?" asked Reia. Icy claws of fear crept down her spine.

"Yes," Terosh said without hesitation. "Gardan stands as a gateway, a stronghold against the GAPP powers. If we want to stay out of that mess, we need them."

Realization slammed into Reia with jarring force. This renewal involved her.

"What do you need me to do?"

Terosh's expression told Reia that he wanted nothing more than to hold her and pretend no problems existed. He seemed torn between laughing and weeping.

"My grandfather wishes to renew the treaty through you."

"How?" asked Reia. Panic and ravenous curiosity filled her.

"He wishes to have one of his children adopt you," said Terosh, forcing a smile.

"How is that possible? My family is here. What would Gardan gain from such a deal?"

"I don't know. That has me worried," Terosh admitted.

"Is your grandfather the sort of man who would lend aid

without hope of repayment?" Reia wondered.

"No. He's the sort of man who spent his children like tretlings. I wouldn't even bring it up if I hadn't seen it among the proposed session questions. How did that go, by the way?" His light tone failed to counter the gravity in his expression.

"Fine," Reia said with great patience, "but you don't really want to talk about that. What's wrong?"

"This whole thing with Grandfather feels wrong." Terosh looked chagrined at having his emotions read so easily.

"Wrong how?" Reia probed.

"Just … wrong. Forget it, you're not going. Let's go eat something." His expression lightened and he stood, reaching to help her stand.

"Who said anything about going anywhere?" asked Reia, accepting his help.

"My grandfather wanted you to stay on Gardan for a year to formalize the adoption."

Surprise sent a new wave of fear through Reia.

Using their clasped hands to draw her close, Terosh leaned down and kissed her tenderly.

"I'm not my grandfather," he whispered when the kiss ended. He leaned his head against hers, waited a few heartbeats, and added, "I would never trade you for anything. We will find another way."

***

Royal Guard Captain Ectosh Laocer watched the king and queen from a respectful distance. He could not make out their words, but he knew the conversation was serious.

He blinked as if seeing the queen for the first time. She looked so innocent. Her concerned expression played his protective chords like a master musician. No matter how hard he tried, he could not tear his gaze away from her.

Chapter 11:
Dark Deals

Kest (October) 6, 1538
The Lady's Estate, Kala Mountains

It took Mavis Altran a few seconds to recognize the odd fluttering sensation in her stomach. She hated the interplanetary call she had to make, but she drew comfort from the fact that if everything worked out well Reshner would be free from the corrosive relationship with Gardan.

Thinking over the reports her people had compiled over the last week filled Mavis with an invigorating sense of righteous anger. That twit of a senator, Gabriel Luvak, had been right: people were disappearing. Perhaps only a few hundred so far, but Mavis had traced enough of the weak links to suspect a far more sweeping plan. Only three of the abductions could be connected to Gardan, but the evidence convinced Mavis something needed to be done.

It took twenty minutes for Mavis to gain an audience with King Padric Creston. While she waited, she debated herself about her motives. If something went wrong one way, she might inadvertently help Gardan harm her people. That was an unlikely but sobering possibility. If everything went wrong in a different way, she might destabilize half a dozen tenuous alliances Reshner needed.

She wondered why she hated Gardan's king with a deep passion. All things considered, he was a very small piece of her distant, painful past. In his position, she might have even made many of the same decisions. As she narrowed her thoughts, Mavis focused on his current plan, if it could even be called a plan. It was sloppy, unprofessional, and desperate. There, she found the core of her hatred for the man: his desperation.

King Padric Creston's greeting cut into Mavis's thoughts.

"Lady Altran, your persistence is rewarded at last. You have quite a reputation. I wonder if you are worthy of it, but such curiosities will have to wait. What matters warrant such secrecy and urgency?"

"I have an offer for you," replied Mavis. She kept her features and body relaxed.

"This is indeed a surprise," said Padric. His condescending tone hit three separate notes of measured boredom that told Mavis he knew, at least in part, what she had in mind.

She forged on, still banishing emotions to a small, unseen part of her. Leaning toward the vidrecorder, Mavis said, "I want you to stop stealing my people."

"That is an offensive request implying wrongdoing," responded King Padric.

"We could spend all morning trading accusations, or you can agree to let your people question my people later. A better use of our time would be to let me explain my proposition."

King Padric tipped his head in a gesture of gracious tolerance.

"You are wise and beautiful, and you have my attention. Do not waste it," said King Padric.

"You seek the anotech powers," Mavis began, enjoying the chance to shock him. "I want to help you."

King Padric's surprise morphed into anger.

"You dare—"

"I dare to try and help my people," Mavis cut in.

"They are not even *your* people. You are nothing but a disgraced former royal."

Even though Mavis had braced for cutting remarks, the words struck her painfully. She sipped a quick breath and let three heartbeats pass before attempting a reply.

"That as it may be, I happen to be in the unique position to nurture or destroy your work here," said Mavis.

The Gardanian king stared at her intently for a long second.

"I find it hard to believe you would aid my cause without proper motivation. You obviously have enough wealth and power to cultivate valuable contacts, so what is it I could offer a lady like you?"

"More power and more wealth, of course," said Lady Mavis because he expected it. His type, though gifted in many ways, could never comprehend some of her reasons so she did not burden him with them. "There is always the motive of revenge against my family, but that has little to do with you. Believe it or not, King Padric, we have a similar goal."

"I find that difficult to believe, but I shall humor you for now." His arched eyebrow asked the obvious question.

"We both seek a clean break from this disastrous union. You seek it by gathering a gift of people, no doubt for some mid-level GAPP bureaucrat to secret away for illegal experiments."

"You have an interesting imagination, Lady Mavis." The king's neutral tone could not mask all of his dismay.

Mavis continued as if he had not spoken.

"You would sell us as slaves. I say sell us as royals."

"Is there a difference?" asked King Padric, obviously aware of how the question would affect Mavis.

"You ought to be a connoisseur of such knowledge," said Mavis evenly. "A slave is useful because of what he does; a princess is useful because of who she is. It is no secret GAPP desires that which makes Reshner unique. If we are to be sold, I demand it be for a higher price than that of a common slave."

"What an odd request," said Padric. "What about your rhetoric of helping people?"

"I meant every word," Mavis assured the king. "Things will go much worse for my people if I let you blunder around taking innocents at will. Allow me to choose the targets in exchange for a few small requests and a treaty of non-aggression between us."

"I assume you mean you and me and not our respective planets," said King Padric.

"Correct, though I would hope Gardan had the good sense to stay out of Reshner's affairs once our dealings conclude."

"Assuming we reach amiable terms, what prevents me from making a captive of you and extracting the information by more conventional means?" asked King Padric.

"You can certainly try," said Mavis, letting a cold edge take her voice lower. "However, time, effort, and convenience favor partnership over hostilities."

The ghost of a smile touched King Padric's lips.

"We have much to discuss, Lady Altran."

Mavis agreed and turned the call over to Dennel so he could work with some of Creston's people on the details.

Alone at last in front of the blank vidrecorder and hologram display, Mavis let herself sink into her chair. Dealing with King Padric was every bit as difficult as she had anticipated.

Let the games begin.

***

Kest (October) 6, 1538
Same Day
Market District, City of Rammon

Talyon Keldor walked beside Nils Clavon in silence. He had nothing against the Terabian man, but he also had little to say to anyone. His best friend was for all intents and purposes a captive, and his body ached and bore ugly bruises from her husband's misplaced wrath. His family likely wanted him dead, and his bosses certainly wanted him brought back under their control.

"The Alliance hold on you will fade with time," said the dark-skinned man walking beside Taly through the crowded market streets.

Taly nodded, hoping the man was right. Before he could respond, someone bumped into him, knocking him off balance.

"Check your pockets," Nils instructed tersely, righting Taly with a firm hand on his arm.

"I'm not carrying anything valuable," Taly protested.

"Check anyway," Nils replied.

Not wanting to argue, Taly reached into each pocket. To his surprise, his fingers brushed a thin, sturdy infopad chip in his left pants pocket. He held it up to study, but Nils stopped him.

"Put it away and follow me. We must not be followed back to our place of rest," said Nils. He turned away from Taly and started walking rapidly down a side street filled with fruit vendors.

Taly's heart raced as he followed Nils, keeping his pace just under a run.

The Wellum's servant led him through a winding set of Rammon streets through the Market District and into the West Quarter. Two streets into the West Quarter, Nils stopped suddenly before a small shop where people could buy any sort of drink imaginable and rent the use of private infopads.

"In here," Nils said.

Once they were settled in a private booth, Nils took out his own infopad and motioned for Taly to give him the chip.

"Why not use the infopad here?" Taly asked, holding up the machine chained to their table. "We don't know anything about this chip," he added, fishing it out of his pocket. He flipped it over a few times.

"The Tarpons have outfitted many of these places with listening devices. I am certain other organizations have done the same," Nils explained. He took the chip from Taly and tucked it into a slot on the side of his infopad.

"The chip itself could be trapped or traced," Taly pointed out.

"You speak truth, but we must investigate," Nils replied.

The head and shoulders of a masked figure shrouded in black appeared on the screen. A man's voice spoke.

"Greetings. This message is for Talyon Keldor only. Please confirm your identity and that you are alone. A simple two sentence response should suffice."

Taly cast a curious look at Nils and received an encouraging nod. Shrugging, he said, "I am Talyon Keldor. And I am alone."

"Error. Multiple presences detected. Please reset and try again."

Taly sat up straighter and stared at the infopad in disbelief.

Nils stood up.

"I will leave you alone. Come out when you finish, and we can return."

Once truly alone, Taly repeated his introduction and declaration of solitude.

"Confirmed," said the infopad. "Young Master Keldor, I represent a party known as the Lady. She believes you are in a unique position to help her, just as she is in a position to aid you. At this point, you may cut off communication and destroy the chip or request further information."

Two small squares appeared at the bottom of the screen. Taly hesitated only a moment before pressing the one for more information.

"You have chosen well. Your instructions are simple, but the rewards will be great. Keep this chip on your person at all times. When the Lady wishes to give you a task, one of her agents will activate the chip. It will vibrate to indicate a message. Upon completion, the Lady will restore Merisia Restler to you at a location of your choosing."

The message ended, and the infopad ejected the chip. Taly tried to reinsert it, but the infopad refused to accept the chip again. Bewildered, Taly shoved the chip into his pocket, picked up Nils's infopad, and left the private booth.

***

Kest (October) 6, 1538

Same Day
Miraz Estate, City of Resh

Lucas Telon waited impatiently by the front gate to the Miraz Estate. When his target finally emerged, bid her friend goodbye, and climbed into the back of a grand hov, he released a breath he had not realized he held. A gesture to the miniature vidrecorder recalled the device from its position hovering three meters above his head. When it touched his palm, he tucked it into a pouch on his belt and mounted his hov bike.

Crouching low, he activated the cloaking shields on his bike and dark outfit. He had avoided using the devices before to minimize the sense of claustrophobia and not tax the batteries.

Each second stretched into the next. Less than a minute later—though it seemed much longer—a dark green hov slid out the gate and turned left.

As the hov passed, Lucas flicked half a dozen trackers onto its back and sides. He braced, not really expecting an alarm but oddly wishing for one. It would complicate his mission, but the excitement would be worth it. The trackers were only a secondary plan anyway, a guard against the unexpected.

Lucas let the hov gain a lead of several hundred meters before starting his slow pursuit. He knew the hov's destination and exactly where he wanted to intercept them. He followed the hov at a gentle pace for five minutes before altering his course. A small part of him disapproved of the recklessness of waiting until the very last moment. A rush of adrenaline blew the pesky thoughts away.

Dropping the cloaking shields, Lucas enjoyed the cold rush of night air that roared past him as he carved a path through the sky. For no other reason than that he could, he weaved back and forth across several rooftops and passed in front of some windows. The hov bike's powerful vibrations pumped through his arms and legs, reverberating in his chest. He felt alive. Lucas cursed the necessity of wearing a mask on this mission. He wanted to really experience the wind on his face.

Normally, Lucas could expect a police hov to accost him, but he trusted the Lady's word that tonight the skies belonged to him. He spared a glance at the moons and dared the three crescents to reveal him to his powerless quarry.

As he whipped around the last building blocking him from the young lady's hov, Lucas cut the bike's power. The bike lurched and dropped, causing his stomach to flip within him. At the last moment, he re-engaged the power and flipped forward onto the hov's roof.

Kolknir would scold him for the theatrics, but Lucas would not be denied the added drama.

After slapping a scrambler onto the hov to prevent cries for help, Lucas drew a pair of kerlak pistols from holsters strapped to his lower back. One pistol would have been sufficient but two was much more fun.

Electricity zipped across the roof, destroying his scrambler and sending a painful jolt through each of Lucas's boots. His lower legs felt like metal spikes had been driven deep into them and spewed liquid fire through every nerve. He grunted but recovered quickly, thankful for the insanely expensive boots and the extra pain tolerance training Kolknir had forced upon him.

Accepting that his legs would be momentarily useless, Lucas dropped his pistols and awkwardly rolled from the roof, letting the pain motivate him. Despite the energy influx, they should still work, but he had no wish to wager his life on that assumption. Instead, Lucas reached for the case of flingers secured to his waist.

Two doors opened and a pair of well-muscled security officers emerged with kerlak pistols at the ready.

Lucas didn't wait for their orders to surrender. He completed another roll and forced himself to his feet. As his body teetered on wobbly legs, Lucas whipped his right arm across his chest then back the other way. At the peak of each wave, he released a flinger. The security men stiffened and fell, neither having time to protest as death claimed them.

An anguished cry of dismay coincided with another door opening. In a moment, Lucas's target stood before him, a shaking serlak pistol in her left hand. She hesitated. Had his orders dictated her death, the mistake would have been fatal. That not being the case, Lucas disarmed her with another flinger and closed the distance between them. She screamed a split-second after his right hand closed over her mouth.

He leaned into her, pressing her back against the hov. When she paused for breath, he said, "Peace, Lady Zelene. My masters wish you no harm. Your presence is required elsewhere this evening."

Without giving her time to reply, Lucas rendered her unconscious. Once certain she would not move, he retrieved his flingers from the dead guards and recovered his pistols. Then, belatedly, he considered how he would get the young woman onto the hov bike idling above their heads. Hefting the lady with one arm, Lucas fumbled at his belt until his hand secured the bike controls.

A few quick commands later, the bike drifted down like a mythical steed ready to fulfill its master's wishes.

***

Kest (October) 7, 1538

Prince Skye Research Center, Royal Palace, City of Rammon

For the first time in many years, Terosh stepped into the largest of the labs tucked in secluded corners of the palace. Cool air wrapped around him, making him grateful for the long sleeves of his formal robes. He had wanted to change into something more comfortable and less imposing, but the Senate meeting had gone on longer than anticipated.

Terosh walked swiftly past many scientists hard at work and willed people to ignore him. He need not have bothered. The scientists seemed completely enthralled by their projects. The few researchers who looked up executed swift bows and returned to their work as if royalty entering their private domain was a common occurrence.

Perhaps it was a common occurrence, Terosh thought, recalling his brother's obsession with Dr. Deanna Koffrin.

He shook his head sadly. The anotechs had informed him they were currently compiling the story for him, but they had also warned him that he would not like several parts of it. He wondered if he would let them tell him the tale. Tate was dead. Deanna was dead. Their daughter was dead. What would it gain him to know how they loved, lived, and died? Perhaps he owed his dead brother the satisfaction of catching whoever had killed his family, but revenge ranked low in matters of running the planet.

At any given time, the Royal House employed about two dozen scientists through research grants offered to professors and students at the University of Rammon. Master Sedir had once tasked Terosh with reading through a stack of proposals and choosing the next year's scientists. The ideas had ranged from slightly odd to boring to downright crazy to an exciting sort of dangerous. He remembered being intrigued by Dr. Atien Belcross's proposal of adding sedatives to kerlak energy packs. Terosh had approved the project and eventually enjoyed the fruits of Belcross's labor.

The door to Dr. Kurt Saddic's private lab opened as Terosh approached. He entered and stopped two steps into the room as a putrid odor assaulted his nose. The anotechs dealt with it almost immediately, but it took a lot of willpower not to clamp a hand over his nose and mouth. The brief taste of the odor filled his entire being, hitting him hard in the gut.

"Welcome, Highness," said Dr. Saddic, rising from his comfortable chair and bowing. "I apologize for the smell. Porit vipers are especially fond of rotten wallay corpses. I find this surprising because in the wild they thrive upon freshly hunted game, but I'm sure that's not what you came here to know. How may I be of service?"

Terosh noticed shelves full of tanks containing every kind of crawling, creeping, and slithering creature.

"Dr. Dentelich says you're an expert on poisons," said Terosh, tearing his gaze away from the tanks.

The scientist nodded vigorously.

"It is so, Highness. I have been studying poison in one form or another for over twenty years. It captured my fancy as a small boy when I saw a widowmaker spider take down a full-grown roakul while I was on a camping trip in the Felmon Desert."

The Terabian reputation for speaking swiftly holds truth, Terosh thought, picturing the scene the scientist described.

He had never seen a real roakul, but Sedir's Native Predators lesson had included several impressive holograms. The three-meter-long beasts had been imported from Nabeloth about three centuries ago. The original intent had been to cull some of the nastier desert creatures, but the reality was a restructuring of the food chain.

We promised to protect her, the anotechs said, sounding miffed.

I just want to be sure.

Smiling politely, Terosh asked, "Can you make someone immune to a particular poison?"

"It depends on the poison, Your Grace," answered Dr. Saddic. His words continued flowing with the cadence of racing ibeks. "Most common poisons already have reliable antidotes, but some of the faster-acting ones have never been studied in sufficient detail to develop an antidote. May I inquire as to the specific poison you wish to conquer?"

"Comaladon," said Terosh.

"The poison that killed the queen," Dr. Saddic's said, sounding surprised. His head bobbed up and down several times. "You wish me to make it so that our new queen does not share your mother's fate, yes? Yes, of course, why else would you be here? I believe this can be done, Highness, but I cannot guarantee swift results. I will have to isolate the chemical, study it, synthesize an altered version, and arrange for experimental trials."

The mention of trials chilled Terosh's blood. His stomach twisted at the thought.

Noting Terosh's expression, the scientist hastily added, "The test subjects are always willing volunteers. In the few cases the experiments have failed, the families have been well cared for."

The words brought little comfort to Terosh.

If you want to bring about change, do so.

"No more," said Terosh firmly. His heart raced with excitement and trepidation for what he would have to face in the Governors Council and Senate if he truly wished to back up his words.

"No more what, my king?" asked Dr. Saddic.

"Study the poison and try to create an antidote, but do *not* perform trials with live subjects." Terosh's tone left no room for argument.

Dr. Saddic argued anyway.

"Highness, please reconsider. The only way to truly know if the counteragent works is to test it upon humans from this planet. No other species or foreign population can claim our unique genetic pedigree."

"I'm trying to save a life, not destroy more," Terosh snapped.

"Your Grace, this is the way science has been conducted for decades," argued Dr. Saddic. "I will need subjects who grew up in conditions similar to the queen. Her sister would be—"

"Find another way," Terosh interrupted, hardly believing he was having a conversation about experimenting on his wife's sister.

That would thrill Reia.

Without another word, Terosh spun on his heel and left the scientist's creepy lair. He had a ceremony to attend.

Chapter 12:
Momentous Moments

Kest (October) 7, 1538
Throne Room, Royal Palace, City of Rammon

Reia barely resisted the urge to leap from her throne and rush to the two Rangers being ushered in. To distract herself, she stole a sideways glance at her husband. He appeared calm, but Reia could tell he felt uneasy. She sent him the mental equivalent of a reassuring smile and received a similar nudge in return.

As per Sedir's instructions, Reia carefully avoided eye contact with any of the soldiers or courtiers. It helped a little, but she still felt their emotions ranging from cool neutrality to simmering resentment. She would have to thank Sedir for his warning to expect as much.

Her composure almost faltered when the Rangers approached and knelt. Knowing tradition dictated each movement could not help her shake the strangeness of the moment.

Why did the Council send Kiata and Todd? Reia dismissed the thought, choosing to simply be thankful.

"The Ashatan Council sends its highest regards and deepest well-wishes," said Todd Wellum. He kept his voice serious in acknowledgment of the occasion, but genuine affection poured from his eyes. "It is thus with great pleasure that we come before you to renew the vows established by Prince Davel's Order of the Nareth Talis with regard to the members of House Minstel."

Kiata voiced the familiar vow with steady, flowing words.

"Essepetraesmeaproc. Isercuessecaiu totmielstom. Enlivetninliv ichonasevpetraminstel." As she spoke, Kiata removed her banistick from its belt clip and placed it on the ground before the throne, a symbol of her willingness to do likewise with her life.

"This house is mine to protect. I embrace this cause with all my heart. In life and death, I choose to serve House Minstel," Todd repeated for those who could not understand Kalastan. He too removed his banistick and placed it before the throne.

"Your aid is most welcome," said Terosh. "I shall hold you no longer than necessary as I am certain you have much to do, but you are always welcome in this palace and in our lives. Before you go, I believe my queen desires a private word. If you would be so kind as to retire to the Upper East Library, she will join you shortly."

Reia's heart leapt. She certainly wanted to speak with her sister and Todd, but she had not said as much to Terosh.

The Rangers acknowledged the request and gracefully rose, retrieving their banisticks in the process.

***

Kest (October) 7, 1538
Same Day
Governor Lord's Estate, City of Resh

Lucas Telon marveled at the ease with which his mission had proceeded. Resh was a relatively peaceful city, as befitted its name, but he thought common sense would warrant greater caution. He silently thanked the relatively uneventful reign of King Teorn for lulling Governor Darmon Zelene into his current state of vulnerability.

Capturing Akia Zelene the previous night had been extremely easy. A short comm conversation had convinced the governor of her tenuous position and gained Lucas this audience.

Despite the governor's promise of complete cooperation, Lucas expected trouble. As he entered the governor's office, Darmon Zelene rose from his chair. His face bore the lines of a worried father, but he said nothing. His chest rose and fell in a regular rhythm, and his eyes flashed with suppressed rage. Large fingers stabbed commands into an infopad. Lucas wondered if he should be alarmed until the muted buzzing of a sound damper reassured him.

"Greetings, Governor Zelene. Your daughter is well for now," said Lucas. He let the obvious threat hang in the air as he crossed the room to stand before the governor's desk.

"Do you have the proof I requested?" inquired the governor.

"I do," replied Lucas, holding out an infopad. "I also have a summary of your instructions should you forget anything we discuss here." He laid the infopad on the governor's desk and retreated a step, clasping his hands behind his back to present a less threatening figure.

Lucas had enjoyed taking the pictures the governor flipped through. Kolknir would caution against emotionally engaging the target, but Lucas saw his task as an art form. He needed to capture the young lady's vulnerability and display it for her father.

Some pictures showed her face relaxed in a state of peaceful slumber, but most showed her bound with stuncuffs. His favorite showed her hanging from the wall, arms secured up behind her head. Lucas had been careful not to leave her there too long, as his purpose was not to physically distress her. However, her expression in that image had been a perfect mixture of pain, confusion, and frustration. Lucas smiled at the memory.

Darmon Zelene's face paled as he scanned the images and instructions.

"I accept," he said at last. He tossed the infopad onto his desk. It landed with a clunk that rang with a note of finality.

The response surprised Lucas. He felt cheated out of the fight he had braced for.

"I sense the Lady's dark hand in this," Governor Zelene said, as if it would explain his easy capitulation. In a way, it did. "She is misguided and dangerous, but she is also true to her word. Now, if you'll excuse me, I have some arrangements to make."

***

Kest (October) 7, 1538
Same Day
Upper East Library, Royal Palace, City of Rammon

The Royal Guards standing outside the library entrance snapped to attention and opened the door for Reia. Nodding to their commander, Captain Ectosh Laocer, she thanked the guards and wondered if she would ever get to touch a door handle again. Once she entered the room, the guards swung the big doors shut. Remembering Sedir's repeated warnings, Reia reached for the panel next to the entrance and keyed in a privacy code. Then, she turned to her guests.

They stood respectfully. For a moment, nobody spoke.

Reia started closing the eight or so meters separating them from her, keeping to a slow and regal pace, but the sight of her sister changed her mind. She spared a sour thought for the shoe designer, shucked the evil creations binding her feet, and sprinted to Todd and Kiata. Once wrapped in Kiata's embrace, she sighed.

"One would think our separation had been months, not days," said Kiata with a laugh. She pulled away enough to plant a kiss on Reia's forehead.

"It has been a long few days," Todd commented.

Reia broke free from Kiata and hugged Todd.

"I read some of the reports from Terab," she said, twisting in Todd's grasp to loop an arm over her sister's shoulder and draw her close. "You two have a lot of explaining to do."

"What's to explain?" asked Todd with wide-eyed innocence. "We went to retrieve Talyon Keldor, and there was a slight altercation at the Deegan estate."

Kiata squeezed Reia's waist with her right arm and scoffed. Then, letting go, she sat on one of the ornate couches.

"That's one way to put it," said Kiata.

"Then you explain it, if you can do better," Todd said. He led Reia over to the couch where Kiata sat and deposited her before retreating to the other couch. He kept his tone light, but Reia sensed an underlying layer of tension in the set of his shoulders.

"Is the young man all right?" Reia inquired, letting her gaze bounce between her sister and Todd.

"For now," Todd said with a curt nod.

"That doesn't sound very convincing," Reia noted.

"He's worried Taly might do something reckless," said Kiata.

Todd's laugh was tinged with bitterness rather than mirth.

"It's more a question of *when* Taly will do something stupid," he clarified.

Reia arched an eyebrow at him.

"It's complicated," Kiata said, rubbing her temple with her left hand. "You were there when Taly and his friend, Merisia, broke free from the Restler-Tarpon Alliance."

"Of course," Reia confirmed. It would be hard to forget such a night. "We were chased all over the Kesler Plains until you jumped from a moving hov to stop our pursuers."

"I'm surprised you remember all that," Kiata commented.

"Taly and Merisia were also at my wedding," Reia said, "but beyond that, I know little of them."

"Merisia is the youngest child and only daughter of Vera and Tyko Tarpon," Todd explained. "She was married to Gareth Restler as part of the formation of the Restler-Tarpon Alliance. From what Taly says, she wanted to break free because she feared her unborn child would become an alliance target."

"They were caught a few days ago in Terab," said Kiata. She took a deep breath and released it slowly. "I came to see you, we went to rescue them, the mission was partially successful, and here we are, a little the worse for wear."

"It's not over though," Todd said. "There are too many unanswered questions."

"Is there anything I can do to help?" Reia asked, feeling oddly powerless.

"Not in this matter," Kiata said slowly.

"What matter may I be of service then?" asked Reia. She sat slightly straighter and slipped unconsciously into more formal speech. Though Terosh had been the one to mention a meeting with Todd and Kiata, Reia suspected they had arranged it for a specific reason.

Kiata and Todd exchanged a meaningful look that confirmed her suspicion.

"Master Niklos," Todd said. He sounded weary, worried, and frustrated.

A jolt of panic shot through Reia.

"Is he—"

"He's fine," Kiata cut in quickly.

"He's quitting and moving to Resh," said Todd.

"Quitting?" Reia asked, dumbfounded. She could not fathom the Rangers without Master Niklos Mikhail McGreven. Her spirit warmed at the thought of the man who had taught her practically everything she knew about being a Ranger.

"He's angry with the Council," said Kiata.

Before she could elaborate further, a chiming noise caught everybody's attention.

A disembodied, apologetic male voice said, "Forgive me, Majesty, the king requests your presence in the throne room. There is urgent news from Resh."

"Thank you. Please tell the king I shall be there shortly," said Reia, rising from the couch.

She tossed hasty farewells to Todd and Kiata before fleeing the library, but they followed her to the throne room anyway.

Chapter 13:
Cause for Concern

Kest (October) 7, 1538
Same Day
Throne Room, Royal Palace, City of Rammon

In spite of the grim news he'd just received, Terosh smiled when the heavy throne room doors burst inward and his barefoot wife made her grand entrance. Courtiers gasped and soldiers suppressed grins. Noting her worried expression, Terosh sobered, feeling bad for alarming her and even worse for the news he had to share.

"I would like a word alone with my wife," Terosh said to the chamberlain.

Dutifully, the man issued the appropriate orders and the throne room emptied with remarkable speed. The Captain of the Royal Guard, Surd Antar, protested but was successfully mollified by the skillful chamberlain.

Terosh barely paid the controlled chaos any attention. His mind scrambled for some way to make the news more palatable. He was still stumped when Reia arrived at the foot of the dais. She drew in deep breaths and looked at him with a mixture of caution and compassion that made him love her even more.

"Governor Zelene is dead," Terosh blurted, knowing of no other way to tell her.

Reia paused midway up the platform steps and closed her eyes against the pain of the news. When she opened her eyes, unshed tears made her green eyes shiny. The next instant, she finished climbing the steps and wrapped him in a hug.

Terosh stiffened instinctively then relaxed and returned the embrace. He wished his roles as king and husband could always intertwine, but often, the king role demanded he cloak himself in an impenetrable emotional shield.

"He took his own life," Terosh said, after allowing himself a long moment of just holding her.

Twisting her head sideways, Reia asked, "Why?"

"I don't know. I'm having Captain Garahad look into it, but I doubt he'll find much," Terosh admitted.

"Who knows?" Reia asked, as she reluctantly drew away.

"Lady Akia, of course—"

"She's here?" Reia demanded.

Terosh shook his head.

"Not yet. She sent a comm message. She'll be here tomorrow to announce her father's death to the Governors Council."

"We should go to her," said Reia.

"There will be time for condolences when she gets here, but there's a more pressing issue to settle." Terosh winced at how callous that sounded. Forming a fist and closing his eyes, he said, "That's not what I meant." He retreated down one step and looked to Reia, as if she held the answers.

"What pressing issue must be settled?" Reia wondered.

"Governor Zelene's successor," Terosh answered, grateful she did not call him on his poor manners. His throat threatened to close, but he forced himself to swallow. He wanted Reia to be a part of these tough decisions.

Brows drawing together in confusion, Reia said, "Sedir said governorships could be inherited."

"They can," Terosh confirmed, "but Lady Akia Zelene has recently spent a lot of time among the Ritand. Fair or not, that does not endear her to the power bases in Resh. If she moves to succeed her father, they could stir up enough trouble for the people to reject her."

"They are wrong," Reia declared.

Terosh agreed but knew that power meant more than personal beliefs in the political arena. He offered Reia a thin smile.

"Welcome to the wonderful world of politics, where words are daggers and right, wrong, and fairness don't matter."

"It can't be all that bad," Reia protested.

"It can when the major contenders for a carefully balanced Governors Council both have little love for House Minstel."

"Cynicism doesn't suit you, dear," Reia said, gently touching Terosh's chin. With him one step down, they stood almost eye to eye. Reia took advantage of the position to kiss him firmly. "Who are these would-be governors?"

***

Kest (October) 7, 1538
Same Day
Throne Room Entrance, Royal Palace, City of Rammon

"They will call us when they're ready," Todd called to Kiata. He stood with arms crossed over his chest and leaned back against the far wall, eyes shut in an attempt to minimize distractions.

Kiata paced back and forth in front of the imposing throne room doors.

"She forgot us." Kiata reached one side of the door, turned sharply on her left heel, and started back the other way. "I hate this."

Todd tried to concentrate on moving anotechs beyond the doors, but he kept meeting electrical resistance. As vexing as he found the situation, it also intrigued him. The obvious reason for such resistance was a royal awareness of the anotechs. He had always known anotechs were heavily involved with House Minstel in the past, but he had assumed the connection had been lost over the years. Kiata's talks with Reia after Terosh's near-disastrous Kireshana had revealed some anotechs at work, but this level of protection spoke of a very deep understanding.

Most of the Nareth Talis Rangers would fail to raise such a defense.

The thought brought him back to the old debates over using the anotechs. Rangers accepting a position among the elite did so with knowledge that the anotech secrets came and went with the job. In other words, retiring from such service meant leaving their mission memories behind. The ceremony, called Remominelstom, literally meant "remembered no more in mind or heart."

Todd understood both positions but had yet to choose a side. Some felt the Ranger mission to guard the anotechs was paramount to everything, even the mandate to protect the Royal House. The other side believed that not using the anotechs was irresponsible at best and morally reprehensible at worst. Having experienced anotech abilities for several years now, Todd gravitated to the side favoring anotech use, but his history lessons were thorough enough to make him cautious.

We need to have a long, serious conversation with our new sovereigns.

As if the thought could summon results, a Royal Guard

announced, "Their Majesties will see you now."

Todd snapped his attention back to the moment and nodded thanks to the guard. Two servants swung the ponderous doors aside. Kiata's sure strides carried her into the throne room, and Todd jogged to keep pace with her. He noted the curious absence of Royal Guards. The heavy thud of the throne room doors emphasized its deserted state.

After quick greetings, King Terosh and Queen Reia filled Todd and Kiata in on the recent turmoil in Resh.

"We want you to investigate Governor Zelene's death," Reia finished.

Kiata glanced sideways at Todd before returning her attention to her sister.

"Our current mandate is to protect you," she reminded them.

Reia nodded like she had expected the protest.

"We will be in Resh for a few months. It should give you enough time to make discreet inquiries and obey your mandate."

"Master Sedir suggested we visit each city over the next few years. It will not be a problem to rearrange the schedule," said King Terosh. "Funeral rites for the governor commence in three days. I must be there to honor him for my father's sake."

"Your willingness to go to Resh speaks much for the weight you give these matters, but what do you think such an investigation will yield?" asked Kiata.

"I suspect either Tyko Tarpon or Damien Luvak forced Zelene's hand," King Terosh answered. "They are the two with the most to gain."

Todd cleared his throat uncomfortably.

"Rangers will hardly help your cause where Master Tarpon is concerned, and House Luvak holds us in fairly low regard as well," said Todd.

"You're the only ones we can trust." Reia's tone underscored the gravity of the situation.

"You might find nothing related to House Tarpon or House Luvak," King Terosh admitted. "Still, the threat they represent is enough to warrant investigations on several levels."

"What about Talyon Keldor?" asked Kiata. "Our responsibility to him continues."

The king and queen shared a long, meaningful look that said Taly had come up in their conversations. Todd found that interesting.

"Leave him here in the palace for now. He will be safe for as long as he wishes to stay," said Reia. She hesitated, then added, "Talk with him though. We cannot hold him prisoner. From what you said before, I suspect he may return to the RT Alliance for Merisia's sake."

Her statements rang uncomfortably true for Todd, especially given the message Taly had received yesterday. He still didn't know what to believe about that mysterious communication.

***

Kest (October) 7, 1538
Same Day
Wellum Home, East Quarter, City of Rammon

The conversation was not going well. Kiata Wellum wanted to reach out and shake sense into the boy.

"You're not safe here, Taly," Kiata declared. "The close call yesterday proves as much."

His defiant expression told her the argument failed to sink in. Talyon Keldor nodded and stood.

"I know and I thank—"

Waving impatiently, Kiata said, "Sit down. We're not kicking you out."

"We're trying to tell you that the queen has offered you refuge at the palace," said Todd.

"Please consider the offer," Kiata added.

Taly cast a pleading look at Nils Clavon.

Nils crossed his arms and leaned against the doorframe as if the less obtrusive position would allow him to escape involvement. After a few moments of awkward silence, he cleared his throat.

"Talyon does have a point, masters."

Kiata grunted and hung her head in temporary defeat.

"Which one?" she muttered, frustrated that the servant chose this moment to assert his free will.

"He must disappear," said Nils. His clipped Terabian accent made the statement sound like the only option.

"It's for the best," Taly said glumly from the seat he had reclaimed. "Every moment I stay here endangers you."

Kiata snorted.

"You're not that important," she said, knowing she was probably wrong.

The Keldor name carried a lot of weight in the Restler-Tarpon Alliance. As far as she knew, Taly's father, Ariman, still held a high rank. In addition, rumor had it that Taly's grandfather, Niktrod, had been captured in connection with the death of Reshner's previous queen. If the public knew, the Keldor name would become immediately famous—or infamous.

"We're not exactly Alliance favorites, Taly. What's one more reason to kill us?" Todd asked with a shrug.

"It's different," Taly protested. "Before you helped me, the Alliance viewed you with the general contempt held for all Rangers, but now, it's personal. I—"

"Tried to help a friend," Kiata finished.

"That's not how they see it." Taly stuck his hand in his pocket and removed the chip. He turned it over several times with one hand before passing it to the other.

Kiata fought the impulse to wrap the forlorn young man in a comforting hug. Even though she and Todd had experienced danger since they were far younger than Taly, it felt wrong for him to have to face so much.

"Perhaps there is a better plan," Nils said, yanking Kiata out of her thoughts.

Every eye focused on the tall, elegant man.

He stopped leaning against the doorframe, uncrossed his arms, and looked at Kiata and Todd, silently requesting permission to speak.

Kiata nodded, wishing she could convince the man his debt of service was not necessary.

"Speak your mind," said Todd.

"My people send youths on a solitary journey, much like the Kireshana. They choose to explore mountains, deserts, forests, or seas," Nils explained. "Travelers carry only what weapons they need for survival and no extra links to the modern world."

"You think it's best to send Taly into the wilds?" asked Kiata, incredulous.

"It is a suggestion only," said Nils stiffly.

Kiata felt a stab of remorse, but she couldn't help thinking Taly would be safer on a farm or even in a Ranger compound. She immediately rejected the idea of suggesting Taly stay with Rangers. Not many people knew enough of Taly's story to sympathize. Most still believed him an RT Alliance agent. On the other hand, the idea of a farm struck her as favorable.

"It's a fine suggestion," Todd assured Nils, "but I'm not—I mean it's probably better if Taly stayed somewhere we can find him."

Kiata fixed her attention on Todd.

"What about your brother's farm?"

Todd tilted his head and considered her question.

"I don't want to put more of your family at risk," Taly said, shaking his head.

"It's pretty remote," Todd reflected, speaking mostly to himself. He nodded, as if answering an unspoken question. "Terik could use the help, too. What do you say, Taly? Would you like to be smuggled out of this dreary city to spend some time pushing dirt around?"

"No one will know you're there," Kiata added, willing Taly to believe the danger would not follow him from the city.

"How do you know he'll even take me?" Taly asked.

"He's always looking for new hands," said Todd. "I'll give him my highest recommendation and leave what you tell him about your past up to you."

"I think I would like to get away from cities for a while." Taly still looked uncertain, but he tried to smile.

"I'll call my brother later this evening, and we can leave in the morning," said Todd.

"What do I do about the chip?" asked Taly, glancing between Todd and Kiata.

"What would you like to do with it?" asked Kiata carefully.

When Taly had confessed the substance of the message delivered in the Market District, it took all of Kiata's willpower to not advise him one way or another. Truthfully, she did not know which advice she would have given him anyway. Keeping the chip could draw unknown enemies down upon Taly, yet destroying the chip would end the best chance of solving the mystery it presented.

Taly looked torn between relief and fear, but he seemed grateful for the freedom to make his own choice.

"I'd like to keep it," he admitted. "I only ask because it is your family I put in danger if something goes wrong." He stared gravely at Todd. "You'll have to warn your brother that I might leave suddenly." His gaze became distant.

Sensing Taly's need for space, Kiata motioned for Nils and Todd to follow her into the kitchen.

Chapter 14:
Camarek Pieces

Kest (October) 10, 1538
The Lady's Estate, Kala Mountains

A deep sense of satisfaction swept over Mavis as she observed Governor Darmon Zelene's funeral procession moving through the streets of Resh. She almost wished she'd spent the effort to secretly attend. Indulging the disappointment, she ran her slender carving knife across a piece of kintral wood clutched in her other hand. A delicate sliver peeled away from the block, curling as it did so.

Zelene had been a popular governor, a cool head among a group of highly opinionated people. Tosh and salt dealers, coral and fish traders, Idonian glass merchants, and farmers had come to expect fair treatment from Resh markets. Had Governor Zelene not been tainted by close affection for Mavis's brother and his family, she would have let him live despite his other flaws. He had provided stability to the region, and unfortunately for him, stability gave the royals too much time to think. Mavis wanted them reacting, not thinking.

Sweet chords from Parioxa's *Last Revelations* filled the room providing a suitable atmosphere for watching the funeral. Mavis liked the original version in the artist's native language best, but any version was preferable to hearing the announcer describe everything the viewer could clearly see.

As Mavis slowly worked the knife over a fresh section of wood, the screen showed Terosh and his precious wife in clothes meant to honor the departed. Terosh's dark blue uniform had him looking ready to lead the Royal Guards on parade. His wife's light blue shimmersilk gown flowed in a faint breeze, making one think of peaceful waves. No tears marred their perfect, innocent, very young faces, but their expressions were heartbreakingly sad.

Mavis focused on her nephew's wife and imagined her at his funeral. She felt no particular ill-will toward the woman, but Kezem could never take the throne while Terosh lived. Under better circumstances, Mavis might even like the young queen who at eighteen barely qualified as an adult. Initial reports had dismissed the former Ranger as a harmless healer, but recent events spoke otherwise.

Several wood shavings tumbled free from the figure Mavis was liberating from within the block. A thought struck her.

What would Terosh look like at his wife's funeral?

Mavis had always assumed a need to deal with her nephew first. She regretted the time and effort the deal with Gardan would take, but it was necessary for building a foundation upon which Kezem could rule.

The focus shifted from the royals to the veiled Lady Akia Zelene who marched directly behind her father's body, which floated down the street on a hov sled. Mavis felt a pang of sympathy for the woman. Sacrifice of any kind was regrettable. The most skilled camarek players could vanquish their opponents without either side losing a piece. Mavis did not doubt her skills at fashioning outcomes, but she also knew the value of a timely execution.

As the funeral dragged on, she let her mind chase the possibilities around in circles while her hands deftly dealt with the kintral wood. Bit by bit, the wood submitted to its new form. When it at last took shape, Mavis blew on it to remove dust remnants and held it up with admiration. The piece looked like any other camarek common soldier, but the face bore a striking resemblance to Resh's late governor. Like the others in her collection, this piece would never be played with. They existed solely for her private pleasure at creating—and sometimes destroying—them.

Mavis slowly traced a finger over the figure's face. As a girl, she had loved camarek. Noticing a strong, strategic mind, her father had insisted she learn the rules. From the first, she had admired the fact that the game could be as simple or complex as the players wished. Any small child could comprehend that attack hounds only moved one space in any direction, common soldiers moved two such spaces but only forward, backward, left, or right, and elite soldiers traveled any number of diagonal spaces.

The king and queen could move any number of desired spaces in any direction except the diagonals. The most powerful piece, the spy, could be disguised as any piece and had to be chosen before each match. The spy could move up to five spaces in any combination of directions and was the only piece able to capture the king or queen. Most people tried not to reveal their spy until the very end. Victory could be achieved by annihilating all enemies, capturing the king and queen, or destroying the opponent's spy.

Who will be my camarek spy? Mavis wondered.

She chuckled at the clichéd notion of likening her plans to the strategy game. She had several options for the part, including Kolknir, Lucas Telon, and Surd Antar, but the analogy was imperfect. Kolknir and his protégé had been revealed as enemies of the Royal House, and Antar was too dull to make an effective spy. All three men were eager to challenge the royals, but they seemed better suited for the attack hound role. Even Kezem was not completely capable of playing the part well.

Mavis tucked the new carving into the specially prepared box. Perhaps she would burn the piece to honor the dead man, but for now, the carving's fate would remain safely sealed away. She had new pieces to consider and new players to tempt to her cause. Antar's protégé, Captain Ectosh Laocer, might be the sort of man Mavis needed, and he had an obvious weakness that could be exploited.

***

Kest (October) 10, 1538
Same Day
Tarpon Estate, City of Kalmata

Lucas Telon hurried through the hallway leading to the master bedroom. His breath felt uncomfortably warm and moist within the confines of the black mask. He was anxious to be done with this mission. After the recent invasion of the Deegan Estate in Terab, he had expected to meet fierce resistance at this Alliance stronghold. The two, half-asleep guards he'd met were hardly worth the bullets Lucas had spent on them.

Complacency's a killer, he thought, quietly opening the door.

A dull scraping noise warned him something was wrong just as the door exploded, sending Lucas hard into the far wall. Searing heat made his mask unbearably hot, but the cloth protected his face from most of the splinters. The impact drove thoughts from him, but his training took over. He rolled onto his back, drew his serlak pistols, and shot the figure rushing toward him through the destroyed doorway.

A woman's sharp, pained cry pierced through the ringing in Lucas's ears. He cursed and scrambled over to the body slumped in the doorway to confirm Nera Tarpon's death. A mass of dark, flowing hair covered her face. The body lay curled across the threshold where it had crumpled under Lucas's gunfire.

His mind reeled. That had not been part of his mission. He was supposed to terrorize and perhaps torture the woman but definitely not kill her. He cursed the need for serlak weapons. It had seemed important to his role as a house intruder, but with a kerlak weapon he could have stunned the woman.

Before he could brush the hair away from the woman's face, pain blossomed in Lucas's left shoulder as a strong hand clamped down and hauled him to his feet.

"Let's go," growled Kolknir's voice.

Shame flooded Lucas, but he forced himself to stumble after his mentor.

***

Kest (October) 11, 1538
The Lady's Estate, Kala Mountains

Lady Mavis Altran let the recording finish its gruesome story before shutting the screen off.

"I told you he could not protect you," she said, working compassion and caution into her tone. She turned toward her guest and studied the young woman's expression.

Nera Tarpon sat stiffly in the comfortable armchair. Her body had the unnatural stillness of a Porit viper preparing to unleash a devastating attack. Her fingers dug into the expensive fabric composing the chair's arms. The force drove traces of blood from her fingers.

Mavis imagined those long, delicate fingers as cold bones. While giving her guest a moment to order her thoughts, Mavis thought about Lucas Telon's test. His performance—exemplary until the end—was marred by the simplest of failures. Mavis shivered at how close she'd come to losing a valuable asset and thanked whatever fortune had pressed upon her the need to have Kolknir implement safety measures. Her designs for Nera Tarpon were only starting to materialize.

"What will happen to him?" asked Nera. Her pale purple irises focused intently on Mavis in a sharp contrast to her hoarse tone.

Resisting the tide of irritation trying to consume her, Mavis said, "If you agree to my terms, your husband will simply remain under guard. When all the unpleasantness is past, you will be restored to him." She left unsaid what could happen if Nera chose not to accept her terms. Imagined threats often held more power than spoken ones.

"What must I do?" asked Nera. Her voice trembled.

Mavis pitied the desperate young woman and wondered whether she possessed the emotional fortitude to finish the task. She pushed the doubt aside. Time would tell. Nera was only one day removed from her old life.

"You will train with my agents for a time," she said.

"Kolknir," said Nera, spitting the name with disgust.

"What he lacks in social graces, he makes up for in skill," Mavis assured the girl. She stopped short of apologizing for Kolknir's brutal ways. "He will not be your only instructor, but I will arrange those details in time. All I require now is a commitment."

Nera hesitated.

"What of the king and queen?" she asked.

"What of them?" returned Mavis.

"Will they come to harm?"

Mavis drew a slow breath and tried not to laugh. The question evidenced the sort of idealism that had caught Mavis's attention in the first place. Nera Tarpon, daughter of Arista and the slain Tobias Restler and wife of the Tarpon heir, should have little love for House Minstel. Her question was a troubling reminder of just how far-reaching Terosh and Reia's popularity stretched. Realizing she had remained silent too long, Mavis forced a smile.

"I cannot predict the future, but your help may be crucial to preserving them."

Suspicion entered Nera's expression.

"But you hate them. You're working with my husband and the Alliance to destabilize their rule. Why would you help them?" Her conflicted emotions caused several expressions to flicker across her face in rapid succession.

Mavis acknowledged each point with a small nod, ignoring the annoying notion of working with the RT Alliance.

"My family troubles are long past," she lied. "I remain too much my father's daughter to let revenge blind me to a threat against my homeworld." She let passion infuse her voice with conviction. "Just hear me out."

Even as she spoke, Mavis knew she'd found her camarek spy.

Chapter 15:
A Matter of Right

Kest (October) 11, 1538
Temporary Quarters, Governor Lord's Estate, City of Resh
The moment Terosh Minstel awoke he felt a dozen matters vie for his attention. A week and a half had passed since his grandfather had issued two orders thinly disguised as requests. Terosh knew his people could pacify King Padric Creston for a short while longer, but he wanted the matters settled for his own peace of mind. He had never seriously considered sending Reia to Gardan, but he changed his mind at least twice a day concerning Niktrod Keldor.

Also, Resh needed a new governor, and his favorite candidate would likely refuse the position. He understood and accepted most of the reasons she would cite, but he still needed to decide how dirty he wanted to fight in the battle of wills yet to be waged.

He wanted answers to the recent disappearances. Task forces had been formed in every major city, and troops had been dispatched from most forts. Still, Terosh felt something more ought to be done. At least no new disappearances had been reported.

As expected, the Governors Council and Senate balked at Terosh's call to reform scientific practices. Their coordinated efforts spoke of forewarning. The more he learned about the guidelines, the less he liked them. People could buy and sell living bodies, so long as *reasonable expectations of care and consent* were met.

Fort Tiree needed a new commander, as the last one perished in a boating accident while on vacation in Chara.

Flooding around Twin Lake had damaged several villages.

Azhel's governor, Leonard Westis, requested aid with the relief efforts.

Thoughts of these matters and more left Terosh feeling helpless. He tightened his hold on his wife, as if clinging to her could blast through the negative feelings.

Reia shifted, pressing her back more firmly against his chest.

He froze—not wanting to wake her—which, of course, did so.

Her hands squeezed his forearms, sending anotechs with a simple declaration of love. The skin she touched tingled pleasantly. She nestled her head into the warm space between his neck and the pillow.

"Sorry," he murmured into her hair.

"Don't be. It's much easier to appreciate your company while conscious." As the anotechs reported Terosh's emotional state, Reia added, "I wish you wouldn't worry so much."

"I wish there wasn't so much to worry about," Terosh replied. He sent anotechs carrying the mental equivalent of gentle kisses across her forehead, nose, and lips.

"Kiss me yourself, you lazy bum," Reia said with mock sternness. She twisted around so she could face him nose to nose.

He chuckled and complied, sticking to the same order. When the kiss on the lips reached its inevitable conclusion, Terosh drew his head back, met her steady gaze, and grinned.

"Is there anything else I can do for you, Majesty?"

Reia traced the curve of his cheek and jaw then placed a finger across his lips.

"Kiss more. Talk less."

***

Once dressed, Reia made the bed. Terosh had laughed the first time she insisted on straightening each corner, but her Ranger training was too thorough to rely on servants. She had never minded the chore of setting her sleep pallet to rights. It helped her prepare for the day by providing a nice metaphor of chaos yielding to order.

"Reia, what do you think about Niktrod Keldor?" asked Terosh, breaking into her thoughts.

"The man who killed your mother?" she asked, tucking in one last blanket corner and smoothing it out. Though she tried, Reia could not keep the curiosity out of her voice. She faced her husband and perched on the spot she had just fixed. "I thought you had settled the matter with your grandfather."

"He thinks it's settled, but I keep changing my mind," said Terosh. He wore a thoughtful scowl but did not elaborate.

Resisting the urge to gauge his mood again, Reia pulled herself further onto the bed and waited for Terosh to continue. She knew only scant details concerning the fate of the former queen. Terosh tended to avoid conversations about his mother and the ill-fated banquet that killed her. Reia had not thought to ask Master Sedir for answers, but she made a mental note to do so.

Eyes fixed on the floor, hands clasped behind his back, and frown still firmly in place, Terosh said nothing for a long time.

"I don't know what is right," he admitted at last.

"Is Keldor guilty?" Reia asked, curious about his lack of anger.

Terosh nodded.

"It's not his guilt I question. The investigation was one of the most thorough ever conducted."

"Then what bothers you?"

"He's a citizen of Reshner," Terosh said. "If I hand him over to Gardan, the people will feel robbed. I feel robbed already, but that hardly matters. And I know my grandfather well enough to feel guilty about sending anyone—even Keldor—to face him."

"They would torture him," Reia said. Even in the Riden Mountains, people had repeated stories of Gardan's Shadow Guard in hushed whispers. Master Kolknir's decision to train with them had nearly sent the Council into hysterics.

A possible—unpleasant—solution occurred to her. She tried to keep it off her face but failed. It would be a sort of suicide rather than murder, but the distinction brought her little comfort. Setting the man free would upset everyone and violate justice.

"What is it?" asked Terosh, unclasping his hands and stretching his arms out to his sides.

Reia drew some deep breaths, hoping to draw in extra courage.

"Call for a public trial," she said, still feeling uneasy.

"To what end?" Terosh's gaze sharpened as his mind turned the possibility over a few times. Cautious hope entered his eyes.

"A public trial may satisfy our people," Reia began. "If the evidence is as strong as you say, the outcome is inevitable." She paused to worry her lower lip, silently questioning the morality of this scheme. With a sigh, she forged on. "His sentence could be execution on Gardan, which would satisfy your grandfather, but for the sake of our consciences, I propose an execution on the way to Gardan."

A slow smile spread across Terosh's face.

"Your compassion matches your wisdom. I will see it done."

With that short speech, he rushed forward for a quick kiss and hurried from the room with a renewed sense of purpose.

***

Kest (October) 11, 1538
Same Day
Communications Hub, University of Resh, City of Resh

Terosh stepped into the pod and activated the security devices. He also activated the personal sound damper. In theory, anything trying to hear the conversation from outside a one-meter radius of Terosh would hear nothing but white noise. His outfit conveyed power and opulence. Though he needed the image, the multicolored robes bothered him.

"One short conversation and you can change," Reia promised, looping her left arm through his right arm and clasping his hand.

They had discussed their beginning pose at length and agreed that Reia would stand a few centimeters behind and to the right of Terosh until he introduced her. Then, she would step up beside him so they could present a united front.

"I feel like I'm about to be executed," Terosh complained, "or suffocated or both." He entered the code to establish a connection with Gardan's royal palace. "Now we wait," he said, entering a command for the console to alert him when someone answered.

"Why?" asked Reia, retrieving her left hand and rubbing it down the side of her dress. Her hands were not sweaty, but she needed to move to ease her tension.

"Because grandfather needs to establish that he's more important than us," Terosh replied. "It probably won't be long. I told him you would be here."

"I thought you wanted to surprise him," Reia said, slipping off the diamond studded shoes pinching her feet.

"You really don't like shoes these days," Terosh commented, eyeing the sparkling heels. "One would think a mountain-raised Ranger would be used to shoes."

"Boots and normal shoes are fine. These are jewel-encrusted torture devices," Reia explained. "When we get back to Rammon I'm having a long conversation with Lady Parné about my footwear."

"Just send her a message. She can—"

A chime cut him off.

Terosh gave his wife a sympathetic, encouraging smile and steadied her while she climbed back into the offending shoes. They took their agreed upon positions and Terosh reached to confirm the connection.

"Just a short conversation and—"

A jeweled toe slammed into the back of his right boot cutting him off. He laughed and squeezed Reia's hand before opening the connection with Gardan. By the time King Padric Creston's imperious form appeared, Terosh wore a neutral expression.

"Greetings, Grandfather," said Terosh, lowering his head in a gracious bow. "In our last conversation you expressed an interest in my wife. Allow me to introduce Her Majesty Reia Antellio Minstel, Queen of Reshner."

Reia slipped forward and tipped her head down respectfully.

Terosh dared not look at her. He felt like they were facing a venomous snake and wanted to sweep her behind his back.

"Where is my prisoner?" King Padric asked, ignoring Reia.

Her lack of reaction emphasized the absence of royal blood. Any queen should be livid at such dismissal. Terosh flushed, offended on her behalf. A wave of calming thoughts descended on him as Reia urged him to let it go.

"You will have him after we conduct a public trial." Terosh did not have to work hard for a cold tone.

King Padric's countenance turned stonier.

"That is—"

"The only way to preserve peace, Your Grace," Reia interrupted, dropping into a full curtsey.

What happened to not giving in to his over-sized ego? Terosh demanded through the anotechs.

She sent him a trust-me nudge.

"Your daughter, our queen, was much loved," said Reia. "If we simply sent her killer away, we would be accused of robbing the people. A trial will allow us to address their anger and acknowledge your right to claim the prisoner."

King Padric's glare lost some of its chill as a spark of amusement appeared.

"She speaks well for a commoner. The speech master should be commended," said King Padric, studying Reia with a critical eye. After a long look, he shifted his attention back to Terosh. "You might even want to invest in a few more lessons yourself, boy." He tilted his head thoughtfully. "Assuming I humor you, how long will this trial delay justice? What guarantee prevents a soft-minded judge from acquitting Keldor?"

"In the unlikely event Keldor is exonerated, we will rejoice that an innocent man has escaped wrongful conviction," said Terosh.

Laughing harshly, King Padric leaned close to the vidrecorder.

"Your simplistic views will get you killed, boy. It's just as well you favor your father. I would hate to be linked to your inevitable failures."

Ouch.

Terosh tried to keep the words from bothering him, but they hurt all the same. He sensed Reia's ire rising and silently willed her to let him handle the situation.

"In blood, sir, I am as much a son of Gardan as a son of Reshner," Terosh said, letting anger stiffen his words. "I am proof that a close relationship exists between our planets."

Disgust rang through King Padric's response.

"Any children you produce with this commoner will receive diluted blood."

Terosh bowed his head, so he could consider his next words. He needed to move the conversation back on course, but the man's attitude rankled.

"Had I wed a distant Gardanian cousin, my children would be three parts your home and one part mine. There is no fair way to share the blood of two lines on one throne, but blood matters less than knowledge. Any child of mine will be well versed in both legacies. This I promise on all honors due my late mother."

Menacing silence fell until finally King Padric said, "I will accept your ridiculous need for a public trial and expect news of my prisoner's pending arrival within four months."

"Trials take a long time, Grandfather, but I shall see matters proceed quickly," Terosh promised.

"See that you do. Now, I will repeat my advice that you annul the bond with this commoner or accept my offer to adopt her," said his grandfather.

If I have my way, you'll never set foot on the same planet she does.

"I will not renounce my wedding vows," Terosh declared.

"And we respectfully decline other offer, Your Grace," Reia said.

"Insolent children," muttered King Padric.

Pompous fool. Terosh fired back silently, glaring so intensely at his grandfather that his head hurt.

"We apologize, Your Grace," said Reia. "For my part, I cannot rewrite my past or recast my loyalty. I was born here, I will likely die here, and I am sworn to protect the interests of this people. Were that something I could lay down lightly, it would be worthless."

Surprisingly, King Padric's lips twisted into a smile.

"Boy, you are ensnared by a silver-tongued enchantress. Move the trial along and see that this harpy does not twist what little good sense my daughter imparted to you."

As the connection cut off, Terosh wordlessly embraced Reia.

Chapter 16: Guarantee

Kest (October) 11, 1538
Same Day
The Lady's Estate, Kala Mountains

Knowing Terosh and his wife had a "secret" interplanetary call scheduled with King Padric Creston, Mavis played a game of camarek against the board's artificial intelligence and waited for the inevitable call that would follow.

It vexed her not to be able to hear the conversation. The latest personal sound dampers currently had her experts stumped. Dr. Quatar had promised to invent a device that could break through any sound damper in the next few months, but that hardly helped her now. Besides, she preferred the good doctor devote his time to the project he was hired to complete. The other professors had issued similar promises, but Mavis had far less confidence in their work.

The camarek board moved an elite soldier against the common soldier she had secretly made her spy. She concentrated on the problem that presented. She could boldly move one of her elite soldiers to block the board's move, thus betraying her common soldier as the spy. Conversely, she could cautiously move her queen to a position that would threaten the board's king to divert attention from her lowly common soldier. She could also have her spy execute a clumsy retreat and delay the revelation. The first move would be reckless but take care of the board's last elite solider, leaving it only common soldiers, the king, and the queen. The second and third moves would only delay the confrontation.

Relishing the idea of recklessness, Mavis decided on the boldest move. She hated losing with a passion that could break stone to tiny bits, but playing the game without risk bored her. As Mavis picked up her elite soldier to capture the board's last elite soldier, a pleasant, triumphant tune indicated an incoming call from Gardan. She smiled to herself, paused the game, and wondered how the board's AI would handle the situation. Determining to find out later, Mavis got up and walked to the communications array.

Activating the vidrecorder and hologram projectors, Mavis met King Padric's glare and permanent scowl with a pleasant smile.

"How may I help you?" she inquired.

"Observe the conversation I will send you and tell me your thoughts on my grandson," said King Padric.

Almost immediately, one of Mavis's vidscreens blinked a yellow light indicating an incoming data pack. She activated the recording and felt a thrill of anticipation. It still bothered her that she did not have the information already, but she was happy to witness Terosh's meeting with King Padric.

The entire recording focused on Terosh and his wife and took less than four minutes to unfold. Mavis controlled her expression, but inside, she longed to see King Padric's expression to her nephew's cool reception. Creston's grumpy tone told her the expression would be both amusing and satisfying. She smiled at Terosh's flat refusal to annul his marriage. Their plan to hold a public trial intrigued her. The reasons made sense, but Mavis wondered if they were really so sweetly naïve or more devious than she had imagined.

"I warned you he would never submit on the issue of his wife," Mavis said when the recording had ended. She had asked Dennel to include the warning as a gesture of good will.

"What do you think of this trial they propose?" asked the king.

Mavis hesitated not sure which light to cast Terosh in. Did she want Padric to think Terosh a dolt or a mastermind? She had yet to fully assign him a role, but eventually, she decided that having Padric underestimate her nephew would be preferable. After all, a time might come when she had to deal with one of Padric's plans. Mavis put a lot of effort into a casual shrug and wished she had more time to think over a response.

"It is a decent plan, and I can attest to their assessment of the situation," said Mavis. "Sending Keldor straight to you would be highly unpopular."

"Will the trial be fair?" asked Padric, spitting the last word like a curse.

"I will see that the trial goes our way," Mavis promised, laughing delicately.

"How will you control the sentence?"

"Trials on this planet are fairly standard, except that the judge wields a lot more power than in most places," Mavis explained. "Very few cases stand before a jury of commoners, though some may stand before a royal or a government committee. However, a trial of this magnitude will likely demand multiple phases."

"What does that mean? How long will I be denied my prisoner?"

The king's questions and tone gave Mavis the image of a petulant child crying foul.

"It means the trial will be a planetary affair," Mavis explained. "Normally, it would fall to the king to appoint a judge, but Keldor's advocate will likely object to any involvement from the Royal House. He or she will then appeal to the Governors Council to appoint a judge. They will—"

King Padric exploded with a word Mavis assumed qualified as an invective.

"It could be years before such an inefficient system renders judgment of any sort!" he shouted.

Mavis raised her right hand in a placating gesture.

"It could, but it will not. Leave that to me. I will arrange for my son to be judge, and you will have your conclusion by the Dalest Nareth of next year."

"How can you make such a grand promise? My astronomers tell me your Darkest Night falls early in the next cycle."

Mavis confirmed it with a nod.

"It is set to fall on the twelfth day of Idela (January) in 1539."

"What will you give me as a guarantee that you will keep your word?"

Denying him would be fatal to their deal. Mavis could read as much in Padric's narrowed eyes. Her mind raced. She knew the sort of guarantee he wanted. Though her father's family had long since ceased trading hostages, several noble families—and even Kezem—indulged in the practice. She did not think she could trust King Padric, but she also knew she had little choice if she wanted him to honor his end of their deal.

"You must claim the guarantee yourself," Mavis said, hating the weakness in her voice.

Padric's gaze never wavered.

"Whom shall my men seek?"

Lifting her chin and staring as hard as she could, Mavis said, "Seek the family of Governor Judge Mitrek Altran of Idonia. He has two daughters and a son. Take the eldest child as your guarantee."

"I take it the judge is your son," said King Padric.

"Yes, he is my son," answered Mavis.

"What of his connection to the Royal House? Your sons are still officially recognized relatives to the king, are they not?"

"They are indeed, but Mitrek has a reputation of maintaining impartiality," said Mavis.

"As for your plan, will not a missing child disqualify him as judge?"

"It depends on how the child's absence is perceived. Strike the last plan. Send your men to Rammon," Mavis instructed, suddenly feeling ill. "I will have people bring them to a safe house and see that the child makes it to that same house. They can wait for the trial's conclusion with a few of my people. As far as my son and his wife will be concerned, their daughter will be safely in my care. That is my guarantee."

King Padric said nothing for a time, and his intense eyes swept Mavis's face again and again, searching for deception. Finally, he said, "I accept your plan. Now, what can you tell me about my grandson and his wife?"

"I can add very little to that which your spies have already told you," said Mavis, trying not to let her relief show. "Terosh is dangerously idealistic, as you have pointed out."

"And the commoner?" asked Padric, for once not quite glaring.

Mavis reviewed her knowledge of her nephew's wife, searching for new insights and trying to decide how much to share.

"The reports on her potential to lead vary, but the facts remain consistent. Her parents owned tosh mines and died when a competitor had them assassinated. The Rangers raised her and an older sister upon the request of a mercenary who could not kill them. She became a healer then got herself banished by marrying Terosh."

"This sister you mentioned, do I know her?" inquired the king.

"I sent you a vid showing the sister and her husband breaking into an estate in Terab to rescue a young man," said Mavis.

Recognition flashed in Padric's eyes.

"I remember. That was a most impressive display. I am eager to meet such powerful beings. Tell me, can I expect such a boon?"

That was my intention, Mavis thought, but now that he asked, she hesitated to make a promise she might fail to keep.

"I can make no guarantee, but I shall set my mind to the task," she promised.

"See that you do," said Padric imperiously.

Eager to be done with the distasteful man, Mavis steered the conversation to a close by promising to have Dennel call with instructions once he worked out the details of securing Mavis's granddaughter.

Alone at last, Mavis retreated to the table holding the camarek board and let the AI battle itself. She had no heart to continue the game and barely paid attention as the pieces moved themselves around the board, challenging and capturing each other.

What have I done?

Mavis tried to fight the thought off, but it kept pricking her conscience. She had just wagered her granddaughter's life that she could control a trial that had not even been called for yet. If Terosh changed his mind, Mitrek lost the bid to judge, one of the advocates stalled, or one of a few hundred other things went wrong, Padric Creston would kill Silvia.

I won't let that happen.

Dreading the call she needed to make but determined not to put it off, Mavis reset the camarek board and went to her thinking chair to consider how to acquire Mitrek's cooperation.

Unbidden, another problem surfaced. A public trial might provoke Eldon to an act of supreme stupidity. Her eldest son claimed to have evidence that she had ordered Queen Kila's death. His clumsy threats to reveal such evidence had been a minor thorn in her side for years, but the problem grew exponentially upon Keldor's capture. She cursed herself for not killing the assassin ages ago.

Mavis sighed deeply. She had no wish to deal harshly with Eldon, but her plans were too important to risk on waiting out his unsteady nerves.

He always was a sensitive boy, she thought sadly.

He hid it well behind coolness, but Mavis knew she had failed to turn Eldon against House Minstel. She hesitated to warn him off though because his natural stubbornness and idiotic pride would provoke him into exactly the sort of behavior Mavis would need to deal with harshly.

***

Kest (October) 11, 1538
Same Day
Governor Judge's Estate, City of Idonia

Delia Altran nervously twisted the rings adorning her left hand. Squeezing hard enough for the Nedis crystal diamonds to dig into her fingers, she watched her husband. His tense stance and vacant stare told her of his agitated state, but his expression failed to divulge more information. Although eager to know what bothered him, nameless fear rendered her mute.

"Mother called today," Mitrek finally blurted.

Delia's heart lurched. It suddenly became clear why Mitrek had ordered the children to bed early. Lady Mavis Altran's calls had the nasty habit of heralding trouble. To say she scared Delia would be a gross understatement.

"We are to return the call tonight," said Mitrek, sounding like he was bracing for a refusal.

Just then, Leah walked in with a comm attached to a vidscreen so they could make the call.

Delia wearily rubbed at her eyes and waited while the servant arranged the communications device. Mitrek took the open seat next to her and leaned close so the tiny vidrecorder could capture both their images. Now that he was so close, Delia noticed the fine sheen of sweat glazing his forehead. Somehow, the observation made her feel worse.

When Lady Mavis Altran appeared, Mitrek cleared his throat.

"Greetings, Mother. Leah said you wanted to speak with us this evening, so here we are."

Lady Mavis's warm smile did nothing to ease Delia.

"I realized I have never truly enjoyed the pleasure of Silvia's company and request the opportunity to make up for the lapse." The way she spoke the word "request" made it an order.

"Vee," whispered Delia, unconsciously using the nickname. Her lower lip trembled as her mind conjured a dozen frightening images. She stole a glance at her pale husband and reached for his clenched left fist.

"What have you done?" Mitrek's question contained more accusation than inquiry.

Lady Mavis's smile dimmed. She looked slightly wounded for a second before her smile turned bemused.

"Why does everybody assume I have ulterior motives?" she wondered.

"Because you always do," Mitrek answered.

"Fair enough," replied Lady Mavis graciously. She stared at Mitrek and Delia in turn. "You deserve the truth, and I shall tell you what I can."

She wasn't going to tell us!

The realization struck Delia like a physical blow, making the pain of the news to come worse. Delia held her breath and griped her husband's hands tightly.

"A trial will soon be ordered for Queen Kila's assassin. You must bid for it," said Lady Mavis.

"Why? Did you order her death? Shall I set the guilty free, Mother?" Mitrek's voice trembled with suppressed anger.

"Bitterness suits you not at all, my dear," Lady Mavis said mildly. "And, as for your last question, my wishes are quite the opposite. You will give Niktrod Keldor a death sentence to be carried out on Gardan."

Mitrek's harsh laughter chilled Delia.

"So you did kill the last queen, and I'm to clean up your mess." He shook his head in disgust. "Do you have any idea how many laws you just asked me to break?"

"Do you have any idea how many lives rest upon your decision?" Lady Mavis returned.

Delia was stunned. She knew her husband's mother could be cold, but she never imagined the woman would threaten them.

Mitrek paled even further. His gaze turned murderous.

"How many lives, Mother?"

Delia's breaths came in short, frantic bursts. Her vision clouded and her hearing wavered. She released her husband's hands to rest her head in her palms, elbows propped on knees.

Mitrek's arms encircled her.

"Breathe deeply," he encouraged, rubbing her back with his left hand.

"Delia, focus," Lady Mavis demanded. "You must follow my instructions explicitly. No one can know there is anything amiss about Silvia's visit to me."

"We don't even know where you live!" Mitrek shouted.

"You will know precisely what you need to know when you need to know it," Lady Mavis said.

"You expect us to pack up our daughter—" Mitrek began.

"I expect obedience," Lady Mavis interrupted. "You will bid for and win Keldor's case, conduct the trial, and hand down exactly the sentence I described. Then, I can send Silvia home."

A few more shaky breaths made Delia feel a little better.

"How can you do this?" she asked, wishing her voice were steadier. "How can you threaten your own family?" Tears that had been pooling finally fell, but she locked away the sobs.

"What if I lose the bid?" Mitrek wondered.

"You won't," Lady Mavis said. "Just worry about your part in this." Her eyes focused on Delia. "I do what I must to protect my family. Silvia will have my finest guards during her short stay."

Delia felt like something was trying to suck her soul out.

Still holding tightly to Delia, Mitrek refused to look at his mother.

"I will do as you say, Mother, but when this matter ends, we're done." He slapped the switch to end the call before she could respond.

Chapter 17:
Tutor

Kest (October) 11, 1538
Same Day
Maladek's Private Retreat, City of Idonia

Lord Kezem spun around and drove his kerlinblade hard against the attacker who stood ready for the blow. The man grunted but absorbed the strike with relative ease. A swift kick to the man's right knee earned Kezem a moment to miss the satisfying weight of his electrified banistick, but he needed the kerlinblade practice.

Another eight attackers stood warily in a loose circle around Kezem and the man climbing to his feet again.

"I don't like this," said one of the mercenaries. The blond woman nervously shifted her grip on her kerlinblade. "It feels wrong. You knew we were coming."

A few of the mercenaries muttered agreement and the occasional curse.

"Do you know who hired you?" asked Kezem.

"Not really," answered the woman who first sensed something wrong. "The broker said only—" She cut herself off and raised her kerlinblade up to a defensive position. White light shone off her face.

Kezem sensed movement from behind and threw himself left a split second before a kerlak beam flew across the circle and struck the wall by a surprised mercenary. Three men drew pistols, one kerlak and two serlak. Kezem mentally cursed and decided to kill them all for breaking the contract. His man had been very specific about the job being completed with kerlinblades only. He never expected them to honor the contract, but the point had been to gain genuine practice fighting multiple adversaries.

He charged the nearest man and plunged his blade into the man's stomach, releasing a near-deafening roar of pain and rage. Before the man could even finish bleeding to death, Kezem gripped his right shoulder and pivoted so the body blocked the incoming energy beams and bullets. The twisting motion of plunging the blade in had helped Kezem turn the man, but now, the blue blade cut itself free. Knowing his makeshift shield would soon be useless, Kezem abandoned it.

A quick lunge brought him within striking distance of a young mercenary. The boy barely had enough sense to raise his kerlinblade to catch Kezem's first strike. The force pressed the boy's weapon into his left shoulder. He screamed and fainted, but Kezem wasn't satisfied yet. With a well-timed flick of his kerlinblade, Kezem removed the unfortunate man's head.

Two down, many to go. His eyes challenged the rest to step forward and test him.

"Who are you?" demanded the talkative woman.

"Don't you recognize me?" Kezem asked, grateful for the break. He felt their gazes scrutinize his features. His man had hired them from Azhel, but if they had paid any attention in school, they should know him.

One dark-haired young woman stood with her kerlinblade held casually at her side. She didn't fit with the rest of the group. Too much certainty shone in her lovely, purple eyes. Kezem expected her to speak, but she said nothing.

"You are Governor General Kezem Altran, Idonia's Third Lord," a man said eventually.

"You are Maladek," said another man. He appeared older than the others.

The woman with blond hair immediately lowered her kerlinblade.

"You hired us," she said.

"Right on all accounts." Kezem lowered his chin in an acknowledging bow.

"Why would you hire us to kill you?" asked a young man.

"It doesn't matter," said yet another mercenary man. "I say we finish the job and loot the house besides." The man raised his serlak pistol and started shooting.

Expecting the man to do just that, Kezem easily sidestepped

the first two bullets and retrieved a pair of flingers from the holder on his belt. The first flinger lodged deep in the man's throat. He died almost instantly, but his finger tightened over the trigger and sent one more bullet flying. The errant bullet caught one of the young mercenaries in the left arm, spinning him around and knocking him back into a wall where he leaned heavily. The body of the man killed by the first flinger teetered before falling backward, but Kezem didn't have time to enjoy the sight. The second flinger barely missed the light-haired woman's head, as she used her blade to redirect its flight.

Despite the blond woman's shouted orders to stop fighting, two mercenaries attacked with kerlinblades, unwilling to risk more friendly fire. Kezem attacked the first man to reach him, driving him back into his friend. The second man steadied the first, and they raised their blades to defend against Kezem's vicious strikes.

Suddenly, Kezem disengaged, stooped, and snatched up a kerlinblade dropped by one of the fallen mercenaries. Energy coursed through Kezem as he activated the second blade. It glowed orange. One of the mercenaries lunged, and Kezem swept the man's clumsy strike aside before bringing the handle of his other blade down upon the back of the man's skull.

A terrifying, eerie scream came from the second mercenary facing Kezem with a blade. The man's shirt exploded outward in several pieces. Two more arms uncrossed from the man's bare chest, each clutching a throwing knife. With unimaginable speed, both arms whipped back then forward, firing the daggers.

Kezem made some quick adjustments to the kerlinblades so they were wider and held them together so they formed a shield. The throwing knives slammed into his kerlinblades with surprising force. Kezem feared the thin energy beams standing between him and death would collapse, but they held. A few more adjustments narrowed the beams and changed their colors to blue and red for one and yellow and blue for the other.

By this time, the Elish mercenary held a kerlak pistol in each of his lower two hands. His upper left hand still held his kerlinblade, but the upper right hand clutched a serlak pistol. Kezem had a sinking feeling he might not be able to escape so many bullets and beams. His mind cast about for options. He could seize the man he had just stunned with his blade handle.

Before he could consider other options, the dark-haired woman who had remained quiet thus far traded her kerlinblade for a kerlak pistol. Then, she calmly released a series of stun beams at her female associate. The blond woman cried out at the betrayal, as a beam knocked her unconscious. Three beams pushed the Elish man toward Kezem who slashed diagonally down across the man's chest with his blue and red kerlinblade.

Shifting his grip, Kezem crouched and stabbed down and back, driving the same blade through the mercenary dazed by a head blow. Kezem froze with his right kerlinblade positioned to intercept any attacks and waited to see what the intriguing woman would do next.

She did not disappoint. More stun beams dropped the two remaining mercenary men, including the one already wounded in the arm. Then, the woman put away her pistol, dropped to her knees, and lowered her chin to her chest.

Cautiously rising, Kezem deactivated the kerlinblade in his left hand and clipped it to his belt, but he kept the other blade in a guard position.

"I did not expect such help in this exercise. Who are you?"

"I am Nera Tarpon, my Lord," said the woman, keeping her head lowered. "The Lady would have me learn a blade from you."

His mother had told him to expect a student soon but not deigned to give him details. The young woman before him fit none of the imaginings he had indulged in. Kezem slowly let the kerlinblade drop to his side even as he wondered if his mother was sane. He could easily have killed the woman during this exercise.

"This was as much a test for me as for you, my Lord," said the woman, finally lifting her head. "Will you accept me as a student?"

Do I have a choice?

Kezem knew well enough that he did not.

"I will," he answered, switching off his blade.

"What is your first order then, my Lord?" asked the woman.

Kezem debated killing the mercenaries that had survived. Four were merely stunned and one of those had a serlak bullet in his arm. The first three might be useful sparing partners, but Kezem preferred not to waste his time with the wounded one.

"Kill that one," said Kezem, pointing to the young mercenary who had been shot in the arm and then hit with a stun beam.

"But he's just a boy," protested the woman, her expression stricken. Nevertheless, she took her kerlak pistol out again.

"Wait," said Kezem, deciding to turn the situation into a true test. He walked over to a medical pack attached to the wall and retrieved a stimulant shot. Then, he went to the young mercenary and administered the shot. In a moment, the boy would return to full consciousness. In the meantime, Kezem considered the weapon choices. A kerlak pistol was far too impersonal to prove his point, but a dagger might be a little too close. He settled on a kerlinblade; after all, he was to teach the woman to wield one.

"My Lord?" asked the young woman. A hopeful note said she thought he might have changed his mind about killing the mercenary.

"Take out your kerlinblade and make the blade thin," Kezem instructed.

The horrified expression returned, but the woman swallowed hard and obeyed. Soon, she held a green blade no bigger around than her little finger.

Kezem activated his own blade and made the blue blade very thin as well.

"Good, now I want you to hold your blade like so," he said, demonstrating a simple two-handed grip. He had her practice different cuts for several minutes, sometimes gripping the blade in one hand and sometimes using both hands.

At first, she moved stiffly, but eventually, she relaxed enough to attack the tasks with fluid grace. Occasionally, her eyes wandered to the carnage around them and a bit of the stiffness returned.

After Kezem determined his student had practiced beating the air long enough, he said, "Now, stand in front of the boy. You have more work to do."

Chapter 18:
Time to Move On

Kest (October) 12, 1538
Tarpon Estate, City of Resh

Ignoring the frantic servant begging him to stop, Brook Tarpon crashed through the doors to his father's office.

"What is the—" his father began. Tyko Tarpon cut himself off sharply, glared at the intruder, and muttered something into the infopad he held.

"I'm sorry, Lord Tarpon. I should—" babbled the servant.

"It's all right, Orius," said Tyko in a soothing tone. "My son is always welcome here."

Brook's blood pumped furiously through his head, making his ears ring. Each footfall reinforced his fury. He halted in front of his father's desk, noting the characteristic state of disarray it was in.

"Where is my wife?" Each word in the question could have been its own living entity.

His father's angry gaze softened.

"Lord Maledek must have need of her," he replied, gesturing for Brook to be seated.

"But where is she?" Brook demanded. "Why was my home invaded? The alliance was supposed to improve things, not complicate them."

"You should be more cautious with your words, Brook. Even here at home careless words could call down trouble," spoke a familiar voice.

Brook turned and bowed as his mother swept into the room.

The hum of the sound dampers suddenly surrounded them.

"Hello, Mother. I have come to inquire about my wife," he said stiffly. A spike of resentment rammed him in the chest.

"I received a missive from the Lady this morning," informed his mother airily.

"What?" asked Brook and his father at the same time.

"I made some inquiries as soon as I heard of the attack," Vera continued in a slightly more sympathetic tone.

Brook's father cursed and threw his infopad down on his desk.

"I told you to keep me apprised of all contact with Lord Maledek and the Lady." His petulant tone was magnified by his soft Charan accent, which only surfaced when something truly annoyed him.

"You were busy, and I thought it best not to interrupt," said Vera.

"What did she say?" asked Brook, tired of being ignored.

"Not much," his mother admitted, sitting primly in an armchair. "She claims that Nera is safe, but that she will have need of her for quite some time, years perhaps."

"Years? What could Nera possibly do for her that could take so long?" Brook pictured his wife's rich, dark hair and expressive eyes and felt a pang of despair at the thought of such a long separation.

"I don't know, but you had better let caution guide your every move," Vera warned.

Brook gave his mother a questioning look.

"After all this time, my boy's an idiot," muttered his father, heaving a sigh and letting his chin fall to his chest.

"Innocence is not idiocy," snapped Vera. Her hands clenched in her lap to keep from placing a comforting hand on Brook's arm. "Sit down, Brook dear."

Annoyed but accepting obedience as the swiftest path to answers, Brook followed the instruction.

"Try not to worry about your wife," said Vera. "Given recent tensions in the Alliance, she will probably be safer with the Lady than with you."

"What tensions?" asked Brook through a stiff jaw. "That mess Merisia caused? I thought that foolishness was behind us."

"That's only part of it," said Tyko, massaging his temple with his right hand. "And it's not quite a closed matter. Talyon Keldor's escape is unsettling."

"How so?" asked Brook. "Surely, he would not return for Merisia. It would be suicide."

"Do not worry about Talyon Keldor," advised his mother. "His fate will be determined soon enough, but heed my advice concerning your own safety."

"Why do you think I'm in danger?" Brook wondered, despising the faint whine in his tone. "Why do you say it like it's something new? I've always been in danger thanks to you two." He had not meant to rant but felt better afterward.

"Don't be impertinent, boy," scolded his father.

"This is something else entirely," Vera said slowly, ignoring Tyko. "The danger you have faced all your life was subtle and mostly from the Restlers. The Lady and Lord Maledek operate in a completely different stratum."

"You fear them," said Brook, grinning with perverse pleasure.

"As should you," said Tyko gruffly.

"But the Alliance—" Brook protested.

"Is dangerously dependent upon them," Vera finished. "They know precisely where and how to pressure this Alliance into executing their will."

Her words scared Brook.

"Is Nera a hostage?" Brook asked.

"No more than you or I." His mother shrugged then waved at the faint buzzing from the sound dampers. "Then again, the threats are growing ever more real."

"Can I go to her?" Brook asked, a crazy idea forming.

"Why would you want to do that?" asked Tyko.

"I will raise the issue with the Lady." A spark of interest shone in his mother's shrewd green eyes. "But I doubt she will consent. We have consistently failed to place someone close to her."

"Nera would help if she knew," Brook said, hoping he was right.

They fell silent as each wondered how to best contact Nera.

***

Kest (October) 14, 1538
Governor Judge's Estate, City of Idonia

Lord Kezem silently renewed his vow to permanently deal with his mother sooner rather than later. He liked it best when she left him to his delusions of privacy. He hated it when she used him, and the order to escort his niece to a safe house in Rammon rankled even more than usual. This little errand would make his brother hate him almost as much as they mutually despised their mother.

Does the contempt hurt you, Mother?

Sometimes he caught glimpses of pain in her face or heard traces of it in her tone.

"I thought she might send you." Delia's cool voice interrupted his thoughts. She motioned Kezem in and shut the door after he entered.

"Where is Silvia?" Kezem asked, figuring it best to leave as quickly as possible.

"She is with Leah gathering a few items," replied Delia. She turned away and led Kezem through several hallways to a sitting room.

Kezem sensed nothing wrong until the faint click of tumbling locks reached his ears. His kerlinblade was in his hands an instant later.

By this time, Delia had walked to a wine cabinet and removed a kerlak carbine. The weapon shook in her hands, but her eyes glittered with feral determination.

"Delia, this won't help." Kezem kept his voice calm and soothing. He angled his kerlinblade so that it could shield most of his body, but he left it off to avoid needlessly spooking his brother's wife.

"Yes, it will," Delia declared unsteadily. "She will leave us alone if she knows we hold her favorite son."

Shaking his head, Kezem stifled bitter laughter.

"You are mistaken. She cares only that her plan succeeds, and if she has determined your daughter should be involved, it will be so." As he spoke, Kezem took small steps toward Delia.

"Why are you helping her?" Delia asked in a pleading tone. "Mitrek has turned away from her, you could do the same."

Kezem's bitter laughter finally escaped him. He took two more steps in Delia's direction.

"You don't need to save me from her, Delia."

I will see to that myself one day.

In one swift motion, Kezem's left hand seized the gun and twisted it from Delia's grasp while his right activated the kerlinblade and brought the indigo blade to her throat.

With a small cry, she stumbled back a half-step, halted by the wine cabinet. She shut her eyes like she expected him to kill her.

Grunting annoyance, Kezem deactivated the kerlinblade and tossed her gun onto the small couch behind him. Taking his comm from his belt, Kezem held it out to Delia.

"Call Leah and have her bring Silvia here," he said gruffly. Softening his voice, he added, "I will call you when we reach our destination and have my people provide regular updates."

Delia eyed the comm contemptuously but reluctantly accepted it and did as he asked.

"Leah, please bring Silvia to the first floor sitting room," said Delia. Instead of handing the comm back, she tossed it onto the couch beside the kerlak weapon. "It's hot in here. Would you like some wine?"

Suspicious, Kezem glanced from the comm to Delia and back again. A few quick steps brought him to the couch where he picked up the comm and noticed it was still on.

"Leah, bring me the girl in the next five minutes or I will kill Delia."

***

Kest (October) 14, 1538
Same Day
Governor Lord's Estate, City of Idonia

Eldon Altran's hands shook so hard he nearly dropped the infopad. He sank onto a reclining chair, feeling like a man swallowed by a maw. Having the ground suddenly open then snap shut around him might have been preferable. The report left a sour taste in his mouth. Kezem always had been Mother's favorite, but Eldon thought his brother was smart enough to stay out of Lady Mavis's schemes.

Apparently not, he mused. *How deeply are you involved, Kezem?*

A sinking sensation in the pit of his stomach told Eldon it was only a matter of time before his family faced a crisis like the one thrust upon Mitrek.

Poor Mitrek, poor Delia, poor Silvia. He thought of his wife and two boys. *How do I protect them?*

Eldon wished he could talk to Calia, but he knew ignorance would be her best defense should his plans draw his mother's wrath down upon them.

As time slowly passed, Eldon's frustration mounted. His one protection against his mother was about to either become completely useless or else tear his life apart like a windstorm in a crystal shop. The king had called for a public trial of Niktrod Keldor. The Governors Council and Senate had both agreed, and Eldon had not dared to protest too much.

His mind whipped through options. He could petition the

Governors Council to investigate, but that would only suspend the problem for a few months. He could privately beg King Terosh to cancel the trial, but he doubted that would succeed. Reliable—and expensive—word had it that a Gardanian deal prompted the trial in the first place. Eldon could publicly release the evidence, anonymously, of course, to avoid falling afoul of the Law of Obligatory Revelation. The plan would save Keldor's life if several key factors panned out, but it would earn Lady Mavis's eternal ire regardless of the outcome. Eldon fought a sudden chill as he dismissed the idea.

As he despaired of a good plan, a wild idea came to mind. He argued with himself.

Get Keldor the evidence.

What would that accomplish?

Tell mother he has it and let her deal with the problem.

He knew exactly how she would deal with it. She would kill Keldor.

Well, if you're going to kill the man, why not just shoot him yourself?

The thought shocked Eldon. He had managed to go his entire life without killing one sentient being, and now, he was plotting murder, just like his mother.

He felt sick, but he could not shake the knowledge that Keldor was the problem. While Keldor had been free, Eldon's knowledge had been valuable. A trial risked exposing his mother's involvement, which would obliterate any tenuous hold he had over her. If Keldor died, then the truth might remain safely buried.

Eldon held his head in his hands. He loathed his mother's ways, but he would employ them if it saved his family.

Chapter 19:
Meetings of Heart and Mind

Kest (October) 17, 1538
McGreven House, City of Resh

Sitting on the couch in her former master's new home, Reia consciously tried not to fidget. She had intended to come much earlier in her visit to Resh, but the week had passed in a flurry of lessons, meetings, and entertainment. She had tried to prepare arguments as to why Niklos Mikhail McGreven should continue being a Ranger, but now that she was finally here, words failed her.

"You can't do it," said Master Niklos with one of his gentle smiles. His expression said he knew her purpose in visiting. "I have made my choice."

"But they need you!" Reia protested. "I need you."

"You still have me, Sela," he replied. Master Niklos looked at Reia steadily. "You will always have me."

Reia was grateful he used the term of endearment meaning both "dear one" and "daughter" instead of a lofty honorific, but his dull tone worried her.

"Why would you leave the Rangers?" she asked. "They were your life."

Please don't say it was on my account, she silently pleaded.

His warm smile cut through her.

"I am getting older and perhaps more cynical. I want to spend more time with my family, watch my children grow. I have seen too much trouble and am entirely done with that quarrelsome Council."

"They're not perfect, but they try," Reia said, surprised to be fighting tears. She could hardly think about the Council and their last words without the pain crushing her again. Her mind frantically searched a few of the fruitless what-if threads. "Was I wrong?" she blurted at last.

The question could mean almost anything, but Master Niklos knew her better than anyone except Kiata. He knew exactly what she meant. His expression shifted from the compassionate countenance of a friend to the sterner visage of a frustrated instructor. He leaned forward in his chair with an elbow resting on each knee and hands clasped as if in prayer.

"Listen to me, Sela. Whether or not you were wrong does not excuse the Ashatan Council's lack of judgment."

"Then join them. Guide them," said Reia.

"I tried that for a time, but it was like trying to shout in a windstorm." Having lost the hard edges to his expression, he just looked weary. "I will continue to help wherever I can, but I will no longer submit myself to the Council."

His words frightened Reia.

"You're going to go rogue?" she wondered.

Master Niklos chuckled, and a spark of humor brought life to his eyes.

"Oh, I'm going to do much worse than that. I'm going to be a tosh merchant."

"But the mines are corrupt," Reia said.

"What better place to start cleaning than with that which is most in need of it," Master Niklos intoned in his wisest teacher voice.

Reia conceded the point and let the conversation flow into neutral territory for a time. They needed the break. Finally, she brought up the second reason for her visit.

"Master Niklos, what can you tell me of the anotechs? Why do the Rangers limit their use?"

"You probably know much more than I at this point," said Master Niklos.

"But you were a part of the Nareth Talis," said Reia. "You must remember something."

"I retain only vague impressions of those years," Master Niklos said. "The mandatory memory alterations bring up yet another issue that plagues the Council." He shrugged. "At least it gives them something to argue about when they cease philosophizing about why the anotechs reject certain Rangers."

"Does it happen often?" Reia wondered, trying to absorb the new information and reconcile it to things she already knew. Rumors long since dismissed floated to the forefront of her mind.

"Despite two such cases in the last generation, it hardly happens at all," answered Master Niklos. "Your old trainer, Kolknir, was the first case in a few generations, and then, more recently, Lucas Telon failed in the joining ceremony."

Reia nodded thoughtfully. She had known of Lucas's failure, but the significance had been lost on her. Sympathetic emotions for her former friend battled indignant feelings from recent encounters.

"Kiata wouldn't tell me anything on the subject of anotechs or the Nareth Talis ceremonies, but Todd told me active members are sworn to secrecy. Why the silence?" asked Reia.

"For the same reason much ill is done anywhere," said Master Niklos gently. "Fear."

"If we knew more, we would have less to fear," Reia argued.

Master Niklos began to nod agreement but then shook his head.

"You speak some truth, but you forget that fear comes in many forms. Our internal fears may be assuaged by increased knowledge of the anotechs, but we would also draw much unwanted attention from within and without."

"You speak of GAPP. Are they that powerful? Would they take drastic steps to understand the anotechs?"

"I have no doubt they would," said Master Niklos gravely. "The anotechs' ability to live up to legend matters little. Keeping them a legend has been our only safeguard for many years. Why do you ask? What has happened?"

"Nothing … yet," Reia said, attempting a smile. A chill sapped her will to put any force behind the smile. "It is just a feeling I have had for a long time, nothing more than a dream really."

"A new dream?" asked Master Niklos. He knew her standard nightmares almost as well as Kiata. "Tell me."

Reia struggled to put her dreams into words.

Understanding that she needed time, Master Niklos excused himself and went to prepare some mintas tea. When he returned a few minutes later, he served the tea and returned to his seat, waiting patiently.

"Drink your tea, Sela," said Master Niklos. "It is good for easing troubled minds."

Reia was surprised to see the steaming cup. She murmured thanks and absently took a sip. The sharp, spicy taste of wuzle roots nipped at her tongue. She swallowed slowly and willed herself to relax.

"It must have been quite a dream," commented Master Niklos.

"Yes," said Reia, letting the word hang in the air. "I asked about the anotechs before because I feel the dream is somehow related to them, but I cannot fathom how."

Master Niklos frowned.

"There are not many accounts of people's dreams being affected by anotechs." A pensive look came over him. "There were rumors that Ranger Gedroo suffered terrible dreams before he lost his mind, but the accounts were too conflicting to be believed."

Reia smiled faintly.

"That's good to know. I would hate to follow in Ranger Gedroo's footsteps or share his fate." She took another small bit of the mintas and wuzle root tea and let the mixture sit on her tongue, causing it to tingle pleasantly.

"There's no chance of that," Master Niklos assured her.

"Thank you for saying so, but if I continue having dreams like this, I may yet want to lose my mind," Reia said. She drew a slow, deep breath and began, "I was completely submerged in cold, clear blue water. I wanted to fight to the surface, but some unseen force held me fast. Panic rose in my chest and my muscles ached. I held my breath as long as I could, but when I could hold it no longer, I let the sea flood my mouth and nose. Everything stung. The sea water scraped my throat raw, but I could breathe the water."

"Do you think the anotechs could accomplish such a thing? Is that what makes you think of them?" asked Master Niklos.

"No, it was more than that," said Reia. "I saw sharp rocks lying below a steep cliff, great waves crashing onto a shore, and a man dressed in dark clothes standing over a cliff cradling something in his arms. He felt familiar. Then, I was back under the water feeling myself drown and yet living. The cycle repeated at least three times."

"You certainly have vivid dreams," said Master Niklos.

"I don't know what it means," said Reia, letting frustration seep into her tone.

"Must it have a meaning?"

Reia began to nod but then turned her head thoughtfully.

"Everything about the dream seemed so real … so desperate. It's the same creepy feeling I get when I try to think of the future. I feel like I'm being watched."

Master Niklos burst into laughter.

"My dear Sela, you are the queen. Everybody will always be watching."

***

Kest (October) 17, 1538
Same Day
Governor Lord's Estate, City of Resh

Lacking a better way to deal with his restless energy, Terosh paced back and forth in the small space separating the heavy armchairs from Governor Darmon Zelene's massive desk. Since it only took about three steps to go from one end to the other, Terosh constantly had to turn around. Finally, he forced himself to sit down and look at the woman stiffly perched on the camrood leather chair behind the desk.

"Is there nothing I can say to convince you?" he asked, knowing the answer that would come.

"Not one thing, Your Grace," replied Lady Akia Zelene. She tried to smile, but it flickered and faded almost as soon as it started. "I am not my father. I have not his gift for finding the best compromise or willing others to accept my ways. I know these people, and they know my heart has long belonged to the people of Ritand."

"Will you return there?" asked Terosh as heaviness settle on him.

Nodding and attempting a smile with slightly better results, Lady Akia said, "As soon as my father's affairs are in order, I shall return. The skills the queen taught me are much appreciated there."

"Is there anything I can do?" Terosh asked, desperate to be of some use. He was tired of feeling impotent when it came to dealing with the Governors Council. There were too many careful balances to maintain.

"We can always use more aid, Highness," said Lady Akia. She kept her tone even like she dared not let her hopes rise, but her dark eyes added a heartfelt plea.

Terosh nodded absently several times.

"I will do what I can, Lady Zelene," he promised.

A look of mild alarm mixed with complex pain crossed Lady Akia's features.

"Do not trouble yourself on my account, Highness," she said softly. "The Ritand—"

"Are still my responsibility," Terosh cut in. An idea struck him.

"It's time we improved relations with them." He cleared his throat to transition into a more formal tone. "Lady Zelene, would you consider accepting an official commission to attend the needs of the Ritand people?"

"What manner of position?" Hope and caution struggled on Lady Akia's face.

"Ambassador from the Royal House," Terosh said.

"They will oppose it," Lady Akia said, referring to the Governors Council and the Senate.

"Not if we present it right," Terosh argued. "With your permission, I will frame the position as a memorial to your father."

"Why would you need my permission?"

Terosh nearly winced at the question.

"Technically, I don't, but I'm trying to be fair. Your father did much to improve opinions concerning the Ritand. You have devoted yourself to their cause. An official ambassador is the next logical step. Will you accept?"

Lady Akia leveled a measuring gaze at Terosh.

"The Ritand will no doubt protest government involvement, but I think a few will see the advantages."

Terosh knew it was not a clear commitment, but it allowed him to turn the conversation to the details.

Chapter 20: Investigations

Kest (October) 18, 1538
Site of the Attack on Lady Akia Zelene, City of Resh

"Todd, it's been more than ten days since the attack," Kiata Wellum said, doing a poor job of masking her impatience. "A couple of thousand people have trampled over this site." She matched Todd step-for-step for another ten paces. "*We've* trampled over this site at least three times."

"I'm going to try something," Todd announced, abruptly sitting down in the middle of the intersection where Lady Akia Zelene had been attacked. He arranged his legs in a crossed position and let his hands hover just above the ground in front of each knee.

A few passersby watched curiously. A young mother snatched up the arms of her two small children and hustled them away. A drunk waved and saluted them with his half-empty bottle of dark ale. Paying no attention to their reactions, Todd uncrossed and straightened his legs, closed his eyes, and eased back until his head rested on the ground.

Kiata blew out an annoyed breath.

"You look like a corpse, and you're going to get us arrested for erratic behavior. Again."

"Almost arrested," Todd corrected cheerfully. He released some anotechs from his hands, arms, and feet and told them to search the area for clues. Sometimes, if he concentrated hard enough, he could connect to anotechs present at the time a specific event occurred. Occasionally, these anotechs let him witness these events as they had seen it. He hoped this might be one such case. Before fully committing to the search, Todd said, "Besides, that was ages ago, and this time we're officially sanctioned by the Royal House."

"Hurry up and finish before a merchant hov makes you a permanent part of the intersection," Kiata snapped.

"I trust you to watch over me, my love," Todd replied, speaking dreamily. He had committed most of his concentration to the task of directing anotechs.

The tiny machines fanned out away from Todd's prone body. The farther they ranged, the harder Todd had to concentrate to control them. He let himself sink further into a meditative state to facilitate such deep concentration. The anotechs flooded him with sensations.

Kiata had once asked him what it felt like. He had tried to explain, but it was difficult. It felt like drawing each impression across his chest and testing it with his heart. Most impressions flew past leaving Todd with only the faintest echo of a vibration, but strong emotions and significant events touched him deeper somehow. He experienced these like a friendly thump on the chest. When that happened, he stopped the flow and let the current anotech tell its tale.

Several false alarms left Todd weary, but he pressed on, knowing of no other way to get the information he sought. He and Kiata had questioned Lady Akia, Lady Orla Miraz, servants from both estates, Governor Damien Luvak, Master Tyko Tarpon, every officer who had searched the scene, and several witnesses the police had conjured. Nobody could shed much light on who might have attacked Lady Akia. Silent witnesses seemed the best course now. Their evidence would never be accepted in a court, but Todd was more interested in identifying the man who had terrorized Lady Zelene and likely killed her father. He would let the police sort evidence and worry about prosecution.

Todd wished Kiata could help him. This would go much faster with less space to cover, but his wife lacked the patience for the work. Even with only part of his consciousness aware of her, Todd felt Kiata's impatience like a burning torch. If he opened his eyes during this state, he would see an outline of her, glowing orange, red, and yellow. He peeked to confirm this and returned to his work, reassured by the moving blur that told him Kiata paced in front of him.

He watched three hov crashes, several fights between gangs, a few shady meetings, half a dozen robberies, and even a murder.

Popular place for crime, he thought.

Not really. This is a relatively lonely place, but many years have passed, so many things have happened. The voice that spoke in his mind sounded young yet wise.

It took Todd a few seconds to overcome the shock of speaking directly with anotechs.

You can use the common tongue?

Of course, we can, but we usually choose silence. Few understand us. Many fear us. Speaking leads to trouble.

I don't fear you. I seek answers. Who attacked Lady Zelene?

We will show you.

Todd felt the familiar thudding sensation, and his heart skipped a few beats. The short scene unfolded behind his closed eyes as clearly as if he watched a vid. He saw Lady Zelene's hov float into the intersection and stop. The view switched to a different angle, and Todd watched a black-clad figure land on the hov's roof and slap something metallic down. The view switched again, and the whole hov shimmered with energy. The masked man tumbled from the roof and rolled a few times, coming to his feet just as two men holding pistols jumped from the hov. The man in black waved and a disorienting view showed a man's neck approaching at rapid speed. Todd flinched as the view switched again showing the attacker shoving Lady Akia against the hov and leaning close. He couldn't make out the words, but Lady Zelene had already reported her attacker's words. She slumped, the man retrieved his weapons, and Todd's mind returned to a blank state.

Todd watched the scene a few times to make sure he saw everything. On the fifth time through, Todd saw the hov light up with energy, he noticed the small metallic object fly away from the hov. The police had sent copies of their reports to his infopad. Nobody mentioned finding a small metal device. Perhaps finding it would provide a clue. Todd tracked its flight path and snapped his mind out of the trance.

He tried to open his eyes, felt a stab of pain, and decided to wait a moment. The presence of flingers disturbed Todd. He thought over the matter while his senses slowly recovered. He had recognized the tiny silver throwing weapons on his second time through the anotech memory. Military and police units might spend a few weeks training with them, but the only people who handled the weapons to much effect were Rangers. Kiata, Lucas Telon, and their old master, Kolknir, were the only three people Todd could conceive of making such swift and deadly throws.

"Kiata," Todd called, irritated that his voice sounded so weak. He blinked and squinted up. A few tears squeezed out of his dazzled eyes. He hauled his aching body to a sitting position and immediately regretted it. His felt lightheaded and his stomach rebelled. He shut his eyes and clenched his teeth to will the pain away.

Kiata appeared at his side.

"I'm here. Did you learn anything?" She gripped Todd's arm to hold him steady.

"Flingers—" Todd never finished his sentence.

A gasp from Kiata cut him off as her arm slammed into his chest, driving him to the ground.

***

Kiata Wellum sensed the stun beams move through the air above her back. After flattening her dazed husband, she rolled off him and grabbed her banistick. It snapped open in her hand as another blue beam headed for her. Leaping to her feet, Kiata timed her swing to plow the stun beam harmlessly into the ground.

Seeing no immediate threat in front of her, Kiata whirled to search for threats to her husband. She hoped his recovery was much swifter this time around. Last time, his reactions had been sluggish for at least an hour. She shook off the disturbing thought.

The sudden lull made her very suspicious. She scanned for signs of danger, and unfortunately, found them approaching from multiple sides. Like something out of a nightmare, five men materialized from the shadows. Furious at not having sensed the danger earlier, Kiata crouched in a ready position, her eyes dared any man to face her in a fair fight.

Each man wore a black RT Alliance uniform and carried a kerlak pistol and a kerlinblade. Two held their kerlinblades in addition to their pistols. The blades were wide and flat, ready to defend the men should Kiata or Todd turn one of the stun beams against them. The other three had only kerlak pistols pointed at the Rangers. Their kerlinblades remained on their belts.

Kiata mentally marked the two with both blade and pistol as the most dangerous and angled her body to face one of these men. The odds did not please Kiata, but neither did they terrify her. She spared a glance at Todd and to her horror, saw him sitting cross-legged in another meditative trance. Sensing Todd needed time to complete a task, Kiata pointed at the nearest man.

"You, state your business," Kiata commanded.

The man's eyes flickered to one of his comrades. A silent message passed between them. Then, the air filled with stun beams.

Panic fueled Kiata as she dodged a few beams. The maneuvers took her about a meter away from Todd, so she fought her way back toward her husband's oddly serene form and slapped at stun beams that came too close to him.

This had better be good, Todd.

Kiata sank into her training and let instinct dictate where her banistick struck. During a brief break, while one of her attackers changed the battery pack on his kerlak pistol, Kiata plucked a flinger from her belt and sent it into the distracted man's head.

It scraped past his left eye, shaving off a bit of his brow. The man had enough time to cry out in surprise before the cormea, radon, and alipo sap combination knocked him out.

Four beams converged on Todd. Kiata had enough time to block two of them but knew the other two would slip past if she didn't do something. So, lacking a better plan, she intercepted the beams with her left leg. It numbed instantly. Kiata hopped on her right leg, trying to maintain her balance and fight. The dead weight of the limb distracted her, and another two stun beams rendered her right arm useless. She briefly wondered why the beams were so weak.

I should be unconscious by now.

The thought was not a complaint, but it did bring up a curious point. Now fighting with right leg and left arm only, Kiata grimly braced for more shots.

None came. It took her a good five seconds to absorb the fact that no one was attacking and identify the reason why. Balanced precariously, Kiata watched as the two attackers in her line of vision groaned and sank to the ground. Two more muffled thumps from behind her said the other two had suffered a similar fate.

"Did I miss anything?" asked Todd, smiling wickedly at her.

"Not much," Kiata responded, torn between laughing and taking a swing at him with her banistick. As adrenaline levels dropped, Kiata's good leg trembled. "But you might want to catch me."

Todd rose gracefully, stepped up close behind her, and pulled her into a tight embrace. Tucking his chin near Kiata's ear, he said, "Nice shot with the flinger."

"You saw that?" Kiata twisted around to peer up at him.

Todd leaned down and kissed her right shoulder.

"I saw everything. Remind me not to anger you while you have a banistick in hand."

"I thought you'd already learned that lesson," Kiata teased.

"I've learned a lot from you, Kiata," Todd said, leaning in for a quick kiss. Sighing, he added, "Including the need to pack stimulants when I travel with you." He shifted his hold on her, pulled an emergency pack from his belt, and fumbled to open it.

"Let me hold it before you dose yourself," Kiata said.

"Yes, dear," Todd said.

Kiata elbowed him playfully with her good arm and caught the emergency pack as he dropped it. After deftly flipping the pack open, Kiata held it so he could see its contents.

Todd selected two stimulant shots and stuck one in her right arm and one in her left leg. Next, he tucked the spent syringes back in the emergency pack and put it on his belt. Finally, he resumed holding Kiata.

"Reia would have a fit if she knew we used these," Kiata said, as the stimulant brought feeling back into her paralyzed limbs.

Todd shrugged, inadvertently tightening his hold on Kiata.

"She will know," he said softly, in case one of the attackers woke up enough to listen to them. "Her knowledge of anotechs is deeper than ours now, and she's not bound by Council rules. I think I found what we need here, and I've got a lot to tell you about the anotechs."

Sensing faint movement from one of the attackers, Kiata said, "That should be an interesting conversation, but first, we should wake one of these men and question him. I would like to know why Alliance soldiers attacked us in the middle of the day. They usually have more sense than that."

***

Kest (October) 18, 1538
Same Day
Tarpon Estate, City of Kalmata

Brook Tarpon shifted uncomfortably on the camrood leather chair and let his gaze rest on the flickering flames waving hypnotically from the fireplace. He tried closing his eyes but immediately snapped them open again to stave off the nightmarish image of his wife's lifeless face. The dreams had begun the night after her disappearance. Each started out differently, but they always ended the same with his hands around her throat and the intelligence in her pale purple eyes slowly fading to cold blankness.

Knowing only that Brook's sleep was disturbed, Dr. Bartul had recommended relsuma pills, but Brook had only taken them once. The medicine made everything worse by forcing him to sleep and doing nothing to stop the dreams.

The infopad shook in Brook's hands, and he consciously set it down in his lap for fear of breaking it. He looked hard at Nera's image, trying to etch it into his memory. If they had to be apart, this was how he wanted to remember her. The picture showed a close view of her lovely face. She did not smile or frown. Instead, her head tilted thoughtfully, and she stared with a haughty, challenging spark in her eyes.

A strong sense of loss and anger at the forced separation swept over Brook. Nera would return once completing the Lady's task, but he wondered why the mysterious meddler wanted his wife. Surely there were other people she could recruit. What special skill or quality did Nera possess? Guilt and regret hit him. He knew so little about his wife. He certainly admired her beauty and enjoyed her company, but theirs was a slow-growing love planted in the rough soil of business.

Disgusted with the emotional tides, Brook sprang to his feet and nearly knocked the infopad into the fire. It bounced off the low table and landed just short of the flames. A spark sprang free of the fire but died harmlessly a few centimeters above the infopad. He needed to get out and clear his head, maybe pick a fight with someone.

After checking to make sure his miniature kerlak pistol was where it should be, Brook sprang up, dodged the low table, snatched the infopad off the floor, and took another long look at Nera's face. Then, he tossed the infopad onto the chair he had vacated and fled the room. About five steps into the long hallway that would lead him to the front door, something hard slammed into Brook's back.

He tried to tuck into a roll like his defense instructor had taught him, but his exhausted body betrayed him. He landed awkwardly on his left shoulder. Sharp pain radiated from the point of impact, and his head knocked hard into the floor, leaving him stunned. Instinctively, Brook's right hand sought his kerlak pistol, but something smashed into the inside of his forearm, knocking it aside with aching force. He barely registered the new pain before something nestled into his neck just below his chin. He froze and followed the weapon's slender trunk up to a man's hand, arm, and face.

"Cease inquiries into your wife's fate," said the man holding the banistick.

Pain, surprise, and indignation fueled reckless anger within Brook.

"You have no authority over me," he declared, trying to ignore the insistent pressure the banistick placed on his neck.

The man smiled and increased the pressure on Brook's windpipe.

"This is my authority."

"The people I serve—"

"Are the ones who sent me with this gentle warning," finished the man. He lifted the banistick off Brook's neck. "The Lady wearies of your questions. Accept that your wife is performing a vital service and continue handling your Alliance affairs."

"What do you know of the Lady?" demanded Brook, suddenly desperate to know more about the figure his parents had enslaved the Restler-Tarpon Alliance to. "Does she serve Lord Maledek, or does he serve her?"

"It is enough to know that they both serve a free Reshner," the man replied.

Brook chuckled bitterly.

"That rhetoric belongs in the Senate Great Hall. Who are they?"

His question went unanswered. The man double tapped Brook's chest with the banistick and whipped it up toward his face. Brook flinched, and the blow grazed his left check, drawing blood. He soon lost consciousness.

***

Lalri (November) 5, 1538
The Lady's Estate, Kala Mountains

Lady Mavis Altran regretted giving Damien Luvak the ability to contact her. He knew nothing concerning her whereabouts, but the ability to call her private line gave the twit an unfortunate sense of his own importance.

"Would that I could see your face and kiss your hand in thanks, my Lady," said the contemptible little man.

Would that I could kill you and still control Resh, but alas, we must both settle for disappointment.

Instead of sharing these honest sentiments, Mavis double-checked that the voice filtration system was activated, and said, "You have my heartfelt congratulations on your election, governor. The people of Resh have chosen wisely. I trust your commitment to our cause will remain ardent."

"Indeed, my Lady, I know well that I have you to thank for my good fortune." Governor Luvak's chest swelled with pride. His moist eyes beamed delight and his jowls shook with vigorous nodding.

"Is thanks all you called to convey, my friend?" asked Mavis, keeping her voice mild.

If you waste too much of my time, I'll improve someone else's fortunes posthaste.

Horror entered Luvak's pale green eyes.

"Not at all, my Lady, though it be a large part of that which I hope to accomplish through this call." His ability to use many words to say nothing was impressive even for a career politician.

Mavis wanted to reach through the vidscreen and throttle the nuisance.

"Do ease my suspense then, Governor Luvak."

Luvak's gaze darted about nervously.

"My Lady does me great honor by addressing me by title, but I wonder if it is quite safe to do so."

If it were unsafe, it would be far too late to worry.

Mavis pinched the bridge of her nose to relieve a sudden idiot-induced headache.

"We are safe enough," she assured the man. "What knowledge have you to share?"

Luvak leaned closer to the vidrecorder so that his face grew uncomfortably large.

"A Ranger pair was here investigating my predecessor's fate," he said, lowering his voice to a whisper.

I know this! They were there weeks ago as well. What of it?

"Did they find anything?" asked Mavis. She let only mild curiosity into her voice.

"I am not sure, my Lady," said Luvak. He pursed his lips and moved his jaw from side to side. "I am certain they learned nothing about your involvement."

Of all the things he could have said, that statement triggered worry and anger in Mavis.

You told them? Yes, of course, you told them.

After a brief period of near panic, Mavis dismissed her fears. Damien Luvak knew only that the Lady might have something to do with Governor Darmon Zelene's death. Mavis silently thanked whatever providence had prompted her to trust very few people.

Taking her silence for disappointment, Luvak blundered on, "I learned something else, my Lady." He paused, nearly breathless with his news. "The Rangers investigating Zelene's death are related to the queen!"

This man was the better choice for Resh's governor?

Mavis questioned her sanity.

I think I preferred Zelene. He would never deal with me, but at least, he wasn't a complete idiot.

"Is that so? How did you come by this information?" Mavis hated feigning ignorance, especially in the presence of such an abundance of the trait.

"I have many valuable sources, my Lady," said Luvak, bowing his head humbly. The movement brought his greasy face dangerously close to the vidrecorder. "Perhaps I shall one day have the opportunity to lend them to you. As I said, I am much in your debt, and I always pay my debts."

Indeed, you always pay, even if you must murder your neighbors and steal their mines to do so.

The thought opened many delightful possibilities. Should Damien Luvak ever prove more problem than profit, Lady Mavis knew exactly how to deal with him.

"I shall look forward to that day," said Mavis, more to herself than Luvak. Before he could find some way to continue the conversation, she muttered inane pleasantries and severed the connection.

Chapter 21: Troublesome Request

Lalri (November) 9, 1538
Wellum Home, East Quarter, City of Rammon

Kiata's eyes widened as she recognized the young man standing at her door. Fear lent her speed and strength as she seized hold of the caller and hauled him into the welcome room.

Slapping the door closed, Kiata whirled to face the man.

"What are you doing here?"

"I'm sorry about—I didn't mean—I meant to—" A very pale Talyon Keldor stood stiffly and stammered through several sentence starters.

Instantly contrite, Kiata hugged Taly fiercely.

"You're always welcome here, Taly," she assured the young man, pulling away to study his face. He'd grown so much that he had a few inches of height on her now. "I hope you know that." She squeezed his shoulders and stepped back. "What brings you back to Rammon? Wait, don't answer that yet." Kiata held up a hand to forestall a response then waved toward the sitting room. "Please, sit down. Your expression tells me you bear quite a burden."

Once they were both seated, Kiata waited for Taly to restart the conversation, using the still moments to study him further. The month or so on Terik's farm had done him good. Physically, he appeared stronger and healthier than ever. Taly would never be a brawny man, but he was fit and seemed more comfortable with his body than before. However, the haunted look in his eyes had only deepened, making him appear much older than someone who had lived less than two decades.

Kiata wished she could fix the troubles in his life, as she had healed him from the Porit viper's poison when he was a child. It had been one of the few times in her life she had healed someone else with anotechs and the only time she had succeeded so completely. She longed for such a deep connection with the mysterious machines to be permanent, but even her Nareth Talis bond paled in comparison. Anotechs obeyed certain commands and occasionally whispered words of advice, but nothing came close to the purity of knowledge that told her they would heal Taly that day.

Turning her thoughts away from the unreliable nature of anotech connections, Kiata considered the string of unfortunate events that composed Taly's recent life. His friend Merisia still lived in danger. His RT Alliance superiors likely wanted him captured or killed. His grandfather's trial would officially begin tomorrow. Her mind fastened on the last problem. Though she admittedly knew little about Taly, he struck her as the sort to value family and friends very highly. His commitment to Merisia had proven the point. Kiata believed his claim that nothing but friendship existed between him and Merisia.

Taly stood abruptly and stared at Kiata with anguish in his eyes.

"I shouldn't have come, and I have no right to ask anything of you. But I need to see the queen. Will you help me?"

"That might be difficult," Kiata said, knowing that she could never arrange for an official audience. The Royal Guards would sooner shoot a man bearing the Keldor name than let him within shouting distance of their queen.

"I would never hurt her. I just—" Sudden emotion cut Taly off. He angrily dashed away a few tears. "I need to beg for her mercy."

Kiata didn't know whether to leave him to cry in peace or comfort him. She hoped Todd would return soon with Nils. She settled for something in between. Rising, Kiata slowly approached Taly, placed her hands on his shoulders, and pushed down until he sat. Then, kneeling before him, she gripped both of his hands tightly.

"I honestly don't know how she will respond, Taly, but I believe in your right to seek such an audience. You have my word as a Ranger and as a friend. I will do what I can to convince my sister to hear you out."

***

Lalri (November) 10, 1538
East Servants' Entrance, Royal Palace, City of Rammon

"Majesty, may I have a word with you?" called a man.

Two steps from the freedom and anonymity of a quiet exit from the palace, Reia reluctantly stopped. Resisting the urge to growl, she schooled her features into the slightly aloof, obscenely polite expression Sedir insisted she master and turned to face the speaker.

A tall, thin, dark-skinned man came barreling down the hallway at a pace just short of a run. The tempo of his words matched the crisp, confident stride. He wore a white lab coat and carried an infopad. Skidding to a halt, the man bowed.

As soon as his head snapped back up, he said, "Dr. Kurt Saddic at your service, Highness. We met briefly during your tour of the palace. I am deeply sorry for disturbing you this way. Normally, I would wait until an audience to seek your favor, but I have exciting news. I have made tremendous progress with the project. We are almost ready to proceed with experimental trials, but the king seems reluctant to grant permission for the trials. I thought perhaps if you knew how close we were to discovering a proper defense against comaladon, you could have a word with the king."

Reia's mind raced with questions and implications. Only about half of Dr. Saddic's words made any sense to her. She remembered meeting him and recalled his specialty being poisons, but beyond that, she knew nothing about the man or his project.

Sedir's warning rang in her ears: *Never admit to ignorance. As queen, you must exude confidence and knowledge.*

Reia bought time with a pleasant smile and chose her words carefully.

"I shall certainly do as you suggest, Dr. Saddic. Do you have specific good news I may relay to the king? Perhaps if you give me a copy of your report I can find a favorable time to present it to him."

"Certainly, Majesty, I have my report right here," said Dr. Saddic, holding up his infopad. "I can beam a copy to your infopad or arrange for a paper copy to be delivered to your private chambers." Dr. Saddic's infopad passed from his left hand to his right then back again as he dithered. "The king expects a report tomorrow. If it would not inconvenience you too much, I think it best if you appeal to him before I deliver my report. Do you have a preference for delivery?" An eyebrow spiked and settled as he answered his own question. "Perhaps I shall do both. Yes, both would be good. That way you can read it at your convenience." His fingers flew over his infopad. "I shall also have Mikael pull up the informal report so you can see the full version with my comments. Will that be acceptable to you?"

Reia merely nodded, still reeling from his verbal barrage.

"Excellent! Thank you for your time, Highness. I shall delay you no further. Riden bless the rest of your day. I must return to my lab and continue with the project. There is much to be done!" The scientist's knees trembled with the need to move. As soon as he received another nod, he retreated down the hallway faster than he had arrived.

Torn between going to her sister's house and finding out what Dr. Saddic had been babbling about, Reia pulled her infopad from an inner pocket and looked down at the blank screen. Coming to a decision, she dashed out the door and into the gardens to find a quiet spot to read. Kiata and her sudden invitation to visit would have to wait ten minutes.

***

Lalri (November) 10, 1538
Same Day
Wellum Home, East Quarter, City of Rammon

As soon as the door closed behind Reia, she leaned back against it and blew out a long, slow breath. Escaping from Saddic then encountering a crowd had taxed her energy reserves. She spread her fingers and pressed her palms against the danesque wood, letting the smooth coolness calm her nerves. The effect was so complete that she didn't even sense her eyes falling shut until Kiata's soft laughter made her snap them open again.

"Come in and sit down before you collapse and crack your head open," said Kiata. Her voice commanded but her silver-blue eyes teased. "I would hate to have to clean up the mess or try to explain that to your husband."

Reia released a noise somewhere between a whine and a groan.

"I'm not sure I can move. You must have a few hundred neighbors standing on your doorstep."

Grinning wickedly, Kiata said, "Well, I'm sure I could call upon a few dozen of them to assist you. Shall I summon them?"

"You wouldn't dare," said Reia. A nagging doubt lodged in her mind. She never really knew what her sister might do when that expression crossed her face.

"Wouldn't I?" Kiata asked, raising an eyebrow. A light in her eyes said she sensed a challenge.

"She would," said Todd, stepping up behind Kiata and

wrapping his arms around her waist. Then, tipping his head into his wife's he added, "Just to see your reaction." After kissing Kiata's left ear, Todd said, "Dearest, it isn't polite to torment royal guests with threats of unwanted company."

"Killjoy," Kiata complained. She twisted out of Todd's grasp and rushed to Reia. "Come, I'll show you the house."

Before Reia could protest, she found herself on a whirlwind tour of Todd and Kiata's small but comfortable home. The large welcome room led to a tiny sitting room and a short hallway to the kitchen. A washroom, a closet, and a multipurpose room rounded out the rest of the downstairs. Upstairs boasted a master bedroom with its own washroom and a slightly smaller guest chamber.

Gratefully settling onto the couch in the sitting room, Reia leaned back and reveled in the novelty of sitting down.

"You forgot to show me that massive closet you said you could hide a horse in, but it'll have to wait until my legs feel like working again." Reia kept her voice light, but she'd sensed the emotional atmosphere thickening.

"I didn't forget," said Kiata.

Noting her sister's serious tone and Todd's absence, Reia raised her head from where it had fallen back against the couch cushions. "I assume Todd went to retrieve your guest," Reia commented, not quite certain if she should be worried or annoyed.

"Yes, I needed a moment alone with you to explain," Kiata said, sounding sad. A grin flashed and faded. "I know you felt him. You know what he seeks, and you probably already know the answer you're going to give him. Still, I'm asking you to hear his plea with an open mind."

Helplessness crept over Reia in exhausting waves. She hated denying her sister, but now that the formal trial had been ordered for Niktrod Keldor, entertaining requests from his kin felt like betraying Terosh.

"Protecting the boy is one thing, Kiata—you know I'm more than happy to do that—but this is different. I'm not supposed to discuss the trial with *anyone*," Reia said. "Like it or not, my every word needs to be weighed and watched because it's sure to be analyzed from a thousand angles." She hated disagreeing with Kiata while sitting down. It left her at a disadvantage.

"I'm not asking you to publicly broadcast your interview," Kiata said impatiently. "Listen to him."

"I don't want to give him false hope," Reia argued, hearing the subtle shift in tone that said she'd surrendered the verbal battlefield.

Kiata must have heard it too, for she inclined her chin.

"Thank you," she said. "Simply listening will give him much-needed hope. He's still hurting from being cut off from Merisia Restler." Kiata vacated the doorway and went to stand behind the reclining chair, so she could observe the pending exchange better.

Todd entered a moment later with Talyon Keldor, waved the young man over to the chair Kiata stood behind, and left the room.

Taly's tense jaw, stiff shoulders, and clenched fists declared his discomfort. He lowered his eyes, tilted his head forward, and rested his elbows on his knees. His breaths were slightly irregular as he gathered the courage to speak.

Reaching out with the anotechs, Reia sensed his mood and received a flood of impressions. She could not claim to be an expert at interpreting such feelings, but she recognized the heady rush of a racing mind and the tightening across her chest that spoke of pent-up emotion.

"What is it you seek of me, Talyon Keldor?" Reia asked formally.

Taly's eyes flicked up before returning to study the floor near Reia's feet. His head lowered even more.

"If it pleases Your Majesty, grant me this one request." He paused a second to bite his bottom lip, as if afraid to go on. "Spare my grandfather's life. A public trial places him in great danger. The accusation alone of assassinating Her Majesty Queen Kila of House Minstel is enough to condemn him to most people."

"We will do everything in our power to avoid that, Taly," Reia assured. "The trial will be available by infopad and vid broadcasts, but the format has been modified to answer your concerns. None save a committee from the Governors Council and the king even know which justice arena will host the trial. The accused will not appear before the public until the trial concludes. Should your grandfather be found guilty, he …"

Taly's head snapped up so fast his teeth clicked. He locked eyes with Reia, causing her to forget the rest of her statement. His lips pressed tightly together and unshed tears glimmered in his eyes.

"He is guilty, my Queen," said Taly in an agonized whisper.

Kiata's expression darkened, but she showed no other signs of surprise or distress at Taly's announcement.

Reia felt the words like a physical blow. She closed her eyes against the mixture of emotions they unleashed. Soon, however, sorrow defeated the elation of knowing the rigged trial and planned execution would be just.

"I wish you had not said that." She blinked to hold back tears her role forbade.

Alarm crossed Taly's features, and his words flowed like a flashflood.

"The day I joined the RT Alliance, my grandfather warned against following in his—and my father's—footsteps. He said if I traveled their path, my friends and family would be nothing but hostages for the rest of my life."

"That is a fair warning, but not an admission of guilt," Reia said, feeling relief spread through her.

"He also said that the better I got at my job, the more dangerous my allies would become," Taly said, speaking slower now. "To prove his point, he confessed his role in Queen Kila's death and showed me an infopad recording of his instructions. It proves he performed the deed under duress. Against orders, he saved the communication as a guard against his employer."

Reia's spirits rose then crashed. The news of an employer shifted some culpability to another, but any involvement in a murder of this magnitude would carry the death penalty.

"Stop talking, Taly," Kiata ordered, her voice tight. She side-stepped out from behind the reclining chair Taly occupied. "Reia, forget everything you just heard."

"I wish I could," Reia said. Her throat was as raw as if she'd swallowed glass shards.

Kiata rushed to the couch and seized Reia's shoulders. Her silver-blue eyes etched the same message her hoarse voice released.

"I mean it! Forget everything! It was a mistake to bring you here, but that is *my* mistake. He should not pay for it with his life, and if you speak, he will be executed for not confessing sooner."

Every part of Reia wanted to deny it, but Sedir's lessons on the justice system told her Kiata spoke truth. A few tears slipped out.

"What else can I do?" Reia asked, choking back a sob and driving further tears away with anger. She hardly noticed the painful grip her sister maintained on her shoulders. "The law is binding. King Rammon—"

"Was a raving lunatic," Kiata finished, releasing Reia's

shoulders. "I'm not surprised that law came about during his reign. If you—"

Taly cut Kiata off by squeezing her shoulder. Then, he dropped to his knees before Reia and looked at her with a mixture of sorrow and guilt.

"I am sorry, my Queen, I should not have come, but if you could convince the king to spare my grandfather, I would count the use of my life worth it."

It took two seconds for his meaning to sink in.

Kiata's gasp halted Reia's thoughts before she could fully comprehend. Kiata looked down at Taly, inclined her head, and clasped her hands behind her back.

"Well-played, Taly," she said with a smile.

The shift in Kiata's manner confused Reia.

"I'm sorry," Taly murmured.

"Why?" Reia asked as nameless dread prickled in her chest. The question was half-addressed to Taly and half-addressed to Kiata and meant something different to each. The answer hit her suddenly, resulting in speechless rage and icy adrenaline. She simultaneously wanted to smack Taly and seize him in a hug.

The Law of Obligatory Revelation dictated that anyone who possessed information on a crime of significant magnitude yet remained silent faced consequences equal to the crime. Thus, Taly's previous silence on his grandfather's guilt doomed him to share in whatever fate awaited his grandfather. By extension, Todd and Kiata, who had harbored Taly, might also be drawn into the legal web. Even if spared from death, they could face serious prosecution. Reia could say nothing and break the law or appeal to her husband for an exception.

Taly must really love his grandfather to take such a risk.

While Reia wrestled with the odd combination of emotions, Todd entered the room like an Ashasten, plucked Taly off the floor, spun him around, and plowed a fist into the younger man's chest. The blow knocked Taly into Kiata who caught him reflexively. Todd drew back his arm for another strike.

"No, Todd!" Kiata cried, stumbling back a few steps and hauling Taly in the wake of her retreat. "Don't you see? This is the only way he could protect himself." She deposited Taly onto the armchair.

The sound of Taly's coughing dominated for a time. Reia tried to absorb the rapid changes. Todd spent the time glaring at Taly. Kiata knelt before young man and checked that nothing had been permanently damaged.

"He used us," Todd said. "He purposefully placed our lives in danger and now—"

"And now the king must hear him out," Kiata broke in gently.

With effort, Reia forced herself to think. A plan formed. She steeled her nerves and turned to Taly.

"Do you have the infopad proving the threats against your grandfather?"

Taly shook his head.

More thoughts tumbled around in Reia's head.

"No matter, we can ask him about it later. I doubt it will do much to sway the king or the judge, but I will submit your account and question your grandfather." Reia rose from her seat, swallowing several angry threats that would gain her nothing. "I must return to the palace to fulfill these words," she added, directing the words to Kiata and Todd. Then, facing Taly again, Reia said, "I admire your courage and family devotion, Talyon, but know this: my devotion to my family is equal to yours. Do not test me on this."

Chapter 22:
Threats Within

Lalri (November) 10, 1538
Same Day
King Terosh's Private Chambers, Royal Palace, City of Rammon

"Where have you been?" Terosh regretted the question even as it came out. He managed to suppress further words but had to think them or risk bursting something in his head. He spared a moment to warn the anotechs not to broadcast his thoughts and then launched into his silent tirade.

I almost sent Royal Guards tearing through the city after you. Why would you leave without telling someone? Don't ever do that to me again!

The door to his bedchamber slammed shut, telling him part of his message probably showed on his face. His wife's green eyes looked ready to fire energy beams. She stood inside the door wearing an expression that flickered between collapse-into-tears and kill-something-with-bare-hands. Her flushed cheeks and slightly disheveled hair lent her the air of a beautiful damsel in distress, but Terosh valued his life enough to refrain from commenting.

To give Reia time to respond, he sat on his bed and removed the belt holding his kerlak pistol and kerlinblade. After a brief hesitation, Terosh dropped the weapons belt to the floor next to the bed. He would not need them for this coming battle, though part of him wished they could solve their problems like the Ereni. Natives of Eren IX dueled until one party yielded. The winner won the argument and the loser had to live with it. A nice Dollan duel would go a long way to relieving anger and would certainly be easier than navigating the mysteries of a woman's emotions.

Terosh's unease grew as the silence stretched. Fearing he would start babbling, Terosh studied the pastoral paintings lining the walls. He wasn't enthusiastic about paintings, but his mother had insisted his private quarters be adorned with something other than colored crossblades champions and vid stars. One traumatic day when he was eleven, Sarie had replaced his treasures with wildlife and nature paintings. At the time—and under threat of his mother's wrath—Terosh had left the paintings up, now he was simply used to them. Usually, he paid little attention to them, but he had to admit they were nice scenes.

At last, Reia activated the sound damper and broke the tense silence.

"I had two very interesting conversations today, one with Dr. Saddic and one with Talyon Keldor." The careful way she spoke said she wasn't exactly happy about either conversation. "We need to discuss both. Do you have a preference as to which we attend to first?"

Guilt seized Terosh, and he tried not to wince. He had meant to discuss Dr. Saddic's project with Reia, but the timing never seemed right. In truth, Saddic's research tended to slip Terosh's mind until the bi-monthly reports. Now that Reia mentioned it, Terosh remembered a lengthy infopad message from Saddic saying he was close to a few breakthroughs and would give a full report on Lalri (November) 11, 1538.

"What did Dr. Saddic have to say?"

"His project is nearing the experimental stage. He seeks your permission to proceed with the trials," said Reia. Her curt tone and grim expression declared disapproval. Frowning, she added, "The report I received also included his notes."

Terosh's mind raced, making connections and drawing conclusions. He stood and held both hands out in a placating gesture.

"It's not what you think," he said carefully.

"What exactly do you think I think?" demanded Reia. Her eyes dared him to defend the research.

That's a dangerous question.

"I think *we* think the same thing," Terosh said slowly. "Human trials of this nature are wrong. Science should never have gone there, and it's time to return to a higher moral position or progress to a different level that will avoid such research."

As hoped for, the speech stole some of the raging fire behind

Reia's eyes.

"What could possibly have possessed you to commission such research in the first place?" she demanded.

That's a dumb question and you know it!

Terosh fought the urge to rush over and sweep Reia into a crushing hug. Instead, he sent her a long look full of more meaning than words could capture.

"I think you know the answer to that."

Confusion melted into clarity and more fire leeched from her eyes. Reia glided over and threw her arms around Terosh, resting her left cheek against his chest. After several moments, she pulled away and stared up into his eyes.

"I am not going to die that way, Terosh. I promise. The anotechs say any poison they have tasted can be mastered. Your mother's death will protect us and our family for generations. Don't you trust them?"

"Trusting them doesn't mean I shouldn't seek other answers," Terosh replied. "The anotechs will only protect our family and most of the Rangers. If Saddic succeeds, then no one will ever share my mother's fate."

Reia nodded slowly. She released her hold on him and took a small step back, letting her hands drop to her sides. After three seconds of deep thought, she tilted her head and spoke.

"You're right. In that case, I will do it."

Alarm shot through Terosh as her meaning dawned on him.

This is exactly what we're trying to fight against.

"What? No! Reia—"

"We're the only ones truly safe from comaladon," Reia insisted.

"We're also trying to prove that experimenting on people is wrong," Terosh snapped. His head hurt from the sudden shift in the conversation.

"Dr. Saddic's report contains applications for the project," said Reia. Her voice tightened and she looked close to tears. "Several thousand of them in fact."

Terosh groaned.

"He knew that would happen." He wanted to wring Saddic's brilliant neck. "It's going to be impossible to stop him."

"Would you want to?" asked Reia. A faint smile added: *You started this.* "You still believe in his work, just not his methods. So define his methods. Use the law to regulate the acquisition and treatment of volunteers for scientific research. The existing laws are shifting, useless shadows with no real power."

Terosh shrugged.

"I suppose that would work," he admitted. His hands found hers and clasped them tightly. "But promise me you won't volunteer. I trust the anotechs and Saddic, but I'll feel a whole lot better knowing you avoided that sort of danger."

"Would it be unfair to make it a conditional promise?"

"That depends on the condition," Terosh responded carefully.

"We should probably sit down for this part," Reia warned.

Terosh agreed and they settled onto his bed.

"The second interesting conversion I had today starred Talyon Keldor," said Reia, once she was safely snuggled in his arms. "To make a long story short, he broke the Law of Obligatory Revelation, and by extension, endangered Kiata and Todd. They didn't know he had broken the law until he revealed as much in my presence, but that would be hard to prove. He seeks an audience with you, so that's my condition. Meet with him and forgive his crime."

Terosh let several heartbeats pass while he mulled over the situation.

"No jury would ever convict your sister or her husband of breaking the law based on Talyon Keldor's words, but he could still cause trouble. I will give him his audience and amnesty." Feeling just as manipulated as Reia, he found the last word painful to utter. Terosh had barely met Talyon Keldor, but the young man had always exuded an air of innocence. It pained him to see that image destroyed.

"Thank you," Reia murmured, sounding sleepy.

"What did Talyon say exactly?"

Reia repeated as much of the conversation as she could remember and then let Terosh view the conversation in her mind via anotechs.

"We should speak with the elder Keldor before entertaining Talyon," said Terosh.

"Why?"

"Because I don't want any further nasty surprises to come up in conversation with the young Keldor."

***

Lalri (November) 11, 1538

Niktrod Keldor's Cell, Palace Prison, City of Rammon

The weary guard shifted his weight from foot to foot and looked steadily back at Eldon Altran.

"My apologies, Governor Altran, but my orders are clear. The king, the queen, Master Abner, and the nine members of the select committee from the Governors Council are the only ones permitted to see the prisoner. I can check the list again for you, but it won't change anything."

Eldon Altran struggled against the panic climbing his spine and exploding in his mind. He glared at the guard and wondered if he could overpower the man. A quick dagger strike might prevail if the guard was distracted enough, but it would have to be across the throat. Soft armorweave protected the rest of the guard's body.

"This is a matter of utmost importance. The prisoner is in grave danger. I demand to see him at once!"

"Appeal to the king or queen for permission," said the guard. "Either one of their Majesties can add you to the list."

Taking a dangerous gamble, Eldon leaned forward and lowered his voice as he said, "I know whom you truly serve. I am trying to protect her. Keldor could reveal some very dangerous information."

The guard's eyes widened in surprise but his cold smile chilled Eldon, and he knew his mother had already spoken with the guard.

"What did she promise you? I will match it if you let me through," said Eldon.

"My deepest apologies, but I cannot help you, Governor." The guard's eyes softened slightly, adding the message: *You don't have her power to make such promises.*

Eldon again wanted to drive a dagger into the guard.

"Please leave, Governor," said the guard, dropping his voice low. "Return to Idonia. Rammon will be a dangerous place for you tonight."

Eldon couldn't believe his ears.

"You dare to—"

"A warning, my Lord, not a threat," said the guard, lowering his head in a bow. "All my instructions were very clear."

The man's meaning wrapped around Eldon like cold fog. Abandoning hope of an easy solution, Eldon spun away from the guard and strode down the long hallway. The prison's white stones seemed to laugh as he fled.

***

Lalri (November) 11, 1538
Same Day

The Lady's Estate, Kala Mountains

Mavis checked and rechecked her security measures. Once certain she would not be disturbed, she retreated to the inner room of her private office, sealed the door, removed her shoes, and sank onto the comfortable cot. She pulled herself back to lean against the cool stones, drew up her knees, rested her elbows upon them, and wept into her hands.

She faced an impossible choice. Eldon's recent actions proved he would interfere. She would have Lucas Telon deliver a final warning, but if her son failed to heed it, he would have to be removed permanently.

The best way to save Eldon from his own foolishness would be to kill Niktrod Keldor. Eldon would undoubtedly feel threatened, but he would simply cut off contact with her, a fine solution and probably the best she could hope for. On the other hand, Mavis needed to deliver Keldor alive to Gardan. If she didn't fulfill the contract, Silvia would die along with any hope of a relationship with Mitrek. While she had long ago accepted that such sacrifices might one day arise, Mavis was not yet ready to estrange all her sons.

As the sobs subsided, the white noise in Mavis's mind coalesced into coherent thought once again.

You can stop this.

One short conversation with King Padric and her plans would crumble but her tenuous family relationships would survive.

Is revenge worth it?

This wasn't true revenge since Padric had failed to ensnare Mavis all those years ago.

It's not only about revenge. I must save Reshner from Gardan's poisonous influence.

Why risk family to save the world that betrayed you? The thought filled her with sharp despair.

Mavis remembered Sedir's long-ago lessons. She frowned, tears spent for the moment.

I was born a princess, my son will rule, and those who dare to enslave this planet will pay dearly.

A surge of purpose entered Mavis. She had triumphed in dangerous games before, though admittedly not with such personal stakes. She vowed to triumph again. Drawing on this strength, Mavis stood and set about composing her clothes, hair, and emotional state.

"Eldon, you fool. You will learn sense, or I will have it knocked into you."

***

Lalri (November) 11, 1538
Same Day
Niktrod Keldor's Cell, Palace Prison, City of Rammon

The condemned man's words came out slowly.

"You are king. You may do as you like, but I warn you that nothing you accomplish here will bring you the peace you seek. For that you need a priest. Your brother found only pain when he looked inside my mind."

"Tate looked inside your mind?" Terosh knew the news shouldn't be surprising, but it released a bevy of odd emotions. After mastering them, Terosh asked, "Did you kill my mother?" He felt Reia's supportive touch via the anotechs.

The Niktrod Keldor's gray eyes locked on Terosh, simultaneously sad and wise.

"That can be a very complicated question, Highness. You have enough evidence to know my part without my lips confirming such. The question then becomes a matter of degree. Who is the ultimate killer, the man who orders a death or the man who achieves the desired end?"

"Both are guilty," answered Reia.

"If you will forgive my saying so, Majesty, I shall tell you that when I was your age I believed as you do." The prisoner looked down at his hands which were cuffed to the heavy table. He slowly flexed his fingers. "Time and circumstances have changed my view. I make no claim to great wisdom, but I daresay you will understand better when you have more to lose."

The absence of threat in Niktrod Keldor's voice kept Terosh from reaching for where a kerlinblade ought to be on his belt. He had surrendered the weapon upon entering the prison.

"Tell us the story as you see it," Terosh commanded.

"My orders came from someone called the Benefactor. This being convinced me that my son and his family would be very easy targets should I decline the job." Niktrod shrugged. "So, I weighed my options and accepted the job."

Terosh felt devoid of emotion. Then, suddenly his mind and body ached with pain and rage. Conscious thought caught up about the time his fingers closed around Niktrod Keldor's neck. He squeezed hard, pouring his rage and anguish into the task, but he succeeded only in hurting his fingers.

"He will answer for killing your mother, Terosh, but not this way," said Reia.

The strain in her voice touched something inside Terosh. Reluctantly, he released his grip on Keldor's neck. Part of him thanked Reia for protecting Keldor and part of him resented the interference.

"Who is the Benefactor?" Terosh demanded.

Keldor's breaths came in quick gasps. He swallowed hard several times. When he finally spoke, his voice was just as steady as before.

"My research led to two other names: the Lady and Maledek, but I know nothing more."

"Your grandson said you showed him an infopad containing your orders to kill Queen Kila," said Reia. "Is this true? Did you realize the knowledge would condemn him as well?"

Keldor chuckled bitterly.

"Joining the RT Alliance condemned him a thousand times over. I considered the risk worth it, and I trust the king to decide what is just concerning the boy." His gray eyes sought Terosh's blue ones. "Taly knew nothing about the job until I told him in an attempt to better direct his life. Destroying him for my sake would be almost as contemptible as what I did to protect him."

A wave of sympathy moved through Terosh, making him feel like a traitor to his mother's memory.

"I believe you." His throat tried to close, momentarily preventing words. "I still count you a murderer and believe you deserve to die, but nobody deserves the sentence you will receive if convicted."

"What sentence might that be, Highness?" asked Keldor.

"Extradition to Gardan," Reia answered.

"I see." For the first time, Keldor's eyes widened in fear.

"You see?" Terosh asked. "Say something, man! They want to send you to a place where night and day will melt into one haze of pain!" He slammed his fists down on the metal tabletop. The resulting pain calmed him a little. "Give me a reason to stop this. Help me find the Benefactor, the Lady, and Maledek, be they one person or three. Let me send them to King Padric. He will accept that."

Niktrod closed his eyes and heaved a weary sigh. When he opened his eyes, they held more regret than fear.

"I investigated as best I could. Despite what Taly thinks, I am no closer to the Lady or Maledek or the Benefactor than I was years ago. I will appeal here as long as I can, and if I must go to Gardan then so be it."

Terosh exchanged a desperate look with Reia. She nodded encouragement.

"If—if it comes to that and you wish it, I will give you the means to an easier end," Terosh said quietly.

"I understand," said Keldor. "You have my thanks for the consideration."

Chapter 23: Questions of Love and Loyalty

Lalri (November) 15, 1538
The Lady's Estate, Kala Mountains

Two huge problems still troubled Lady Mavis Altran. The danger posed to her granddaughter increased as Niktrod Keldor's trial continued. A trial of this nature threatened to linger on and on. Mavis trusted Mitrek's skills, but even he could not exert much control over the speed with which the advocates presented their cases. After listening to more hours of trial recordings than she cared to count, Mavis knew she needed to move Silvia out of danger without Mitrek knowing. Her other problem—that of King Padric Creston's growing impatience for research subjects—would also need to be addressed soon.

Sitting in her office drinking rielberry tea, Mavis closed her eyes and concentrated on breathing. An elusive thought had haunted her night and day since her private breakdown several days before. The harder she pressed her mind for it, the more the thought teased her. Trusting her instincts, Mavis kept her mind as blank as possible, knowing that the thought would be fully realized soon.

As her mind fought the false peace she imposed, she wondered what messages Dennel blocked at this very moment and worried about what Silvia thought of everything. Would the child's sense of innocence survive the experience? The agents had orders to use only minimal force and to keep Silvia distracted where feasible, but by now, the girl had to wonder why they would not let her contact her family.

Solve both problems simultaneously.

But how?

At first, Mavis felt annoyed, but the more she pondered the idea, the more she liked it.

Let the Rangers solve the problem.

Mavis almost dropped her teacup.

Could it really be that simple?

She drained the rest of the rielberry tea in one long gulp and set the cup aside. Then, she rested her elbows on the desk and let her warm fingertips massage her temples.

How unfortunate that Lucas killed Hiram Alikron.

Mavis had never liked the pompous little Ranger, but if she chose assets based on likes, she would never work with anyone.

The recent, disastrous dealings with the Rangers had burned most of her ties with them, but she still had a camarek spy or two stashed away for desperate times. Players kept only one spy per board, but no rule prohibited several games from being played simultaneously. Multi-board games offered another layer of challenge for serious players. For all their mysterious powers, Rangers possessed common wants and needs. Mavis had devoted many resources to knowing these details, turning her knowledge into power.

Sliding her fingers down her face, Mavis folded her hands when they met at the point of her chin. Her mind raced over the broad details, and she determined to discuss the situation with Dennel later. The man's insights had proven invaluable many times, and moreover, Mavis trusted him.

In theory, the Nareth Talis Rangers numbered in the dozens. In reality, very few showed the sort of power King Padric sought. James and Kelsa Celdin kept busy raising their child and teaching apprentices. Esther Penoi and Adji had good track records, but they avoided using anotechs wherever possible. A self-healing here and a wall scaling there hardly made for grand news. Zed Laverit was not shy about using his powers, but reports spoke of his powers failing at key times. That alone might prove interesting, but certainly not as the first delivery.

Mavis needed Rangers with strong connections to anotechs who didn't fear using them. Kiata and Todd Wellum were certainly candidates. A vid of them rescuing Talyon Keldor had caught King Padric's attention in the first place. Something in Mavis hesitated to involve them, whispering that she should keep them close rather than ship them to Gardan. In the end, practicality triumphed, for few Rangers had the skills to free Silvia.

Mavis stood. Her mind filled with the orders to issue. Lucas and Kolknir could handle the first phase, and hopefully, Kiata and Todd would handle the second phase. She smiled at the irony of twice kidnapping her own granddaughter to save her.

***

Lalri (November) 17, 1538
Ashatan Council Chamber, Riden Mountains

Mentally bracing himself, Todd Wellum bowed to the Ashatan Council, eased onto the nearest cushion, folded his legs into a comfortable position, and silently bid farewell to the rest of his evening.

Sensing Kiata's burning curiosity, Todd shot her a reassuring smile and hoped one of the Council members would speak soon.

Why summon us? Why not just send a comm message?

Their grim countenances told Todd the answer.

To prove a point.

"Thank you for coming so quickly," said Master Jolinda Ekris. "I'm sure you are both eager to know why you were summoned. I will let Master Deliad explain."

Deliad leaned forward and gazed imperiously at Todd and Kiata.

"About a month ago, we received a report from the Resh police concerning an altercation with some RT Alliance thugs. Why did we not hear the same report from you?"

"With respect, the Council issued no orders to report every incident," Kiata replied.

"You should always report anything that could affect the Order," Deliad snapped.

"Captain Von informed us he was filing a report," Kiata said.

"We read and approved of his findings," Todd added. "A report from us would have been redundant." He suddenly hated sitting on the floor like an apprentice waiting for crumbs of wisdom. "We knew they were Alliance thugs, but they carried no identification cards and had their fines paid by an anonymous source."

"Fines as punishment for an attacking Rangers ought to be a crime," muttered Master Corida.

"Why were you in Resh?" asked Master Deliad, shooting Corida a look that demanded he focus.

"What does your report say?" Kiata asked coldly.

"Mind your tone, Ranger Wellum," Deliad warned.

Todd could feel anger streaming off Kiata in palpable waves.

"The report says that you spent several weeks investigating the death of Governor Darmon Zelene," said Master Corida. "Why?"

"That was not your mandate," Deliad added.

"The Royals requested our help investigating the governor's suicide. He was a personal friend of King Teorn," explained Todd.

"What did your investigation reveal?" inquired Master Ekris.

"Unfortunately, very little," Todd admitted. "Governor Zelene ended his life to ransom his daughter. Lady Akia Zelene was kidnapped the evening before by a very skilled man using flingers."

The three Council members drew in sharp breaths.

"A Ranger?" Master Ekris asked.

"How do you know it was a man?" asked Deliad.

"Kolknir or Lucas," said Corida, frowning deeply. "Their flinger skills were unparalleled. Kiata comes close, but few men certainly."

"We think it was Lucas, but we have no evidence to support the claim," Todd reported.

"He was a good Ranger," Deliad commented.

Corida grunted.

"He was a traitor."

"Masters, please. This isn't helping," said Ekris. She raised her right hand to her forehead like she had a headache. "Kiata, Todd. We want to know that you're sticking to your mission in Rammon."

"Our mission is to protect and obey the Royals," Kiata said shortly.

Todd placed a calming hand on her right knee.

"We understand our mission, Masters," he said.

"Good." Deliad gave them each a long, acidic look as he dragged out the word. "Do be mindful that you obey the Order first, for the good of the Royals, of course."

Kiata stiffened, and Todd fought the urge to seize Deliad and tell him to shut up for his own good.

"Now that we've cleared the air, we have a separate mission for you," said Master Ekris, "a secret mission."

"Nobody can know, not even the Royals," added Master Corida.

"Can you handle that?" asked Deliad, studying them like specimens in a jar.

Todd met Kiata's eyes and saw a reflection of everything he was feeling: curiosity, fear, and excitement. He sat up straighter.

"What is the mission?" he asked.

***

Lalri (November) 21, 1538
Roniak Warehouse, City of Huz Mon

The Lady gets what she wants, Lucas Telon thought wryly, marveling at how well the plan had proceeded. Though not privy to the whole plot, he knew it was wider than him.

The Lady had given him the layout of the Rammon Safe House and a list of agents guarding the child, four RT Alliance agents and two Gardanian Shadow Guards.

The Alliance had become an ungainly beast. Lucas's soldiers had no idea they cut down unfortunate allies. Regret pierced him as he remembered the slaughter. He enjoyed a good kill as much as any man, but sacrificing allies seemed wrong.

His mind locked on one woman's expression when he'd planted his dagger in her chest. Her dark eyes had been pain-filled and curious but not condemning. Lucas cursed those eyes. Why didn't she hate him? The lack of anger only made him condemn himself.

The tap-tap of boots on concrete interrupted Lucas's reverie.

"She's whining about her mother again," complained Alden Tarpon. "What should I do? I'm not here to play nursemaid."

"I'll speak with her," Lucas promised. "Have your men begin preparations. Lord Maledek wants this place to be a fortress."

"I will see to it, Master Telon," Alden said. He partially turned then paused.

"Something else you need?" asked Lucas.

The young man hesitated.

"My brother would like to be involved in the mission." Alden did not sound enthusiastic about the idea, but his tone suggested that alternatives would be worse. "I think he's a bit stir-crazy with his administrative duties, especially with his wife … occupied with the Lady's business."

"One should avoid speaking of the Lady's business even in passing," Lucas said, staring steadily at Alden. "But I agree. Have Brook help with the warehouse, but tell him nothing of the girl. Tell no one. Those who need to know will hear it from me, understand?"

"Yes, Master Telon," Alden said with a slight bow. "May I send him a message now? It should only take a few minutes."

Lucas nodded permission, wishing Kolknir were still around. Things could get interesting if Brook Tarpon recognized him. While not exactly relishing the meeting, Lucas would not shrink from it. If Brook caused trouble, Lucas would kill him. With his mind humming with various killing methods, Lucas set off to find the child.

Chapter 24: Unexpected Audience with the King

Lalri (November) 24, 1538
Justice Arena, City of Idonia

Mitrek Altran wanted to drop the Niktrod Keldor case. The presentation of evidence and testimonies seemed pointless. He could hardly believe he'd once enjoyed listening to advocates bicker and shred each other's cases. Under different circumstances, he would have quit the case, the job, and even the planet. He vowed to do precisely that as soon as this case concluded.

Once we get Silvia back, we'll go, but where should we go?

Balar, Riab, Wirsh, and even Gardan were viable options. Balar consisted of three hundred and forty-six separate countries on eight continents with a population close to nine billion people. Blending in would be extremely easy. Having destroyed their natural environment several centuries back, the people of Riab developed self-contained pods to inhabit. Disappearing there would be slightly more challenging, despite the massive influx of tourists. Wild, almost lawless Wirsh would be hard to get used to, especially since it lacked moons. Provided Mitrek could leave his surname behind, Gardan might be a pleasant place to live, and certainly, the transition would be simple since Gardan and Reshner had very similar political structures.

Mitrek did not give much thought to other planets farther away. Long distance space travel required preparations of the sort that would leave a trail for his mother to follow.

"—my client's best interests," concluded Master Isaac Marin.

Mitrek cleared his throat to stall.

"I think it would be in our best interests to take a short recess. When we return, you may continue your presentation, Master Marin." Mitrek typed the appropriate order into his infopad and stood up before anyone could object. Feeling the weight of many eyes, he fled to his private office.

Focus on the case. Every moment you dither, Silvia spends in danger.

These thoughts filled him as he collapsed onto his chair. He let his fingers brush the expensive zalok leather and wondered what stories lay in its history. What life had the beast that once owned the hide lived? What adventurer had illegally poached it, or had it come from one of the rare merchants licensed to scour the mountains for dead zaloks?

A timid knock and a gentle chime both indicated someone's desire to enter his private sanctum.

"Enter," called Mitrek, straightening and trying to look busy.

A tow-headed young man entered and bowed.

"Apologies, Lord Altran. His Highness King Terosh of House Minstel would like a word with you," said the boy.

Mitrek silently cursed in three languages. He could not fathom what Terosh wanted. Normally, he could dodge the conversation under the guise of avoiding a conflict of interest, but one did not lightly cast aside the king's request.

"Send him in, Andel, and extend the recess an extra ten minutes."

"As you wish, my Lord," said Andel with another bow.

About two minutes later, Mitrek rose with all the grace he could muster from his trembling knees. After the customary bow, he stepped away from his chair and gestured toward it.

"Please have a seat, Your Highness. Shall I—"

Terosh waved off the invitation like a man swatting flies.

"I'm not here as your king, Mitrek. I am here as your cousin. What's wrong?"

Mitrek leaned heavily against his desk. His thoughts tripped over each other, but he clenched his teeth to hold them inside.

"What makes you believe something is wrong?" he queried.

"Delia has been at every session with Sullivan and Arabeth, but I've not seen your eldest child for some time," Terosh said slowly. "Given our family's history, I thought it best to inquire. Where is Silvia?"

The question hit Mitrek like a throwing dagger. He stumbled

back to his chair and flopped onto it before his knees could completely fail. Avoiding Terosh's gaze, Mitrek said, "She is in my mother's care." The effort to control his emotions left his voice lifeless.

"Where?" asked the king. "Would your mother keep Silvia with her at her private home?"

"I doubt it," Mitrek replied bitterly. "Besides, nobody knows where my mother truly calls home. It's in the Kala Mountains somewhere, but few venture there."

"Should I be concerned, Mitrek? The recordings of Delia say I should. Natural beauty aside, she looks like death warmed over."

Mitrek winced. He'd noticed the terrified look in Delia's eyes, but he had hoped others would see only her brave smile.

"There is nothing you can do, Highness. Pursuing the subject will only complicate matters. I can do my job."

The king frowned.

"I could withdraw the charges and stop the trial."

Mitrek tried to clamp down on the alarm but knew his countenance betrayed him.

Before Mitrek could respond, Terosh continued, "But stopping the trial is the last thing I want." He fell into moody silence, then changed the subject. "Do you find it odd that nobody knows where in the Kala Mountains Lady Mavis makes her home?"

"If I had a kef for every idealistic reporter who begged for an answer, my fortune would pave a path to our farthest moon," Mitrek said with a dark chuckle. He pressed his fingertips together. "It seems like both of us are in a bit of a bind. Let me finish this trial quickly. He's guilty. Everybody, including him, knows it. The only remaining question is how he will be sentenced."

"You already know the answer to that too, don't you?" asked the king.

"I will weigh every option," Mitrek said carefully. "But the political winds are blowing hard in one direction."

"I want to help, Mitrek," King Terosh said. "Ours is a strange family. If we fail to defend each other, we will fall that much sooner."

Before he could think, Mitrek blurted the first thing that came to mind.

"You can aid my family best by helping us leave." Feeling lightheaded, Mitrek knew blood was draining from his face. If Terosh spoke to the wrong person, Mitrek and his family would die, but the younger man had never struck him as reckless or ruthless. Figuring the damage had already been done, Mitrek forged on. "As soon as this trial ends, I want to leave Reshner. Permanently."

Chapter 25: More than Simple Smugglers

Lalri (November) 29, 1538
Roniak Warehouse, City of Huz Mon

Despite the discomfort of the white and black mask, Kezem enjoyed the euphoric rush of being Maledek again. It had been a mistake to let Belcross borrow the identity. Kezem had nearly perished from boredom during those long months.

I was meant for this life.

Kezem checked the weapons arrayed on the table, eyeing each like a proud father. Picking up the electrified banistick, he turned it over a few times and reluctantly put it down again. Bringing it to bear against a Ranger would be lovely, but a sentimental part of him wanted to save the banistick for a royal. Shutting his eyes and breathing deeply, Kezem cast his mind back to Deanna's death. He'd not killed her with the banistick, but he had wounded her with it.

After a moment's consideration, Kezem picked up two kerlinblades and clipped them to either side of his belt, tilted at an angle for easy cross-draw. He would leave the shooting to his men. He sensed they were just as eager for a fight after many days dodging the king's soldiers, police, and Rangers. It had been cruel to bait so many traps and not spring them.

You were right again, Mother, he thought, mentally saluting her.

Kezem hated being wrong, but this did not bother him as much as usual. The thought of a challenging fight thrilled him. He still questioned his mother's sanity in having Silvia brought here, but he trusted something significant would happen soon.

***

Ranger Kiata Wellum did not like the odds. If they were detected, she and Todd would have a tough time escaping even with the anotechs' help. Her knees complained and every muscle she owned begged to be uncoiled. She closed her eyes and pressed her back against a large crate, mentally bidding her husband to hurry. She clutched her banistick to her chest and resisted shaking Todd for answers.

Why couldn't I have been born with Reia's patience?

The steady thud of boots announced an approaching guard. Kiata instinctively crouched lower, shifting to a better position in case she had to attack. She prayed her ankles wouldn't crack and give her away. The footsteps stopped for an infuriating moment, and Kiata fought down the suicidal urge to leap over the crate and take out the RT Alliance soldier. As she exhaled the last of a calming breath, Kiata heard the welcomed thud of receding footsteps.

With the danger temporarily gone, Kiata eased one knee to the ground and looked at Todd. He sat exactly as he had the last two dozen times she checked. With his left leg tucked close to his body, right leg stretched out, eyes shut, and head leaning toward his left shoulder, Todd looked far too relaxed for their current situation. Without warning, his head snapped up, his eyes sprang open, his body stiffened, and he moved to rise.

Despite being ready for this, Kiata's heartbeat quickened. She clamped her left hand over Todd's mouth while her right hand braced the back of his head so he wouldn't bang it against the crate.

"Wake up! It's me!" she whispered, leaning close to his ear. She pulled her head back and tilted it enough to come into his line of vision. With a wry smile she added, "Remember me?" She saw only confusion in his hazel eyes. Kiata shrugged. "You will in a moment, but please refrain from loud greetings. We're in a bit of trouble here. The next time the Council has a dangerous secret mission on offer, I say we skip it. We're getting too old to skulk behind crates."

Todd's eyes finally cleared. When Kiata didn't immediately let go, he narrowed his eyes and shook his head impatiently.

Releasing him, Kiata whispered, "Welcome back. What did you find?"

"They're definitely smugglers, but I'm still not sure why the Council sent us," Todd reported. "The crates have everything from firfe spice to zalok scales to kerlak and serlak rifles. They're obviously illegal, but that doesn't explain the number of guards around here or the Ranger interest."

Kiata bobbed her head in agreement.

"They were a little sparse on details. I credited that to their anonymous informant. Now I wonder if there was something more to it."

"Shall I look again?" asked Todd. "I only got through about half the warehouse. We'll probably find more in the offices at the far end anyway."

After helping Todd up, Kiata waited impatiently while he stretched some feeling back into his limbs. Then, they picked their way to a new position closer to the offices. They passed three patrols, but nobody came close to discovering them.

There was no shortage of crates to hide behind. They settled down between a sturdy set marked: Charan wine. A side wall sat within touch to their right and another set of crates blocked their left side. The close fit made Kiata feel both protected and trapped. She hunched her shoulders against an uneasy prickling at the back of her mind and again clutched her banistick for comfort. She almost pitied the first thing to jump her tonight. The tension coiled inside her would not be gentle when unleashed.

***

As soon as he found a comfortable position, Todd Wellum slipped into another anotech trance. His senses heightened to a disconcerting level. The floor felt painfully hard. Faint drafts carried the too-sweet scent of Charan wine, the tangy odor of a few thousand wooden crates, and the musky scent of human apprehension. His ears identified twelve distinct pairs of boots beating different rhythms on the floor. He also heard Kiata's carefully controlled breaths and felt each heartbeat that thundered in his chest.

Pushing past the sensations, Todd sent anotechs to explore the area around his body. They skittered from crate to crate and reported the contents. As before, he found weapons, food, and spices. Telling them to ignore items already noted, Todd sent the anotechs through crate after crate until they reached the wall shared with the warehouse offices. Concentrating so hard his head throbbed, he pressed on, instructing some anotechs to enter the nearest office.

Several minutes passed while the anotechs swept through one office after another. In the fourth office, Todd sensed something different. The anotechs buzzed excitedly in his head. He spent another thirty seconds sorting the impressions they sent back, feeling fear and discomfort. The sound of ragged, shallow breathing and small whimpers filled Todd's mind. He sensed a form lying on a thin carpet. A quick query identified the individual. Stunned, he recalled the anotechs and told them to wake his body slowly.

Todd waited impatiently for his consciousness to fully return and his senses to revert to normal. He opened his eyes to Kiata's concerned face hovering nearby. Her expression demanded answers. His mouth felt uncomfortably dry.

"There's a child here. Silvia Altran," he whispered. "She must be the reason we're here, but who knew they had her? Why do they have her? Do you think it has to do with the Keldor case?"

"We can theorize later," Kiata said. Her low tone could not mask her tension.

The worry he heard summoned a rush of adrenaline that woke Todd nicely.

Abruptly, every light in the warehouse snapped on to full brilliance. Todd blinked furiously and scrambled for his kerlak pistol. Footsteps made thunderous noise for a few seconds then deafening silence fell. Seconds later, a man shouted orders. Several men responded. A high-pitched yelp rang out from one corner and half a dozen excited barks answered.

This was no ordinary search but a hunt, which meant trap.

Todd's mind cycled through their options. They could elude detection by hiding among the crates, but that would not last long. The trained korvers would find them far sooner than soldiers. A direct fight did not offer favorable odds. They could climb to the highest crates and try to leap out with anotech powers, but that would make them nice targets.

We must save the girl.

No sooner did the thought brush Todd's mind, Kiata said, "Go get Silvia."

Todd opened his mouth to argue but she was gone. Growling in frustration, Todd leapt to his feet.

A triumphant shout told him the men had spotted Kiata.

When we get out of this, we're having a chat about your plans, Todd promised his reckless wife.

Knowing Kiata would be unable to distract all the RT Alliance soldiers, Todd carefully picked his way between crates. Several times, he had to backtrack. Going over the crates would have sped up progress, but it would also nullify the advantage of Kiata's diversion.

He only encountered one soldier desperately hanging onto a korver's leash. A command to the anotechs rendered both the soldier and the korver unconscious.

A dizzy feeling gripped Todd. Leaning heavily against the nearest crate, he ordered his feet to carry him forward. He couldn't afford to do that again. As his legs reluctantly obeyed, Todd drew his kerlak pistol and adjusted to medium stun. Normally, he would have left the power on full, but he did not want to accidentally kill the child.

***

Silvia Altran's skin felt alive with unseen things. A scream caught in her throat. A flood of tears was all she could release. Then the korverhide ropes binding her ankles and wrists fell away and a reassuring wave of calmness cradled her. The sobs that tried to form burned hot then disappeared, leaving behind gentle sniffles.

A man appeared and reached for her.

In the darkness, she could not see him, but somehow, she knew him as the source of the calmness.

"Be brave, Silvia. Silent and brave. I'm going to get you out of here, but you need to run to safety." The man lifted her to a sitting position as he spoke. "I need you to stand on my knees and jump as high as you can. Will you do that for me?"

Unable to form words, Silvia nodded.

"Once you're out, you need to be even braver still. Rub some dirt on your face and go where your feet take you. Have Captain Armith contact the palace. Tell him Ranger Todd Wellum told you to speak to no one but the queen or king."

The man spoke so fast Silvia feared she would forget his instructions, and she really wanted to remember them. The wave of calmness turned to cool confidence that she would remember everything. She nodded again.

"Come then, let's get you out of here," said the Ranger. In one smooth motion, the man lifted Silvia up and turned her around, bracing her feet on his thighs. "When I count to three, I'm going to toss you up. You need to jump then, okay?" He started counting without waiting for a reply.

When he reached three, Silvia jumped as high as she could. Another scream died an unnatural death in her throat, but inside her mind, she screamed with terror and joy. As she thought she ought to start falling, an unseen wind propelled her up with frightening speed. She watched the glass skylight rush up, but before her head could slam into it, the skylight shattered outward.

Silvia squeezed her eyes shut and covered her head with her arms, but not one glass shard touched her. Her stomach lurched as she hovered over the broken skylight. Reassured by that inner calm, Silvia stretched her hands wide and enjoyed floating on the air. Then, she felt very sleepy, but she remembered the man's words. She needed to be on the ground if she wanted to obey them.

As if the wind supporting her body agreed, she floated down to the ground, tumbling head over heels to a standing position. When Silvia's feet touched solid ground, strange energy filled her with an irresistible need to run.

Chapter 26:
Hunted

Lalri (November) 29, 1538
Same Day
Roniak Warehouse, City of Huz Mon

The energy coursing through Kiata Wellum went far beyond the usual adrenaline rush of entering battle. She recognized the anotechs and welcomed their aid. Knocking a man's kerlinblade aside with her banistick, Kiata crashed her right fist into his chin. The man cried out once and toppled into the soldier behind him. The other man had just enough time to catch his friend before Kiata's banistick clobbered him at the base of his neck.

Energy beams flashed toward Kiata. She dropped to the ground, rolled, and scrambled behind the meager cover of the two soldiers she had just felled.

A rat screeched at her for bringing trouble to its home.

Now would be a good time to consider other warehouses, she thought as the rat turned tail and beat a hasty retreat.

"Surrender and save yourselves a lot of pain. Escape is impossible. I have dozens of soldiers guarding every door and window." The synthesized voice boomed from speakers in the ceiling.

Kiata didn't need to see to believe the message. For each of the many RT Alliance soldiers and korvers chasing her through the stacks of crates, she sensed two or three lining the perimeters.

Why don't they kill me?

The thought wasn't exactly a complaint, but she felt unfriendly eyes peering at her through rifle scopes. She crawled behind a crate and hunkered down to catch her breath.

"My orders are to keep you alive, but they were a little vague as to *how* alive." The voice sounded pleasant and cajoling. "Come, face me. I will be at the center where there is a slight clearing. If your fighting skills please me, you will enjoy my protection against the Alliance men."

Who are you? Who gave you those orders? Why are you working with the Alliance? You seem to be in charge, but for how long? Do you mean what you say? She crushed the last question. Surrender could not be considered. Kolknir had taught her that much a lifetime ago.

Five serlak bullets thudded into the crate Kiata hid behind, tearing a chunk off one corner and raining splinters down on her head. Knowing the shots were meant to rattle her did not prevent the tactic from working. She gripped her banistick tighter, incensed by being toyed with. A tingle creeping down her spine told her a tremendous amount of anotech activity took place very close at hand. Cold fear followed closely on its heels.

"Over here!" shouted a man.

Four excited barks answered.

"We know!" snarled another man. He cursed and one of the korvers whined in pain.

"Have a care with your shots, gentlemen," spoke the voice from the ceiling. "I need them alive."

"If he wants 'em alive so badly, he can haul his backside over here and give us a hand," grumbled a third man.

"I think it's a woman," said the first man. "What should we do?" He sounded uncertain.

"Climb over that crate and drag her out here, or I'll let Alaios have your legs for chew toys," snapped the second man.

His korver rumbled an eager growl.

Hearing the unmistakable sounds of a man climbing, Kiata closed her banistick and attached it to her belt. Still torn between moving toward the increased anotech activity or away from it, Kiata took two quick steps and jumped toward the crate in front. Her hands gripped the top and held while her knees, legs, and feet struggled for purchase.

More serlak bullets punished the crate for helping her, but she ignored them, reasonably confident that the man in charge would keep a tight rein on his trigger-happy snipers. Kiata's arms ached from bearing her weight and stung from scraping along the rough top edge.

Pushing the discomfort aside, she pulled her body up and rolled to a kneeling position.

Banistick back in hand, she lunged to her feet and sprinted across the top of the massive crate. When she reached the far edge, Kiata called on the anotechs to lend strength to her legs and leapt. More shouts and surprised gasps filled the air behind her. At the height of her arc, she tucked into a forward roll that carried her about four meters from where she'd jumped. Bending her knees to absorb the landing shock, Kiata assessed her surroundings.

Stacked crates formed a cage around her. The space was four meters wide and five meters long. A small opening provided the only break in the solid line. Men shouted conflicting orders at each other. A moment later, three scrappy little korvers slipped through the hole and charged at her.

Kiata glared. She'd never liked korvers, and she liked them even less having heard of the attacks during Terosh's Kireshana. A familiar wave of controlled rage blossomed in her chest. Attacking Terosh would have been bad enough, but threatening Reia earned korvers Kiata's eternal ire.

The well-trained beasts surrounded Kiata, moving as she turned so that two constantly flanked her while one pranced about in front. Movement from above and to her right drew Kiata's attention to a soldier peering down from a stack of crates close to the side wall. Four more joined him. She suddenly felt like a spectacle in a pit fight. Her concentration wavered as more soldiers appeared.

Cheers rose from the RT Alliance soldiers. They stood or crouched on the edges, eyes bright with anticipation. Most had kerlak pistols or rifles leveled at her. The few with serlak weapons held them across their chests or left them casually hanging by their sides. This small confirmation that they intended to capture her brought Kiata little comfort. If they all fired upon her simultaneously, the combined stun beams could kill her, but she could not spare the effort to worry.

Sensing her distraction, the korver behind and to her right darted in to snap at her legs.

Kiata swiped at the korver, catching it at a glancing blow across the snout. It yelped and retreated, glaring balefully at her. Too late, she remembered the other korvers. Pain exploded in her lower left leg, at first sharp then dull then indefinable. Tossing her banistick to her left hand, Kiata whipped the weapon down.

A muffled crack and thump preceded a blessed relief to the

level of pain in her leg. Warm blood gushed out of the wound. Shifting her weight to her right leg, Kiata paused to instruct the anotechs to staunch the blood flow. Murmurs from above told her the soldiers noticed the healing effort.

Tasting victory in the blood-tinged air, the other two korvers came at her, one aiming for her good leg and the other intent on her throat.

Instinctively, Kiata hopped back and made some adjustments to her banistick. The grip slid to the center, and she twirled the weapon in rapid circles. The instant before the korver's teeth would sink into her right leg, Kiata's banistick slammed into its head. Suddenly, she stopped the twirling and rammed the full length of her weapon up into the korver headed for her throat, pushing off her good leg. Pain and panic lent extra strength and the korver flew away from her into the top of the crate that now lay in front of her.

Three more korvers eased into the space. They moved cautiously, sniffing at their fallen friends and growling at her.

Feeling her strength ebbing, Kiata snatched three flingers from the belt case and sent them flying with deft flicks of her wrist. She could not swing her arm as violently as necessary to give the shots her usual devastating speed for fear of unbalancing herself, but her aim was true. The first two korvers dropped with pitiful cries. A blue energy beam collided with her third flinger, sending it off on a new course where it slammed into a crate.

The third korver stopped short, confused by the sudden light. It danced about excitedly trying to find the new threat.

"Call them off," commanded a toneless, metallic voice from behind Kiata.

"Adean, Endel, heel," called a soldier.

The korver Kiata had thrown and the one that narrowly escaped her flinger froze in place looking disgruntled. One whined a pitiful complaint to its master.

The soldiers fell eerily silent.

Kiata tensed.

"You fared well against the beasts, but I say again: this fight is futile. Do you intend to best a hundred men?" The synthesized voice sounded close.

Wearily, Kiata pivoted to face the speaker and changed her banistick so the handle again rested at one end. Despite everything she had seen and experienced over the years, the sight of the expressionless white and black mask chilled her considerably.

"Who are you?" she asked.

"I have many names and faces, but you may call me Maledek."

She recognized the name of course, but Kiata could not comprehend why a mysterious figure that generally plagued Idonia, Azhel, and the surrounding areas would show up in Huz Mon.

Her confusion must have shown on her face, for the man spoke again.

"Save your strength for our duel. Questions will keep until later. It's a pity you're injured. I wanted to truly test your reputation."

Kiata's right leg complained about holding most of her weight and her left leg still throbbed from the bite wound. She shuffled back so she could lean against a massive crate as far from the dangerous man as possible.

"Why should I bother fighting you?" she asked, angry enough to be contrary.

The man folded his arms across his chest and tilted his head in an amused nod.

"Would you not do it to satisfy my curiosity, dear lady?" he inquired.

The mechanical words crawled over Kiata's skin.

"Come and claim your duel, and we'll see how satisfied you are afterward." If her wrath could turn into fire, the man would have burned to ashes.

With a mocking bow, the figure hopped down into the makeshift dueling arena, landing lightly. His movements were characterized by a fighter's fluid grace.

"Would you prefer we move to the wider area? The lighting is better, and there will be less korver blood and fewer bodies."

"This will do." Kiata worked frantically to shunt the leg pain to an obscure corner of her mind where it would least inhibit her ability to fight.

"Should we wait for our other honored guest?" Maledek asked, drawing a kerlinblade from either side of his waist.

Kiata gritted her teeth against the pain still radiating up her leg and the knot forming in her stomach. Against her will, she followed Maledek's gaze up to the crate she'd just hurled a korver at.

Soldiers jostled each other, steadily forming a gap. More soldiers filled the gap, dragging something between them.

Todd!

Kiata's heart lurched. Her husband's head hung limply. The agitated flutter of anotechs in Kiata's chest declared him deep in an anotech trance rather than simply unconscious. His features were frozen in an expression of intense concentration.

At a wave from Maledek, the two soldiers holding Todd draped him feet-first over the side of the crate and let him slide to the ground.

Kiata flinched as Todd's body flopped to the floor near the subdued, grumbling korvers. Her fingers longed to cast down her banistick and rush to her husband. Though he looked completely insensible, Kiata still felt the heightened anotech activity. She only hoped he succeeded in getting the girl away.

***

Eager as he was to start the duel, Kezem knew he would gain more satisfaction if more soldiers could watch. He did not relish dodging korver bodies and patches of floor still slick with blood. Besides, the woman looked ready to collapse. The short rest would do her good. Perhaps he would even give her a stimulant to make the fight fairer.

"I'm afraid I must insist on a change of venue," Kezem said. The synthesized voice he used for Maledek sounded too loud, but he enjoyed the vibrations the voice modulator sent through his chest.

The pale woman rested her head against the crate supporting her and shut her eyes. Sweat glistened on her face and arms. A fraying braid of light brown hair curled over her left shoulder. The lower portion of her left trouser hung in strips. The leg itself did not fare much better.

Kezem winced at the sight. Disappointment spread through him. She would require treatment before even attempting a duel. Perhaps her husband would oblige him with the fight he desired.

"You've gone and hurt yourself worse than I thought," Kezem commented. "Be reasonable and surrender or it will go worse for you."

"Worse?" the woman scoffed. "I'm not sure that's possible."

Nodding in a friendly manner, Kezem said, "I could set the korvers on your other leg and let them play with your husband."

Shutting her eyes against a wave of pain, the woman frowned at his words. Opening her eyes, she said, "You're well-informed. What do you want?"

"Answers in time. For now, surrender will suffice."

Their eyes met and measured each other. As Kezem raised his hand to motion the soldier to set Adean and Endel on the woman's husband, she let her banistick slip from her grasp. It clattered to the floor.

"What now?" asked the woman Ranger.

Kezem was pleased to hear defiance in her voice.

"You will be escorted elsewhere," he replied. "Welcome to Huz Mon, Kiata. I'm sorry you won't get to see much of the city."

Chapter 27:
Reflections and Hard Choices

Ferrim (December) 4, 1538
Mount Hakan, Kala Mountains

Ignoring the two Royal Guards hovering nearby, Queen Reia sat down on the cliff's edge and swallowed great gulps of thin, cold mountain air. She wished for Master Niklos's comforting presence. The few comm conversations with him had been nice, but she dared not involve more people she loved while so little was known about why Kiata and Todd never returned from their last mission.

Reia's feet touched nothing but air. The sight of land dropping away so suddenly would unnerve most people, but Reia felt only a flutter of apprehension that could easily be taken for excitement. She had grown up in mountains, and though these were not her mountains, something about the rugged isolation comforted her.

Remembering the awful night she'd been roused from a rare, restful sleep, Reia let her thoughts dwell on Kiata and Todd. The little girl they had rescued ought to be tucked away in the palace, safely in Sarie's care. Reia still didn't know what to think about that situation, but the memory of Silvia Altran's fierce embrace and fantastic story would not release Reia. Lady Mavis had insisted that the child's rescue be kept a secret, but Reia thought the decision cruel to Lord Mitrek. Lady Mavis's reasons made sense, and Reia certainly had no wish to further endanger Silvia. Still, the thought of Mitrek thinking his daughter remained in danger threatened a tide of tears.

Reia pushed past the emotion by appealing to the questions that drove her here.

Is it my fault Kiata and Todd were taken? How do I save them? Are they even alive?

They live, answered the anotechs.

Where are they? How do you know they live? Reia demanded.

Don't know. Just know, you know? Dark Ones guard their plans well. Give many false signals, but their life sense is very real.

What would the Dark Ones gain by holding Todd and Kiata?

Not main plan, we think, but Dark Ones seeking those strong with Light Ones.

Terosh? Me? Rangers? Who are they after? Who else has the Light Ones in them?

We choose many. Many choose us. Some do not know. Some do.

Ambiguous as always. Can you tell me anything useful? Or shall I return to my worry?

Do not worry, Queen of the Chosen. Probability is very high the Dark Ones do not intend death for them.

No matter how many ways Reia phrased her questions, the answers remained consistently vague. Finally, she cut off communication with the anotechs. As expected, worry crept back in. She tried to focus on the natural beauty around her, but even that cure had its limits.

Reia let her gaze trace a path down the jagged gray cliff to the sprawling valley below where a carpet of kintral trees clothed the mountainside. In the distance, she saw flocks of cannafitch riding gentle wind currents, but she could not hear their screeching cries. For the moment, everything was so completely quiet that her heartbeat echoed in her ears and the ragged breaths of her two guards sounded like the start of a windstorm.

"If it would please Your Majesty, there's a better view from up here," said Captain Ectosh Laocer. He really meant "back here," as in well away from the cliff's edge.

"I'm fine, Captain," Reia said with as much warmth as she could muster. She still felt half-dead inside, but he meant well. "I'm sorry to drag you and Lieutenant Zareb so far from your normal duties."

"No apologies," Zareb scolded gently. "Queen Reia of House Minstel honors us by sharing grief. Elish know grief shared lighter."

Nothing against the two loyal Royal Guards, but Reia longed to share this grief with her husband. A stab of guilt followed the wish, for she knew it was her own fault Terosh stayed away.

He would come if you asked.

The truth shielded her against the cold wind. She remembered the flight they'd shared across part of the Riden Mountains. Her desperate plan had almost killed them, but together, they had made it. The crash landing hurt but facing the subsequent cold with Terosh made the pain bearable.

Before Reia realized exactly what her fingers were doing, she had completely undone the braids holding her hair tightly to her head. She raked her fingers through the hair until the braids unraveled. A gentle breeze picked up the newly liberated strands and sent them flying.

When will Todd and Kiata experience something like this? Are they scared?

Images of Kiata's concerned face came to the forefront of Reia's thoughts, and she understood some of the burden her sister carried over the years. Never before had Reia recognized the full measure of responsibility Kiata had carried since their parents' death. The thought turned Reia's mind to the duties that dictated her own life.

Your life is no longer your own.

Her sister's words had never been truer. Reia could not even worry without involving other people. The Royal Guards flanking her at a respectful distance proved that.

Can I go on like this? Reia shivered against the thought. *What kind of a stupid question is that?*

Life might have been easier had she chosen to stay a Ranger, but for all the annoyances and terrors that came with her new life, Reia knew Terosh and the people were worth it. The spark of anger triggered by the stupid question flooded Reia with determination to forge on. She had things to accomplish. Kiata and Todd would give her an earful if they knew she neglected her duties to worry for them.

***

Ferrim (December) 7, 1538

Prison Level, RT Alliance Safe House, City of Huz Mon

The low-level pain and heavy doses of criessa coursing through his body slowed thinking, but Todd Wellum finally understood why he and his wife still lived. Hundreds of conversations and facts gathered by the anotechs added up to one conclusion. Their captors wished to study the anotechs. He wanted to deny it, but he also knew his duty was clear.

Fighting the chilling numbness of criessa and ignoring the pain, Todd snapped his eyes open and looked to Kiata. She lay on her cot watching him and tapping her left fingers in a regular rhythm. The pain was probably worse for her because of the leg injury. The ugly white gloves and foot covers responsible for the pain looked oddly benign.

For Todd, it felt like sticking his hands and feet into a sonic cleaner set dangerously high. The pain wasn't constant, but it struck whenever their captors' frustration peaked. They pretend to have a purpose besides waiting for transfer orders, but the questions they posed were inconsistent and pointless. Todd did not know where they would be transferred to, but he gathered that it would happen soon, which meant he had little time to consider his moral dilemma.

Noticing his gaze, Kiata tried to grin but it turned into a grimace. She sighed.

"I'm getting really tired of waking up like this." She raised her white-gloved hands and studied them. The muscles in her arms clenched violently then relaxed as another shock charged through.

Todd looked at her and loved her so much that his resolve wavered. He instructed the anotechs to jam the door so they would have more time for discussing their situation.

Recognizing the conflicted expression, Kiata swung her legs over the side of her cot and sat up.

"Out with it," she ordered, swaying gently as her body adjusted to the new position. Her hands gripped the thin mattress. She winced and bit her lower lip, indicating that the shock must have gone through her left leg this time. When the pain faded, Kiata fixed her silver-blue eyes directly on Todd.

"I've been eavesdropping. They're after the anotechs," he announced, sitting up and facing her. "I can't tell who the leaders are because something strange keeps diverting the anotechs away from them." He shrugged and said no more but avoided eye contact.

"It doesn't matter. You know what you have to do," Kiata said. Her voice was steady and commanding, but she swallowed hard and paled.

"It could kill us," Todd argued half-heartedly.

In more ways than one, he added.

Having never experienced decommissioning, Todd had only other Rangers' accounts that the process could be traumatic. The mere thought of being without the heightened senses filled him with dread.

History lessons held a tale or two of Nareth Talis Rangers who never recovered from the loss. It would also be hard to hide the change from their captors who could decide they were worthless without the connection.

"Our vows are clear," Kiata said.

An angry, muffled shout from outside the door caught their attention. Kiata's head whipped toward the door then back to Todd. His did pretty much the same thing, and their eyes met.

Kiata spoke quickly, tears pooling in her eyes.

"Todd, listen to me. I'm not strong enough to break our links. They're going to know that. You must be." She paused to brace against another shock. "Promise you'll carry through with it. No matter what threats they breathe or what they do."

Todd felt time grind to a stop along with his ability to breathe or think. The next wave of pain broke the momentary spell. He gasped, feeling something in his heart being squeezed to death. He honestly did not know if he could give her such a promise. There was only one solution. He had to break the connection before his resolve could be tested.

Tears streaming down his face, Todd muttered the ceremonial words and settled in for the fight of his life.

***

Ferrim (December) 9, 1538

Kaypree Springs, Felmon Desert, between Osem and Terab

Terosh Minstel was not in the best of moods. Kiata and Todd Wellum were still missing, and he could do little more than demand the Royal Guards work quickly to find them. He had let himself get trapped arbitrating a dispute for water rights between the Osem Rangers and Terabian water traders.

If Reia had insisted, he would have led a room by room search of Huz Mon to find clues, but she told him their work must continue. While he understood the logic, his heart ached to offer more comfort. He hated that she suffered alone. Reia chose not to join him on the peace mission to avoid provoking the Rangers. He missed her, even though less than a week had passed apart.

The next arbitration case is taking place in the palace, he thought, knowing the promise would be hard to keep.

Outside, the wind made an incessant thumping noise as it pushed hard then let the heavy canvas material spring back with a muffled crack. Occasionally, the wind would slip a small puff of sand under the tent walls. Terosh watched the new sand slither along like sidewinders and pass through the other side or else form miniature pillars along the edge.

"Both sides have valid points," Terosh muttered, wishing it were not so. He scratched at a bit of stubble he'd missed while shaving and absently bid the anotechs to fix the problem. A cascade of hair fragments rained down onto his dark blue shirt. Even though the hairs were invisible against the dark fabric, Terosh brushed at them anyway.

The Rangers had discovered and maintained the Kaypree Springs for far longer than the Terabian water traders. However, the water traders spoke truth in saying that the Rangers had more options than they did. If they would travel a bit, the Rangers could even draw water off Twin Lake. That would solve the Osem-Terab problem but create a new one between Osem and Azhel. Terosh knew of only one way to completely solve the problem and neither side would be wholly pleased in the end, hence his foul mood.

It's the best option.

"It's the most dangerous option," Terosh said, feeling pathetic for talking to himself.

You know it works. You and the queen pulled water from the Morden Lowlands.

"That was different. We only needed a little water," Terosh said, not even realizing the thought wasn't exactly his own. "We've never tried anything on this scale."

Terosh felt a tingling sensation in his head that indicated the anotechs' amusement.

You pulled water from the air, too. That was much harder than this will be.

Terosh rubbed at his tired eyes.

Now you speak? I've been wrestling with this dumb debate for three days and this is the first time you've deigned to speak to me about it.

We thought you knew. The problem is very simple to solve but warn them of the dangers.

Thanks, I feel so much better. Terosh shook his head, stood up, and walked to the tent entrance. *Might as well get this over with.*

After flinging the heavy flaps aside, Terosh said, "Covin, please fetch the representatives. Tell them I have reached a decision and would like to explain it to them before making a formal announcement."

"Right away, King Terosh of House Minstel. Covin honored to

carry message," said the Elish. He bobbed his head three times and hurried off to summon the chief representatives.

In less than ten minutes, Ranger Knight Caius Drake and Master Milo Carlangas sat cross-legged on the floor in front of Terosh's sturdy travel chair.

"Before I render a judgment in this matter, I need answers to a few questions," said Terosh, after the exchange of customary greetings. "Covin will keep a record of my questions and your responses. The first question is obvious but must be stated for the record. Do you agree that the forthcoming judgment will be final and completely binding upon yourselves and the parties you represent? If so, please say 'I do.'"

"I do," chorused the representatives without hesitation.

"Good. Now, this part is important. Ranger Drake, can your Order spare several dozen volunteers with the rank of Knight or Healer to accept special instruction from myself or the queen?" Terosh fixed his gaze upon the young Ranger.

I hope Reia agrees to this, Terosh thought belatedly.

He did not look forward to that conversation but decided to worry about that part later.

"It may take a day, a week, a month, or many months. I have no way of knowing how much time will be required, but each volunteer would need to agree to certain … security measures."

The Ranger frowned.

"With respect, Highness, I will say that gaining volunteers should not be a problem, even with the security measures. I assume you mean to teach us a new technique. We—especially those sworn to the Nareth Talis—are well acquainted with taking precautions to guard our powers. However, there will be great opposition for accepting instruction from Her Majesty the queen." The man's cheeks reddened.

"That is why I asked," said Terosh. "Will your people let themselves be bound by your word, Ranger Drake?"

After a brief hesitation, the Ranger said, "Yes, Your Grace. I am authorized by the Osem Ashatan Council to seek an end to this dispute. The Rangers are peacekeepers. If attaining peace requires us to swallow our pride, then we will do it."

"Very well, I accept your word," said Terosh. He turned his attention to the other representative. "Master Milo Carlangas, can your people survive on half rations of water until such a time as instruction to the Osem Rangers is complete?"

"Half rations? What is to become of the rest of the water?" cried Carlangas.

"I will explain shortly, but I first need confirmation that your people will accept my proposal," said Terosh.

Master Carlangas drew his shoulders back and spoke quickly.

"My people can survive almost any condition." He hesitated, staring up at Terosh. "I am authorized by Governor Edeline Pallav to accept terms of arbitration on behalf of the city of Terab. We trust House Minstel will do right by the Terabian people."

"I accept your word, Master Carlangas. Then, if we are all in agreement, I shall render judgment." Terosh paused a moment for each man to nod. "Please allow me to finish before protesting a particular point. In the matter of control over the Kaypree Springs, judgment is decided in favor of the Terabian water traders upon several conditions."

The Ranger looked stunned. Master Carlangas looked relieved, triumphant, and then cautious.

Before they could speak, Terosh continued, "The conditions are as follows. The Terabian Water Trading Union is fully responsible for supplying both Osem and Terab with adequate water for the indeterminable time until the Rangers can raise their own supply. The Rangers are obligated to work to master such lessons in a timely manner, as both cities will be operating on half rations until then."

Master Carlangas raised a hand, indicating a wish to speak.

"Forgive me, Highness, but I fail to see the necessity of half rations. Even at the height of this dispute, both cities operated at close to unrestricted water status."

"The half rations are to spare your people from exhaustion, Master Carlangas," Terosh said, trying not to sound patronizing. "With the Rangers devoting several dozen members to the studies I have in mind, they will have no time to retrieve water. In essence, the Water Trading Union is using labor to purchase the Kaypree Springs from the Osem Rangers."

"What if they never master the lessons?" asked Master Carlangas, his voice dangerously close to a whine. "We will be slaves for this indeterminable time!"

Ranger Caius looked insulted.

"I assure you we are quick learners, Water Master. We do not accept charity lightly either. The Rangers will put every effort into returning both our cities to normal. You have my word on that."

"Good. Before you leave, compile a list of contacts for Covin." Terosh rose signaling an end to the matter. It had gone much better than anticipated, though as predicted, neither representative looked entirely pleased.

***

Ferrim (December) 9, 1538
Same Day
Maladek's Private Retreat, City of Idonia

This is bad.

"Why would he take such a risk?" Kezem wondered, working hard to keep his voice steady.

"I do not know, Lord Maledek. I only know this will foster peace between Osem and Terab," said Aster Captain Surd Antar, speaking swiftly and softly.

"What exactly *is* he doing?" Kezem wondered.

"I know nothing more, Lord Maledek," said Captain Antar. "The king promised to teach the Rangers how to form water. He mentioned the queen would help, but I do not think he's raised the matter with her yet."

"Keep watching and update me regularly," Kezem instructed, cutting the link before Antar could utter farewells.

Needing to kill something, Kezem drew a kerlak pistol from his desk, growled, and shot a target dummy seven times. It helped a little. He couldn't believe how quickly things could change. A week ago, he had two perfect Ranger prisoners and a tidy feud between two powerful cities. Now, he had two broken, useless prisoners his mother insisted he keep alive, and Terosh had somehow gotten both cities to back down. Grunting, he shot the dummy in the nose one more time for good measure.

Unbidden, his mind fixed upon the memory of the chaos in the Rangers' cell. The man had been in some sort of trance then racked with seizures. Kezem's men could do nothing but hold the man down and wait. When the strange fit passed, it truly had been over. The man had looked positively triumphant. Lucas Telon had guessed at what transpired, and the man admitted to severing his link to the anotechs. Kezem had ordered proper retribution, but it could not change the fact that the Ranger had ruined his mother's plan. While he might once have been happy about that, this scheme would have greatly aided his cause.

A pleasant chime signaled an incoming call that interrupted his woeful recollections. Stifling a groan, Kezem smacked the accept button and waited for his mother to speak, staying well out of vidrecorder range and leaving the screen blank. He did not need to deal with her condescending looks today.

"I have need of the Ranger prisoners," Lady Mavis said coolly. Her tone conveyed sympathy for his feelings but enough warning to tell him not to argue.

"Why?" Kezem demanded, grimacing at how childish he sounded.

"I am returning them to the queen to foster goodwill," said his mother.

"You're buying trust?" Kezem asked incredulously, not sure if he wanted to laugh or shoot something. He flicked the kerlak pistol's safety on and off several times.

"I am," his mother confirmed.

"How will you do it?" Kezem demanded, lacking the good cheer for a verbal duel.

"Dennel will send you the details," said Lady Mavis. "This is why we keep our resources separate. I wanted to keep you informed since you complain I don't tell you enough."

Kezem bristled at her last statement. He certainly never complained to her, which confirmed that her spies were literally everywhere.

"How did King Padric take the news?" he asked, redirecting the conversation.

"Not well, of course, but I shipped him some intriguing commoners to pacify him."

That news surprised Kezem. His mother usually shied away from involving commoners.

"He hopes I'll send him the queen one day," Lady Mavis continued. "I need to keep that hope alive for the time being."

"Will you send him the queen someday?" Kezem asked innocently. It seemed his mother changed her mind every other day with regards to keeping Terosh and Reia alive. He wondered which side she leaned toward today.

"If necessary," said his mother.

Kezem shook his head and cursed under his breath. He knew she lied, but he had entertained hopes of recording something he could turn against her one day, even if it meant dealing with King Padric Creston.

Chapter 28: Aunt Mavis's Gift

Ferrim (December) 18, 1538
Prison Level, RT Alliance Safe House, City of Huz Mon

Life went on without the anotechs. It felt strangely quiet, but slowly, Kiata Wellum had adjusted to normal senses. Retraining her thoughts took longer, for she had not realized how much she anticipated receiving anotech answers to the simplest questions. She pitied Todd and wished she could ease his suffering. His stronger connection to the microscopic machines made the loss of them many times more painful. In addition, their captors' wrath fell twice as heavily upon him.

"I wish there was some information we could betray," Kiata whispered.

She cradled her husband's head in her lap, gently brushing at his fiery hair and tracing his face with her fingertips. She kept her touch light and slow so the stuncuffs engulfing her forearms would not consider it a threat and shock her. While annoying, she found the stuncuffs an improvement over the gloves and foot covers that had inflicted pain at their captors' whims.

Todd's cracked lips spread in a faint smile.

"You would never do it. Too stubborn."

The weariness in his hoarse voice slipped tendrils around Kiata's heart and pulled tight. She blinked back frustrated tears. A noise consisting of one part choking sob and two parts bitter laughter escaped her constricted throat.

"Yes, but perhaps you would show enough sense to give them what they want and save us."

He rocked his head back and forth once as a substitute for shaking his head.

"Want nothing. Just angry." Todd breathed the explanation so softly Kiata's ears strained to catch the words.

"Even if we still had the anotechs, what could they gain by studying us?" Kiata wondered, not really asking Todd. Feeling his lips part to offer an answer, she shifted three fingers across them. "Hush, that was rhetorical. Rest."

His lips spread in a grin beneath her fingers then pushed up in a gentle kiss.

Kiata pulled her fingers away and chuckled.

"You get romantic at odd times, my love."

"Prisoners can't be picky," Todd mumbled.

"In that case, I'm glad it's me you're stuck with," Kiata said, flicking some stray hairs off his forehead. She meant it in a light-hearted manner, but felt tears forming anyway. She wanted to throw her arms around this man and hold him forever. "I love you, Todd Wellum." Her fingers found the stubble along his cheeks and chin. "Scruffy beard and all."

Todd peered up at her with first one warm hazel eye then with both.

"Love you, too. No beard. Good thing."

Kiata's laughter held genuine warmth this time.

"I would look terrible with a beard."

"Neviasuakayleen," Todd said solemnly.

Never. You're beautiful forever.

The words wrapped themselves around Kiata's spirit and cradled it gently, sinking in and lending a new kind of strength. Kiata's cheeks flushed and her eyes stung.

"Stop that or I'll cry all over you," she said.

"Please do," he whispered with a long look.

Direct communication through anotechs had never worked consistently well for Kiata and Todd, but she needed nothing to translate his look. It meant: *I want to know every part of who you are. I vowed to love you. Let me prove it.*

Before Kiata could respond, the sound of the locks cycling open made her flinch. She drew her hand away from Todd's face in case the temperamental stuncuffs decided the sudden movement warranted a shock.

Four people rushed in wearing black from head to toe. Two

paused at the door, kerlak pistols ready to challenge anyone daring to follow them. The other two converged on the trussed-up Rangers.

Kiata immediately started calculating which looked easiest to take out. Her eyes darted between the two but fixed on the one aiming a pistol at her forehead. Her pulse quickened. She had been in many bad situations before, but this one ranked high in hopelessness. Usually, she had a weapon or at least the energy to think straight. Two and a half weeks of mistreatment and inactivity severely taxed her energy reserves. She felt Todd trying sit up, but out of the corner of her eye, she saw a figure pressed a palm firmly into Todd's chest.

"Just listen. I'm here to deliver you to the palace," spoke a woman's voice from beneath the black mask.

"They're releasing us?" Kiata asked, uncertain whether to be overjoyed or worried sick. The scene didn't exactly have the markings of a rescue, especially the eye-level pistol.

"Not exactly," the woman said dryly. "But my people will handle any resistance."

"Who hired you?" Todd croaked, sounding short on breath.

"Questions must wait," said the leader. "For now, we must render you unconscious and move you to a hov sled. Please don't struggle."

The words "render you unconscious" did not sit well with Kiata. She stiffened, ready to spring.

"You can accept the sedative or take a stun beam," snapped the woman. "Your choice, but the sedative shouldn't hit your head as hard as the beam will. I highly recommend it."

Kiata willed her shoulders to relax and leaned back to prove her reluctant compliance. She watched the woman's companion unfold a second pair of arms and pull out a small black object. Instinctively, she shut her eyes and leaned back against the wall as the Elish figure stepped forward.

With two hands gripping Kiata's head just below her ears, the Elish used a third hand to place the device close to her neck and activated it while a fourth hand kept the pistol trained on her.

She was unconscious before the object's pleasant beeping sound faded.

***

Ferrim (December) 18, 1538
Same Day
Royal Gardens, City of Rammon

Despite Lady Mavis's assurance that everything would be fine, Nera Tarpon really hated this part of the plan. She knew at least four different plans that would accomplish her goals without this ridiculous risk.

It's like she wants me to be discovered.

She dismissed the thought. Why would Lady Mavis wish her unmasked after spending so much time and effort on training?

"Halt!" shouted a young Royal Guard. "Who trespasses on the king's land?"

Nera's soul tried to leave her body through the top of her skull and got stuck in her throat, making her teeth tingle. It took tremendous effort not to clasp a hand over her heart.

"Speak quickly!" yapped the young guard, striding into view with another man close on his heels.

"Dillain," drawled the man behind the young guard. "It is usually best to quietly confront intruders so as to not wake the entire Market District." He placed a calming hand on the younger man's shoulder and gave a gentle squeeze. The gesture said: *let me handle this.* Stepping around Dillain, the other guard bowed to Nera, and said, "Welcome, Lady Nera, I have informed the queen of your arrival. She will meet you by the Fountain of Nouvirn shortly. This way please."

I'm expected?

The shock overrode the disturbing news that the man knew her name. Knowing she had little choice in the matter, Nera followed the two guards through a maze of paths meandering through the palace gardens. Evenly spaced sticks topped with something soft and gooey looking lined the path and attracted hordes of flitnits and shiners to light the way. If a display required brighter light, glowcrystals were artfully arranged in intricate patterns that made them appear alive.

Nera longed to rip off her mask and gaze around in wonder. They passed dozens of plants, trees, and creatures she had never dreamed of seeing in person. Fireblooms from the Ash Plains surrounded cormeth trees from the Talmeth Mountains. The path turned and dayde flowers from the Felmon Forest lit the way, their glowing heads slowly turning to face her as if they felt her presence. A colana bird whistled a warning then darted into a hole in a cormeth tree.

The path turned again and sloped gently down to Nera's destination. She paused and took a moment to admire the sight. Light from the three moons—Marishaz, Corid, and Gemuln—streamed down and blessed the Fountain of Nouvirn. Though only half-full, the moons shone down from different angles, throwing light about in such a way that the colorful Nedis crystals winked back. The combined effect created the impression that the entire fountain shimmered with inner magic.

"This was my favorite fountain," said a female voice to Nera's right.

Nera gasped and jumped. Her hands flew to her waist where a kerlinblade would have rested had she brought one.

The Royal Guards whirled and leveled kerlak pistols at the woman stepping up next to Nera. The lady drew back her hood, and the guards immediately put their weapons away.

"My apologies, Lady Mavis," said the older man. He bowed deeply. "We were only informed that the queen would come here tonight."

"There is nothing to apologize for, Lieutenant Brycen," Lady Mavis said graciously. "I had not intended to come in person, but these matters are much too important to be delegated."

Nera felt the statement like a well-placed shot to her pride. She shrugged off the feeling in favor of paying attention to the conversation. She longed to demand a reason for Lady Mavis's presence.

"Shall we attend you, my Lady?" asked Lieutenant Brycen.

"Thank you, but that will not be necessary," Lady Mavis said, sweeping past the two guards and approaching the fountain. She dipped one hand and skimmed it along the water's surface before turning back to Nera and the two guards. With a gentle smile, Mavis said, "You may return to your patrol. The queen should be along in a moment. We will be fine until then."

"As you wish," chorused the guards. They clapped right fists to left shoulders and tucked their chins as a salute.

Then, much to Nera's relief, they left.

Irritation and curiosity buzzed within her. Nera slowly approached the fountain. Her heartbeats slowed, and she noticed more about the famed Fountain of Nouvirn.

A statue rose out of the center featuring two men with fierce expressions brandishing swords at one another. Each man grasped one side of a golden chalice, lifting it high above the stone pedestal it had once rested upon. Water flowed out of the chalice and arced over the two combatants, providing an underlying, urgent splashing noise. More water trickled down the sides of the stone pedestal and spewed out of spouts around the fountain's gently curving sides. Each smaller stream added a different nuance to the rush of water. Nera could easily imagine how this fountain became Lady Mavis's favorite.

"I spent most of my childhood beside this fountain," Lady Mavis said. She sat primly on the wide edge and let one of the side spouts spit water up into her palm.

Nera watched Lady Mavis thoughtfully study the water. An odd feeling sputtered to life in her chest. She had never seen Lady Mavis appear so open and vulnerable, and she couldn't decide why she found this image of her patroness frightening.

Sensing her attention, Lady Mavis peered at Nera and offered a small, knowing smile.

"So, at last you see the princess who was, and you don't know what to make of her."

Nera's voice failed.

Lady Mavis's smile brightened, and she laughed.

"I did not always exile myself beneath a mountain, my dear." Her smile dimmed. "I was once young and carefree." The smile completely melted away. "And now I have returned, somewhat heavier of heart." She looked down at her right hand which was still wet and slowly curled the fingers in, forming a loose fist. After a moment, she dropped the fist into her lap and cleared her throat. "But enough of these pointless reflections. Take off your mask."

Nera hesitated for half a second then ripped the mask off and breathed deeply. The cool night air filled her, pleasantly chilling her lungs. Sweet and sharp flower scents converged on her. The choirs of night insects sounded louder. She nearly wept with relief at regaining such freedom.

"The queen must know you and trust you. This will go a long way in earning her favor." Lady Mavis's voice contained no trace of uncertainty or vulnerability now. "Ah, here she comes. Rely on your training, my dear. Keep to the script I gave you. This is the true test."

***

The beauty surrounding her meant nothing to Reia as she ran full tilt down path after path. Her bare feet slapped against the cool stones, nimbly navigating each turn. The sound of her breath rasped in her ears, but not from the run. The message had said to meet at the Fountain of Nouvirn for news of Kiata and Todd.

Thudding footsteps behind her warned of Terosh's pursuit.

"Wait! Reia, this could be a trap!"

"In our own gardens?" She tossed the question over her shoulder as she plunged on.

"Anywhere!" Terosh shouted in exasperation.

"Let us check the area first, Majesty," called Aster Captain Surd Antar.

"You will find no trap tonight, Captain," said Lady Mavis.

Sheer surprise succeeded where shouting had failed. Reia came to a jarring stop as the path entered the clearing surrounding the fountain. Terosh bumped into her and they stumbled forward a few steps, his arms firmly around her waist.

"Aunt Mavis? This is quite a surprise," said Terosh.

"A pleasant one I hope," replied Mavis.

"Where are they?" Reia demanded, desperation making her voice waver. Suddenly grateful to have Terosh close, Reia folded her arms across his.

Mavis rose gracefully from her seat on the fountain's ledge.

"They are safe, Your Majesty. My agents found them in a compound beneath a Restler-Tarpon Alliance warehouse."

"Antar, draw up some warrants," Terosh ordered. "I want every high-ranking Tarpon and Restler brought in for questioning."

Lady Mavis held up a hand to catch their attention.

"Wait, there's more, but I will let my agent explain." She nodded to her left and waved a figure forward.

Reia's attention riveted upon the young woman dressed completely in black. She could not see much of her features until the woman cautiously stepped into the pool of warm light cast by the portable lightbars carried by Antar's men.

Blinking rapidly, the woman knelt on one knee and endured the collective stare for several long seconds.

"I am Nera Tarpon, daughter of Arista and Tobias Restler and wife of Brook Tarpon." At a wave from Terosh, Nera rose and clasped her hands in front of her body. "The men who attacked the Rangers were traitors to the Alliance, villains who wore the uniform without the honor behind it."

"You're connected to the Alliance?" Terosh asked. His arms tightened around Reia as his body went rigid.

The question confused Reia until Lady Mavis answered.

"My agents come from many backgrounds. Any connection to the Alliance is coincidence. I typically deal in information, but this mission required a more direct approach. So, I activated my best."

"We tried to take the traitors alive, but they fought to the end," Nera said slowly. Her hands unclasped and fell to her sides. "Our priority as per Lady Mavis's instructions was, of course, the safe recovery of the Rangers." She looked directly at Reia. "To that end, we succeeded. They are convalescing in their home tonight. My people can watch over them the rest of this night, or if you wish, I will have them stand down in favor of Royal Guards."

Reia felt her knees weaken with relief, but she willed them to continue holding her upright.

"Thank you, Lady Tarpon, Lady Altran. I am greatly in your debt," said Reia.

Terosh issued a series of orders that sent Royal Guards scurrying.

Mavis and Nera bowed and took their leave.

Reia let Terosh lead her over to the fountain and settle her on its edge. The next thing she felt was Terosh's hands warm upon hers.

After a few moments, his concerned voice finally pierced the fog in her mind.

"Reia, they're all right. I called for a hov to be prepped. You'll be with them soon."

Chapter 29:
Keldor Conclusion

Ferrim (December) 19, 1538
Fountain of Nouvirn, Royal Gardens, City of Rammon

"Sit down, Taly," said Queen Reia Minstel. She sat on the fountain's wide shelf and patted the space to her left.

Talyon Keldor mutely obeyed. His stiff legs carried him forward with the grace of a wooden soldier with gummed up joints. Her weary tone and sympathetic expression ripped his heart out and crushed it. Hands clamped tight to the shelf he sat upon, Taly braced for her next words.

"Common sense speaks against this conversation," the queen began, speaking swiftly yet softly. She paused to take a deep breath. "But Kiata insisted I say something to prevent you from getting yourself killed. I believe her concern is warranted, so here I am. However, I will only continue this conversation on one condition. You must not attend the sentencing hearing tomorrow."

Despite bracing, the pain brought about by the condition left Taly short of air. Fountain mist chilled him. He trembled under the strain of reining in his emotions.

"Why?" he managed to croak at last.

"Do you agree to this condition?" inquired the queen. "If not, then you may go your way. If so, as soon as we finish here Royal Guards will escort you to your grandfather's cell. You may stay with him as long as you like, even until the hearing tomorrow if you wish."

The chance at a protracted farewell seemed a better choice than seeing his grandfather at the hearing, but Taly wasn't sure how much time passed before he finally spoke.

"I agree."

"I trust you understand the enormity of what I am about to say, but promise you will never speak of it," Queen Reia pleaded. "I have ways to ensure your compliance, but I would rather have your word."

"You have my word," Taly responded automatically, unsure whether he meant it.

"You know the sentence that will be handed down," said the queen. "What you do not know is that the king and I will not abide it."

Taly's head snapped right with painful force.

"What do you mean?"

Queen Reia gravely met his gaze.

"Your grandfather will be sentenced to death according to Gardanian custom to be carried out on that planet."

"But you said—"

"We said he would not suffer, and we will honor that word," the queen replied, not waiting for him to finish his protest.

"Gardanian law condones executions by torture," Taly spat.

"And Reshner's laws do not," said the queen, before Taly could work himself into a frantic state. "Nor do moral and natural laws, and those three dictate our actions. For reasons you need not know, we must appease Gardan's king, so your grandfather will be sent there."

"How will he die?" asked Taly with a sinking heart. "Can you call for mercy? There must be something you can do!" Taly leapt to his feet and turned to fully face the queen.

Queen Reia glanced into the shadows behind Taly, held up a hand, and shook her head.

Taly figured a dozen weapons were leveled at him, but he didn't care.

"Sit down before you unbalance one of my guards," Queen Reia ordered. She waited until Taly reluctantly complied before continuing, "I wish I could do more, Taly, but the truth is that justice too must be met. Under duress or not, your grandfather murdered my husband's mother and your former queen." Tears pooled in the queen's sea green eyes, but she held them in. "He is rightly sentenced to die, but no man deserves the end Gardan would give him." She drew a shuddering breath, like the forming words sickened her. "In fulfillment of our promise, we will give him the means to choose his end. I pray you will one day understand."

Wild thoughts thrashed about in Taly's mind. He imagined

lashing out and striking the queen then sprinting into the surrounding gardens as fast as his legs would carry him. He wanted to throw his head back and scream himself hoarse.

He did none of these.

Instead, he sank to his knees and surrendered to the sobs clogging his chest. The next thing he felt was the queen's arms gathering him close.

***

Ferrim (December) 20, 1538
Justice Arena, City of Idonia

Silence covered the arena. The faint hum of vidrecorders and lightbars loomed loud.

Every eye fixed upon the judge.

Governor Judge Mitrek Altran stared grimly at the condemned man. Niktrod Keldor returned the gaze with resigned weariness etched into his features. As expected, the evidence had left no shred of doubt that Keldor had poisoned Queen Kila Minstel. Pleas for leniency based on circumstances might have persuaded a jury in some cases but not this one. The discussions took longer than Mitrek wanted, but finally, he could hand down the sentence and have his daughter returned. Knowing the crowd expected a grand speech, Mitrek gathered his notes and courage and stood.

"Master Niktrod Keldor, you stand convicted of the gravest sort of crime. The people of two planets have cried out for your blood. It falls to me to decide which of them has a greater right to it, but first, I will ask you to state your preference. For the record, please say your name then indicate which planet you would rather carry out your execution."

"I, Niktrod Keldor, choose to die on the planet of my birth. If I must die for my actions, then let it be at the hands of my people."

Mitrek nodded slowly in acknowledgement of Keldor's choice. Fervently hoping his mother had spoken with his cousin, Mitrek addressed the king.

"Highness, you have heard the doomed man's wish. As the one most wronged and as Reshner's voice, I ask what say you in response to his request?"

"I object!" shouted Ambassador Valad Neldro of Gardan. "King Padric lost a daughter. You have no right to claim that King Terosh's loss is any greater than that suffered by my king."

Anticipating the outburst did nothing to stop anger from

burning hot within Mitrek.

"We are not here to debate degrees of loss, Ambassador Neldro. I will appeal for your opinion in a moment, but until that time, I shall ignore your objection." Returning his attention to Terosh, Mitrek asked, "What will you do, Your Grace?"

King Terosh stood, looking paler than usual.

"Were I free of responsibility, I would grant his wish, but the good of my people must come first. King Padric Creston of Gardan has claimed my mother's killer since before we knew his name, face, or story. Therefore, Reshner forfeits her right to the life of Queen Kila's murderer."

The announcement released cries of outrage and rumblings of agreement. Mitrek had to call for order four times before it could be restored.

After waiting out the expected outburst, Terosh continued, "Some will cry foul for sacrificing one life on the altar of peace, but perhaps a few will understand that I do not make this decision lightly."

Mitrek's stomach clenched and twisted with distaste as he spoke the next line expected of him.

"Are you aware of the execution protocols employed on Gardan?" he asked.

"I am aware of them, yes." Terosh shivered like a cold wind swept through the room.

"Are you also aware that by submitting to Gardan on this issue, you may set a dangerous precedent?" asked Mitrek, battling to keep the strain from his voice.

"I am," the king intoned again.

"Furthermore, do you acknowledge that your actions seen in light of your foreknowledge come perilously close to violating our laws against cruel deaths?" Even as he asked the question, Mitrek prayed Terosh had prepared a very good answer.

"Governor Judge, I am perilously close to violating the moral law of my own conscience, but I will not allow anything to jeopardize the safety of this people," declared the king.

"How do the two have anything to do with one another?" Mitrek asked. The question flew out before he could think about it.

"You don't need to know," King Terosh insisted. "Nobody here needs to know the mechanisms behind the measures keeping them safe. Such knowledge would be a burden to them. It is part of the price I must pay for the privilege of my birth."

"Thank you, Highness. Your words have been recorded and will be afforded due consideration." Heaving a mental sigh of relief, Mitrek addressed a stunned Ambassador Neldro. "You have heard my king forfeit his right to the prisoner's blood in favor of King Padric Creston's claim. How do you respond?"

Drawing himself up to his full height, the blustery little man sucked in a giant breath before launching into his speech.

"Gardan gladly accepts the responsibility for carrying out the execution. We do not fear to give criminals exactly what they deserve. My king shall be most pleased. May the relationship between our two great planets continue many thousands of generations."

Eager to be done with the matter, Mitrek looked to Keldor.

"It was never really a question of guilt, but more a question of what to do because of that guilt. You have heard the exchange that took place here in your presence. I will now make it official. Niktrod Keldor, you are hereby sentenced to death by execution through methods deemed appropriate by King Padric Creston of Gardan. Your execution will proceed with all due haste as soon as you arrive on that planet. May Riden have mercy upon your soul, for the king shall surely have none."

***

Ferrim (December) 21, 1538
House Minstel Private Hangar, Spaceport, City of Rammon

"May I have a private word with him?" Terosh asked.

Ambassador Valad Neldro wore a harried expression.

"As you wish, Highness," said the ambassador. "I will discuss final details with the pilot." He motioned for the two Shadow Guards flanking the prisoner to follow him.

Once they were relatively alone, Terosh activated his personal sound damper and stepped close to Niktrod Keldor.

"I did not forget my promise, Keldor," he said, ducking his head in case some vidrecorders escaped his initial sweep.

"Nor did I think you would, Your Grace," replied the prisoner, likewise addressing the ground between them. "But while I have your ear, I will make one last request. Watch over my grandson. Talyon is a good but troubled lad. Politics mean so little to him. For my part, I understand the mercy you offer. It is a cold mercy but better than none."

Carefully keeping his hands at his sides, Terosh sent some anotechs to Niktrod Keldor.

"The queen's sister has already taken an interest in Taly's well-being. We will as well. As long as he will stand for it, he will be welcomed at the palace. Taly already knows this. As for you, I can ask no more but that you wait until you reach Gardan."

"Have you more to say?" inquired Keldor, after waiting several long seconds through silence.

Their eyes met.

Terosh's mouth felt like it had never touched a sweet drop of water. His lips moved slowly as he forced them to shape words.

"I have spent too much time hating you, Keldor. It has made me miserable. My mother is still gone. Riden knows I wish things were different between us. This justice feels hollow."

"You'll get no argument from me," said Keldor. "I have made peace with my choices. Horrible as it sounds—and Riden as my witness—I stand by my decisions. Hate me as you will, but I face my death knowing I did what I could for my family. When your end comes, may you be able to say the same."

Feeling cold disquiet creep over his heart, Terosh nodded solemn farewell to his mother's killer.

***

Ferrim (December) 27, 1538
The Lady's Estate, Kala Mountains

Lady Mavis Altran shook her head and groaned. Several blissful months had slipped by with only scant communication with King Padric Creston. The timing concerned her. Niktrod Keldor probably just arrived on Gardan. The trial and sentencing had taken place much as expected, yet Mavis found her thoughts disturbed by the nagging notion that Terosh would somehow ruin her plan. With a sinking feeling, Mavis activated the interplanetary communications unit.

"He's dead!" roared King Padric, glaring into the vidrecorders. He flushed crimson from the tips of his white hair down through where his neck disappeared into his shirt collar. "I will not stand for this treachery!"

"Was not killing Keldor the point?" asked Mavis. She wrapped her arms close around her body partly to aid the image of disdain and partly to hide her shaking hands.

Terosh has done something, but what?

"He was to die on my terms!" cried the enraged king. He leaned forward and lowered his voice to a hoarse, menacing whisper. "What have you done?"

"Everything I said I would," Mavis said evenly. "I arranged for Keldor to be sent to you. Anything that transpired once he reached Gardan is not my responsibility." She narrowed her eyes, deciding to go on the offensive. "And speaking of treachery, reports have arisen of citizens disappearing again. Have you an answer for such reports?"

"Your deliveries have been sparse, my scientists grow impatient," grumbled King Padric. "I sent agents to your planet and some of them got ambitious. I am still restraining most of them, but I also figured you could use the motivation."

"My word is motivation enough," Mavis said slowly. "In time, I will send all the subjects you need, including the queen herself if necessary, but do not question my timing."

A battle of will ensued as each stared deep into the other's eyes. Finally, Mavis flicked her eyes down in well-calculated submission.

"You have my condolences on the justice denied you this day. Let us have no more of these petty disagreements. Keep your agents in line, and I shall move my plans forward. To prove my utmost commitment to our cause, I will allow you to study my son while you attend that part of our bargain."

"I could do with him as I liked," Padric said darkly. "What makes you think I would not?"

"You are very powerful. Such power does not come through foolishness," Mavis explained. "You know that I am the best means to the ends you seek and that I did not gain my position through letting myself be manipulated by emotions."

"What makes you believe I would even wish to study him?" Padric persisted peevishly.

Mavis let a faint grin touch her lips.

"You are obsessed with this planet, desperate to discover our secrets. You would study a wallay so long as it came from here. Shall I send you one with my compliments?"

King Padric considered that with a stony stare then grunted. With visible effort, he shook off the dark mood gripping him.

"Were we operating on the same planet, one or the other would be dead. You would make a formidable enemy, Lady Mavis. Tell me, in your opinion, is that insolent boy, my grandson, responsible for robbing me of my prize?"

Most definitely, yes.

Mavis did not respond immediately. Her mind raced ahead to what he might say to the various responses she could give.

Why do you wish to know?

"I think it very likely Terosh would interfere any way he could, but I could not tell you how," said Mavis. "I know he had a private conversation with Keldor before the ship left, but he did not even touch the man."

Padric pressed his fingertips together and leaned forward, a gleam in his eyes.

"What would you say if I told you I wanted my grandson removed from the throne?"

Get in line.

"I would first inquire as to your reasons," Mavis said, again speaking slowly to give her mind a chance to cope with the twist. She peered curiously at the vidrecorder, letting her confusion show. "I must admit you baffle me, King Padric. You spent a great deal time, effort, and resources to extradite your daughter's killer and now you request my response to harming her son. What am I missing?"

"Who would inherit the throne?" demanded Padric, ignoring her question.

"Queen Reia, of course," Mavis said.

Padric waved his hand dismissively.

"Yes, yes, suppose she is gone as well."

Taytron's daughter, Mavis answered silently.

Kezem thought himself quite clever keeping the girl alive, but he had yet to master the art of keeping his people loyal.

"If they had a child before such misfortune befell them, the child would inherit the throne, but a regent would rule until his or her sixteenth birthday. If no such child existed, the Senate would conduct a search for the nearest living relative. My father's line would be spent but he had a brother."

"What about you, my lady. Do you not still possess Minstel blood?" asked Padric with affected gentility.

Mavis gave him a tight smile.

"You know my history well enough to understand the impossibility of ever claiming the throne for myself, so I wonder where your questions are going. I have much to do, King Padric, as I am certain you do as well. Please ask what you wish to know."

"Your history does not taint your progeny. One of your sons stands to inherit Reshner's throne should some accident befall my grandson and his wife before they bear a child. Why have you not moved against them?"

His tone brought Mavis the image of a little boy cocking his head in innocent curiosity.

I am not rid of you yet.

"So far, my nephew has proven himself a capable if somewhat idealistic ruler and my sons have their own lives to lead. I see no immediate reason to change the situation."

Afraid she might say too much, Mavis closed the conversation as quickly as possible.

Chapter 30:
Safe Service Act

Ferrim (December) 29, 1538
Queen Lissa's Ballroom, Royal Palace, City of Rammon
Terosh Minstel cast a furtive glance at his wife. She sat beside him watching the Terabian Dance Troupe throw their bodies about in rhythmic waves. The lively, percussion-heavy beat reverberated in his chest, but nothing could shake the disquiet shrouding his heart.

Over a week and a half had passed since Kiata and Todd Wellum's miraculous rescue by Aunt Mavis's agents. The drama surrounding the end of Keldor's trial had occupied Terosh much of the week, but now that he could think, he admitted that something about the rescue bothered him. Despite this, he worked hard to hide his misgivings from Reia. Right now, Lady Mavis Altran could do no wrong in the queen's eyes, but Terosh knew his aunt never did anything without a convincing reason.

Just how compelling are her reasons?

Terosh worried how much this rescue would cost them in the end. It also disturbed him that neither the anotechs nor his own agents could say much about the whole Ranger capture-and-release saga. The former told him they knew not where or how to conduct such a search for truth and the latter returned with only baffling pieces of conflicting accounts.

What if Aunt Mavis set them up in the first place? Her resources are adequate to the task.

Terosh braced against the thoughts and shook with denial. Aunt Mavis could be both sneaky and self-serving, but part of her soul still carried the Minstel name. She loved the people with a fierce passion unique to those born royal.

Love for the people does not equate to love for you. She still resents the family for casting her out. Could it be that simple?

Terosh's grandfather, King Salen, had cast Aunt Mavis out, officially disowning her in every legal and emotional sense. Terosh's father, King Teorn, had cautiously welcomed her back emotionally, but the legal distance remained. Terosh could, in theory, rescind some of the legal ramifications.

It would be dangerous, whispered the anotechs.

How so?

She has many secrets.

As the music ended, Reia's hand landed on Terosh's forearm and squeezed gently. She leaned close.

"Something bothers you. Shall I press you for it now or later?" Her expression stayed true to the aloofness Sedir had drilled into her for formal entertainment occasions, but her cool green eyes promised unwavering support and love.

"Later," Terosh murmured. His voice sounded painfully loud in the relative silence caused by the cessation of drumbeats.

"I shall hold you to that," Reia whispered, releasing his arm.

Terosh silently hoped she enjoyed the next song.

Master Wesley Roth loudly thanked the performers and announced the next phase of entertainment.

"Royal Highnesses, honored guests, it is my pleasure to present Lady Gianna LeCross. Tune your ears and prepare to be swept along by musical talent the likes of which have not graced the palace in many years."

The ballroom doors opened to reveal a young woman with flowing black hair. Head held high and soulful, dark eyes full, she glided in with grace enough to make any princess jealous. She stopped short of the dais and curtsied. The crowd fell silent as she smiled and drew a deep breath. She held it a long moment, letting the air fill with anticipation. When she finally sang, it was the crowd's turn to let breath linger long. Her voice needed no musical accompaniment, but soft, heartfelt, stringed notes played in the background anyway. Terosh and every soul present listened as Lady Gianna sang:

"Love shall find whom it will.
Dear father mine, need I remind?

You taught me what a man should be.
Strong, brave, kind, and truly free
To love, honor, serve, and save.
What matters his lowborn birth?

Love shall find whom it will.
Flee not, my love. Stand with me.
I hear their words and care not.
They hold no power over me.
Should they call for my crown
I would pay that price for you.

Love shall find whom it will.
Let learned men say otherwise.
From the way my heart cries
I know this love will pass
Test of time, trial of birth,
All reasons declaring it foolishness.

Love shall find whom it will.
I should know. It found me
When I wanted nothing more
Than to flee this strange new pain.
For the world I stand to gain
I choose you and our love."

Midway through the song, Terosh's eyes slid away from the singer to his wife.

I would pay any price for you.

His fingers found hers and intertwined.

***

Though she could not hear Terosh's thoughts, Reia felt their meaning when he picked up her right hand and folded his fingers through hers. Lady Gianna's song filled the room at first pleading, then reflective, and finally declarative. The story belonged as much to Reia and Terosh as to Princess Sora Ann and her Royal Guard lover, Quinard. Knowing Terosh had chosen the song for her touched Reia deeply.

I guess I'm lousy at hiding my insecurities.

She sent her husband a small rush of anotechs to deliver her approval.

Terosh responded with the mental equivalent of a relieved sigh.

Turning her attention back to Lady Gianna LeCross, Reia was struck by the woman's youth and something else, something indefinable in her eyes. Curious, Reia reached over with her left hand and patted Terosh's arm affectionately before extricating her right hand. Then, she tilted her head down and pretended to examine a nonexistent spot on her purple shimmersilk gown. While doing so, Reia sent a stream of anotechs to the young singer.

When the first anotechs returned, a few hundred impressions bombarded Reia's senses. She felt the weight of deep concentration and heard the traces of passionate anger under the songs. Dozens of words beat at her as different anotechs tried to describe the singer: desperate, hurt, weary, and scared seemed to dominate. Out of the confusion flew a new name: Carla Segore.

Reia's eyes flew open and she flinched. She swiftly wiped her expression of all traces of surprise, but she noticed a few curious glances from the crowd.

Check again, she ordered, sending them back to the girl.

No mistake.

There must be some mistake! What do I do?

The easiest answer would be nothing, but Reia knew that was no answer. The girl radiated terror. Reia happened to possess the attuned senses necessary to pick up on it. Ignoring Carla now would be a crime only slightly less repulsive than whatever first put the fear in her.

Save her.

That's easy for you to say. You're not the ones the senators and governors are going to verbally slaughter.

Reia's mind skipped ahead to other possibilities. The harder answer would be confrontation, but the situation demanded tact. If done improperly, she might heap greater harm upon the girl rather than help her.

Then save her here.

The anotechs spoke so confidently that Reia could not help but feel her courage rally. She did not bother asking them how. She had worked with them long enough to know they rarely answered "how" questions. Reia contemplated the problem so hard that she barely heard a word of Lady Gianna's last two songs. When the final note faded, she joined the polite applause as the performer curtsied again.

Master Roth stepped forward to announce the next act.

Before he could speak, Reia shocked everybody by standing. The crowd drew a collective breath and fell strangely quiet. With heart thudding in her ears and cheeks burning, Reia mustered a brilliant smile and leveled it at the people.

Praying her voice didn't fail, she said, "I find myself deeply moved by that wonderful performance. Would you count me selfish if I begged for a few moments alone with the young woman?"

Conversations burst out over the ballroom as guests discussed the odd request, attempting to divine the queen's meaning. A few people started to move toward the exit.

"That won't be necessary," Terosh called after them, appearing at Reia's side.

The conversations died as abruptly as they had started as people strained to hear Terosh's next words.

He did not disappoint them.

"Please, stay and enjoy yourselves. The queen and I shall retire to the Central Library. Master Roth, please send in the next performers. Lady Gianna, would you grace us with your company?"

The young woman's eyes darted to a man in the crowd, but she nodded.

"I would be honored, Your Grace," she murmured.

Reia calmly grasped Terosh's elbow and sent him silent thanks for trusting her. They exited the ballroom at a painfully slow pace, but she managed to look unconcerned. What she really wanted to do was tear out of the room at a full sprint. When they reached the hallway, the urge to run intensified, but Reia forced herself to maintain the regal pace all the way to the Central Library.

As the doors swung shut behind them and their bewildered guest, Reia stepped to the sound damper controls and activated the security measures.

Terosh quirked a curious eyebrow at her and waited for Reia to explain.

"What is your name?" Reia asked. She kept her tone as kind as possible, but the girl looked ready to flee right through the doors.

Terosh's eyes shut as he sent anotechs to investigate the strangely terrified young lady.

"We're not here to hurt you," he assured the girl. "We will help you if you wish."

The girl backed into the door looking ready to burst into tears.

"Let me return. You can't help me. He would know."

"We *can* help you, Carla, but you need to trust us," Reia said, wagering that hearing her own name might rattle the girl just right.

Carla drew a shuddering breath. A soft whine escaped, and she sank to the floor and gripped her knees. She clenched her eyes shut but a tear slipped out. One tear turned into two, three, and a flood. Within seconds, her shoulders shook with suppressed sobs.

"How did you know something was wrong?" Terosh asked Reia in a whisper.

"Her eyes," Reia answered. She slowly approached Carla and knelt beside her.

After a brief inner debate, Reia laid her hands on Carla's right shoulder and bid the anotechs to encourage the girl to share her burdens.

Carla needed this chance to cry.

Eventually, the suppressed sobs morphed into unsuppressed sobs then subsided to gentle weeping. Terosh paced the room impatiently, and Reia stayed by the girl.

"How old are you?" Reia asked. The anotechs had already told her, but she wanted to hear the girl's response.

"Fourteen," Carla admitted at last.

Terosh's pacing came to a violent stop.

"Where are your parents? How did you end up with Master Nazhu?" he asked.

"My parents are dead," said the girl.

"Dead how?" Reia wondered.

"My mother died when I was ten. Father borrowed money from a man in Meritel to buy some hovs for his delivery business. Somebody robbed him before he could make the purchase. The man he borrowed from killed him when he could not repay the debt and sold me to recover some of the loss."

"How did you come to sing, Carla?" Terosh asked gently, trying to distract the girl from her pain. He sat on the floor where he was, so he would not tower over her.

"My mother taught me." Carla's gaze turned distant. "She died of Candela Fever. Near the end she said the best legacy she could leave me was the gift of song. She said I could heal any hurt if I found the right song for each type of pain. Master Nazhu discovered my gift when I used it to help another servant."

The conversation stretched several hours. In the end, Reia knew more than she wanted to and less than she needed to about indentured servitude and the slack regulation thereof.

***

Idela (January) 10, 1539
Senate Great Hall, City of Rammon

Terosh struggled not to smile and wondered why he had worried about Reia facing the senators and governors today.

It's natural to worry when your wife enters a korver's den.

Despite obvious animosity from certain parties, the discussion remained remarkably civil. Even Senator Gabriel Luvak and his oafish brother, Governor Damien, had stayed miraculously quiet thus far.

Only Sedir's advice kept Terosh from showing his support more openly. Politically speaking, Reia needed this cause to strengthen her position. Should the unthinkable ever happen to him, she would need a strong base of supporters from both governing bodies. The people needed to understand her as a compassionate, capable queen in her own right, rather than merely an accessory to Terosh's power.

Understanding the reasoning did not make it easier to calmly play moderator. Terosh's control panel blinked and flashed in a riot of colors as governors, senators, and reporters vied for speaking rights. His head ached from thinking so hard about the balance of speakers. Few would be completely satisfied and favoritism complaints would air anyway, but Terosh's sense of honor required he let a wide variety of people have their say.

Idonia's senatorial light blinked blue. Intrigued, Terosh entered his approval code and all lights returned to white except the one belonging to the person to whom he'd granted speaking rights.

His mind wandered to how he would spend the evening. Perhaps he would ask Reia to walk the gardens with him. He couldn't remember the last time they had spent an entire evening together. Meetings had dominated the last couple of weeks, and before that, Reia's attention rested with Todd and Kiata's recovery.

Senator Victoria Turrel's bold voice rang forth.

"Royal Highnesses, fellow Senators, Honored Governors, I think we can agree the queen's ideas are noble, but how shall our great cities continue to function without the indentured workforce? What shall become of those unfortunates who find themselves in great debt? And how shall we integrate these non-citizens back to citizen status? Will these steps not plant seeds of rebellion?"

Murmurs of agreement rose around them. Terosh sat up straighter and silently thanked Senator Turrel. At last, someone had raised the right questions. Many others had come tantalizingly close, but so far, none had worded it just the way Reia wanted.

The faint, thoughtful smile on Reia's face said this might be the turning point where the governors and senators quit posturing and finally declared sides. Terosh waited a few heartbeats in case Senator Turrel had more to say. When the senator ceded the speaking rights by sitting down, Terosh simply ignored the blinking lights and waited for Reia to respond. As the one to call for this joint session, she had full speaking rights throughout.

"Senator Turrel raises many interesting questions, which I shall address soon," Reia said with an acknowledging nod toward the senator. "Before I get there, however, I think we can agree that the seeds of rebellion already exist. Were we to offer free food, water, shelter, and medicine, people would still complain."

Several heads nodded reluctant agreement.

Reia shifted to address a different section of the crowd.

"Contrary to popular belief, I am an ardent supporter of maintaining tradition. However, I do not approve of indentured servitude as an institution because it is vastly unsupervised and impossible to regulate under the current guidelines. Something dies within a sentient being robbed of freedom. We as rulers of this people are responsible for their well-being in body, spirit, and mind. Indentured servitude seeks only care of body at the cost of spirit and mind. We can change this."

Despite not possessing speaking rights, several spectators raised the obvious question.

"How?"

"It will take time to explain my plan in detail, but I shall summarize," said Reia, turning to yet a new section of people. "What we require is a Safe Service Act, a comprehensive series of laws regulating an alternative to indentured servitude as it stands now. In essence, those seeking aid for a debt will hire their services to the cities. Contracts will dictate what sort of work each is qualified to do and how long a term is necessary to absolve their debts."

"That will never work," scoffed Governor Holum. "You're adding a complicated layer of bureaucracy to the very institution you claim to despise."

"The forms and files will no doubt land on the governor's desk," grumbled Governor Naverick.

Reia gave Holum and Naverick each a sympathetic look and a

gentle smile.

"You might have more work for a while, but I am certain adequate help could be found. In any case, it would be work done to directly aid others. What better way to fulfill our vows?" Reia's smile turned a touch ironic. "Besides, if set up properly, the programs will soon be self-sufficient. Funds will be generated two ways. First, businesses and private estates wishing to hire temporary servants can still do so through the cities, and second, anyone wishing to deal directly with a particular person may also do so for a price. Yes, my friends, I realize it comes down to money in the end."

The unexpected admission drew a warm chuckle from the crowd.

Reia's expression became earnest.

"Minus necessary administration costs, the vast majority of kefs generated will be funneled into programs for ensuring the safety of each servant." She paused to stare at each section. "Some people will not like the changes, and if we accidentally put the wrong people in positions of power over these services, we may do more harm than good. Unfettered slavery will probably always exist, but none of these facts ought to dissuade us from trying to save at least some from the tyranny of indentured servitude as it exists today!"

Terosh wanted to cheer along with most of the onlookers, but he settled for a small smile.

She had won.

The discussion would likely continue for days, but a quick glance around confirmed that Reia would have plenty of support in the detail battles ahead.

***

Idela (January) 11, 1539
The Lady's Estate, Kala Mountains

"How would you suggest handling this situation?" asked Kezem, his tone curious.

Mavis allowed one eyebrow to climb a little higher. Her youngest son must be extremely baffled to seek her opinion. Usually, she had to wring reports from him or pay off his agents. She had devoted much thought to the situation, but thus far, taken no real interest in it. The queen's grand plan to ease people's suffering struck Mavis as highly naïve but ultimately harmless. The thought of having missed something crucial bothered Mavis.

"Opposing our dear queen on this issue will leave you in a

morally weak position." Mavis stopped to consider her feelings. "However, this may prove useful. Do you know where everyone stands with regards to the Safe Service Act?"

"So, I should support the queen?" asked Kezem, avoiding her question. "Would that not work against my ultimate designs?"

"Quite the opposite, I believe. Outwardly support the queen. In fact, secretly support measures that inconvenience the governors and senators. I must emphasize the secret part because you must also subtly let those governors and senators know that you sympathize with their causes, whatever they may be."

"It is a slow plan," Kezem complained.

Laughing, Mavis said, "It is not even the main plan, darling, but only fools risk everything on single strategies. Consider that the next time you send an assassin blundering about my mountains."

Kezem shrugged.

"He had too high an opinion of his skills. I had to humble him. Did your people leave him whole?"

"Unfortunately for him they did, but I deemed him too great a threat to keep around," said Mavis.

"What a waste," Kezem murmured.

"Were I in your position, I might show such signs of impatience, but you still need me, Kezem. Suspend this nonsense between us at least until the Gardan campaign ends."

"Speaking of Gardan, I received some new reports of people vanishing. I assume you are aware of such. What are you going to do about it?" Kezem's cobalt eyes flashed with indignation.

Your people should be shot for slowness.

"I have spoken with King Padric, and naturally, he claims the responsibility belongs to a few rogue agents. I told him to control his people, but I do not know how long that will work. Patience is not a strength for him. The Rangers were supposed to appease him, but we both know how that ended," Mavis said with a small frown. "I am taking certain measures to ensure no one important vanishes, but hopefully, this too will work to our advantage. We shall simply have to choose targets for the Shadow Guards."

A new thought struck her, and she smiled broadly.

"What does that look mean?" Kezem demanded.

"Perhaps nothing, perhaps everything," Mavis whispered. She ended the call with Kezem and stared into empty space.

I wonder how closely King Padric keeps watch over his Shadow Guards.

Chapter 31: Ambassadors

Idela (January) 17, 1539
Restler-Tarpon Safe House, City of Meritel

Kolknir raised a hand to stop his protégé from punching their prisoner.

A rebellious look crossed Lucas Telon's face, but he straightened and reluctantly stepped back.

"We want to turn him," Kolknir reminded the younger man.

The man hanging from the wall glared but said nothing.

Lucas touched the sore spot on his jaw where the prisoner had clouted him during the take down.

"I am sorry for the restraints," said Kolknir. "We have an offer for you and wish to deliver it in peace."

"If the Lady did not find you useful, I would kill you," Lucas added. He folded his arms across his chest and leaned against the far wall.

"My friend would enjoy persuading you to our cause the traditional way, but I would like to try words first," Kolknir explained. "What is your name? Surely you can tell me that."

He knew the name but wanted to see what the man would tell them.

The prisoner studied the floor.

"I can be a very patient man, but I would like to let you down from that uncomfortable position," said Kolknir. "The sooner our conversation progresses, the sooner we can release you."

The man grunted, managing to convey derision and bitter amusement.

"It is in your best interest to cooperate with us," Lucas said, fiddling with a dagger retrieved from an arm sheath. He flipped the dagger several times before slowly slashing it through the air in front of the man.

"You are well-trained and suspicious; I respect you for both. Allow me to lay out the Lady's proposal, and then you may make your decision." Kolknir tapped a command into the control panel and a metal footrest slid under the prisoner's feet. "Be comfortable for a moment so you can concentrate on my words."

The prisoner's contemptuous look carried several curses.

"Relax," Kolknir advised. "You'll hurt yourself hating so hard."

"This is pointless," Lucas muttered, attention still fixed on his dagger.

"As I am sure you can guess, my patroness would like to buy your services as an informant and agent," Kolknir said, pausing in case the man decided to respond.

The man barked a short, humorless laugh.

"Her sources are already good. You would make them better, Nolan," Kolknir said. He said the name lightly like it was a known fact, not a piece of information dearly bought.

Surprise flickered across the prisoner's face, but his training slapped it away almost instantly.

"Join us. Why let your precious sister toil long days in a field in some sun-cursed part of Gardan, when she could join you here and live like royalty?" Kolknir spoke slowly to let the words stoke the fires inside the prisoner.

The man jerked against his restraints and clenched his teeth.

"I have no sister," he lied.

Kolknir's sympathetic look meant little for the man would not meet his eyes.

"There's no use denying it. She may not believe she still has a brother, but you know you still have a sister. Your parents and grandparents are dead. You have chosen no wife. You have sired no children, and you keep few enough friends. Your unmarried sister, Kara Demilak, is really all you have left. Did you know she's pregnant by her master?"

"Do not involve her," said the prisoner.

"Do you hear what I'm telling you, man?" Kolknir snapped. "Not involving your sister is the worst thing I could do. I am offering to help her—to rescue her from the terrible situation in which *you* left her." His voice struck at the man like a banistick.

The man glared at him.

"If you're so well-informed, then you know I did not simply leave her."

Kolknir smiled and nodded. They had reached the turning point.

"Indeed. You were taken from her, sold as a soldier while still just a boy. You owe Gardan nothing, save your training. You owe your king nothing. Your only loyalty ought to be to your elder sister who protected you the best way she knew how. She who sold herself—body and soul—to save you from horrors that would have crushed your innocence to dust."

The Shadow Guard's cautious expression, now devoid of the anger, told Kolknir they had won. The conversation would naturally go around and around, for one does not switch loyalties on a whim. Nolan would take some time to fully convince, but he would accept the Lady's offer and become her spy.

***

Idela (January) 28, 1539
Docking Bay 17, Spaceport, City of Rammon

Reia halted the hov bike about twenty meters from the shabby-looking ship and dismounted, absorbing the entire scene in a glance. The ship rested serenely at the hangar's center, looking prepared to endure a siege. Royal Guards formed a loose perimeter around the ship, kerlak rifles in hand but not quite pointed at the ship. Several mechanics gawked.

A grim-faced Captain Donald Garahad strode toward her.

"You should not be here, Your Majesty. It might not be safe. My men can handle this."

"I was informed the ambassador requested an audience with a royal. The king will be in a Senate hearing for another few hours, so I am here to welcome our guests," Reia explained, affecting calmness she did not quite feel.

"That ship hails from Rorge II," Captain Garahad said, as if that were a condemning fact.

"All the more reason to attempt peaceful overtures, Captain," said Reia. "Have your communications officer inform the pilot of my arrival."

A soft metallic whine sounded, and a ramp descended like a mouth slowly opening in a yawn.

"They are aware, Your Majesty," Garahad said tightly. He turned to face the ship and shifted to a better position to defend Reia from any danger that might come down that ramp.

Having chosen the Healer's path early in her Ranger training, Reia had not been sent on many missions to protect people, but Kiata and Todd had shared many of their experiences. Needless to say, the people being protected did not always welcome the help. Part of her had always wondered why, until now. Too much protection could be a nuisance.

Reia took stock of the situation. A Rorgen stood with all four limbs flush against the deck and had his head lowered in a defensive posture. Dark eyes darted around, measuring the various threats. He presented no sign of weapons but wore pride like a personal shield. His movements were the slow, measured steps of a natural predator exploring a new place. Black fur covered much of his body, and three streaks of silky, golden hair sprouted from his head and ran down his back.

Stopping at the bottom, the Rorgen bowed low then sat down as if unimpressed by the significant number of Royal Guards surrounding his ship.

"You must be the dominant female. I am called Nirrolik Tul. I am sent of my people to request aid. The star that warms our planet will die a violent death." His smooth, strong voice rumbled from deep in his chest.

Dominant female? I've never thought about it quite so literally, but I suppose it fits. Well, at least they don't mince words. That's refreshing.

Reia eased past a very tense Captain Garahad.

"Greetings, Nirrolik Tul. I am Queen Reia. Welcome to Reshner. I hope this may be the restful place you seek for your people, but for now, all I can offer is an introduction to my husband, King Terosh of House Minstel, and our ruling bodies. I will call for a special session to take place tomorrow. In the meantime, Captain Garahad can escort you and any of your people to the palace to await an audience with the king."

"There is only me. Two dozen of my kin went forth to other life spheres. Some are captives. Some are dead. Many returned home with no good news. People fear. Few want to stand against our masters. The masters say my people are not worth saving." The rolling cadence marking the Rorgen's speech softened the terrible meaning of his words.

"Who are your masters?" Reia asked, still trying to wrap her mind around telling any people that they were not worth saving.

"Masters are many. They are of the Galactic Alliance of Populated Planets," answered Nirrolik Tul. "They come many years ago and say our resources are theirs in exchange for care. Resources gone now. Taken to other life spheres. We say to masters take us to other life spheres. Masters say find new minerals, new technologies, new slaves, and maybe we save you."

"I do not wish to give you false hope, Ambassador," said Reia. "My people have long sought to avoid entanglements with GAPP."

"You are dominant female. Make them listen," said Nirrolik Tul.

"As I said, I will call the governing bodies to order and let you present your case, but I do not know if we can help you. Rest now, we can deal with these heavy issues later." Reia could picture how the Senate Great Hall would look on the morrow and tried not to wince.

***

Idela (January) 29, 1539
Senate Great Hall, City of Rammon

Terosh sympathized with Rorge II's plight, but he also knew his first duty must be to his people. The GAPP ambassador had conveniently arrived an hour after Nirrolik Tul. Terosh found the ambassador and her timing unsettling.

Senator Gabriel Luvak held speaking rights for the moment.

"Your Highnesses are suggesting we risk the lives of our citizens to help strangers!" He said the last word in a tone that added: *they're a race of overgrown korvers.*

"We are suggesting you hear the ambassador's request and evaluate it in light of moral and natural laws, Senator Luvak," Terosh said. "We are asking you to decide whether we have an obligation to help the people of Rorge II, and if so, how we can best acquit ourselves in that regard."

The lights for both guests blinked. Terosh swallowed some of the tightness creeping across his throat and pressed the button to transfer speaking rights to the GAPP representative. Sabrina Raquel stood and immediately drew every eye. Terosh noticed most of the males straightening in their seats. With his own pulse quickening, he couldn't really blame them.

The ambassador wore a deep red gown more suited for a ballroom. Her wide eyes shifted shades from a warm, friendly gray to a mysterious, murky green. Her seductive smile said she knew how to wield her natural beauty well. Sabrina Raquel swept her gaze slowly over the crowd.

"Honorable people of Reshner, we are each committed to averting a tragedy. The solution is simple. We are not your enemy. I do not blame Ambassador Tul for painting us in such a light, but I do mourn the miscommunication that has tainted our reputation." Her voice gushed forth with a breathy softness that caressed every ear.

"If you have a solution, Ambassador Raquel, please share it," Terosh said, though he knew full well what her suggestion would entail.

"Join us. Add Reshner's voice to the largest power base in this galaxy. With your strength and resolve, we can address the terrible fate looming over the Rorge system." Sabrina Raquel somehow managed to make it sound absolutely foolish to consider any other option.

"Why don't you address it anyway?" asked Senator Victoria Turrel.

Several others—mostly females—echoed the question.

Sabrina Raquel tipped her head toward Senator Turrel and smiled in a self-deprecating manner.

"With great power comes great responsibility. We are handling delicate situations that span the galaxy. We lack the physical resources and people to address every concern. The Rorge II settlements are sparsely populated compared to places like the Olic Cluster. Our choices may seem heartless, but we must deal with the stark reality of sacrificing a few billion to save hundreds of billions elsewhere."

"Ambassador, I am not certain I follow your reasoning," Reia admitted. "How exactly does Reshner factor in? Whether we join you or not, you still face the same resource deficit."

"That is an excellent question, Your Majesty," Sabrina Raquel crooned. "In this case, I am happy to inform you that we are not immune to politics. What the honorable Nirrolik Tul has said about recruiting holds true. I can divert evacuation ships to Rorge II if I offer your joining our cause as justification."

Murmurs arose, and lights danced across Terosh's control panel. He selected Senator Byron Price to summarize the people's sentiments.

"I believe I speak for my colleagues when I say that you have given us very interesting insight into GAPP politics," said Senator Price. "We will discuss the matter at length before rendering a decision. Unless either of their Royal Highnesses objects, I move to break down into regional discussion groups."

***

Lanolin (February) 8, 1539
Senate Great Hall, City of Rammon

Reia steeled her heart against the words she must speak. The discussions over Rorge II's plight had dragged on for days. The governors had polled the people. Then more discussions took place. Finally, a decision was rendered, and while opinions still varied, most senators and governors believed the decision embodied the will of the people.

Reia did not hear a word of Terosh's introduction, but she felt the crowd shift attention from him to her. Standing, she belatedly hoped her voice still worked.

"Ambassador Nirrolik Tul, it is with deepest regrets that I must inform you that Reshner will decline to join the Galactic Alliance of Populated Planets. However, six cities have offered to accept up to ten thousand refugees and seven more believe they can harbor five thousand each. The Rangers will take an additional thousand people into their care in the Riden Mountains. Finally, House Minstel will accept responsibility for fifty thousand people to be sheltered in new settlements in the Frozen North, the Kevloth Plains, and the Felmon Desert."

Both ambassadors leapt to their feet.

Terosh granted speaking rights to Nirrolik Tul first.

The Rorgen ambassador slid to the room's center with stealthy movements. Once exactly in the center, the Rorgen walked a tight circle and sat directly facing Reia and Terosh.

"There is only me. My kin return home. This place was our last hope. Five years is long time. Life star not explode for five years. Keep talking about Rorge II. Remember us."

"We will commission a subcommittee to annually revisit this issue," Terosh promised. "You will not be forgotten. As the queen has said, we offer refuge to some of your people. We do not have many large ships, but we will put out contracts to hire a few freighters. Working steadily, we should be able to complete the evacuation in time."

Ambassador Sabrina Raquel stabbed an impeccably painted fingertip at the button to request speaking rights. Her pale gray-green eyes looked almost feral. When granted the floor, she put on a frosty smile that immediately bothered Reia.

"Honorable people of Reshner, I humbly urge you to reconsider," said Ambassador Raquel. "While we may lack the resources to implement an effective evacuation of Rorge II's entire population, we will certainly safeguard our remaining interests there."

"Speak plainly, Ambassador," Reia said. "What interests can GAPP be keeping on a planet with a dying star? Do you mean to say you will interfere with an evacuation?"

"Rorge II is still considered a colony, and several teams of scientists maintain research outposts there. Some of them have military contracts." Her smile grew colder still. "Speaking plainly, Your Majesty, Rorge II belongs to us. I fear the commanders stationed there may misinterpret your philanthropic efforts."

Dead silence reigned for several seconds as Ambassador Raquel's words crystallized in everyone's mind. Reia could not have been more stunned if the sleek ambassador had whipped out a kerlinblade and brandished it at her.

Chapter 32:
Lull

Lanolin (February) 9, 1539-Temen (July) 30, 1539
Tour of Reshner: Cities of Rammon, Chara, Kalmata, Ritten, Meritab, Meritel, Calsola, Idonia, and Azhel
After the stresses of the first four months as Reshner's rulers, Reia and Terosh threw themselves into the task of exploring the various cities. In addition to keeping up with Senate and Governors Council meetings, they attended banquets and balls, entertained ambassadors, held court to arbitrate disputes, studied galactic and local politics, and visited with countless people. While touring, Reia often spoke to generate support for her Safe Service Act. She especially enjoyed talking with indentured servants benefiting from the programs.

While in Chara, they visited the surrounding vineyards, fruit farms, and traditional farms. They saw how hovs could be turned into water hovs and spent a few days on various fishing boats. Reia had her first real experience with a beach and stepped into the cool waters of the South Asrien Sea. Students from the University of Chara impressed them with a beautiful fireworks display and a play about the miraculous rescue of Princess Lystran from her father, King Rammon. Terosh discussed new irrigation plans with Chara's governor while Reia continued her lessons with Sedir.

Before moving on to Kalmata, they escaped their duties for four whole days at a private house along the Glass Coast. Royal Guards maintained a perimeter but kept well away from Reia and Terosh. The royals threw their efforts into swimming, exploring, and foraging. Each meal became an adventure to share, enjoy, and mutually conquer. Each day as the sun set and the moons rose, they spent precious moments in blessed silence, watching the waves roll in and enjoying each other's presence.

On the way to Kalmata they stopped at the Imberg Tosh Mines where Reia sensed something familiar. They toured the mines and used the anotechs to ascertain some of its history. Imagine the queen's surprise when she realized her parents had once owned part of the mines and died for it. The discovery set off a legal battle which resulted in Kiata Wellum owning part of the mines and signing the shares over to Reia for the benefit of indentured servants with mining skills.

Finally, in Kalmata, Reia and Terosh saw how workers reclaimed salt from the West Remon Sea. On a visit to Fort Tiree, they talked with many of the Royal Guards stationed there. Reia noted that most soldiers were human, so she added diversification of the armed forces to her list of causes. At the Kalmata orphanage, they discovered an overworked, underpaid, and generally worn out staff. Naturally, the king ordered immediate changes and set Master Roth to the task of improving things. Lady Akia Zelene offered her expertise, and soon, the orphanage stood in much better stead. Though the aid recipients could only pay in smiles, the royals considered it more than enough.

The factories in Ritten turned raw materials from the Riden Mountains and Imberg Tosh Mines into everything from comms to hovs to ground vehicles to small starships. Reia and Terosh both enjoyed learning to fly klipper fighters, but their enthusiasm paled in comparison to the young lieutenant instructing them. Soon thereafter, Reia also learned how to drive a hov. While she liked the experience, she still felt more comfortable with the natural rolling gait of a horse.

The people of Meritab and Meritel hosted a huge festival in honor of Reia and Terosh's visit to their fair cities. Games and contests abounded. Reia politely declined to participate but encouraged Terosh to do so. He entered a serlak pistol shooting contest and fared well, though he did not win top prize. Todd and Kiata Wellum both entered several competitions. Although they had rejoined with the anotechs, both avoided enhancing any senses or reflexes during the competition. Nevertheless, Todd won top honors in kerlinblade combat and several kerlak shooting contests. Kiata soundly defeated her challengers in banistick and unarmed combat and earned great recognition for her skills with flingers. Each evening in Meritab or Meritel featured a new play or dance demonstration, sometimes both.

Although they found the twin cities enthralling, Reia and

Terosh tore themselves away in early Enis (April) to return to Rammon and oversee the Festival of Future Fighters, sending the next wave of Kireshana travelers on their way.

Next, the horse lords and ladies in Calsola proudly displayed their steeds. Reia marveled at how much she had missed the previous year by rushing through Calsola in hot pursuit of Prince Terosh and his Royal Guard entourage. Practically every man, woman, and child they met in Calsola could competently ride a horse. Most could even race them, a fact proven time and again in both official and unofficial races. Reia found the wild spirit of Calsola's citizens infectious. They reminded her of Rangers. Though that thought brought pain, she loved being around the unpretentious people who taught her to love racing of any sort. Before her time in Calsola, Reia viewed hovs, hov bikes, and horses simply as means of transportation, but afterward, she appreciated the joy that drove people to pit their skills against one another.

On the way down to Idonia, Reia and Terosh camped a few days in the Clear Mountains and then again in the Ash Mountains. While the two mountains invoked vastly different feelings within her, Reia was thrilled at being fully immersed in wild lands and breathing free air. They narrowly escaped a windstorm, but the experience challenged them to continually defy the weather. A large korver pack took mild interest in them as well, but the Royal Guards used kerlak stun bolts to good effect. Despite chilling memories of the korver attack in the zalok cave, neither Reia nor Terosh were eager to slaughter korvers outright.

The weeks in Idonia returned the king and queen to refined culture. On separate occasions, they visited with Governor Lord Eldon Altran and his family and Governor General Kezem. With their help, Governor Judge Mitrek took his family to Balar the week after Keldor's trial ended. Being in Idonia caused them to think of Mitrek, but they dared not speak of him for fear of somehow betraying him. They had routed the family through several pods on Riab due to Mitrek's insistence that no one—especially his mother—be able to trace them. Lady Mavis surprised Reia and Terosh by seeking them out one afternoon.

Around the family visits, the king and queen toured crystal factories and the Nedis Crystal Mines. The mine owner admired them so much that he readily accepted Reia's proposal for having former indentured servants work some of the packing lines. An assassination attempt dampened their experience a bit, but they found most Idonians pleasant people. Senator Victoria Turrel bestowed a lovely pair of glass swords upon the young royals and arranged for a demonstration of their use by Idonia's colored crossblades team.

The last stop before the long-awaited Colored Crossblades Tournament in Korch was Azhel. There they met Father Morgivesh Niktol and communed with the man who had presided over their marriage. He admitted a desire to see them as motivation for his current spiritual journey and guided them around the a few of the temples. Naturally, a serene, deep spirituality marked the people of Azhel. Reia found the time among them very relaxing. Their music seemed to mean more whether provided by the Azhel Grand Percussion Band, the Children's Choir, or the Gentle String Quartet. This last portion of their trip around Reshner left Reia feeling refreshed and confident that she could face most anything. She would need that feeling in the months and years to come.

Chapter 33:
Colored Crossblades Tournament

Allei (August) 1, 1539
Colored Crossblades Arena, City of Korch

Queen Reia Minstel braced against the thunderous noise crashing down upon her from the frantic crowds. She marveled that so much of her life could pass without hearing of colored crossblades, a series of sporting events that dominated a good portion of the culture. Master Colander had immediately rectified the sad deficiency in her education, but she had all but forgotten the games until Sedir reminded her of this duty to grace the events with her presence.

Although almost a year had passed since inheriting her role as queen, Reia still found crowds unnerving, especially crowds as large and enthusiastic as this one. A wall of harried Royal Guards kept the people at bay, but she still felt closed in by the sheer number of people. Upon reaching her designated area, Reia resisted the urge to fling herself into the nearest seat. Instead, she steadied herself on a railing and scanned the crowds.

As she soaked in the sight of rank upon rank of colorfully attired people, inexplicable pride filled her. One could tell which section belonged to each city by the banners and flags and blinking arrangements of coordinated infopads.

Korch's dark green and black banners with the image of a goritor dominated because of the location. Reia was surprised goritors did not represent Meritab or Meritel since those cities were closest to the Lotrian Fields, the place made famous for its goritor infestation. Green and brown banners bearing the emblem of a horse represented

Calsola, and green and yellow banners bearing the likeness of a cannafitch represented Osem.

It took Reia a moment to find the purple and green, zalok-bearing banners representing the Royal House and the red and gold, korver-bearing banners from the city of Rammon. Master Sedir and Master Colander had both warned her against favoritism, but the majestic images of her new home and family secretly held her loyalty. It amused her to think of a korver as a noble symbol for once. In obedience to good advice, Reia bestowed her smile and attention as equally as possible.

The section claimed by people from Azhel shimmered with orange and red flames. One of their signs read: FLAMES BURN ON. The Idonians held their banner of a helmeted soldier aloft and rhythmically chanted a warrior's cry. A large number of those from Estra wore dark blue outfits studded with white pieces of glass that reflected the sun sharply. The people of Kalmata were a riot of colors in tribute to their mascot the kyrie bird. They contrasted with the black and silver worn by Meritab natives whose symbol of a sharp dagger hardly needed the garish trappings of multiple colors. The Charans roared with the challenging battle cry of a mythical dalagon.

Exceedingly glad not to have to speak at the opening ceremonies, Reia thoroughly enjoyed the team parade and the show that followed. The songs and traditional dances from the various cities were expertly performed, but they could not match the splendor of the portion put on by the city of Korch. Reia especially liked the part where two teams of five hov riders performed a series of acrobatic maneuvers, often flipping from one bike to another high above the crowd. The welcoming speeches were far less exciting but mercifully short.

Her favorite part did not come until the very end. Though it consisted of nothing more than a simple recitation of the vow to fight for the honor and glory of each home city, the sight of nearly a thousand kerlinblades raised over the players' heads could not fail to inspire awe. Reia wished Terosh could have joined her. He had promised to watch a recording, but no vid could adequately capture such a moment.

***

Allei (August) 7, 1539

Colored Crossblades Arena, City of Korch

King Terosh watched the Kamarachi Duel with interest. It wasn't his favorite duel to participate in, but he admired the skill it took the four teams of five to fight in a hundred-meter-long, half-gravity field. This match featured teams from Meritab, Meritel, Azhel, and Osem. As expected, the Meritab Blades and Meritel Vipers were allied at the moment, which left the Azhel Flames and Osem Cannafitches to either unite or lose.

Terosh couldn't help but compare the teams to their respective governors. Beady-eyed, suspicious Governor Holum of Meritab and silent, somber Governor Naverick of Meritel were practically inseparable. Azhel's venerable Governor Westis tended to keep to himself, and Osem's good-natured Governor Ella Price kept her affairs neat and unobtrusive. Terosh spared a wish that Governors Council meetings could be solved like colored crossblades duels.

"Stop that," Reia scolded, slipping her left hand into Terosh's right.

"How do you always know what I'm thinking?" Terosh wondered, giving her a guilty grin.

"You're wearing that special, slightly sickened expression you reserve for the Governors Council," Reia said. "No more politics. Enjoy your one month of complete freedom from councils and meetings. It only comes once every three years."

"I'll try," Terosh promised, tightening his grip on her hand.

On the field, two Meritel players had the Osem current flag bearer trapped against a barrier that had materialized on the seventy-meter marker. Before the barrier could form a roof and complete the trap, the Osem player executed a backflip onto the barrier's frame and used it as a launching point to spring over his attackers. While still in the air, he casually tossed the flag to a teammate. Despite its name, the "flag" was really a lightweight glowbar a little smaller than a standard kerlinblade handle. The throw was a little wide and the other Osem player lunged to catch it before it touched the ground. The Osem fans drew a horrified collective breath then let it out in a rush once they realized the flag was safe.

"They make it look so easy," Reia commented. "There's so much to keep track of. How do they do it?"

"Long hours of intense training for a start," Terosh said, watching a Meritab player bat aside strikes from Azhel and Osem duelists. "It's meant to be chaotic. Kamarachi Duels began as war games to train soldiers to fight in space."

"The inventor must have been quite a commander."

"Don't say that to Master Sedir unless you want to suffer through his three-hour lecture on the history of colored crossblades duels," Terosh warned. He took the opportunity to lift his wife's hand and gently traced her fingers. His interest in the duel waned as he enjoyed the simple pleasure of being near her.

"Only three-hours? You must have gotten the short version," said Reia, pulling her hand free of Terosh's loose grip to clap politely. "I thought he would talk on straight through the evening meal, but Master Colander rescued me."

Feeling bereft, Terosh returned his attention to the field where the Meritab team was celebrating the successful capture of the flag. The bar changed from green and yellow to silver. Seven separate duels still raged around the field.

One brave Azhel player fended off three opponents at once. Despite her obvious skill, the Azhel player slowly found herself corralled toward a barrier. She tried to leap free, but two Meritab Blades blocked her efforts. A moment later, a Meritel player knocked the Azhel woman into the barrier and it held her fast.

Terosh flicked his eyes to the scoreboard. Meritab led by a mere ten points with a score of two hundred and twelve, followed by Osem at two hundred and two, Meritel at one hundred and seventy-eight, and Azhel at one hundred and sixty-two. Three minutes remained in the second round.

Although he did not really care who won the game, he silently cheered for the Azhel team just because they were so behind. He wasn't worried. Leads changed almost by the second in this type of duel. Captured flags were worth twenty-five points, strikes against opponent players were worth one point, and captured opponent players were worth five points for the first up to twenty-five points for the last.

"Is there a limit to how many times the flag can be passed within a team?" Reia asked.

"Not under these rules," Terosh answered. "There are several very similar games where passes matter, but here players can hold the flag the whole time or continually pass countless times."

The round ended, and Terosh and Reia rose to stretch.

The barriers released their prisoners, and the players retreated to their respective corners to regroup.

Two more rounds, Terosh thought, suddenly anxious to be done with the match. Then, he could spend some quality time with his wife.

"Patience, love," Reia whispered, leaning over and wrapping him in a friendly, one-armed hug. "The world is watching."

Four giant vidscreens displaying their image to every eye in the arena emphasized her words. Terosh forced himself to smile and wave, but inside, he cringed at the attention.

***

Allei (August) 30, 1539
Colored Crossblades Arena, City of Korch

Ariman Keldor eagerly anticipated the coming duel. It would change everything. The king would finally receive his due for that mock trial and the subsequent death of Ariman's father. He knew it was dangerous to be here, but he had to see the plan unfold. He shook his head, trying to shake off a sudden chill. A year ago, he would have never even considered assassination, but the year had changed him.

As soon as he witnessed the king's death, he would keep his promise to Dr. Nabern, an old, brilliant friend.

***

Lord Kezem Altran dutifully waved to his cheering supporters. Inside, he battled rising resentment. His patience with his mother's endless schemes was all but spent. He could not shake the uneasy feeling that this plan would fail. Trying to predict the people's reaction to the pending accident left him cold.

He marched over to his starting area and let the officials inspect the sensors built into his black dueling suit. He did not have to look to know Terosh was also submitting to a similar inspection. He listened with half an ear while one official dutifully listed the rules he had memorized since childhood.

"This is a Dollan duel to an Ideal Fifty. Three ground strikes may be used to change the blade color, but additional ground strikes will incur a five-point penalty. If the officials determine you are using additional ground strikes to purposefully lower your score, you will be disqualified, and your opponent will be declared the victor. Do you understand?"

Kezem grunted and glared at the man.

The official hurried on with his recitation.

"Blade colors will follow the standard rainbow from red to violet through white and back to red. Red strikes are worth seven points, orange six, yellow five, green—"

"Get on with it!" Kezem demanded.

"Apologies, my Lord Kezem, but I am bound by the rules of

my office," said the stuffy little man.

Kezem gritted his teeth and endured the rest of the man's speech.

"Green strikes are worth four points, blue three, indigo two, violet one, and white ten. Score panels to the sides will show the current scores as the duel progresses. You may refer to these at your own risk. Sensors in your suit will register valid body strikes. Please avoid blows to the head, neck, and other vital areas as they carry no point value and may result in disqualification. Also, please respect the boundaries of the dueling circle. Violation of these boundaries will result in disqualification."

"What colors will we start with?" asked Kezem. He could not remember whether Dollan duels started with red or randomly. It had been quite some time since he had indulged in an officially regulated match.

"You are the challenger, my Lord Kezem; therefore, the choice rests with the challenged, His Majesty, King Terosh."

"I know this," Kezem snapped. "What did he choose?"

"Random, my Lord Kezem," answered the official, blinking slowly like a sunning sand lizard.

Once the tiresome official was finished with Kezem, the babbling announcer picked up the cause to annoy him. The man introduced Kezem and the king and spewed facts everybody knew about them. He tried to emphasize the deep rivalry between the cousins. Though he spoke truth, Kezem wished the fool would get on with the duel.

At last, the match moderator stepped into the center of the dueling circle and beckoned to Kezem and the king. Kezem pulled on sensor-lined cloth gauntlets and tightened the straps. Then, snatching the modified kerlinblade from the boy holding it out, Kezem entered the circle and saluted his young cousin with his unlit weapon. Terosh returned the gesture. They bowed to each other, and the match began.

Kezem activated his kerlinblade, and it blazed into orange life. Terosh's blade lit green. Their blades crashed several times as each tested the other's defenses. The rapidly changing colors dazzled Kezem's vision enough to allow Terosh first strike, a red glancing blow off Kezem's left forearm. It did not hurt, but the tingling sensation from the sensors further distracted him. He retreated several steps, blocking eager strikes from Terosh as he went.

As the duel continued, Kezem relaxed into the rhythm of the

fight. Anticipating Terosh's strikes grew easier. The color changes ceased to bother Kezem, though he did have to pay close attention to them to plan his strikes. Dollan duels were especially useful exercises for they forced the combatants to constantly think several moves ahead.

After using a particularly hard over-the-head blow to unbalance Terosh, Kezem scored twice, once with a violet blade and once with a white blade. Terosh answered a moment later with a yellow hit.

From time to time, Kezem switched his grip from right hand to left hand to a two-handed hold on his kerlinblade. Each new hold allowed him to attack Terosh from a slightly different angle. The duel ebbed and flowed as they further provoked each other by changing the speed of their attacks. Slashes met parries. Their kerlinblades locked together and pressed close, draining each man's strength. Kezem disengaged but attacked right away, lest anyone think him the weaker party.

Suddenly every joint in Kezem's dueling suit stiffened. When Terosh's blade next connected with Kezem's, both weapons emitted a bright flash of light followed by the sizzling crackle of raw electricity. Kezem saw Terosh fly backward just before pain crashed in on his senses from head to foot.

He barely had time to wonder why his mother would betray him before consciousness deserted him.

***

Reia watched in horror as the spirited duel between Terosh and his cousin turned deadly. A sharp crack like a danesque tree trunk snapping in half preceded a series of lesser pops. Twin whips of energy, one white and one green, flew between Terosh and Kezem. The charge lifted both men bodily, cradled them for a second, and flung them away from each other with the force of a windstorm.

Kezem landed on the boy who had given him the kerlinblade, killing the child instantly. Reia felt the loss of his life like a cold wave of water across her whole body. Still glowing green from energy pouring out of his kerlinblade, Terosh's body hurtled through a small cluster of officials judging the match. Their pained cries were immediately lost in the cacophony of confused shouts.

Reia's skin tingled, practically buzzing as agitated anotechs flooded her senses with information. Memory took her back to the korver attack on the zalok cave. A sickening sense of helplessness flooded her. She reverted to Ranger training to continue to analyze the situation when she really wanted to collapse in despair.

A feeling of dread seized her stomach. Kezem's body bounced off the crushed boy like a stone skipping across a calm lake then skidded another five meters. Another four unfortunate bystanders were knocked aside. Terosh's body finally set down hard against the ground. Both men still instinctively clutched the smoking handles of their destroyed weapons.

The dread multiplied, driving Reia to her feet with sudden clarity burning through her skull. Terosh and his cousin still lived, but something else was about to happen. Sedir's dire warnings against using anotech powers were banished by the panic that fueled Reia to action. Clenching her hands around the metal bar in front of her, Reia closed her eyes and slumped forward as if in a dead faint.

Reaching out with the anotechs, she pried the weapons from the two stunned men now lying on the arena floor far below her. She had two choices. She could have the anotechs carry the hazardous handles high into the air, risking an explosion over the frantic crowd, or she could try to contain them while still on the ground, risking her husband and his cousin. Much as it sickened her, she chose the second option, frantically bidding the anotechs to diffuse whatever danger still lay inside the kerlinblade handles.

Not knowing what else to do and having very little time to do anything, Reia wrapped each weapon in a shield of anotechs and braced for pain. An agonizing second passed in terrifying anticipation. Then, Reia felt two sensations. The first was like a thousand glass shards trying to rip through her, and the second sensation was like being bathed in firebloom extract. Her whole body convulsed as the twin torments punished her for saving the two men and the crowd.

As suddenly as it had started, the pain cut off. She moaned as her body began falling. Warm hands caught her and held on tightly.

"Don't worry. I've got you!" declared Captain Ectosh Laocer.

Welcomed blackness slipped over Reia's vision. She had just enough time to command the anotechs to protect her husband and his cousin before truly fainting.

Chapter 34: Aftermath

Allei (August) 30, 1539
Same Day
The Lady's Estate, Kala Mountains

Mavis Altran relished the fresh air that met her as she stepped out onto the carefully hidden balcony she had ordered built into Mount Corith's side. The extensive airflow system kept her underground estate supplied with fresh air and even a passable imitation of cool breezes from time to time, but it could not replicate the wild spirit of natural wind. She breathed deeply several times, trying to force the tension from her body.

Though well-acquainted with fear and anger, Mavis was not used to experiencing them in such toxic quantities. Her cheeks flamed and her head pounded with the force of her boiling blood. She wanted to kill the man who had failed her. She would kill him, but she needed to calm down enough to deal with him properly. If she faced him now, she would probably riddle his body with serlak bullets, and that would be a terrible waste. Proper punishment always took time. She had already issued the necessary orders and now had only to wait.

A cannafitch screeched a hunting cry as it soared past Mavis's balcony. She admired the impressive wingspan of the leathery creature, a male with a splash of white across the crest of his forehead. Then, she shot its skinny head off its slender neck and felt a little better. She watched the body float along on the wind current for several meters before twisting awkwardly and tumbling out of the air stream. It then plummeted toward the rocky valley below. Some korver or mountain lion would feast without having to work tonight.

Mavis returned the small, sleek kerlak pistol to its holster hidden beneath her heart. Dennel would not question her, but he would frown that deep, disapproving frown if he knew. Mavis smiled at the thought of the faithful old servant's reaction. For a second, she almost wished he would scold as he had done during her childhood. He had long since abandoned scolding aloud, but Mavis read him well enough to know when one of her actions displeased him. It bothered her that she cared so much for his good opinion, but she accepted the weakness.

In addition to dealing with the failed scientist, she had vid recordings to watch, a protégé to check on, false sympathies to prepare, and a wounded son to ship to Gardan. Thinking about the list of tasks made her weary, so she let her thoughts brush the recent near disaster. The resulting spike of anger woke her muscles, and Mavis found herself wishing another cannafitch would fly by.

Kezem almost died.

The resulting rush of helplessness turned her anger cold. A sudden, fierce wind whipped strands of her graying black hair painfully across her face. She closed her eyes and leaned into the wind, letting it rake its cold claws along her cheeks.

Reia saved him.

That set some mixed emotions loose in her. She silently thanked the young woman and experienced an odd guilt that they could never be friends. She opened her eyes and fixed them directly on the sun, squinting against the glare. It bothered Mavis to not know exactly what the young queen had done to save Kezem, but she had seen enough recordings to recognize when anotechs were at work.

She saved them both.

The reminder that her nephew also still lived gave her a confusing twinge of disappointment and relief. It had not been her design, but she could have easily adjusted plans to accommodate Terosh's unfortunate demise. Her nephew and his wife had thankfully not produced an heir yet. Kezem might have inherited the woman as well as the throne. Mavis shook her head at the ridiculous notion.

They should not have needed saving.

The thought brought Mavis full circle back to her anger. She nursed it this time, letting it wash through her and enjoying the safe emotional ground it offered.

***

Allei (August) 30, 1539
Same Day
Royal Palace, City of Rammon

Reia awoke mere moments after losing consciousness and forced herself to action, issuing dozens of instructions to see order restored.

Terosh, his cousin, and the other wounded people received immediate care. The dead were covered. The stunned crowds were calmed and ushered out of the arena by police and soldiers. Bolstering what little courage existed in the crowd to prevent panic took every scrap of reserve energy and concentration Reia had left. When she finally collapsed in exhaustion, Todd and Kiata took care of the remaining details.

Reia spent the hov ride back to Rammon in fitful sleep by Terosh's side.

Kiata and Todd parted from the company as soon as it reached the palace, informing the queen they would issue public statements in her stead.

Reia nodded absently and followed the four Royal Guards surrounding her husband's hov sled. She quickly fell behind their rapid steps. Several other Royal Guards, including Captain Laocer, hovered at her side and kept pace with her, ready to catch her should the day's events prove overwhelming.

No one dared utter a word, so the somber procession proceeded through the palace hallways in silence.

Head and heart pounding, Reia feared she wouldn't make it to Terosh's private quarters. The gentle rocking motion of the elevator almost made her sick. Somehow, she held herself upright until the guards had placed Terosh's still form on his bed. Then, she ordered everybody out and sank to the ground beside the bed. Only then did she allow the aching sobs to collapse her emotional defenses.

She woke up with her head resting in her arms and the right side of her face creased from the sheets. Her eyes swept over Terosh's body, seeking a sign of life. He lay on his back with his hands folded neatly across his stomach, appearing so much like the peaceful dead that Reia's heartbeat quickened with dread. She levered herself to a standing position and tenderly laid her hand on his chest. The brief moment before she felt the gentle rise of his chest was one of the longest in her experience.

Her headache returned as a tight band around the top of her skull. It was tolerable as far as headaches go. Reia shut her eyes and directed anotechs to explain the damage done to Terosh's body. Before they could report, the outer door slammed open with a solid crash.

Reia's eyes flew open, but she left her hand hovering over Terosh as she lifted her head to face the intruder.

"What are you doing?" demanded Ezzai Dentelich, rushing into the room. His face flickered between anger and astonishment.

"Trying to see what's wrong with him," Reia replied, lacking the energy to be irritated with the doctor.

"That is my job, Your Majesty," said Dr. Dentelich, recovering a bit from his shock. "Please allow me to do it," he added, stepping around the bed and motioning her to move aside.

Reia was not sure she could safely move at all. Her legs refused to respond to the first few impulses she sent them. Finally, she managed to stumble back and nearly fell over. Only Dentelich's strong grip on her upper right arm kept her upright.

Dentelich shouted for a Royal Guard to help him, and said, "Tell me what you're feeling."

"Tired," Reia mumbled, as her knees buckled.

Dentelich slipped his left arm around her waist and draped her right arm over his shoulders so he could support her. He grunted with the effort and shouted for the guard again.

"You are more than merely tired, my Queen."

Reia didn't hear if he said more, but she felt strong arms pick her up like a child, carry her around to the other side of Terosh's bed, and lay her gently next to him. Letting her eyes close, she reached out to grip Terosh's right hand. Her hand found his wrist instead, and the steady beat of his pulse sent waves of comfort through her.

***

Pirua (September) 1, 1539

Central Communications Room, Royal Palace, City of Rammon

Kiata Wellum stood to the side, out of range of the vidrecorders and hologram projectors, wishing she could do something to help her sister. It pained her to watch Reia's slow, stiff movements. She seemed to be holding herself together through stubborn will alone. While this did not surprise Kiata, it did frustrate her.

"How fares the king, Your Grace?" asked Lady Mavis Altran, her elegant face lined with worry.

"He has not regained consciousness yet, but Dr. Dentelich believes he will," Reia answered without much inflection.

"You are a healer of the finest degree," Lady Mavis gently

reminded her. "What do you believe?"

Kiata could not see her sister's face, but she heard the uncertainty and desperation in her voice.

"I have never seen anything like this," said Reia. She gripped the back of the chair in front of her for support. Her voice dropped to a whisper. "I don't know what to do."

An emotion Kiata could not identify flashed across Lady Mavis's face and was gone in an instant. Genuine compassion took its place.

"You will know what to do when the time comes," said Lady Mavis. "You will save our beloved king."

"Thank you for the kind words, Lady Mavis," said Reia, reluctantly releasing her grip on the chair and standing slightly straighter. "How is Lord Kezem?"

Kiata could tell Reia wanted to assure the older woman that she had done everything she could to protect Lord Kezem. To Kiata's great relief, Reia had the sense to contain any statements that would lead to awkward questions.

"I suspect he fares exactly as our king." Lady Mavis's words were heavy with sadness. "I am sending him to some specialists on Gardan."

"What do these specialists do?" asked Reia. Her tone finally had some life to it.

"I am not quite sure," said Lady Mavis. "I only know their practices are dangerous yet have near miraculous results. If you like, I shall keep you apprised of their progress. Should their methods work with my son, perhaps we can risk them with our king."

Reia's shoulders slumped slightly.

"I see. Will Lord Kezem be all right?"

"We can only hope and pray it is so," replied Lady Mavis.

"Is his situation really so desperate as to warrant such risks?" Reia pressed.

"Unfortunately, I fear he was struck by something more than simple electricity," Lady Mavis announced.

What makes you say that? Kiata wondered, thinking it an odd observation.

Dr. Dentelich said the samples taken from King Terosh would require a full day to analyze, even with several top scientists devoting their full efforts to the task.

Reia tensed.

"What causes such fear in you?" she asked, echoing Kiata's sentiment.

The lady responded with a small, self-deprecating smile.

"Your Grace, I have lived long enough to know that things are never quite as simple as they seem. So, when I see my son fall in a flash of light, I know to expect a complicated explanation."

"What more do you expect? A poison?" asked Reia, horrified.

"We will not know until the results are in, and I think it best we not worry until then," Lady Mavis advised. "Now, if you'll excuse me, I must see my son off personally."

"Certainly," Reia said with a nod. "Thank you for taking the time to call."

"It was my pleasure, Highness," responded Lady Mavis.

A moment passed while the two women silently regarded each other, waiting for someone to end the call. When the connection had been cut and the machines stopped humming, Reia finally turned around and leaned wearily against the chair she had been gripping for support.

"What is it?" she asked, probably in response to Kiata's expression.

What is it? Kiata silently repeated. Something bothered her, but she could not fathom what.

"I'm worried," she admitted, lacking words to better define her feeling.

"Well, that's specific," said Reia.

"Something's not right here," Kiata said, frantically trying to make the scattered feelings give her answers.

"Not much is right," Reia answered, leaning her head back and shutting her eyes. "My husband's in a coma, the councils are outraged, the people are worried, and I'm not ready to do anything about any of it."

Kiata's helpless feeling returned, but she stepped forward and swept her sister into a firm embrace.

"You will do fine," she whispered.

***

Pirua (September) 1, 1539
Same Day
The Lady's Estate, Kala Mountains

After changing out of the drab outfit she had put on to contact the queen, Mavis found herself back in the communications room once again. She ran her hands down the front of her bright red shimmersilk gown and idly wondered how many more times she would be burdened with talking to Gardan's king. Though she doubted anything would impress King Padric, Mavis favored the dress because of how well it worked with her light skin and dark hair. She tapped in the proper commands and waited.

As usual, King Padric made Mavis wait to prove his importance. When he finally answered, he eyed her critically and skipped the pleasantries.

"I am told your plan has gone somewhat awry. Is this true?"

That's an understatement.

"Not at all. My plan has proceeded quite well," Mavis answered.

"I always knew you to be an ambitious woman, Lady Mavis, but nearly killing your own son is a dedicated step indeed," said Padric with a rare smile. "I commend your strategy, and I take it you are ready to proceed to the next phase."

"Almost ready," Mavis corrected. "I believe I have underestimated the length of time it will take for you to properly repair my son. His wounds will have to be answered for before the improvements can be implemented, and I am told those alone can take a year or two to complete."

The smile melted into the usual scowl.

"That is unfortunate. This partnership seems plagued with delays. What added incentive will you offer in exchange for the extra time and effort I must waste on behalf of your son?"

Mavis smiled carefully, trying not to seem too eager. Having Padric believe the suggestion a concession rather than something she deeply desired was crucial.

"I have had my people do some research on our young queen, and I believe she would provide your scientists with some fascinating results."

Despite the scowl, Padric looked intrigued.

"I have thought as much for a long time, but how will you deliver her without bringing our respective peoples to war?"

"It will not be easy, but I believe I will soon be in possession of the proper leverage," said Mavis.

"The sister?" asked Padric. "Did you not try and fail at that before?"

"The incident you refer to was some of my men trying to

acquire a target-of-opportunity, and yes, they failed at it," said Mavis. "However, I do not have to force the queen to do anything. If I can convince her to learn some special healing techniques found only on Gardan, she will come to you."

"You possess a very dangerous mind. Take care to not bring harm to yourself or your own in the process," Padric warned with a hard stare.

"That is sound advice, King Padric," Mavis said evenly. "I shall heed it. I only called to inform you that my son should arrive in a little over a week and advise you that I may be unreachable for a time. Dennel will be here to receive any reports your people send."

Padric blustered for a time, but Mavis calmly nodded at the right times and ignored the childish rants. After a few minutes, she concluded the conversation and signed off.

She had some frustration to work off, and she knew the perfect cure for it. A few instructions to the right people set things in motion nicely. Mavis decided to grab some fresh mountain air to clear her mind while she waited for Kellen to make the necessary preparations. He had indicated there might be some delay. She hoped not, but she trusted his judgment.

Chapter 35:
Anotech Assessment

Pirua (September) 1, 1539
Same Day
King Terosh's Private Chambers, Royal Palace, City of Rammon
"Are you sure there is nothing more I can do, Majesty?" asked Captain Ectosh Laocer.

"I am certain, Captain," answered Reia. "Ensure that the guards around this chamber are refreshed every few hours."

"It will be done," said Laocer solemnly.

Reia returned her full attention to her husband. She folded Terosh's hands neatly across his stomach, tucked her knees up to her chest, and wrapped her arms around them. Her forehead hovered over her knees. She held the position for a few seconds as the anotechs' disturbing words floated through her mind.

We sense much poison in him. Very powerful poison, but also very familiar.

What does that mean? Reia demanded.

We know this poison. We can fight it.

What aren't you telling me? Reia asked, feeling their hesitation as a fluttering in her stomach.

It is a form of comaladon. It changes structure to prevent eradication.

Reia's throat constricted, jamming her breath inside her chest.

Not again! Her mind protested the possibility that Terosh would die by the same poison that had claimed his mother. *Can you heal him?*

Not alone, but you can.

How? Her breath escaped in a rush, ending in a strangled sob.

The anotechs explained the task they required of her. They needed Reia to direct complete transfusions of anotechs so they could continually remove the poison from Terosh's system. The reality could not easily be explained with words. They could not tell her how many times she would have to lay her hands on her husband's burning hot chest and feed fresh anotechs through one hand while ones saturated with poison entered her through the other. To be fair, they did warn her about the discomfort she could experience during the process.

Reia accepted the role with grim determination and a sense of elation. She would not have to sit idly by while her husband's fate rested in others' hands. Worry about all that could go wrong tried to press in, but she crushed the half-formed thoughts and concentrated on directing the anotechs.

***

Pirua (September) 4, 1539

King Terosh's Private Chambers, Royal Palace, City of Rammon

A cool hand brushed Reia's forehead. She opened her eyes to find Dr. Dentelich leaning over her.

"How do you feel, Highness?" asked Dr. Dentelich. "Well rested, I hope. You've slept for more than two days."

Slept more than two days ... Terosh! The thoughts jolted her wide awake and she struggled to sit up.

Dr. Dentelich quickly straightened to avoid a collision.

I didn't dream, Reia realized, before pain engulfed her head. She knew she was falling back but could do nothing about it.

The doctor reached out, caught her, and eased her back to a prone position.

"Lie still. Your fever's gone, but you need to eat and drink," said the doctor.

"How is Terosh?" Reia asked, ignoring the reproving tone but obeying the good advice. With much effort, she turned her head to look at her husband.

He wore a simple pair of black pants and a loose white shirt. It surprised her that he wasn't tucked tightly under the covers.

"No change," Dr. Dentelich admitted. "We will need to discuss treatment options, but first, you must take care of your own needs."

"What options do we have?" Reia asked, turning back to Dentelich.

Before the doctor could answer, Sarie Verituse appeared in the threshold.

"May I enter, Your Majesty?"

"Yes, of course," said Reia, wishing she were not lying flat on her back.

"Thank you, I would hate to return to Lady Wellum with nothing to report," said Sarie. She bustled in carrying a large tray with fresh fruit and a glass of water.

"Kiata's here?" Reia asked, surprised. She tried sitting up again, slower this time.

After asking for and receiving permission, Dr. Dentelich helped Reia to a sitting position and tucked three pillows behind her.

Sarie shook her head.

"She said she or Master Todd would return this evening for a report, but I planned to tell her sooner." Sarie walked over to the table beside Reia.

Dr. Dentelich ducked out of the way and retreated to the foot of the bed.

Sarie reached with her left hand and tapped a few commands into the control panel near Reia's head. The table extended and a pair of slender stands descended to the floor. Sarie expertly swung the tray around and placed it on the table.

"Thank you," Reia said, not really interested in the food.

Dr. Dentelich opened his mouth to bluster more orders to eat, but Sarie stopped him with a gesture.

"Lady Kiata also said that she would give you a rather large piece of her mind if you refused to eat," said Sarie. "She added that if need be she would break into the palace and spoon feed you. It may not be my place to say anything, but I believe she would keep her word."

Reia rubbed at her temple to fight the weariness.

"I agree, and I surrender to your good will." Reia picked up a grape and rolled it between her thumb and forefinger. Her eyes flickered between Dr. Dentelich and Sarie who watched her intently. She raised the grape in a small salute before eating it. "You may tell my sister her persuasion skills have not waned."

"I will do so, Your Majesty," said Sarie, as a bright smile lit up her dark face. "I shall leave you to finish your meal in peace, and I believe Doctor Dentelich would like to speak to you alone."

One look at Dentelich's expression confirmed as much. Reia continued to pick at the fruit array and waited for the doctor to share his thoughts.

"You may speak your mind, doctor," said Reia, once it was clear he would not speak first.

Dentelich straightened.

"Your Grace, I have been a physician for the Royal House for more than thirty years," he said gravely. "I watched Queen Kila fall to comaladon mixed with poison from a gully fish." As he spoke, his expression melted from inscrutable to stricken. "I have never seen a poison like this. It is comaladon, but it has been modified." He stopped speaking when he noticed Reia nodding.

"I know. It changes form, so it's hard to treat," Reia said, repeating what the anotechs had told her. "But I can help him."

From Dr. Dentelich's distant expression, she doubted he had heard the last part.

"There are certain methods practiced on Gardan we could try," Dr. Dentelich offered. His hesitant tone conveyed deep reservations.

"Lady Mavis mentioned them in passing," said Reia. "She is sending Lord Kezem to Gardan for treatment. I assume it is for the methods you speak of, but you sound uncertain about them."

"They require sacrifice," Dr. Dentelich informed her.

Reia's hand froze midway to the fruit tray.

"What manner of sacrifice?" She let her hand flop down and rest in her lap.

Dr. Dentelich reluctantly explained the process of transferring blood from one person to another.

"It would kill Terosh to know someone died for him," said Reia.

Dentelich nodded wearily.

"I expected as much, which is why I hesitated to tell you about it. I can keep him sedated to let his body rest as much as possible, but it won't cure him."

"I can help him," Reia said again.

"How?" asked Dr. Dentelich.

Sedir's warnings against sharing about the anotechs came to the forefront of her mind.

"I cannot tell you how," said Reia. "It would break a vow I have made."

The doctor flushed with a fresh tide of anger.

"We are talking about your husband's life! I am his physician. I must know every treatment he receives!"

His tone provoked some anger in Reia, but she had not the energy to indulge it.

"I am aware of the topic," she said slowly, coming to a decision about how much to tell him. "As I am sure you are aware, members of the Royal House have access to power most people do not. I can help Terosh through this power, but no one can know the details of it, not even you."

"Saving him would be a miracle. The medical implications would be—"

"Doctor, no one can know," Reia repeated. "I don't know if I can save him. I think I can, but it won't be easy. It must remain a secret because if it were known everyone would expect a miracle and chaos would ensue upon any sign of failure."

They exchanged long, solemn looks.

"I will do what I can to help you," Dentelich promised. With the assurance hanging in the air like a blessing, he bowed to Reia and departed.

Chapter 36: Retribution

Pirua (September) 4, 1539
Same Day
The Lady's Estate, Kala Mountains

"I want you to tell me exactly how you failed me." Mavis had not liked the idea of waiting, but now that it was over, she did not mind half as much.

Sweat beaded on the man's brow and glistened in the bright light. He smelled powerfully of sour fear. Dr. Edwin Nabern ran his tongue across cracked lips.

"The charge was too strong," he whispered.

"Exactly." Mavis knew everything worth knowing about him, but she preferred to think of him in the detached sense. She mopped sweat from his face with a clean white cloth. Each gentle pat resulted in a muffled whimper. She contemplated offering him water but remembered the unfortunate incident where he had spit at her and decided against the small comfort. "And what else?"

"And I added a comaladon derivative I stole from Dr. Saddic," the man reluctantly admitted.

Mavis shut her eyes and swallowed the sudden rage that threatened to boil over and kill the man. When she spoke, her voice was almost lifeless.

"Why would you do such a thing?" Her eyes opened and stabbed into the man. "Why would you alter one of my plans?" The two questions unfolded in slow, rhythmic waves.

The man's lips trembled as he tried to keep a confession in. A few more seconds baking under her withering glare crashed his defenses and words poured forth.

"I was afraid of what you might do to them. When he contacted me, he said he knew exactly how you worked and that if I wanted to save my family I would do as he said."

"Who contacted you?" Mavis asked. Her tone cracked like a serlak rifle.

The man flinched.

"Keldor," he said.

"Which one?" Mavis asked, though she knew precisely which one.

"Ariman Keldor," answered the man.

He has finally chosen a side. Too bad. I had high hopes for him.

She was getting answers at last. They had been over this many times in the last couple of days. At first, the man had protested any wrongdoing and even defended his faulty calculations with scientific theories and experiments. Mavis had let Kellen and Lash explain the error of trying to justify mistakes and outright lying. They had clearly done well. She nodded appreciatively at the two who stood respectfully out of the way.

Lash, a lovely young Terabian woman with an unhealthy attachment to a plain, korverhide whip, lowered her eyes shyly. Kellen crossed his right arm across his chest in a salute and executed an elegant half bow to acknowledge Mavis's unspoken praise.

"Do you remember what I promised when I hired you?" asked Mavis. She took one more swipe at fresh sweat on the man's forehead and tossed the sullied cloth to the ground by his feet.

The man nodded miserably, but Mavis was pleased to see a touch of anger glitter behind his watery blue eyes. Stepping back, she lifted her right hand like someone lifting praise, then twisted her wrist with a flourish, and held her thumb and pointer finger about a centimeter apart. Lash's whip cracked into the wall by the man's left ear.

He yelped as if the blow had struck him. His hairless chest heaved, displaying the scars where some of Lash's other lessons had landed. The muscles in his arms and legs tensed instinctively, straining against the restraints securing him to the wall. He twisted his head as far to the right as it would go, inadvertently exposing his neck.

Feeling Lash's eagerness to strike, Mavis shook her head, sorry she had to disappoint the young woman.

"Do try to remember how much I loath unresponsiveness," said Mavis with a small sigh.

"Yes, I remember. You said you had a job where the rewards and risks would be extraordinary." The man's eyes darted about the room not daring to meet hers.

"And my promise?" she prompted.

He swallowed hard. The little color left to him drained from his face.

"Continuous work for me and protection for my family, pr-provided I succeeded."

"But you did not succeed," Mavis said slowly.

The man met her eyes as the statement yanked him out of the discomfort-induced stupor.

"Don't hurt them," he pleaded.

Mavis was impressed by the weight of will the man put behind his words.

"I'm going to let your work speak for itself." She pulled a controller from a pocket and tapped in a few instructions.

A vidscreen slid out of the ceiling behind her head to the left. She did not have to turn to see what it would show. Her instructions had been quite explicit. The man's wife and two children would be bound. Dressed in colored crossblades suits, they would each be seated with knees tucked up to their chests and hands and feet secured to one of the man's inventions.

The man renewed his attack against his unyielding restraints.

"No! They're innocent! You can't—"

Kellen's fist slammed into the man's gut, cutting off the rest of his protest.

"Speak civilly to the Lady," muttered Kellen.

The man sucked in great gasps, trying to catch his breath. Tears flowed freely down his face.

"Please, please, let them go. They are nothing to you."

"If they survive, I will set them free," Mavis promised. Then, she tapped in a few more commands to activate each device.

***

Pirua (September) 5, 1539
Village of Kerimia

Lucas Telon kept his senses alert for trouble as he walked through the deserted village streets. Boards covered most of the windows and shifting shadows covered the rest. Lucas felt nervous eyes follow his progress down the street. A faint breeze kicked up puffs of dust and brushed against Lucas's pants. He breathed deeply, enjoying the thrill of the hunt.

"These people are accustomed to fighting," said Kolknir, "but we are not here to destroy the village."

Lucas cast an annoyed glance at his mentor.

"I read the orders," he said.

"Yet you're still trying to provoke them," Kolknir pointed out. "We do not have time to indulge—"

"You want to kill them as much as I do," Lucas said. "Don't bother denying it. We're too much alike."

"If you were less brash, humbler, and better looking, I'd agree."

Lucas stopped, stunned by Kolknir's uncharacteristic flash of humor.

"Where—"

A red kerlak bolt slammed into the ground in front of Lucas, cutting off the rest of his question. His serlak pistols were in his hands an instant later, but by that time, Kolknir had drawn his serlak rifle from the holster across his back, aimed up, and fired into the inky blackness of a window.

A man's cry of pain sounded just before a satisfying clatter and thud. Then, relative silence fell again. A distant korver howl punctuated the eerie feeling that struck Lucas in the gut.

"You knew," Lucas said, torn between anger and relief. "How did you know the man was there? How did you know I'd stop?"

"Keep your senses alert," Kolknir advised. He started forward again, still gripping his rifle.

"My senses are alert," Lucas muttered, holstering his pistols and falling into step beside his mentor.

"You're distracted," said Kolknir. "If it continues, you will die. The Lady has little patience for repeated failure." He spoke almost pleasantly.

"This time, if I fail, you fail," said Lucas, noting that they were nearing their destination. He wished they could have ridden hov bikes to Keldor's door.

"Which is why you will not fail this time," Kolknir assured him. "But I cannot hold your hand on every mission. You had better shake off whatever has wrapped around your mind."

"It's nothing," Lucas insisted. A quick search of his feelings proved him a liar, but he forced the irritation aside.

You're pathetic. She's moved on.

His thoughts froze on the last three words. He wondered at his inability to do the same. His love for Reia Antellio had never even been fully realized.

"Focus," Kolknir snapped.

Lucas shivered and forced himself to concentrate. Channeling his frustration, he kicked the door. It flew open and banged against the wall.

"Try the handle next time," Kolknir said.

Lucas ignored him and stepped into the cozy front hallway. Signs of a female presence were everywhere. Wildflowers arranged in simple vases added bright spots of color. Scented candles filled the air with the pointed, yet pleasant, fragrance of kintral trees. Baskets of varying sizes were stashed in nearly every conceivable space, holding everything from clothes to wood to drying ira petals. Lucas wondered what the rest of the house looked like if all that was packed into the first hall.

He was just about to ask which direction they should search when a female voice spoke from the darkness beyond the candlelight.

"Leave my home." Her voice held enough command that Lucas suspected she had something to emphasize her order.

"Where is Ariman?" asked Kolknir, shifting his rifle toward the voice.

"I haven't seen him for months," said the woman with enough bitterness to lend credence to her statement. "I've barely seen him since the Alliance formed. What makes you think he'd come back now?"

To protect you, Lucas thought as his danger senses flared.

He snatched up one of his pistols and threw his body toward the left wall just as Kolknir fired several shots into the darkness above the woman's head.

She screamed.

Something heavy dropped to the ground. Light flooded the hall from glowpanels built into the walls and ceiling.

Lucas squinted into the glare.

The woman screamed again, a cry of anguish and disbelief this time. She knelt beside Ariman Keldor and threw herself across his chest, sobbing.

Kolknir reached over and plucked a kerlak pistol from the holster tucked in the small of Lucas's back. Then, he calmly shot the weeping woman twice. Both blue stun beams slammed into her right shoulder. A sharp cry from the woman was answered by a groan from the man on the floor. Kolknir returned Lucas's pistol and walked to where the woman still lay atop her husband. He rolled her off, gripped the man by the shoulders, and hauled him into the hallway.

Each of Kolknir's moves tonight had been marked by swiftness and decisiveness. Lucas sighed, feeling silly with his serlak pistol raised in the air.

I guess I do have a lot to learn yet.

Kolknir knelt beside the man and checked his wounds.

Meanwhile, Lucas searched the small house to make sure they were truly alone. He returned as Kolknir administered a stimulant shot. The man gasped as the stimulant temporarily held off death. A quick visual assessment said it would not work for long.

Most men would be dead already.

Two holes in the man's chest, one near his left shoulder and the other a little lower but on the right side, formed pools of blood steadily working their way toward each other.

"Your … mission done," the man said haltingly. "Don't … hurt—"

"We're not here to kill your wife, Ariman," Kolknir assured him. "The Lady sends her regrets and asks why you betrayed her."

The man shook his head.

Kolknir looked up at Lucas and nodded toward the woman's still form.

Understanding his meaning and eager to be of some use, Lucas contemplated the best way to accomplish his new task. Though short, the woman looked solidly built. Lucas collected a stimulant shot from the case Kolknir had left open on the floor and stuck it in the top part of the woman's right arm. He returned the spent dispenser to the case and closed it. Then, he stepped over the groggy woman, knelt behind her, and pulled her up to a kneeling position so her husband could see her face. He considered adding a dagger to the picture but both his hands were occupied propping the woman up.

"Give me an answer, or we will have to question your wife," Kolknir said.

"She … doesn't know," Ariman protested. His voice sounded weaker than before.

"For his father," answered the woman.

Ariman grunted but nodded.

"Revenge," he confirmed, his voice fading even further.

Kolknir glared down in disgust.

"You are a fool, Ariman Keldor, and you deserve your fate. I should kill your wife here in front of you just to make your last moments as miserable as possible."

Lucas agreed. He didn't know the details, but he knew Keldor had endangered one of the Lady's recent plans. It had something to do with the Colored Crossblades Tournament accident, but Lucas had not been privy to the original plan. Therefore, he remained uncertain as to how Keldor had caused the plan to go awry.

"Kezem … is … Mal—" Death cut off the rest of Ariman Keldor's words.

"Ah," said Kolknir, as if Keldor's last words explained everything.

The woman's soft sobs held off the silence that tried to fall.

"What did he mean?" Lucas studied his mentor intently.

"He knew," answered Kolknir. "I wonder that the Lady did not tell us he knew."

Knew what? Lucas glared the question at Kolknir.

The woman fought his grasp suddenly.

Lucas held on for a few seconds, but eventually, he let the woman struggle free and stood up.

"He knew Maledek's real identity. He also knew the Lady," explained Kolknir.

"Why does that matter?" Lucas asked. "I know. You know. I'm sure a lot of people know."

Kolknir shook his head.

"Only a privileged few had access to that knowledge. It matters because it explains the Lady's anger."

A sniffling noise drew Lucas's attention to the floor where the woman clutched at her husband's bloody shirt and wept.

Lucas cocked a questioning eyebrow at Kolknir.

His mentor spared only a glance at the woman before he picked up his case of stimulant shots.

"Leave her," he said.

Chapter 37:
Healer's Return

Pirua (September) 5, 1539
Same Day
King Terosh's Private Chambers, Royal Palace, City of Rammon
Dr. Ezzai Dentelich finished his examination of King Terosh Minstel. The burns, bruises, and cuts decorating the king's body had largely disappeared. Though it pained Ezzai to admit it, he knew nothing he had done could account for the rapid healing.

The queen's words sounded in Dentelich's mind.

Members of the Royal House have access to power most people do not.

Her words troubled Dentelich for several reasons. Needing to think, he sat down on the chair he had set up to keep vigil beside the king. His scientific mind was simultaneously intrigued and vexed by not knowing how she intended to heal the king. If he could convince her to let him understand, perhaps he could find a way to utilize the power without compromising the secrets. He shook his head, amazed to find himself accepting the queen's strange healing powers as legitimate science. Not long ago, he would have fought fiercely to defend the purity of conventional medicine.

A thought struck him, and he gasped. Sitting bolt upright, Dentelich pressed his fingertips to the sides of his temple to concentrate. Besides Queen Kila and now Terosh, Dentelich rarely ever treated members of the royal family. Years ago, when he had been young and eager to impress his mentor, Dentelich had pored over the palace's medical records. With close to a thousand regular staff and about half that number in Royal Guards and security officers plus any current guests, Dentelich and his staff kept very busy.

He searched his mind for actual encounters with the royals and recalled about half a dozen occurrences throughout his term as head physician. One of them was a birth. He frowned, remembering the scandal surrounding Prince Taytron's birth. As per Gardanian custom, the queen had confined herself to quarters throughout her term, refusing all medical aid except that rendered by her personal maidens.

King Teorn had protested so strongly that the queen had acquiesced to Reshner customs by Terosh's birth. Besides that, Taytron broke his left arm and right leg on separate occasions, Terosh punched through a glass window, Kila had been poisoned, and Teorn had been depressed when she died. Dentelich did not count the last incident as his case because he had turned it over to Dr. Briella Ender.

Taytron walked on that leg far too soon, and there wasn't enough blood around Terosh and the broken window. Both realizations made Dentelich's stomach lurch. *What else have I missed?*

Before his thoughts could spin toward panic, the sound of the inner door opening interrupted Dentelich. He dropped his hands to his sides and stood hastily as the queen entered the room trailed by her sister. The Ranger wore simple black pants, black boots, a white blouse, and a blue and black travel cloak that fell to her waist. Something about her looked different. She was halfway across the room before Dentelich realized she wore no weapon. A Ranger without a banistick seemed as awkward as a cook with no food.

The queen wore a black cloak that engulfed her body from the neck down. The cowl framed her face as she entered, but she threw it off as she approached Terosh's bed. Then, slowly, her left hand appeared from under the cloak, reached up, and unfastened the clasp holding the cloak together beneath her chin. With practiced ease, she swung the cloak off, rolled it into a bundle, and placed it on the foot of the bed. The cloak's removal revealed a simple purple night dress.

Dentelich's cheeks flamed as his breath caught in his throat. Before the king's accident, he had hardly seen the queen in anything but an elegant gown or a combat training outfit. During the two days she had slept straight through, the servants had clothed her in loose pants and a long-sleeved nightshirt. He had never seen her like this. The thin straps revealed gentle, sloping shoulders connected to thin, toned arms which bore a few faint scars.

"I thought it best to save someone the trouble of changing me should this healing venture have similar results to the last time," said

Queen Reia. Her eyes lowered. "I apologize if I'm making you uncomfortable, Doctor."

Her words brought Dentelich back to his senses. He drew his shoulders back like a soldier coming to attention.

"No apology necessary, Your Majesty. I am thankful for the opportunity to witness this … momentous event." He searched for the proper term.

"Healing," supplied the Ranger.

Dentelich flinched, wondering how he had not noticed her standing right next to him. He cast a questioning look her way.

"I am here to translate for you, Doctor," said the Ranger, looking at King Terosh's still form. Her voice was low and calm. "You may call me Kiata. I have no need for titles. Tonight, I am not here as a Ranger, merely a guide."

Ah, that is why she bears no weapons.

"If you are to be my guide, then please call me Ezzai," said Dr. Dentelich. "Tonight, I am not a doctor, merely an observer."

Kiata smiled as he mimicked her phrasing. She turned her attention back to the bed and nodded.

"She is almost ready to begin. We should retreat to avoid disturbing her."

When they reached the windows, Kiata motioned for Dentelich to be seated then settled onto the wide cushion nestled beneath the window with the clearest view of the bed.

Dentelich watched as the queen climbed up onto the bed and crawled over to the king's still form. Kneeling beside the king, she leaned over and ran her left hand down the side of his cheek twice. The glowlamp set beside King Terosh's head presented her somber expression in stark detail.

"To honor tradition, she prepared a song for him," Kiata whispered. "Healing is a gift given to very few. No matter what our Council says, she will always be a Healer and a Ranger."

Dentelich's heart lurched as the queen's voice floated to him.

"Shelsuoresfet abriesepalasu," sang the queen. (Shell-soo-ore-ez-fet ah-bri-eh-say-pal-la-soo)

"Should your ears fail to bear these words to you," said Kiata.

The song continued with the queen singing a line and pausing while her sister translated.

Queen: "Sansemasuspira." (Sahn-say-mah-soo-spy-ear-ah)

Ranger: "Feel them with your spirit."

Queen: "Peremscritonsuelstom." (Pear-rehm-screet-on-soo-el-stowm)

Ranger: "Let them write upon your heart."

Queen: "Peremlevesusalua alieucongrasi." (Pear-rehm-lev-eh-soos-ah-loo-ah ah-lie-oo-con-grah-see)

Ranger: "Let them carry your soul to a place of safety."

The queen shifted her knees to one side so she could sit closer to the king and face him. She picked up his left hand, clasped it tightly for two seconds, drew it to her lips, and kissed it. Then, resting her left cheek on the back of his hand, she continued, "Idesuon mekeroesus." (Ee-day-soo-on may-care-oh-ee-soos)

Ranger: "I told you once my love is yours."

Queen: "Prasuoramantomoa." (Prah-soo-ore-ah-man-toh-moh-ah)

Ranger: "May you hear it many more."

Queen: "Difetesasehsuliese." (Dee-fet-ez-ah-say-soo-lie-esse)

Ranger: "Hard as it is to see you like this."

Queen: "Cremploraidesicry." (Crem-plore-ray-day-see-cry)

Ranger: "Please believe me when I say."

Queen: "Kerosimsusninqwirmessecam." (Care-oh-seem-soos-nen-qwhere-eh-say-cam)

Ranger: "A love like ours cannot be conquered this way."

The queen lifted her head off her husband's hand. Next, she returned the hand to its resting place across his stomach. Then, she maneuvered her knees close to her chest and folded her hands around the left one, so she could hold the position. Her head slumped down in a gesture of grief, and when she sang again, Dentelich had to strain to hear her.

Queen: "Selvafelshelsupertosovali." (Sell-va-fell-shell-soo-pear-toe-so-val-ee)

Ranger: "Part of me feels, should you perish so would I."

Queen: "Efnonencorponamin." (Ef-noh-nen-corp-oh-nah-min)

Ranger: "If not in body then in mind."

Queen: "Etoiknoivalirencresonta." (Et-toe-ee-know-ee-valley-rain-cray-son-tah)

Ranger: "Yet I know I would go on living."

Queen: "Jusalevteparosucompleame." (Joo-sah-lev-tay-par-oh-soo-com-play-ah-meh)

Ranger: "Just to carry the part of you at one with me."

The queen's voice subtly changed, becoming stronger and more determined.

Queen: "Ehvikerohatotpuntier." (Eh-vie-care-oh-ha-tot-poon-tie-eh)

Ranger: "If ever love had any power."

Queen: "Praetonsufietahiasu." (Pray-ton-soo-fie-et-ah-ee-ah-soo)

Ranger: "May it be enough to heal you."

Queen: "Idesuon mekeroesus." (Ee-day-soo-on may-care-oh-ee-soos)

Ranger: "I told you once my love is yours."

Queen: "Prasuoramantomoa." (Prah-soo-ore-ah-man-toh-moh-ah)

Ranger: "May you hear it many more."

The queen held the last note until her sister's quiet translation had finished. Then, she repeated the song in the common tongue.

Dentelich had found it touching the first time through, even with the translation pauses, but the second time made his eyes sting. It presented the desire to heal and strengthened it with the underlying promise to go to great lengths to succeed.

"Now, she will draw the poison out of him," Kiata explained.

"How long will it take?" asked Dentelich, watching with interest as the queen climbed off the end of the bed and walked around to the chair set up next to the bed.

Pulling the chair closer, Queen Reia sat down and placed her left hand high on the king's chest and her right hand on his stomach, just above his folded hands. Body tense, the queen leaned forward and bowed her head as if resisting the urge to pull her hands away.

Dentelich took two swift steps forward before the Ranger pulled him to a halt.

"I don't know how long it will take," Kiata said, speaking rapidly. Her clipped tone and strong grip said she was holding a lot of emotion at bay. "It could be minutes; it could be hours. We will know when she's done." She released her hold on Dentelich's shoulder but looked ready to stop him again if he moved to interrupt the healing.

"How? What is she doing?" The need to do something helpful made Dentelich's questions come out harsher than intended.

"She said she will rest when she finishes," Kiata answered, appearing equally as frustrated. She spun away from him. "As for what she is doing, you know about as much as I, Doctor. Our role is to tend to her when she finally rests."

The bitterness in her voice stunned Dentelich.

"You disapprove," he said when the ability to speak returned.

"I disapprove," Kiata agreed with a nod. She took a position beside the chair where the queen sat and knelt. "I hate seeing her like this, and I hate waiting and wondering whether or not a healing like this will kill her."

"Surely, it cannot be that dangerous," Dentelich protested. He waited for her to agree. When no agreement was forthcoming, he stepped forward again. "We should stop her at once! We cannot lose them both!"

Kiata intercepted him again, this time by stepping into his path.

"We will not lose them both," she promised.

"How can—"

"She is taking the poison out of him. If anything, I worry more for her than him. She knows exactly what he means to the people." The Ranger looked very near tears.

Words twisted around in Dentelich's stomach.

Would she trade her life for his?

Dentelich did not know much about the queen, but what little he had observed told him she would.

They watched in silent agony as Queen Reia held her position. When Dentelich could stand it no more he paced the wide bed chamber. He lost count of the times he crossed and re-crossed the room. His legs ached as much from the tension as from the unexpected exercise. Watching the Ranger woman stand vigil to the right of and a little behind the queen did not help Dentelich's nerves.

How can she stand to stay still so long?

Dentelich quickened his pace unconsciously trying to balance the Ranger's inactivity.

"It is done for the day," Kiata declared at last.

Dentelich turned so fast he nearly pulled something in his back. His eyes immediately fell upon the queen who lay draped over the king's body with her head resting between her hands. The sight touched him. They looked so terribly young.

Our hopes rest on them.

Dentelich might have wept if he knew how many days he would witness a healing battle fought for his king's life. He could have delegated the duty of watching, but he learned much by seeing the queen work and listening to her address the king's still form. It did not take long for his admiration to morph into genuine affection.

When the king finally shed his unnatural sleep a few months

later, Dentelich had more to do to get his charge fully healed. Even with the queen's faithful ministrations and Dentelich's finest work, King Terosh's health remained fragile for several years.

Chapter 38: Save the Queen

Pirua (September) 6, 1539
The Lady's Estate, Kala Mountains

"Welcome back," said a rich, female voice from behind.

Nera Tarpon stiffened and reached for her kerlinblade. She stopped just short of drawing the blade but let her hand rest a second upon the hilt.

"Lord Kezem said you had studies of a different sort for me to attend to," said Nera, turning to face Lady Mavis.

"To succeed in your mission, you must study the queen," said Lady Mavis.

"To what end?" asked Nera. Her heart fluttered. After all this time, she still could not fathom why Lady Mavis had chosen to train her.

"To become her for a short time," answered Lady Mavis. "Come with me, and I shall explain."

The flutter in Nera's heart turned to a frantic pounding as she followed Lady Mavis out of the waiting room and through several long halls in the labyrinth that was the Lady's lair. Nera resisted the urge to skip with girlish delight. She had always loved exploring new places. As a child, she had driven her mother and the servants mad looking for her.

As Nera began wondering when they would reach their destination, Lady Mavis stopped and ushered her into a room filled with three wide vidscreens, a few hologram projectors, two vidrecorders, several comfortable chairs, and a very strange floor. The far side of the room had simple, smooth wooden floorboards, but the rest of the room was a patchwork of small squares featuring every sort of walking surface from loose sand to hard-packed dirt to fresh grass. Nera took two cautious steps into the room and stopped.

"Here, you will learn to walk as the queen does," said Lady Mavis. "There's a control panel that will allow you to simulate nearly any terrain. Dennel will instruct you in its use later. The vidscreens can show you many hours of the queen walking to or from some function. Eventually, you will record your work and compare your gait to the queen's."

"Why is it so important to master how she walks, my Lady?" asked Nera.

"It is of no greater or lesser importance than learning how she speaks or dines, but success depends on mastering everything," said Lady Mavis.

"But why must I pretend to be the queen?" asked Nera.

Lady Mavis glided past Nera to the desk holding a lot of the recording equipment. There she reached down and pressed some buttons Nera could not see. The door swung shut with a click of heavy-sounding locks.

"You must pretend to be the queen to save her," said Lady Mavis without turning.

"What threatens her? Why did you choose me? What can I do?" Nera was about to spew more questions, but Lady Mavis halted her with a delicate gesture. Strange anxiety made Nera's fingers twitch to hold her kerlinblade.

"You are perfectly safe here," said Lady Mavis, sounding slightly weary. She turned and swept her eyes over Nera from head to foot. "My reasons for choosing you are many and varied, not the least of them is that I believe you can accomplish the ends I seek. Your physical build is a close match for our queen, and you possess a spirit conducive to learning new skills."

Nera still felt lost.

"What are we fighting for, my Lady? You keep saying we shall save the queen, but I know your heart is not truly committed to that end." Nera paused as thoughts coalesced in her mind. "I do not believe saving her is your end at all, so when does the end come? When may I return home?" The last question surprised her for it conjured a mixture of strong emotions. She missed her husband, but she enjoyed the challenge of this new life. Having seen and done so many terrible and wonderful things, she could never simply return to her life as Lady Tarpon, wife of Brook.

"Rescuing the queen from this current threat may not be my ultimate end, but that is indeed your end. Once you finish, you may go with my blessing," said Lady Mavis. "Like my reasons for choosing you for this task, my motivations concerning the queen's welfare vary. You know what you need to know and must trust me on the rest. For now, I bid you study well and lay other thoughts aside." She executed a graceful turn and again pressed some buttons.

Nera heard the locks snap open and felt her heart jump with more inexplicable fear.

Chapter 39: Awakening

Lanolin (February) 13, 1540
King Terosh's Private Chambers, Royal Palace, City of Rammon

The darkness lightened.

A familiar voice reached down through the remaining darkness.

"Terosh, I know you're awake," said Reia. "The anotechs told me as much. Please open your eyes and drink. I want to hear your voice. I'm getting tired of talking to myself."

It took tremendous effort, but Terosh finally gathered enough strength to force his eyes open. The sight of Reia leaning over him took some of the meager breath left to him. Her soft hands brushed his cheeks, chin, and neck. Her left hand settled over his heart and fresh anotechs flooded into him, restoring a sense of energy and vitality. Relieved tears streaked her face, but a brilliant smile lent her a beauty that no tears could diminish.

"Don't even think about rising," said Reia. She dashed some tears away. "A newborn kyrie chick could knock you flat with a look. You've slept over five months."

Five months?

Her hand left his chest, and soon, he found a waterbag spout between his lips. Cool water poured slowly down his throat. He gulped it down as quickly as possible.

"Take it slowly," Reia said, easing the bag back so the water gently trickled. "The anotechs kept you in good repair, but you've had nothing but Dr. Dentelich's nutrient injections for a long time."

Terosh drank his fill and rested his head back against the

pillow. His body tried to drag him down to sleep again, but his mind fought for consciousness. The effort left him short of breath. He closed his eyes.

"What did I miss?" he asked.

Reia's gentle laughter wrapped around his sinking consciousness and held him fast. She picked up his left arm and moved it aside then curled into the space created.

"You do realize this is going to take a long time, right?"

"Hope so," Terosh murmured. Despite the high energy cost, Terosh curled his left arm up to draw his wife closer. He had missed feeling her for five whole months and come close to never laying eyes on her again. He wasn't about to let another moment be wasted.

Once settled, Reia sighed.

"Let's see. While you slept, Fort Savad suffered some structural damage from a windstorm. We received enough sympathetic messages to nearly crash the network. The Huz Mon salt mines had a riot. A maw was reported on the Kevloth Plains, but thankfully, no one was hurt. The Morden Lowlands flooded. Mount Kelleth had a minor eruption, covering Korch and its surrounding villages with ash. GAPP delivered a few more sweetly worded threats not to interfere in the Rorge System. Kiata and Todd left a couple of days ago to undergo a ceremony so they can have a child. Oh, and I politely declined at least three marriage invitations."

Terosh stiffened.

"Marriage invitations?"

Reia's laughter vibrate pleasantly against his side as she tightened her one-armed embrace.

"Yes, it seems if you were conveniently gone, Reshner could forge strong alliances with Benata, Riab, or Praxitti VII," Reia said matter-of-factly. She nestled her head to a slightly different position on Terosh's shoulder. Her voice softened. "I could have had an emperor, a sultan, or a high king. Call me selfish, but I think I'll keep the king I've got."

***

Lanolin (February) 14, 1540-Jira (March) 1, 1542
Royal Palace, City of Rammon

One would think the healing process would have sped up once King Terosh regained consciousness, but it took over a year to fully purge the poison. About that time, he took to reading Senate and Governors Council reports and making some of the decisions necessary to run the government. Over the next year or so, his body slowly regained most of the strength lost during the months of inactivity.

Terosh could not know how fierce the battle would be inside his body as the Linonos and Dalonos—light and dark anotechs—fought for him. Although the Dark Ones knew they could not kill him, they kept him weak.

For her part, Lady Mavis Altran spent the anxious months of Kezem's recovery, arranging things for the final stages of her grand plan. As Terosh slowly mended, countless days passed while Mavis struggled to stick to her plans. It would have been simplicity itself to assassinate Reia and Terosh, especially with the anotechs subduing him, but the king and queen had a key role to play in other plans.

Chapter 40: Return of the Restler Raiders

Jira (March) 2, 1542
The Lady's Estate, Kala Mountains

Shadow Guard Nolan Demilak had proven himself invaluable time and again. Mavis replayed his message twice to let the good news settle fully upon her. In the privacy of her office, she indulged in a gesture of profound relief by placing her hands over her heart. Her fingertips brushed the pendant bearing the symbol of her father's house. She tipped it up to examine. Its smooth metal soothed her by reminding her why she had spent most of her life planning to destroy the Minstel name.

Kezem will leave Gardan within the week.

The message repeated countless times in her mind and heart. To her dismay, she felt tears prickling her eyes. The depths of her relief surprised her. She had not realized how much she longed for Kezem's return. Mitrek's cowardly flight to an unknown planet hurt more than she wanted to admit. Eldon and his family still resided in Idonia, but as expected, he had withdrawn emotionally, hiding behind his work.

It is time.

The three small words thrilled her. Mavis snatched up her comm and called Dennel. They had a lot of calls to make. The next phase needed to be executed with precise timing to provide a diversion.

Within minutes, Kolknir's hologram appeared before Mavis.

"Is Lucas with you?" Mavis asked, before Kolknir could bother with greetings.

"I am," said Lucas, stepping into view.

"What are your orders?" queried Kolknir.

"It is time to move against the Restler-Tarpon Alliance," Mavis announced. "Dennel will send you instructions. Kolknir, you will strike at the Tarpons while Lucas harries the Restlers. Remember, I want them scattered and broken, but no names must be released until the time is right! Many of the key people will need to be eliminated, but leave the lower ranks alone. My son will have need of them one day. Turn those you can and kill whomever you must, except Brook Tarpon and Merisia Restler. I have further need of them."

"As you wish," said Lucas.

"Yes, my Lady," said Kolknir a half-second later.

Mavis ended the communication.

Now, we shall see if all those visits to Terosh's bedside were worth it.

With a giddiness she'd not felt in years, Mavis went to find Nera Tarpon. The young woman would need to be put in isolation. Despite her orders, Mavis did not trust that no names would be leaked. If necessary, Brook Tarpon and his sister, Merisia, would persuade Nera to continue with the plan, but Mavis really wanted to avoid that kind of persuasion. Her plan would work best if Nera Tarpon believed in the cause.

***

Jira (March) 4, 1542
Restler Estate, City of Meritab

Life had not been particularly kind to Merisia Restler. Even as she gazed upon the peaceful face of her infant son, she wondered what her unborn daughter would have been like had she survived the fight at the Deegan Estate. The familiar ache of guilt wormed its way through Merisia's chest.

I'm sorry, her mind cried to both children.

She longed to turn back time. Had she known the cost, she would never have run away. She also wished her scarred heart knew how to truly love this little life before her.

What sort of man will you be, Daniel Restler?

Her thoughts flooded with terrifying images. She imagined Daniel as a boy catching frogs and mice as she once had with Talyon Keldor. The image smiled sweetly and lifted up a squirming frog. The scene gave her peace until the boy tripped and fell headlong into the shallow stream. Pure, impotent fear and rage nearly burst her heart as she watched him slowly drown. Next, she saw him as a young man wounded through the side with a kerlinblade, slowing bleeding to death. Finally, he was a grown man, looking just like Gareth, glaring down at her in arrogant disapproval.

She could almost hear him say, *"You let my sister die!"*

Merisia burst into tears and dropped to her knees by Daniel's crib. The noise woke him, and he cried. Standing, Merisia leaned over the crib.

"I'm sorry!" she said, rubbing a trembling hand across the baby's chest and stomach. Tears poured out of her and rained down on Daniel. He fussed some more. "I'm sorry," she whispered again, trying to turn her head away and let the tears fall elsewhere.

"Don't be," said a male voice behind her.

Too stunned to scream and almost too tired to care, Merisia slowly turned to face the man. Daniel wailed but her heart numbed to the plaintive cry. Feeling faint, she braced herself against her son's crib. Strangely, the kerlak pistol leveled at her chest had a calming effect on her. She sniffled and wiped at some tears, wishing she could conjure enough emotion to be upset.

"My apologies, Lady Restler. Please make no sudden moves," said the man. "I did not bring a pair of stuncuffs for you, and I have business to conduct with your husband. He should be along in a moment."

"Kill me," Merisia dared. It took three seconds to recognize the hoarse, desperate voice as her own. She remembered saying the very same thing to Talyon Keldor and prayed he was somewhere safe. Gareth and his henchmen could tell her a hundred times that he died, but she knew Taly was alive.

Before the man could respond, a commotion in the hallway caught Merisia's attention. A few muffled curses and a thump sounded. Then the door flew open and three men burst into the baby's room. Gareth stood between two men with thick stuncuffs covering his forearms. To Merisia's surprise, her heart lurched with sympathy.

"I demand to know—" Gareth began. His protest turned to a pained grunt when the men holding him each kicked a knee and put pressure on his shoulders.

Merisia glared at the two men and received a second shock. The man holding Gareth's right shoulder refused to meet her eyes, but she knew him. Merisia gasped and stared, dumbfounded.

Nobody spoke.

"Hello, Meri," greeted the familiar man.

She drew short quick breaths, but none of them gave her

enough air to speak.

"It's not what you think," said the lead man kindly.

If he'd not pointed a gun at her, Merisia might even have believed he cared.

"What should I think?" she asked.

The man on Gareth's right snapped his head up, finally meeting her gaze.

"I'm here to protect you," said her brother.

"You can imagine why I'm having some trouble believing you, Alden, a lot of trouble actually," said Merisia.

"I can vouch for him," said the leader. He braced the gun against the crib's railing. "The RT Alliance is failing. Alden chose the right side and wanted to make certain you do as well, Lady Merisia."

"We are an alliance of legitimate businesses," Gareth said.

"You are an alliance of thieves and thugs," responded the lead intruder.

Gareth laughed sharply.

"That's interesting from a man threatening my wife and son! Who are you? Who sent you? What do they want?"

The attacker laughed mirthlessly.

"We want justice, Master Restler," said the attacker. His kerlak pistol darted away from Merisia's chest and sent a brilliant red beam toward the child.

"No!" cried Merisia and Gareth.

Unaware of her actions, Merisia threw herself at the man, pushing him back a few steps. Her limbs flailed and her fingers sought blood from any part of the man she could reach. One nail caught the vile man just below his left eye. He screamed. The sound of shattering glass struck Merisia at the same time burning pain engulfed her stomach and sharp pain exploded from her head. Neither pain could match that gushing from her heart. She welcomed darkness.

***

Jira (March) 4, 1542
Same Day
Tarpon Estate, City of Kalmata

Kolknir hoped Lucas finished his mission well. The man had sounded truly distraught when he checked in, but at least he'd included adequate vid footage to convince Brook Tarpon not to be an idiot.

"Good evening, Master Tarpon," Kolknir greeted entering Brook's office.

"Who are you?" Brook demanded, right hand sliding under his desk.

"I am a servant of the Lady. She requires your presence and sent me to fetch you. Will you come peaceably?"

"What does she want with me?" asked Brook. "She already has my wife."

"It is not my place to question the Lady's will, neither is it yours. I ask again, will you come peaceably?"

"No," answered Brook, his features hardening.

Kolknir waited, wishing the man would hurry up and use that pathetic gun under his desk. With a shrug, Kolknir tossed his infopad onto Brook's desk.

"You're welcomed to verify those images if you like."

Brook reluctantly picked up the infopad and flipped through the images. His lips pressed tightly together, and his eyes flashed with anger.

"What makes you think I care?" he spat. "The brat probably deserves whatever you have in store for her."

Kolknir raised both eyebrows. He had never known the Lady to misjudge a situation, but if Brook truly did not care about his little sister then Kolknir would have to deal with him the hard way. Kolknir met Brook's glare until the man looked away, and in that moment, Kolknir understood. Brook truly cared. He just did not wish to let Kolknir hold the knowledge over him.

"That's not a very brotherly thing to say," Kolknir scolded. "And I can tell you care because you look queasy. Don't worry; she's perfectly safe with my men. Your brother is watching over her."

"Why would Alden help you?" Brook asked.

"He helps for the same reason you will—to save your dear sister from something worse than death." Kolknir didn't know what that would be, but he figured Brook would fill in the gaps as he liked. He couldn't permanently harm Merisia if he wanted to since the Lady wanted her alive, but Brook did not know that. Seeing Brook consider going for the gun, Kolknir added, "Leave it. You don't want to test me."

Brook leaned back in his chair looking resigned.

"Where are we going?"

***

Jira (March) 4, 1542
Same Day

City of Meritab

Gareth Restler wandered the dark streets. Several shady beings started to approach him, but one look at his expression made them back away. He should be dead. His wife and son were dead. Things had not always been smooth with Merisia, but they had grown closer in the last few years. She might not have been perfect, but their son certainly did not deserve to be shot in his crib. Gareth wanted to fight something; perhaps killing would assuage his grief.

He had sought refuge in a friend's tavern where he watched story after story of strange attacks unfold. Reporters glowed with excitement as one RT Alliance safe house and estate after another fell under attack.

Gareth did not know which stories told whole truths, which told half-truths, and which contained no truth, but he knew for certain the Alliance was no more. His heart shattered to little sharp shards. He melted them in the fires of his anger, knowing eventually they would crystallize into something unbreakable.

Chapter 41: Subdue and Switch

Jira (March) 6, 1542
Upper East Library to King Terosh's Private Chambers, Royal Palace, City of Rammon

"Pardon me, Your Majesty," said Aster Captain Surd Antar. "Lady Mavis Altran has arrived to visit with the king. She is with him now."

The usual mixed feelings fluttered through Reia as she put down *To Conquer the Sea: A History of Osem.* While grateful Terosh's eccentric aunt visited him often, she could not help feeling some resentment. Some warning would have been nice so Reia could arrange a proper welcome and give the impression she knew what transpired in her own home.

Thanking Captain Antar, Reia dashed from the room, her bare feet slapping the polished floors. Midway to her destination, Reia halted and considered whether or not she should change. Since no important meeting or audience had been scheduled, Reia wore only plain white pants and a light blue shirt with silver patches artfully arranged across the neck and down both sleeves. In an effort to remove herself from the palace trappings, she had left both weapons and jewelry in her room.

Antar would throw a fit if he knew her loose sleeves held neither the miniature kerlak pistol nor a tiny dagger in a sheath. Her training had been too thorough for her to simply forget them, but she felt reasonably secure in the palace. She paused to consider what Lady Mavis would think of her casual attire and lack of queenly accoutrements. Reia decided she didn't really care. Her pride minded a great deal, but since she tried not to indulge that less-than-admirable emotion, she would leave the judgment up to Lady Mavis.

Inner equilibrium restored, Reia finished her journey to Terosh's private chambers at a respectable pace. She quietly greeted the two Royal Guards flanking the door. They saluted her in unison and the one nearest the control panel immediately pressed the button to open the door. Reia hesitated the necessary second for the door to finish swinging aside.

They looked awfully serious, almost grim, Reia thought once she was three steps into the outer room.

Dismissing the thought, she strode toward the main bedchamber. Upon entering the middle room, Reia heard the sound dampers activating. She crossed the room in a few quick steps and reached for the door's control panel. The door opened before she touched the panel.

At first, she saw nothing unusual. Terosh sat up with a pillow propped behind him and the covers tucked neatly around him. A figure Reia assumed must be Lady Mavis stood next to the bed. A heavy maroon cloak with a deep cowl hid most of the figure's body. One look at Terosh's pale face and furious expression stopped Reia cold with one foot across the threshold. She had expected the pale part, but the fury surprised her. Terosh ranked among the most even tempered, affable men she knew. She had never seen him this angry. The dark emotion thickened the air.

"Welcome, Your Grace. I trust you know my companions," said Lady Mavis. She waved gracefully at the space to Reia's right.

Heart nearly freezing in her chest, Reia stumbled forward two steps. When her heart started beating again, it pounded on her ribs painfully. Her throat constricted and her hands instinctively searched her waist for a banistick. Even after a few years, her fingers ached to hold a Ranger weapon. Conflicting impulses warred for control. One impulse told her to whirl and flee while the other bid her to comfort Terosh. She did neither. Instead, she looked where the woman indicated.

"You'll have to forgive me for the theatrics," Lady Mavis said, affecting a humble tone. She removed her hood, revealing the intensity in her blue eyes.

Three figures lined the wall. They wore black cloaks with deep hoods. The two farthest away moved to where Reia could see them better. After a two-second pause, the figures reached up and removed their hoods.

"This is not right!" Terosh protested. "What use is it to bring up her past?"

"That is not my intent," Mavis said. Her silky voice slid over Reia's senses.

Feeling cold and dizzy, Reia regarded the three figures. Her mind numbly spoke the names as if that would make them less like a living nightmare.

Kolknir, Lucas, Nera.

The first two fit the role of haunting specter very well. Both had entered her life as trusted instructors. Kolknir had quickly destroyed that image, but she had once counted Lucas a friend. Once upon a time, they had even been on the cusp of becoming something more, until Reia realized Lucas's possessive nature would only cause her grief. She wondered how he had come by the angry-looking scratch beneath his left eye. No matter how hard she tried, Reia could not comprehend what Nera's role would be.

Finding her voice at last, Reia whipped her attention back to Lady Mavis.

"I know them." Her eyes searched Mavis's face. "But *why* are they here?"

"Lucas and Kolknir are present to ensure you and Terosh remain cooperative. Nera is here to replace you," Mavis explained casually.

"Aunt Mavis, this is madness. What do you hope to accomplish by it?" Terosh wondered.

Reia hated how tired he sounded.

"Explanations shortly, Terosh dear," Mavis said, patting him lightly on the shoulder. "Do not spend your energy worrying. You have my word that she will not be needlessly harmed."

Needlessly harmed? As in, you might have a legitimate reason to hurt me?

Reia's mind was too busy racing to prompt her to breathe. When something touched her right arm, she gasped and jerked her arm away. Something caught her wrist and pinned it to her left shoulder. Drawing breath to scream, Reia looked at the "something" which turned out to be Lucas. He dropped her hand and stepped away, but a strong arm encircled her throat and a hand slammed against her mouth hard enough to hurt her teeth. Her head snapped back, resting partly on Kolknir's shoulder and partly on his neck.

Helpless but not yet hopeless, Reia jerked forward and

screamed. The scream died a muffled death in Kolknir's palm, and the effort to break free only strained her neck. Desperate, Reia bent both knees so Kolknir suddenly bore her full weight, trying to throw him off balance. He must have expected the move because he released her suddenly, planted his hands on her shoulders, and pushed down until she landed hard on her knees.

Next instant, Reia lay flat on the floor with Kolknir's knee digging into her lower back and tingling, fiery pain shooting from her right shoulder. Ignoring the pain, Reia gathered energy to spring free at the first opportunity.

A hand landed gently on her left shoulder and gave a friendly squeeze.

"Stop struggling before you kill him," hissed Lucas.

Against her will, Reia tuned her senses to the things happening around her. She felt Mavis's frustration, Nera's helplessness, and impatience from both Lucas and Kolknir. The impression she received from Terosh combined rage, panic, and intense pain.

She froze. Angry tears slipped out as Reia gritted her teeth, stilled her body, and said two painful words.

"All right."

***

Seeing Terosh's violent reaction to Reia's captivity, Mavis Altran feared she might have miscalculated. The stupid boy was likely to break something vital in his head if he didn't calm down. While her plans might eventually call for his death, the timing mattered a great deal, and right now, she needed him alive. Even with Nera leaning across his shoulders, the wretched boy thrashed violently enough to almost roll free.

This was not how the scene should have panned out. Growling low, Mavis clamped both hands on Terosh's right shoulder and leaned forward.

"Calm down before you kill yourself," she ordered. "So help me, Terosh, if you die now, I will inflict unimaginable horrors on your precious wife!"

Nera gasped and withdrew her hands like she'd been scalded.

Mavis glared a warning at her then returned to staring absolute sincerity into Terosh's eyes.

"I truly intend no harm to you or Reia, but I have plans much grander than both of you," said Mavis, softening her tone. "I will not take kindly to interference."

Terosh sagged, gasping for breath. His fit had carried him halfway down the bed where he lay on his back.

"What do you want with her?" he asked, staring up at Mavis like a wounded puppy.

Mavis sighed as she released his shoulder. She had seen her nephew stoically endure battle after battle against the poison, yet one tiny threat against his wife reduced him to a state just shy of blubbering idiocy.

This sort of sentiment will undo you one day, Terosh, Mavis thought as a pang of sympathy touched her.

She wished things could be different. He reminded her so much of his father, her baby brother. Like Teorn, Terosh had a heart that could abide no pain in others.

"My Lady, the queen is yours to command," Kolknir called.

"Or at least try to control," Lucas said dryly.

Mavis turned, shaking off her reverie.

"Thank you, gentlemen. Bring her here so I may avoid shouting." She waved to the foot of the bed and waited for Kolknir and Lucas to guide Reia to the indicated spot.

Besides casting death glares, the queen seemed to accept her new lot. She wore the stuncuffs with an ease that indicated familiarity. For some reason, Mavis found that upsetting. Aside from having the poor judgment to marry Terosh, the girl struck her as intelligent and innocent, the sort of person easy to love.

Kolknir and Lucas gently lifted Reia and deposited her on the edge next to Terosh's left leg.

Mavis noticed they had bound her ankles as well. The short chain linking the two cuffs allowed for slow walking but would stop her if she tried to run. While the measure seemed excessive, she trusted Kolknir and Lucas knew their business. If she remembered correctly, both men had briefly instructed Reia in Ranger ways. If anyone could predict her capabilities, they could.

"Nera, please have Captain Antar send the message to Gardan," Mavis instructed.

"Captain Antar works for you?" Terosh asked, sounding horrified.

Reia looked equally shocked.

"Many people work for me," Mavis replied. "And you must understand that I can say no more on the matter. What I will explain is that I need you both to remain here for about a week."

"Why?" inquired Reia.

Terosh said nothing, but Mavis could sense his mind frantically working. His breath hitched, and he shut his eyes as if he could not bear the thought.

"No," he said miserably.

"You have piqued my curiosity, Terosh," Mavis admitted. Teorn had often touted Taytron as the swift thinker, but Mavis suspected Terosh was quite capable of solving this little puzzle. "What precisely do you think my plan entails?"

"Grandfather," Terosh said.

Mavis smiled down at him.

"He has ruled Gardan far too long," she said.

"If King Padric Creston is your true target, why bother with us?" Reia wondered.

"My grandfather has wanted you as a captive for years," Terosh explained, shaking his head slowly. "Aunt Mavis intends to give him Nera in your place."

Turning to the young queen, Mavis said, "Do not worry; your part is easy. I need you to stay here within Terosh's chambers until the deed is done."

***

Jira (March) 12, 1542

King Terosh's Private Chambers, Royal Palace, City of Rammon

Terosh wept quietly when Kolknir showed him the vids covering his grandfather's death, trying not to wake Reia. He had feared King Padric and even hated most of what the man stood for, but the burden of foreknowledge weighed heavily upon him.

I could have stopped it!

The anotechs could have warned enough people to get a message to Gardan in time, but Mavis had anticipated such a possibility and issued appropriate threats. Tarnished honor or not, Terosh refused to risk his wife's life. The assassination's success meant that Reia too had believed Mavis's threat and done nothing as well.

The week had been tremendously stressful. They barely ate enough to keep themselves alive. Days passed in quiet conversation or strained silence. Occasionally, one or the other or both would struggle to stand and pace the room for a while. Nights passed side by side yet chained to the bed frame while Lucas or Kolknir grimly stood guard.

Aunt Mavis entered the room, and Terosh wondered if she would kill them now. His expression must have explained his fear.

She gave him the sympathetic smile he'd come to expect.

"And now we will take our leave, Terosh," said his aunt. "How you handle the fallout that will surely come is up to you, but a word of warning before I go: say nothing."

He shot her an incredulous look.

"Telling everybody on this world and the next how vulnerable you are would be extremely foolhardy," Aunt Mavis said earnestly. "You will have aspiring assassins clogging your hallways. You are more than welcome to search for me. Try to bring me to justice if you must, but by all that is holy, do it quietly."

She actually made sense.

Terosh's head ached. He looked to Reia who slumbered beside him then back to his aunt. Relatively assured at last that Mavis truly meant to leave them alive, Terosh cleared his dry throat.

"Before you leave, tell me why. You must have planned this for years. Was it worth it? What did you gain from his death?"

"We are all pieces of a greater camarek game being played, Terosh. That might sound stupid, but one day, you—or perhaps a descendant—will understand." Her expression changed becoming reflective before returning to neutral. "My part is finished for now … perhaps forever. This is likely the last time we will speak, so I will leave you with these lessons. Never love so much that you cannot lose and live. You are a king. Like it or not, even family must bow before duty."

Terosh felt a needle bite into his arm. He barely had time to groan before a warm darkness descended upon his head and drew him to restful sleep.

Chapter 42:
Records

Jira (March) 22, 1542
The Lady's Estate, Kala Mountains
Back in her lair, Lady Mavis Altran stared down at the report her spies had compiled for her concerning her son and his treatment on Gardan. She'd not moved against King Padric until certain Kezem was finished with the planet.

> Pirua (September) 9, 1539: Unconscious male subject arrives from unspecified location off planet. Landing permission granted to automated ship by authority of King Padric Creston. Security clearance level nine required to access any information concerning this case. Subject checked into Panosh Facility under identification #195183. Blood, bone, hair, and muscle samples taken from the subject. Head physician: Dr. Ian Noir. Head scientist: Dr. Tasha Amie.
>
> Pirua (September) 16, 1539: Dr. Noir orders three blood transfusions. Immune suppression necessary. Donors 154322 and 154324 expire; notifications prepared for next of kin. Dr. Amie works with samples acquired from subject to build a stock of friendly blood to work with.

Pirua (September) 23, 1539: Dr. Amie reports adequate stock of subject's blood to attempt first friendly transfusion. Subject responds well but remains unconscious. Dr. Amie adjusts medium subject's blood is grown on.

Lalri (November) 5, 1539: Subject regains consciousness. As per instructions, King Padric informed immediately.

Lalri (November) 19, 1539: Dr. Noir reports subject has adequate strength to attempt height modification. Surgery delayed. Dr. Amie reports bone growth from subject's samples proceeding slower than projected.

Ferrim (December) 10, 1539: Subject's upper and lower leg bones replaced. Additional sections of enhanced synthetic muscle woven into existing muscle matrix. Height gain upon standing estimated to be 12.64 centimeters.

Ferrim (December) 17, 1539: Subject indicates readiness for additional modifications. Dr. Noir argues that subject needs to recover further first. Dr. Amie reports additional time needed to grow more synthetic muscles.

Idela (January) 1, 1540: Dr. Noir is pleased with subject's physical therapy and agrees to perform arm surgeries if subject can walk down to Dr. Amie's office and back. Subject succeeds but exertion proves too much for his body.

Idela (January) 8, 1540: Subject's right and left arm bones replaced. Additional sections of enhanced synthetic muscle woven into existing muscle matrix. Reach gains estimated to be 6.85 centimeters.

Idela (January) 15, 1540: Subject's left arm develops infection. Dr. Amie takes sample and reports simple bacterial problem. Subject treated with standard antibacterial agents.

Lanolin (February) 13, 1540: Subject's right and left hands injected with bone growth serum.

Jira (March) 4, 1540: Dr. Noir performs surgery to lengthen subject's trunk and broaden subject's shoulders. Dr. Amie reports improvement in bonding time between synthetic and natural muscle.

Jira (March) 11, 1540: Subject still very weak from modifications to trunk and shoulders. Subject reports aching pains throughout modified areas. Dr. Amie takes samples for further study.

Jira (March) 25, 1540: Dr. Amie finds new bacterial strand in subject's sample and treats with modified antibiotic agent.

Enis (April) 9, 1540: Subject begins coordination training.

Enis (April) 16, 1540: Subject begins endurance training.

Retsi (May) 14, 1540: Subject begins building muscle mass. Dr. Amie supervises cautious use of chemical aids.

Zeri (June) 12, 1540: Subject begins training with Shadow Guard Captain Jonas Ri.

Lalri (November) 15, 1540: Subject injured during training exercise. Dr. Noir treats wounds.

Lanolin (February) 28, 1542: Subject indicates desire to return to home planet. Dr. Amie protests. Subject appeals to king.

Jira (March) 5, 1542: Subject checks out of Panosh Facility. Subject returns to single passenger ship. Exit clearance granted by authority of King Padric Creston.

Welcome home, my son. I am eager to see what you have become.

Chapter 43:
Final Gift

Lalri (November) 16, 1542
Karanak Falls, Kala Mountains

Confused and angry, Kezem Altran bellowed a question into the comm clenched tightly in his hand.

"Why?" He could have left the comm on his belt and still carried on the conversation, but he needed to feel its slender casing straining in his strong grip.

Cold wind tore at his dark clothes, ripping through them as if they did not exist. It clawed at his eyes like a cold-hearted beast, freezing tears to death before they could fully form. His modified bones ached which registered as sharp pain in his head. The roaring rumble of rushing water crashed into Kezem's senses, trying to sweep his courage down into the Kala River. Traitorous legs trembled. He knelt beside a large boulder, seeking shelter behind its bulk and peered out at the heavily shrouded figure poised on the cliff's edge.

Not more than ten meters separated them, but Kezem knew he would never reach her in time. He didn't even know if he wanted to reach her. The conflicting emotions left his mind battered. This woman had controlled his life since before he was a thought. Every scrap of knowledge he possessed about manipulating situations and people he owed to her. He'd also tried to kill her several times, and each time, she had survived and turned it into a life lesson. His love and hate roiled about so strongly that they became inextricably linked.

"Why now? Why this way?" Kezem whispered hoarsely.

The figure turned to face him, smiling one of her knowing

smiles.

"You have always known the answer to those questions, Kezem." His mother's voice entered the receiver fastened just below her chin, flew through the space separating them, and crawled up through the comm he clutched. "All creatures are simplistic, humans in particular. What makes any human heart beat?" She paused to let him answer. When he said nothing, she said, "Love." Her tone held amusement, irony, and a hint of bitterness.

Love.

The word seared Kezem, burning through his heart.

"You called me here!" he shouted, concentrating hard on forming words. "What do you want of me? Am I not the son you wanted? Have I not learned enough?" The questions surprised and shamed Kezem. They sprang forth from the wounded child within, and he despised them.

Mavis shook her head slowly. She stood taller and lifted her chin imperiously, seemingly oblivious to the wind hurling itself at her. Loose strands of hair and clothing writhed and thrashed under the assault, but Mavis stood rooted to a broad rock that jutted out over the Karanak Falls.

"I want you to accept your destiny."

"Destiny?" Kezem asked, genuinely confused. His shallow breaths sounded loud in his ears.

His mother's proud features softened a trifle.

"You were always the best and brightest of my boys, Kezem." She removed her infopad from an inner pocket. "Mitrek has chosen his path, and I wish him well. He is a selfish fool, but alive and hopefully prospering. If you reject my plea, I will force Eldon to act, but he would be a poor substitute for the sort of leader you could be. If I have raised you right, then you will want this as much as I do."

"You want me to rule." It was more the echo of a shell-shocked heart than a question or a statement. A spark of anger flared. "How? You destroyed most of my informants before I returned."

"Not destroyed, only purged of weakness as your body had to be," answered Mavis. "Complete instructions are here and with Dennel should you lose this." She waved her infopad and flung it at him. "He will find you if necessary."

Kezem instinctively snatched the infopad out of the air before it could crash into his face. It clattered against the comm in his right hand, nearly causing him to drop both.

"That's it? You're just going to leave me some instructions and quit life?"

"Not exactly how I would have phrased it, but yes," said his mother. "I have given you everything. You are finally ready, and the last steps must be taken completely alone." She started to turn away, but hesitated and glanced back at him. "When you finally achieve our goals, find a good woman and settle down." Then, with one more smile, Mavis reached up and unclasped the heavy pendant she had always worn around her neck. Finally, she wrapped it in the chain, kissed it, and threw it at Kezem.

He caught it as she turned her back on him and dove off the cliff.

***

Mavis Altran heard only the first note of her son's anguished cry. It warmed her even as mist off the falls soaked her. Tucking her arms across her chest, she tried to quiet her screaming mind. She hoped the anotechs did their part well, for despite the impression she wished to leave with Kezem, she really wanted to live. Her entire life was wrapped up in that man. She'd finally given him the last gift she could: freedom. Dying before seeing what he would do with it did not fit her plans.

The anotech shield around her made her skin shimmer but did nothing to ward off the terrible cold. Her body sliced through the air like a living scythe. Most of the way, she hurtled headfirst, but a split second before impact, the anotechs managed to flip her. When Mavis's feet struck the water, it felt like she had landed on concrete. Sharp pain shot from both legs up through her stomach and slashed through her brain in an instant.

She gasped a great lungful of icy water and experienced all the horror of drowning. Then, peace descended on her mind, and she felt nothing of the cold or pain. She floated deep below the Karanak Falls at the foot of the Kala Mountains. Mavis had just enough time to realize her plan had succeeded before darkness claimed her senses.

***

Lalri (November) 16, 1542
King Terosh's Private Chambers, City of Rammon

Every anotech in Terosh stilled at once, and he knew something drastic had changed. His entire body felt somehow lighter and less conflicted. He considered the possibilities but could think of no reason for the change.

Two days later, when Kezem grimly recounted his mother's death, Terosh thought of the lightening of his spirit. Careful reflection upon the timing convinced him. Profound relief and sadness pulled his aching heart in different directions. He tried to cling to righteous anger birthed during the brief captivity many months before, but pity proved stronger.

Chapter 44:
Beautiful Forever

Lanolin (February) 3, 1543
Wellum Home, Riden Mountains

The unforgiving wooden floor outside the Wellum's private quarters made Todd's legs and backside sore, but a small part of him welcomed the discomfort. It would feel completely wrong to be comfortable while Kiata suffered so intensely. Master Jolinda Ekris had gently, yet firmly, tossed Todd from the bedroom into the antechamber soon after her arrival with Master Niklos some four hours prior. Todd had been allowed to hold Kiata's hand until a complication had arisen.

Do they not understand my terror?

For the thousandth time, Todd wished they had not undergone the ceremony to temporarily relinquish control over the anotechs. At least then he could have comforted Kiata and perhaps even eased her pain. Tradition older than the banning of relationships with royals dictated that Nareth Talis Rangers take measures to avoid passing anotechs on to their offspring. Todd understood the logic, but he disliked the implication that anotechs were a heritable disease.

Todd forced himself to stand and started pacing. A moment later, he grunted as he slammed into one wall in the tiny front room. Muttering to himself, Todd turned around and stared around his temporary prison. Normally, the dwelling's front room held only a collection of spare cloaks and dirty boots.

At Reia's suggestion, Kiata had brightened it with sprigs of fragrant mintas and dried ira petals. Todd had no idea where the apprentice sent to fetch the flowers managed to get the ira petals.

Though abundant on the Riden Flats and Kesler Plains, flowers of any sort were rare this high and deep in the mountains. Even the lower hills, which played host to many tretling herds, could only boast scattered patches of flowers.

Unlike most of the Ranger dwellings, this temporary-quarter cabin sat above ground, rather than in a converted cave. The Ashatan Council likely wanted to keep the Wellums as far from others as possible.

A pain-filled moan sliced through the closed door and pierced Todd's heart. Terrifying helplessness gripped him, almost as bad as those first seconds after losing his connection to the anotechs. It wasn't a normal feeling for him, and he hated how much it reminded him of the dark days as an Alliance prisoner. His knees felt weak, and cold sweat broke out over his body.

What's taking so long?

His muscles coiled and uncoiled every time he heard his wife's muffled moans. Occasionally, a sharp cry would break the steady groans. Then, the worst would come: silence. Each time silence fell, Todd felt like the universe stopped. His breath caught in his throat, choking him with fear.

She can't die. She can't die.

A sense of uselessness replaced some of the fear with frustration. Todd had sent a young apprentice to notify the queen, but that left nothing for him to do. Master Niklos had traveled in from Resh two days ago to share this time but even he had agreed with Master Ekris's decision to exile Todd.

The inner door swung open and crashed into the wall with a bang like a discharging serlak gun. Todd spun to face Master Niklos.

"What's wrong?" Todd barely refrained from clasping the older man's finely stitched tunic and shaking him.

Retired from the Rangers or not, the man would always be Master Niklos to Todd.

Smiling wearily, Master Niklos reached out a calming hand toward Todd and gripped his shoulder.

"Nothing's wrong. This is all quite normal. It could be seconds or hours though. Why don't you inform the palace that everything is fine before Reia dispatches Royal Guards?"

That's normal?

Todd's ears burned, turning almost the same fiery color as his hair. He recognized the dismissal. His feet responded by planting themselves more firmly.

"I sent Addin to contact her a few hours ago. I want—"

Master Niklos's grip on his shoulder tightened.

"You're distraught; you'll only upset her."

A long scream sent chills through Todd. Then, eerie silence fell again. Todd couldn't take it anymore. He shouldered Master Niklos out of the way and rushed to his wife's side. Master Jolinda Ekris gave him a disapproving look but didn't interfere as he fell to his knees beside Kiata.

She lay on a mountain of coarse blankets and quava feather pillows with her knees drawn up and her night dress draped down to mid-calf. Her eyes opened as soon as Todd took her slick right hand between his own and kissed the knuckles.

"Hi," she greeted with a weary grin. "I missed you."

Todd leaned forward and said he had missed her too with a long, insistent kiss. A small part of his mind remembered that others were in the room, but he didn't care. The woman he loved was here and safe, nothing else mattered. After the kiss, he settled on the bed beside Kiata and clutched her hand again.

"You're just in time," said Master Ekris.

Suddenly, another cry split the air. Todd's head whipped up and around with wonder and alarm. He squeezed Kiata's hand out of pure reflex. This cry was different: younger, newer, and thoroughly annoyed. Todd's lips formed a silly grin. He twisted further for a better look and nearly fell off the bed.

Master Ekris stood in the corner by the wash basin cradling a freshly cleaned and wrapped infant.

"She's beautiful," she murmured, slowly approaching Todd and Kiata. With infinite care, the older woman deposited the baby into Kiata's waiting arms.

She's beautiful, Todd's mind repeated numbly.

He took in the sight of his daughter's wrinkled, bright red face and fell in love instantly. Wisps of soft damp, red hair crowned the baby's head. Her eyes were still screwed shut. The loose fabric Master Ekris had tucked around the child writhed as she squirmed. The infant's cries lessened in intensity, then subsided when a tiny thumb found its way into her mouth. Kiata tucked her close, and the child promptly fell asleep.

"What's her name?" Master Ekris asked in a whisper.

Todd and Kiata exchanged a deep look. No words could

recreate its entire meaning, but in essence, it meant: *our love is pure and whole and perfected in her; it will last forever through everything she comes to love and cherish.*

They had prepared both boy and girl names, but right now, none of them seemed right for their first child.

Kiata nodded and smiled, reading his thoughts. After gazing at her newborn child for a long, tender moment, she said, "Kayleen."

Beautiful forever. That fits her perfectly.

"Well, don't just sit there, boy. Tell everybody!" Master Niklos ordered.

Todd needed no more encouragement. He dashed out the door and down the mountainside hollering for all to hear. He sprinted so fast that one slip would have broken his neck, but nothing could touch him today. He had a daughter.

Chapter 45: Treasured Eternally

Enis (April) 8, 1543
Royal Gardens, City of Rammon

If Reia wanted proof of his health, Terosh would give her proof. He stood below the balcony leading to his wife's private chambers. He could not blame her for the fear. After all, he had almost died countless times during the last few years.

Carefully tucking a fresh rose into his belt, Terosh smiled and remembered the last time he'd performed this feat, minus the rose, of course. That time, romance had been the last thing on his mind. Proving a point to Tate was closer to the mark. Terosh mentally calculated the time it would take and privately promised to beat that time.

Are you with me tonight, friends? He felt a little stupid for not realizing they had helped him up the wall the first time.

She is going to yell, they replied.

She will understand, he assured, hoping it was true.

We liked you better deathly ill, more sensible, they complained.

He chuckled.

Just have her come out to the balcony when I tell you to.

As you wish, King of the Chosen.

With the anotechs strengthening his limbs and increasing the grip on the smooth palace walls, Terosh made good time climbing the seven floors to his wife's balcony. As he reached the top, Reia's voice floated out from the shadows next to the light streaming from her bedroom.

"You know very well that this is not what I meant."

"Permission to board the balcony, Your Majesty?" Terosh asked cheerfully.

Reia sighed.

"You're idiot enough to climb back down the way you came if I refused you, so come on in," she said imperiously.

Terosh wasted no time scrambling onto the wide balcony and closing the distance between them. He pulled her close as if he'd not seen her in ages.

"I missed you."

Her arms encircled his waist then flew wide.

"Ow!"

He released her suddenly and groped behind his back for the rose he had stashed there.

"Sorry. That wasn't exactly the surprise it was meant to be. They're beautiful, but they can be painful." He opened his mouth to say more then cleared his throat awkwardly. "Well, that was smooth as a mountain range." He sighed. "Here, this is for you." He shut his mouth with an audible click of teeth, thrust the rose forward with two hands like a sword being surrendered, and sucked in a deep, bracing breath. "I need more practice talking intelligently. Can I still claim the 'recently ill excuse'?"

Reia laughed and graciously accepted the rose with two hands, being careful to avoid the thorns this time.

Seeing the faint scratches marking her forearms, Terosh ran his palms over them and used anotechs to soothe the skin. The healing took only a few seconds; then Terosh awkwardly removed his hands to let her admire the gift.

Twirling the rose once and raising it to her nose to inhale the rich scent, Reia smiled and gracefully swept back into her room. A few seconds later, her voice floated back to Terosh.

"You can claim whatever you want."

Terosh stood on her balcony puzzling through possible double meanings when Reia returned.

"You're not angry? The anotechs thought you might yell."

Reia sighed again, hooked a finger into the collar of his shirt, and tugged gently.

"Why can't men take hints?"

"Why can't women speak clearly?" Terosh asked, rising to the defense of his gender.

Reia lifted herself up on tiptoes and encircled Terosh's neck with her arms.

"Focus, dear," she said, once they were eye to eye. "There was a reason you climbed seven levels of the Rammon palace tonight. Do you remember what that could be?"

His arms fell into place around her, and he answered her question with an ardent kiss that made his heart soar and ache. During his long recovery they had been close many times, but not like this. His senses filled with awareness of everything about her.

When the kiss finally ended, Terosh rested his forehead on hers.

"This balcony is feeling far too public."

"I completely agree." Reia chuckled, kissed him shortly, and pulled him further into the room.

***

Idela (January) 13, 1544

Reia and Terosh's Private Chambers, Royal Palace, City of Rammon

A cool cloth brushed Reia's forehead and cheeks. With eyes shut, she enjoyed the novelty of not being in pain.

"Imagine doing that without the blessing of anotechs," Kiata said.

Reia's eyes shot open and she groaned in sympathy as her mind did as bid.

"Sorry I was not there for you. We could have cheated the pain a little."

Laughing, Kiata shrugged and perched on the bed beside Reia. Her left leg rested on the bed and her right leg braced against the floor.

"I understand. You had other things occupying your mind, like a husband to heal and a planet to run."

"No, really, I should have been there," Reia said.

Kiata picked up her left hand and held it in her lap.

"Reia, I long ago gave up the notion that I could always save you from every danger you might face. Now, I'm going to have to ask you to do the same."

Reia shook her head, feeling like a silly child.

"Why?" she asked, not caring how petulant she sounded.

Scooting closer, Kiata tapped Reia on the nose with the side of her index finger.

"Because your family is growing now," said Kiata. "Besides,

birth order still dictates that it's my job to worry about you, not the other way around. How are you sleeping these days anyway?"

A wan smile tugged at the corners of Reia's mouth.

"I will say one thing for pregnancy. The anotechs worried for the child, so they taught me some useful lessons in controlling the nightmares. Guess my own struggles for sanity mattered less to them."

"They have their own brand of logic," Kiata said. "It doesn't always make sense."

"How is your connection with them?" asked Reia.

"Mine is still unpredictable, but Todd's connection seems to be stronger, at least stronger than it was after the first separation."

They fell silent as both thought back to that horrible time when Kiata and Todd had been captives and needed to cut ties with the anotechs. Kiata's grip on Reia's hand loosened as her distraction increased.

"I … can help with that," Reia offered tentatively.

Kiata's expression said *I wish it were that easy.*

"The Council would have a conniption. While I wouldn't mind watching Master Deliad's reaction, I'm still kind of fond of Master Ekris and Master Corida. I'll just have to prove I can do my job without relying so heavily upon anotechs. It's not impossible, only harder. Speaking of harder, enjoy every peaceful moment you can. Kayleen just started sleeping well, which means *we* just started sleeping well again."

"I shall keep that in mind," Reia promised. "Given that first wail, I believe Teven will be very vocal."

Kiata futzed around with Reia's sheet, neatly tucking it along her left side.

"What made you call him Teven?"

Sadness wound cool fingers around Reia's heart.

"He was the youngest McNoughten child, the one who did not survive the Heskrin attack." As usual, she felt the ache of that failure despite knowing she and Terosh had done absolutely everything they could to save him.

It had been Terosh's idea, but Reia still had mixed feelings over the whole situation. On the one hand, it was a good, strong name with solid meaning. On the other side, it could not change the past, nor replace the life lost.

Kira McNoughten had shed quiet tears when Reia asked permission to name her son Teven. The older woman seemed to understand the need and feigned deep honor, but Reia knew the wound caused by losing her Teven still bled.

Kiata gently tipped Reia's chin up.

"It is a fitting name for any prince." She leaned forward and kissed Reia's forehead. "No more second thoughts tonight. Your life has changed forever."

***

Idela (January) 24, 1544

Chamber of Wisdom, Loresh Cave System, Frozen North

Queen Reia Minstel marveled at how very young and innocent her first—and only—Loresh recording sounded. So much had happened since then; she could not decide where to start. She could easily have stayed hours describing each event that had transpired, but in the end, she decided to focus on her reason for coming.

Instructing the anotechs to keep her first message safe, she tried recording a new message. Several failed attempts later, she stopped and spent several minutes thinking about Terosh and Teven and how much they meant to her. Other concerns tried to rise, but she pushed them back.

Finally, with Teven's sweet little face firmly fixed in her mind's eye, Reia let every scrap of joy shine through her smile.

"We have a son!" There, her news stood delivered, planted like a joyous banner. What more should she say? Her enthusiasm dimmed a little, but she forged on. "Terosh could not come with me this time because one of us had to stay to receive the representatives from the Galactic Alliance of Populated Planets. But I had to come." She spared the mental energy to protest the lousy timing, then pictured her son's face again. Her spirits recovered. "Teven is beautiful. He has his father's black hair, my green eyes, and a scream that can penetrate every corner of the palace! I know I am supposed to be recording bits of wisdom here, so here is my lesson for future generations: enjoy every moment you can basking in the love of family."

Reia silently bid the anotechs to stop recording then dashed out of Loresh. She loved being here among the pillars of Terosh's family, but the satisfaction paled before the prospect of spending time with her family. She would just have to collect Aster Captain Laocer and Captain Zareb, and they could be back in Rammon in half a day. She thought about the former Captain of the Royal Guard. Reia had liked Surd Antar, but his obvious betrayal left them little choice but to imprison him. Unable to help it, Reia wondered how many more betrayals would assail them and what sort of damage it would cause. She determined to be ever vigilant to protect her growing family.

Terosh and Reia would spend most of the evening entertaining their GAPP guests, but then, they could spend a few precious moments watching Teven sleep. She faintly dreaded the day when that simple act failed to tug her heart so strongly.

Chapter 46:
Contested Refuge

Idela (January) 25, 1544
Upper East Library, Royal Palace, City of Rammon

King Terosh usually relished quiet moments in the library sipping wine with a beautiful woman, but this time, several factors marred the experience. First, the woman was not Reia, and second, the woman was a GAPP agent. Third, she made decent arguments. Fourth, she had a companion with all the personality of a granite statue.

As if summoned by Terosh's desperation, Reia swept into the room wearing a gorgeous gown of green shimmersilk that skimmed along the ground. She even wore matching heels. A deep purple wrap caressed her shoulders then wove down and around her otherwise bare arms. Her green eyes sparkled with sympathy, amusement, understanding, and love.

Terosh and his guests hurried to their feet. He could not have wished for a more fitting or beautiful guardian angel to watch over his sinking spirits. Terosh swiftly handled the pleasantries.

Once they resumed their seats, Terosh said, "Ambassador Raquel, would you kindly repeat your new proposal for my wife?"

"Certainly, Your Grace. I would be delighted," answered Sabrina Raquel in her smooth, measured voice. "During the years since my last visit to your lovely planet, the Galactic Alliance of Populated Planets has added a new kind of member state. As an Associate Member State, Reshner would have no voting rights in our ruling councils, but would otherwise receive full membership rights. This would, of course, allow your agents to move freely about on GAPP worlds, which should aid your cause in rescuing the Rorgen people."

"There is the small matter of the fee, but I am certain we can work out a mutually beneficial deal," said Barlo Elaird.

"I am certain," Terosh echoed.

"What sorts of membership rights exist?" asked Reia.

"The obvious right members receive is the safety of the name," responded Barlo. "We live in dangerous times. Pirate nations exploit lonely worlds, but they usually think twice once they know the united might of GAPP stands ready to defend a planet."

"We have gone more than four centuries without a serious threat from the galaxy at large," Terosh pointed out.

"All the more reason to fear such a possibility now," Sabrina Raquel reasoned. "Members also receive free trading privileges. Safeguarding the trade of information and resources is a vastly expensive undertaking. By sharing the costs among GAPP worlds, the burden is made lighter for everybody." Raquel's perceptive eyes traveled from Terosh to Reia and then back again. "However, I can see that these arguments hold little appeal for you, so I will reiterate my earlier statement. By joining GAPP you would be free to offer aid to planets in the Rorge System."

"Our people have already answered the question about joining GAPP," Terosh said. "However, in light of this new possibility, we will bring it up in the next session." He rose, effectively ending the conversation. "In the meantime, please enjoy your stay in the palace. If you would like to visit any particular city, I can have Master Roth make the arrangements for you."

***

Enis (April) 27, 1544

Prince Teven's Private Chambers, Royal Palace, City of Rammon

"I feel like a coward," Reia admitted, gently rocking her son.

"That is utter rubbish," Kiata said.

"Rubb-eesh!" declared Kayleen.

Both women looked down at the toddler who looked perplexed but delighted. The child had her right index finger stuffed into her mouth and had clapped a hand to her left cheek.

"Rubb-eesh!" Kayleen repeated, enjoying the sound of her own voice.

Bothered by the noise, Teven whined and wiggled in Reia's arms.

"Don't mind her, Tev, she means well," said Reia, redoubling her rocking efforts.

"Hush, Kayleen, your baby cousin is trying to sleep," Kiata gently scolded.

"Why?" asked the child. She grinned from ear to ear at getting to use her favorite new word.

Reia tried to hide a smile as Kiata winced. She failed at it rather handily but sobered enough to share a long-suffering look with her sister.

"We're going to regret teaching her that word, aren't we?" Kiata asked.

"Probably," Reia answered.

"Why?" Kayleen wondered again. She made a strange noise that did not really qualify as a word, but it was loud and she loved it. She made the noise again and threw herself sideways stretching her arms wide, flopping about like a fish out of water and reveling in peels of laughter.

"I'm getting tired just watching her," Reia said. She walked the four steps to the bed and rested Teven on her knees to relieve her aching arms.

"Wait until he's Kayleen's age," Kiata said. "Our neighbors have three children, one girl and two boys. They said their boys were much more active than their girl."

Reia studied her sleepy son. His black hair stuck out in multiple directions. Green eyes blinked at her slowly. Chubby little cheeks flushed as he flailed his arms about and did an odd dance on her legs.

"Did you hear Aunt Kiata, Teven? In this one regard, you have my permission to be more like a girl," Reia told him.

He drooled in her lap.

"I think that's an ambiguous response at best," Kiata said, chuckling.

Kayleen screeched, impatient at not receiving answers.

Teven leaned back and twisted, trying to find the source of the racket.

Reia grunted.

"I don't think we're going to be allowed a civilized conversation in their presence. Here, take him for a moment." She handed Teven off to Kiata and went to summon Sarie, grateful the woman had a plan for such an occasion.

The Melian Maiden bustled in a few minutes later and immediately took charge of Kayleen.

"Come, Lady Kayleen, we shall explore your aunt's fine collection of clothes while she and your mother speak." She held out her hand and waited for the toddler to stagger to her feet. Then, she scooped her up. "Shall I take the other little one on our tour as well?"

Reia raised a questioning glance at Kiata who still held Teven.

"We'll be fine. Thank you, Sarie. Kayleen, you mind what Lady Sarie says," Kiata said.

Kayleen bobbed her head vigorously.

"Okay!" She raised both hands to her mouth, kissed them noisily, and flung her arms wide, almost falling out of Sarie's arms in the process. "Bye!"

"Who taught her to blow kisses?" Reia wondered.

"Three guesses," Kiata said dryly.

They settled down facing each other on the window seat and sat in comfortable silence for a while. Teven slept in Kiata's arms.

Finally, Kiata nudged Reia with the foot that hung off the seat.

"So, back to the coward comment uttered ages ago," Kiata prompted. "I'll give you one minute to explain it before I tell you each and every reason why it's rubbish. Fair enough?"

"Since when were you ever interested in fair when it comes to proving a point?" Reia asked.

Kiata shot her a grin.

"Since you became queen, and I discovered the usefulness of letting you think you can get your way."

"That's the supportive sister I remember," Reia said. "You had me worried."

"And you *have* me worried," Kiata admitted. "You usually don't avoid a subject so long."

"I should be with Terosh," Reia said, hating how much it sounded like a whine. "He's fighting this GAPP thing by himself, while I hide here. Truth is, I don't even think he really wants to join GAPP even under their new provisions."

"Why would he raise it in the Senate and Governors Council if he did not support it?" Kiata inquired.

Reia stared into the seat's cushions and traced some of the flower pattern before answering.

"Duty. He—we feel it's our duty to aid those thrown into need by the destruction of the Colza Star."

"Do you trust GAPP?" Kiata asked, striking the heart of the matter.

"It depends on what you mean by trust," said Reia. "If by 'trust' you mean 'place hope in,' then, no, we do not trust them. If by 'trust' you mean 'depend upon them to reliably act in the same predictable pattern,' then, yes, we trust them."

"I see you have given this deep thought," Kiata commented.

Still tracing the flower, Reia tried to decide how much to tell her sister.

"I know that expression, Reia," said Kiata. "You might as well tell me the rest now. Todd and I will probably find out whatever it is anyway."

"It's … nothing really," Reia hedged.

Kiata narrowed her silver-blue eyes.

"'Nothing' has never put that look on your face."

Reia winced, hoping she wasn't that readable in public.

"I am concerned with how much opposition we are getting to this GAPP question and where it centers. Lord Kezem seems to be turning the issue into a political storm. That places us in the awkward position of possibly having to pick the opposite side just to keep the discussion alive. Moral reasons alone dictate that this should not be an issue dealt with as lightly as Kezem would have it treated. Then again, by default, the position opposite the one Kezem holds is as GAPP proponent."

"I gather from your tone that you're not pleased with that," Kiata noted.

Reia rested her head in her hands.

"We trust GAPP to act dishonestly in its dealings, but they are still a bureaucracy. If we deal with them cautiously enough, their own words and laws should prevent them from harming us."

"Is it worth it?" asked Kiata.

"I do not know," Reia said, picking up her head and letting her hands drop into her lap.

"Do you think you could ease the situation by standing at Terosh's side?" Kiata asked, tuning her tone to contain more tenderness.

A helpless shrug was all Reia could conjure.

"Then, you're not a coward," Kiata concluded. "You're just unsure which arena would best serve your husband. My advice is: do both. It sounds like Kezem wants an image battle. If you think you can handle it, then give him one. Take Teven along on good days, not that you want to subject an innocent child to senators and governors for very long, but let the reporters see him. Let them see the royal family united in raising a question about compassion. Do not commit to one side or the other; simply raise the question as you did five years ago. The people will eventually return a definitive answer for you."

Chapter 47: Restful One and Restless One

Enis (April) 21, 1545
Reia and Terosh's Private Chambers, Royal Palace, City of Rammon

"Are you comfortable, Your Majesty?" asked Dr. Ezzai Dentelich.

The tender tone coming from the usually gruff man caused Reia to look up at him and smile.

"Yes, Ezzai, I am much better than an hour ago. You can go rest your ears now." She remembered a time when she thought the doctor nothing more than an arrogant fool, but the years nursing Terosh back to health after the kerlinblade accident had formed a bond of respect and even affection between them. "At least this little one was less stubborn about coming out than Teven."

The doctor returned her grin and glanced down once more at the sleeping newborn.

"She's as well mannered as any princess born in the palace in the last few decades," he pointed out.

"I suppose it helps that she's the only princess born in this palace in the last few decades, but thank you anyway."

"I should go rescue your poor Melian Maidens from our dear king," said Dr. Dentelich. "Shall I retrieve the young prince as well?"

After careful consideration, Reia shook her head.

"Have Sarie bring him by in an hour or so. I'd like a few moments with Terosh and my daughter. We still have an important decision to make."

"I understand your wishes completely, Your Majesty, and as

your doctor, I completely concur with your desire for rest." Ezzai bowed and left to inform the king of the happy news.

A few minutes later, Terosh sprinted into the room with Teven clutched to his chest.

Reia stared at him in alarm but had to laugh when two pairs of wide eyes stared right back at her, one pair brilliant blue and the other pair deep green.

"Terosh, you'll shake his head right from his little body," she scolded, ruining the effect with a smile.

"Mommy!" Teven pointed at Reia, turned in Terosh's arms, and began fussing.

Dr. Dentelich entered the room, breathing hard.

"My deepest apologies, Majesty, he would not wait for me to explain your wishes," said the doctor.

Reia sighed and leaned back against the pillows.

"It's quite understandable, Ezzai. We both know he can be hard to reason with," she said, giving her husband a look of mild reproof.

"Are you all right?" Terosh asked, breathing hard.

Just then, Sarie Verituse rushed in with the skirts of her heavy, dark green Melian Maiden robes clutched in her hands to facilitate running. Most of the younger maidens favored the simpler tunic and pants uniform or the flowing green shimersilk dress as they proved much easier to fight in, but Sarie liked the formal robes.

"What do you need me to do?" asked Sarie.

Teven's whining woke the baby who added her scream to the racket. Reia shifted her hold on the baby and gently rocked. Then, tucking her into the crook of her right arm, Reia reached with her left arm for Teven.

"Are you sure it's safe?" asked Terosh, holding Teven back as the boy lunged for his mother.

"Pass him to Sarie. Then, you can take the little one, and I can safely take Teven," Reia instructed.

The child swapping proceeded as smoothly as can be expected, which means it got more chaotic before relative peace returned. Teven screamed and squirmed in Sarie's grasp, nearly breaking free twice, but she recovered him both times.

"Stop that squirming, child," Sarie admonished. "You'll knock your poor mother senseless, if you keep up that nonsense."

As Sarie spoke, Terosh tentatively stepped close to the bed, leaned over, and slipped his left arm gently underneath the bundle nestled against Reia. When the infant's head rested in his palm, Terosh straightened and brought the bundle to his chest. His face shone with the solemn wonder of a man holding a new child for the first time. His eyes stayed transfixed on the infant's face.

"Watch me!" shouted Teven, tired of being ignored.

Reia pried her gaze from Terosh's face to smile at her son. She held up her empty arms and beckoned to Sarie.

"We didn't forget you, love," said Reia.

Sarie gratefully surrendered Teven.

He immediately threw his arms as wide around Reia as he could and rested his head against her heart.

Reia returned the embrace, relishing the warmth of his body and the tugging sensation where he gripped her shirt.

"Would you like to be alone, Highnesses?" asked Dr. Dentelich.

Terosh appeared not to have heard the question.

"Please wait a moment, Dr. Dentelich," said Reia. "Teven will be asleep soon."

"No sleep!" cried Teven, lifting his head and reaching for Reia's mouth. He pressed his small palm over her mouth and giggled.

Twisting her head to free her mouth, Reia used her left hand to capture Teven's hand.

"You keep that up and I might just decide to eat your hand," Reia said, her eyes twinkling as she teased her son. She pulled his hand close to her mouth, slid her grip downward, and planted a small kiss on each tiny finger.

Teven squealed and tried to pull his hand away.

Reia let his hand go but raised her knees under the loose sheets and penned him in with her arms.

"Where do you think you're going?" she asked.

The boy didn't answer. Instead, he leaned back on her knees and looked to his father.

"What's that?" he asked, pointing to the small bundle in Terosh's arms.

"Your sister," Reia answered, feeling sleepy but perfectly peaceful.

"Have you named her yet?" asked Sarie.

"I'm not sure," Reia murmured, casting a curious glance at her husband. "We spoke of many names."

As their eyes connected, Reia felt a hundred wordless messages pass between them.

Terosh looked down at their daughter and whispered, "Rela."

"What does it mean?" asked Sarie. "It's a lovely name."

Rela. Rela.

Reia tested the name with her mind several times before explaining.

"It has several meanings, but the most common meaning is 'restful one.'"

We certainly need more of that sentiment, Reia thought, as thoughts of the GAPP debates rose.

"I'd say that fits the princess rather well," said Dr. Dentelich.

Reia agreed.

***

Zeri (June) 3, 1545
Spaceside Inn, City of Rammon

It is treason, whispered an inner voice.

"It is necessary," Aster Captain Ectosh Laocer muttered into his ale tankard. His gaze darted around the room even though he had already swept for listening devices and had a personal sound damper activated.

It is madness.

"It is the only way," he argued.

You'll never do it. You're a coward.

"I am here," Laocer said.

"I must admit I did not think you would come," said a man.

Laocer's head snapped up, and his kerlak pistol centered on the speaker's chest in less than a second. He recognized the man as one of the Lady's agents, a former Ranger called Kolknir. His mind locked on the long list of crimes laid at Kolknir's feet. For an instant, he wanted to pull the trigger.

Kolknir chuckled.

"Very good reflexes, Captain, but you can put your weapon away. I see that you recognize me, but remember, you called for this meeting. I am merely the response. Lord Maledek was very surprised about your proposal and sent me to test your sincerity."

"It is no trap," Laocer assured. "I desire the king's removal, and I have heard rumors that your master possesses the resources to see to it. My reasons are my own."

The man took the seat to Laocer's left and ordered a drink

through the control panel built into the table.

"Your reasons are as clear as the Crystal Lake, but I am not here to critique them," said Kolknir. "For what it is worth, this is no trap on our end either. Lord Maledek understands and even sympathizes with your cause."

"Queen Reia must not be harmed," Laocer said, clutching his ale tankard tightly.

A buzzing noise indicated that Kolknir's ale was ready. Laocer turned to his right and slid the hidden panel aside to reveal the drink.

"I will get that if you don't mind," Kolknir said, reaching across the table and plucking the drink out of the delivery window. He took a long pull of his ale then resumed his seat. "As for not harming the queen, my master wishes to know what you propose to do with her. He cannot come to power if she lives. Upon the king's death, she alone will inherit the throne—at least until the children come of age."

"Fake the queen's death, and I will take her away. Count her part of my fee if you must," Laocer said, eager to move on.

"And the children?" Kolknir asked.

I don't care about the children!

Laocer drank some ale to steady his nerves. If he answered this question wrong the whole deal would fall through. He suspected Lord Maledek wished the heirs gone as well, but the thought of assassinating toddlers and infants naturally unsettled him.

"Kill them," he answered hoarsely.

"You do not sound very certain on that point," said Kolknir.

Laocer let cold anger enter his eyes and voice.

"I believe Lord Maledek would be a better ruler for Reshner. I don't have to pretend to enjoy the idea of destroying the royal family. Necessity does not make it any less distasteful."

"Why not fake their deaths as well?" Kolknir asked with a knowing grin.

Laocer longed to punch the grin off Kolknir's face.

"It will be hard enough to fake one death and smuggle the queen off the planet."

Kolknir drank part of his ale then set his jaw and stared hard at Laocer.

"How far would you go to get her?"

Glowering, Laocer said, "You know exactly how far I would go." His teeth clenched so hard his head hurt. "I am here offering my services and my access codes to Lord Maledek. I have already admitted a desire that my king and his heirs die. This conversation is enough to condemn me to death. *That* is how far I will go."

"No, that is how far you *think* you will go and even that may be fortified by the ale," Kolknir said rising. "If that is all, I think our time together is at an end."

"Wait!" Laocer said, holding up his left hand.

"How deep is your commitment to this cause?" Kolknir asked again.

Laocer felt sharp emotion tear through his chest.

"I have loved the queen since the day I laid eyes on her. The king and his brats are a burden to her. I hate how she has suffered these long years. I want to take her away from the danger and the pain that comes with the position. But for the light that would cast me in her eyes, I would kill the king with my own hands. That is why I sought your master. I need him, and I can ease his path to the throne."

"Better answer," Kolknir acknowledged. "Please continue."

Chapter 48:
Traveling Fire

Lalri (November) 15, 1546
Prince Teven's Private Chambers, Royal Palace, City of Rammon
Two shrieks cut straight through Terosh's ears and into his head. The shrieks morphed into triumphant screams then challenging yells then dissolved into giggles. Little feet frantically pounded past him first one way and then the other as Rela chased Teven around the room. From his seat on the foot of Teven's bed, Terosh felt like a spectator at a piroball match.

Teven stopped suddenly in front of Terosh. Rela howled victoriously and slammed into him. Both children tumbled to the soft carpet and rolled until they crashed into their father's legs.

Bending down and gathering them in his arms, Terosh asked, "What sort of strange beasts have I captured?"

"Daddy!" Screaming, Rela wriggled around until her arms were free before throwing them around Terosh's neck.

Teven heaved his whole body back and slammed himself full force up into Terosh's chest, trying to knock him back. Laughing, Terosh fell back on the bed.

"Yield, villain!" cried Teven, pushing himself off Terosh's shoulder.

"Never!" declared Terosh. He slipped his right arm up under his son's body, hooked his hand around, and lifted him up with an exaggerated roar. With Teven clinging to his arm like a burr, Terosh slammed it onto the bed at his side, effectively pinning the boy.

Teven giggled.

"Me too, Daddy," Rela pleaded.

Terosh hesitated, not wanting to hurt his daughter. He smiled.

"Princesses are not made for tackling," he said, pulling her further onto his chest. Before she could cry, he added, "They fly." Saying such, Terosh grasped under her armpits and lifted her high, sliding his palms closer together so they formed a sling to support her tiny body. Spurred on by her laughter, he hummed and made sputtering engine noises while waving her back and forth, up and down above his head. When his arms started aching, he lowered her back to his chest.

"My turn!" Teven declared.

Terosh groaned.

"Ride's over. Machine's broken."

"Where's Mommy?" Rela asked, sliding off his chest and landing on her knees next to him. She swatted his stomach when he didn't answer immediately.

Terosh's mind went painfully blank for an awful second. He propped himself up on his elbows and tried to think of a delicate explanation.

"Mommy's busy," he answered lamely, looking from one child to the other.

Teven blinked at him with expressive green eyes that were pure Reia.

"Mommy's baby coming?" asked the boy.

"That's right," Terosh confirmed. He finished sitting up. "The baby's coming today."

"Wanna see!" said Rela.

"Soon," Terosh said, praying it would be so. He hated the thought of Reia in so much pain. Absently, he hugged Rela close with one arm and drew Teven in with the other.

I should be with her.

No, you belong—

Teven squirmed free, scrambled to his feet, and leapt from the bed.

"Where are you going?" Terosh asked, trying to untangle his legs enough to stand.

"Find Mommy," Teven answered.

"Wait! You can't see her right now," Terosh said. He clutched Rela to his chest like a shield and formed a ledge with his right arm for her to sit on.

Seemingly oblivious, Teven ran to the door and looked up at the control panel. Finding it out of reach, he pressed his palm to the button near the floor. The door promptly opened revealing a Royal Guard in resplendent dark blue uniform.

"Sorry, Seth, false alarm," Terosh told the guard. "He's not allowed where he wants to go right now."

Noticing the guard's distraction, Teven slipped through his legs and headed for the last door before the hallway.

Seth started to pursue him but then hesitated.

"Stop him," Terosh said, hoping to clear up the debate apparent on the young guard's face.

Seth caught hold of Teven just before the prince could touch the button that would summon another Royal Guard to open the door.

"Hold there, Young Prince. You're not allowed out there yet."

Teven screeched a wordless protest and threw himself to the floor, kicking and screaming his way into a full-fledged tantrum.

Seeing her brother crying, Rela started fussing too.

The nervous expression on Seth Rolik's face made Terosh laugh.

"Perhaps it might be best if you summoned one of the Melian Maidens, it seems you and I are outmatched here." Terosh shifted his hold on Rela, turning her so she faced him. "Chin up, lass," he said affecting the accent one might expect to hear around Ritten or the Kevloth Plains. "There's no sense crying over nothing."

"Tev cry," Rela pointed out.

Terosh couldn't argue with her logic.

"Well, we'll just have to cheer him up. How should we do that?"

"Kiss?" Rela suggested. She wriggled to get down.

Instead of lowering her to the ground, Terosh tightened his grip. Teven's fit was subsiding, but Terosh didn't want his daughter getting accidentally clobbered by the last vestiges of tantrum.

"That would be nice, but this probably isn't the right moment for that approach," said Terosh.

"What shall I do, Highness?" asked Lieutenant Rolik.

"Wait until he's done thrashing. Then pick him up and bring him here," Terosh ordered.

A few minutes later, a red-faced, exhausted Prince Teven stood sullenly before Terosh.

Although he sympathized with his son, Terosh knew something

needed to be said about the fit or there would be many more. Kneeling, Terosh looked his son directly in the eyes.

"Bad Tev!" Rela shouted.

Nearly choking on suppressed laughter, Terosh instinctively clapped his hand lightly over her mouth.

"Not helpful, Rela."

She mumbled something into his hand.

"Hush, I need to have a word with your brother," said Terosh.

Rela huffed but leaned back and eyed the accused.

"Teven, I know you want your mother, but she cannot be disturbed right now," Terosh said, wishing Reia was there to explain better.

"Why?" Teven asked.

Terosh groaned inwardly. He should have expected that question. His mind scrambled but came up with nothing. The sound of the door opening rescued him.

"Sarie!" Rela announced. She broke free of Terosh's loose grip, hopped down, and raced to the Melian Maiden.

Teven whipped his head around and stared up at Sarie.

"Where's Mommy?" demanded Teven.

Terosh felt his heartbeat quicken.

"Is she all right?" he asked, standing.

A brilliant smile spread across Sarie's dark face as she stooped, gathered Rela into her arms, and straightened.

"She is more than all right, Your Highness. You should go see her and the new prince," said Sarie.

The anotechs could have told them the child's gender, but Terosh and Reia felt it was more fun to simply pick names for either.

A boy!

That meant his name would be Tavel, meaning "traveling fire" in Kalastan.

Feeling as if he would burst if he didn't move, Terosh scooped Teven off the floor and dashed for the door.

Chapter 49:
Fiery Trap

Ferrim (December) 27, 1546
Upper East Library, Royal Palace, City of Rammon

Terosh frowned and entered the code to repeat the message.

A frightened female voice surged forth again.

"Your Highness, I have information concerning Maledek and his long reign of terror. He is someone close to you! I dare not trust any more than that to technology such as this. Meet me in Estra between Cartan and Hiver an hour before moonrise tomorrow. I can tell you more then."

A meeting tomorrow could be arranged, but Terosh questioned the wisdom of it. The obvious questions swirled around his head, leaving him frustrated. He supposed the woman could have faked the fear, but he doubted it.

In the end, the chance to know more about Maladek proved too tempting. Terosh summoned Zareb and Laocer to plan his trip. The attack on the way to Fort Savad last month left him wary enough to take travel precautions.

***

Ferrim (December) 28, 1546
Reia and Terosh's Private Chambers, Royal Palace, City of Rammon

Reia did her best to fight the sorrow and weariness making a mess of her emotions. She frowned down at the baby in her arms surprised to find herself crying again.

"It's not your fault, little love," she assured Tavel, swallowing a sob. She forced a dim smile. "Women are complicated."

"I wholeheartedly agree," Terosh murmured in her left ear. As he spoke, his arms wrapped around her waist and pulled her close. "But they are also soft." He kissed her neck. "And smooth." He ran his fingers over her forearms which still cradled Tavel. "And intelligent, compassionate, and beautiful."

"Terosh!" Reia said unable to keep the surprise out of her voice. She twisted her head left.

"Were you expecting some other man to sneak up on you in our private quarters?" he teased, catching her lips with a tender kiss before she could respond. Then, he loosened his grip so she could turn and face him fully. He kissed her again, leaning forward so as not to smother their son in the process.

"I thought you had left already," Reia said hastily between kisses.

"Officially, I did," Terosh replied, trading passion and length of kiss for frequency and the ability to talk. "Unofficially, I could not bear to leave without a proper farewell."

A fit of laughter welled up in Reia.

"I—am—glad." She gave up speaking and leaned into his next kiss.

Tavel whined.

Reia broke the kiss off with a soft groan and leaned back.

"Let me just put him down."

"May I?" Terosh held his arms out for the child.

Reia eased the baby into his arms, feeling suddenly cold without the tiny bundle.

Terosh cradled Tavel for a few minutes, pacing the room until the baby fell asleep. Then, he kissed the soft cheek, murmured a goodbye, and laid the infant in his crib.

"He'll probably grow three inches by the time I return tomorrow," said Terosh.

"I thought you'd be back tonight." A pang of dismay shot through Reia.

"Night crossings can be tricky," Terosh said with a shrug. "We'll be safer spending the night in Estra and crossing to Chara in the morning."

While Reia could not argue with the logic, she dreaded spending the night alone. She gazed bleakly down at Tavel.

"It's only one night, my queen," Terosh promised, pulling her into a tight embrace. He kissed the top of her head.

"Let me come with you," she urged.

For a moment she thought he would consent, but he said, "It's too dangerous."

Reia leaned back, straining against the circle of his arms.

"If you suspect danger, then send someone else!" she said, feeling tears rise again. "Why go if you expect a trap?"

Terosh moved his hands to her shoulders and held her at arm's length so he could meet her eyes.

"I suspect no more danger than usual, especially since Todd's traveling with me. I should be safe enough. I meant only that it is dangerous for us to travel together." He squeezed her shoulders. "Reia, we have more to live for than ever. I want to know you are here and safe with the children."

Feeling her heart might crack under the strain, Reia fought off a tide of bitterness, stepped up to Terosh, and nearly crushed him with the force of her affection.

"Alosoolsusonana, my love," she whispered, pulling his head down for a long kiss. (To success on your journey.)

***

Ferrim (December) 28, 1546
City of Estra

Memories of holding Reia provided Terosh with bittersweet company during the long trip down to the city of Estra in the Frozen North. Illness had cheated him of approximately half the years spent with her. Every moment apart felt like a cruelty.

Terosh generally distrusted anonymous contacts, but he understood the necessity of such given the soaring political tensions. The Colza Star explosion had been but a tiny flare in Reshner's sky, but Terosh suspected the true extent of the ramifications would be acutely felt for years. The more he learned about GAPP the less he felt inclined to champion their cause, but at the same time, he truly believed in the absolute rightness of aiding Rorge II. If GAPP proved the easiest means of lending aid, then they still warranted consideration. The debate had waxed hot and cold for years now. Terosh couldn't decide whether he should hope for heated discussion or cold indifference. He only knew that something would need to change soon or the Senate and Governors Council would splinter into ineffective messes.

The anotechs warned Terosh of danger two seconds before a massive explosion launched his hov many meters into the air. He immediately encased himself and his guards in thick anotech shields. A desperate scream merged with the explosion's roar, and Terosh knew that the driver's shield had failed. The hov flipped several times as it rose then hurtled nose-down toward the ground again.

Feeling like his chest and head would split open, Terosh threw his awareness outside of the hov. Once he saw where the hov was headed, he seized it in a mighty anotech grip and slowed the descent enough to avoid fatal impact. The crash bent metal and broke glass. The hov's interior filled with smoke and dust. Terosh's ears rang. The anotechs filtered the air going into his lungs, but his guards were not so lucky. Even though he could not hear them, he saw their bodies convulse with violent coughs. Dazed, Terosh instructed the anotechs to filter air for his two living guards.

Sensing danger approaching from several directions, Terosh bid the anotechs to find him a quick exit and grabbed hold of his two semi-conscious guards. Part of the hov's roof peeled away above his head. Relying on adrenaline and anotechs, Terosh clutched the guards one under each arm, clenched his eyes shut, and imagined rising. Much as he had done to escape the maw ages ago, Terosh continued lifting all three of their bodies until they cleared the hole in the hov's roof. Then, he released the guards and let them tumble to the ground.

Hoping his energy reserves held, Terosh aimed his body forward and landed on his hands and knees. Two kerlak shots warned him the danger had not passed. Terosh flinched as the anotech shields still encasing his two guards shuddered under the influx of energy. His gaze flickered toward them, and he allowed his dismay and worry to shine clearly in his expression.

Todd!

The Ranger lay unconscious beside Zareb. Terosh tore his attention away from them but demanded a report from the anotechs. Both had been shocked unconscious by the first explosion. The additional kerlak shots would have killed them, but the anotech shields held. Terosh entertained a lightning quick debate with himself before issuing his order.

Keep them unconscious until it is safe. Convince everyone they're dead, and then send them home.

Unfortunately, the plan could not work for him. The fact that no kerlak beams or serlak bullets riddled his body meant the figures he sensed approaching intended capture, a contradiction considering the force of the initial explosion.

"I see you have survived," said Kezem.

"Kezem?" Terosh asked, whipping his head up to look at the dark figure that stood before him. His cousin's physique had grown quite impressive during his time on Gardan. Questions crowded Terosh's head.

"Welcome, Terosh," Kezem greeted. "We never did complete our duel all those years ago. I believe it is time we finished the matter." He pulled two kerlinblades from his belt and activated them simultaneously. A green blade with a yellow core and a blue blade with a red core sprang into existence.

"Doesn't this strike you as a tad unfair?" Terosh muttered. He staggered to his feet and took out his kerlinblade. After brief contemplation, he left the blade unlit.

"I couldn't decide whether I wanted you to die in the explosion or kill you myself. Now that the explosion has failed, I am grateful," said Kezem.

Glad I could make you happy.

Terosh gingerly shook each limb to make sure they worked properly.

"What happened to the woman in the message?" he inquired, trying to stretch out the moments before the inevitable duel so the anotechs could conduct emergency repairs on his battered body. "Was she real?"

Next time, avoid explosions! the anotechs scolded.

Just make sure there is a next time, Terosh answered.

"Oh, she is quite real," Kezem said darkly, waving to his left with the blue and red kerlinblade. "I present Lady Merisia Restler, to whom I owe great thanks for setting these events in motion."

A door hissed open, and three figures emerged. Two men supported a woman bound hand and foot with stuncuffs. Terosh recognized the man on the woman's right as former Ranger Lucas Telon. A faint scar marked the space below his left eye. The woman's dark hair hung limply around her shoulders. A red, black, and blue welt decorated her left cheek. Her purple eyes glittered with tears, bleakness marring their beauty. She would not meet the king's gaze. Her expression declared both helplessness and hopelessness.

Some of Terosh's weariness vanished beneath a tide of anger. Whether she had willingly or unwillingly participated in this trap, he hated to see her as Kezem's prisoner.

"The trap worked fine. Let her go," he commanded.

Kezem's smile filled with paradoxes. It contained aspects of ice and fire, kindness and cruelty, love and hatred, sympathy and contempt.

"I always knew your compassion would kill you. I just did not know how. Now I have my answer." Kezem motioned toward Merisia again with his lit kerlinblade. "For what it's worth, she did not betray you. She betrayed me, and for that she will die here and now."

The men flanking Merisia Restler shoved her onto her knees.

Knowing he could stall no longer, Terosh activated his kerlinblade and turned his body to face the woman and her captors. He thrust an open palm toward them and made a fist, all the while issuing frantic orders.

The anotechs answered his commands with relish. Lucas Telon cried out in terror as his body hurtled toward Terosh's blazing white blade. Terror turned to pain as blade met and triumphed over flesh. Meanwhile, Lucas's partner hurtled backward through the open doorway they had emerged from and crashed into something hard somewhere beyond.

Merisia dove to the ground, but not before several kerlak beams converged on her, struck the anotech shield surrounding her, and reflected back to their startled sources. Three unlucky men fell to the ground with pain-filled cries. A fourth man caught the reflected beam in his left arm and dropped to the ground with a stream of curses. Merisia ran dazed eyes over the chaotic scene.

With another thought, Terosh released the stuncuffs binding her wrists and ankles and imbued her with the urge to flee.

Several of Kezem's men started to pursue Merisia, but Terosh hauled them back with invisible anotech tethers. They started to rise only to be cut down by a hail of kerlak beams.

"Merisia!" called a young man. He waved frantically and shot at a few more of Kezem's soldiers.

"Taly!" shouted Merisia Restler. The cry was two parts a plea for help and one part stunned greeting.

"Get gone!" Terosh ordered. He drew his kerlak pistol and covered their retreat long enough to see them disappear into a hov and speed off.

Good luck, my friends.

An inarticulate roar warned Terosh as Kezem's blades descended toward his head. Hoping Taly and Merisia would make it, Terosh yanked his concentration back to the moment and raised his kerlinblade to parry the blows. The force of them shuddered through

Terosh's tired arms. He successfully blocked three more swift strikes, but each drained a little more of his precious energy.

Kezem's remaining men formed a loose circle around them. The duel proceeded in an abrupt, desperate manner. Terosh and Kezem lashed mercilessly at each other with blades, fists, and feet.

As the moons rose, a kick from Kezem knocked Terosh into the crowd. Many hands fell upon him. A desperate swipe with his kerlinblade separated several of those hands from their respective owners, but more hands took their place.

Terosh screamed his frustration as his kerlinblade was plucked from his grasp. His eyes caught a flash of metal arcing toward his face. He threw his head right but a kerlinblade handle slammed into his jaw anyway. He tasted blood. His head ached. Something knocked hard into his chest, driving breath from his burning lungs. Another head blow set off a storm of lights behind his eyes. The anotechs cried out for orders, but he could not think straight. Images of his children filled his mind as he lost consciousness.

Chapter 50:
Sweet Servant

Ferrim (December) 29, 1546
Maledek's Private Retreat, City of Idonia

King Terosh Minstel's return to consciousness was not a pleasant experience. Despite the anotechs' best efforts, most of his body hurt. Everything ached. His head throbbed so badly his teeth tingled. He tasted blood. Every breath felt like swallowing a dagger. The few parts of him that didn't ache stung horribly.

His mind jumped back to the explosion and the fight that followed.

Zareb. Todd.

He hoped both friends still lived. They would be understandably furious with him, but he did not regret his actions.

I'm sorry, Reia.

A wave of sadness brought an ache to his chest that almost drowned out the physical pain coursing throughout his body. He beat back the tide of self-pity by focusing on anger. Very few people knew about the meeting in Estra. Fewer people still had the contacts to bait such a simple, almost elegant trap.

Kezem.

The dungeon's heavy door swung open before he could fully follow his thoughts to completion. He gathered his strength to face his cousin. To his surprise, a girl about nine or ten years old entered hauling a bucket and carrying a sponge. She said nothing as she gently washed his wounds, and she kept her expression neutral. She could have been anybody, but Terosh recognized the icy blue eyes and gentle, innocent features.

Elia! Oh, Tate, if only you knew. She's alive!

He wanted to speak to her but could not work up enough energy. His efforts went into sucking in one more fiery breath and forming useless tears. He wept for his long-dead brother, his niece—this child tending his wounds—himself, his children, his wife, and his unsuspecting people.

When the girl leaned over to clean the blood off his neck, she whispered, "I'm not supposed to talk to you, but I like you. I hope you fight well."

Terosh longed to tell her about her father, but she was almost done cleaning him. Pouring his will into the gesture, he lifted his hand. Instinctively, the child took hold of the hand. Terosh closed his fist around her tiny hand and willed some anotechs to leave him. When the time was right, they would explain the child's heritage to her. He could do no more, and the effort drained him.

He released a few anotechs into his surroundings and felt the hard stone floor in a new way. This was no modern prison. It was a dungeon, carefully preserved throughout the centuries to crush the hopes of its occupants. Terosh idly wondered how many people's blood had filled the cracks between the stones digging into his back. When the scouts returned, they told him news that broke his heart anew.

Lord Kezem killed Princess Deanna Koffrin Minstel here. The stones still echo with her presence.

But why kill her?

Dark man, First Maladek, likes power and pain.

There must be something more to warrant such lengths of cruelty, Terosh argued.

He has promised to destroy House Minstel.

But he's a part of it. His mother once carried the name. Why hate us so much?

The anotechs remained strangely quiet, but Terosh knew the answer. He had known the answer for most of his life. Knowing in his mind and being here—feeling the traces of Deanna's despair—were completely different matters. His father's sister, Princess Mavis Altran, had been disowned by her father. Her hatred had obviously been cultivated in her sons.

Terosh would have laughed at such petty hatred, but two thoughts sobered him. He lay atop the very place his brother's wife had been murdered, and his own family would likely be consumed by the same hatred that had killed her so many years ago.

The threat to his family caused Terosh to rally some strength, organizing the anotechs to maximize their healing efforts. He wished for his wife's presence then immediately regretted the thought. He would never wish such danger upon her. She had been through too much already.

He closed his eyes to rest while the anotechs began their healing works on him.

Chapter 51:
Ralose Charm

Lanolin (February) 30, 1547
Princess Rela's Private Chamber, Royal Palace, City of Rammon
"I want to put the Ralose Charm on Rela," Reia announced calmly from where she sat on the edge of the large bed. She cradled the sword Terosh had given her years ago. Her left hand rested atop the scabbard and her right hand cupped the hilt from underneath.

Kiata Antellio Wellum closed the inner room's door and stared hard at her little sister. Her instincts had warned that the early morning summons did not bode well, but nothing could have prepared her for that proposal. She opened her mouth to speak but could not find words to respond. She settled for several long, slow breaths as she organized her thoughts.

"I know the plan is dangerous," Reia said, not daring to meet Kiata's eyes. "That is why I need your help. I need you to live." The last statement came out almost painfully slow, yet it bore an edge of conviction.

And everybody needs you to live, so why can't you listen to reason?

"Reia, you're talking crazy," Kiata snapped. "Even if the Ralose Charm works exactly as it is supposed to, what do you hope to accomplish by it?"

"Should the palace fall, my daughter will survive," said Reia, raising her chin defiantly.

Should? Of course, it's going to fall if you keep sending its defenders to all corners of the planet!

Kiata glared the message at her stubborn sister.

"She would survive if you abdicated. Kezem wants the throne and—"

"And he cannot have it while even one of Terosh's children draws breath," Reia finished, rising from her perch on the bed. She clipped the sword onto her belt, walked past Kiata to the cradle tucked into the corner, and gripped its edge. "If I surrender, he will kill them. If I escape, he will tear apart many lives in the pursuit of them." She lingered a moment longer staring at the child, and then, she shifted her gaze back to her sister. "This way, perhaps part of his bloodlust will be sated, and he will be thwarted by the inability to harm Rela."

You're still talking crazy.

"The last two people to be connected by the Ralose Charm died the same day," said Kiata harshly, trying to shock her sister back to sense. "How can you be certain Kezem won't kill her before he even realizes the connection?"

Reia flinched.

"I … cannot be certain of anything, but I believe Sarie will agree to warn him." She leaned back against the sturdy cradle.

Hearing the bewildered then slightly hopeful words crushed some of Kiata's will to resist.

"And what is my part in this scheme?" asked Kiata, though she knew what her sister would ask. "Please say, go kill Lord Kezem."

"You must sever the connection when the time comes," said Reia.

"How will I know when the time comes?" Kiata asked, trying valiantly to keep her tone gentle.

And how exactly does one sever a Ralose Charm?

"You will know," Reia said cryptically.

Kiata simultaneously feared and respected the tone.

You do not even know if I will live long enough to be of use in this.

Pushing the sobering thought aside, Kiata sighed.

"When do we begin?" Before she knew what was happening, Kiata was caught up in a fierce embrace. The hilt of Reia's sword bumped into Kiata's left thigh.

"I knew you would help," Reia whispered, arms still locked around Kiata.

I always did have trouble denying you.

A tingling sensation emanated from where Reia's hands and arms touched her back. Kiata knew she ought to recognize the feeling, but the impression eluded her attempt to identify it. Deciding to worry about the feeling later, Kiata returned her sister's hug.

"You always did get your way, even before you were queen," said Kiata with forced levity. "There's no sense breaking with tradition now."

Reia tightened her grip even more before suddenly releasing her hold on Kiata and pulling away.

"Thank you," she said. Her voice trembled with suppressed emotion.

"You can thank me better by letting me help you escape," Kiata said wearily. She fought the impulse to knock her sister out cold and cart her away to somewhere safe. She put a half-step between them, drew in a fortifying breath, and concentrated on releasing it slowly. The last bit flew out in a frustrated rush. "But since you seem bent on this path, I will help you any way I can. What provisions have you made for the boys?"

"Teven will go with the McKnights, and the Osem Rangers have agreed to shelter Tavel," said Reia, her voice recovering some of its strength for having something to report. "Todd sent the news yesterday. He said he had a few more things to take care of in Osem, but he hopes to return tomorrow. He also sends you his love." Her lips formed a sad smile.

Kiata's expression darkened. She mentally railed against her insensitive husband for inadvertently reminding her sister of what she had lost.

Reading Kiata's annoyance in her narrowed eyes, Reia's smile broadened.

"Don't hold it against him. It is good to know love still exists."

Kiata grunted, still miffed at Todd.

"Do you trust the McKnights?" she asked, needing to redirect the conversation.

"I trust them less than I would you, but you and Todd have Kayleen to think of," said Reia. "Surrounding my son with soldiers would only catch Kezem's attention. Pria and Nathan have the best chance of moving about anonymously, and they are good people besides. I will send Laocer and a few others to guard them from a distance."

"The captain will not take kindly to that order," Kiata pointed out.

"But he will obey it," Reia said confidently.

Seems to be the only thing to do around here, Kiata thought darkly.

She leaned over her niece's cradle and envied the girl's peaceful repose.

"Should we wake her for the ritual?" asked Kiata.

"No, let her sleep," said Reia. "She would not remember it anyway."

A chill climbed Kiata's spine at those words, but once again, the exact reason for the worry eluded her.

***

Reia's emotions threatened to spill over and send her into a sobbing fit. Each heartbeat pounded painfully in her chest. Knowing if she hesitated any longer she might fail to do what was necessary, Reia pressed a code into the cradle's railing and watched it slide down. Then, she drew the thin sword and placed it next to her daughter. Not satisfied with the layout, Reia scooped up the child, adjusted the sword so it lay diagonally across the cradle mattress, and gently laid Rela on top of the sword's flat edge.

The child stirred and almost woke up, Reia touched her daughter's right shoulder and sent some anotechs with soothing thoughts.

"That was close," Reia said. She glanced at her sister. "Please repeat the words in Kalastan."

Kiata gave her a strange look but nodded.

Reia closed her eyes and placed her left palm on Rela's chest and the tips of her right fingers on the sword.

"Bind the intended souls together." She stopped so Kiata could speak.

Clearing her throat, Kiata said, "Tinetonenkalaensem." (Tin-et-on-en-kal-la-en-sem)

"May their bodies reflect any harm," Reia said. As she spoke, she instructed anotechs to enter both the sword and her daughter. Then, she bid them each to divide and send the new copy to the other form.

"Praesucorpraltonmal," Kiata repeated. (Prah-eh-soo-corp-ral-ton-mahl)

"Where one bleeds, so shall the other," Reia intoned. Her arms, shoulders, and neck tingled as anotechs flowed up one arm and down the other in both directions. Some of the anotechs argued about leaving her, but she willed them to obey.

"Quelunsans cosaletotre," said Kiata. (Kel-lun-sans co-sal-et-oat-ray)

"May this preserve them both," Reia finished. She waited for the anotechs to finish moving. Then, she slowly removed her hands from Rela and the sword.

"Praeseprimalosamb," Kiata translated, sounding relieved to finish. (Prah-esse-pre-mahl-los-am-be)

Remembering she needed to instruct the anotechs on which code to listen for, Reia returned her hands to Rela's chest and the sword. The anotechs stopped their flurry of activity to listen as she sent them the proper phrases to end the Ralose Charm. When she finished, she again removed her hands and told her sister the same phrases.

"Prietal? Why that dialect?" Kiata asked, surprised.

Reia shrugged.

"It sounds better than regular Kalastan. It's also easier to memorize." She winced. She had not meant to mention that last part. She braced for the question Kiata would inevitably ask.

"Why should that matter?" Kiata's voice was saturated with suspicion.

Reia ignored the question, using the careful extraction of her sword from beneath her slumbering daughter as an excuse to do so. Her emotions once more threatened to sweep away her senses. She frantically searched for something reasonable to say. Unfortunately, by the time she had the sword safely sheathed, she had still come up with nothing to allay Kiata's suspicions. Reia stared at her daughter, trying to buy a few extra seconds to think.

Kiata grabbed her right shoulder and turned her so they stood face to face.

"Reia, what aren't you telling me?"

The tide of Reia's inner battle shifted, and her vision suddenly clouded with tears. A sob caught in her throat and burned.

I love you too much to lose you!

She squeezed her eyes shut so they would not send that message, but it was too late.

"No!" Kiata's voice was a fierce whisper, and she held her sister by both shoulders. "Whatever you've done, Reia, undo it right now. Don't you dare waste any effort trying to protect me!"

The admonishment shattered the barriers Reia had carefully erected around her heart.

It's too late.

Her knees went weak, and she dissolved into tears. She would have fallen, but Kiata wrapped her in a tight hug.

As the need to sob slowly drained away, Reia debated how much to tell Kiata. She could barely explain it to herself, let alone anyone else. Losing Terosh had been the single most painful experience of her life. She almost wished Kezem had not sent her his body. Then, at least she would have some irrational hope he still lived. She could not bear the thought of Kiata dying as well.

Or Todd or Kayleen or any of my children.

The next time she saw them she would do for them what she had done for Kiata, but she could not tell her sister anything about those plans. She would not risk provoking her Kiata's anger in what could be their last moments together.

Finally pulling out of the hug, Kiata said, "Reia, please. You have enough to worry about without adding me to that list." Unshed tears made her eyes shiny. "Concentrate on saving yourself."

Can't. I have to save you from you.

Reia couldn't help but smile as she used her knuckles to dash a few late tears from her eyes.

"I love you. Remember that," she whispered.

"You're not going to tell me, are you?" Kiata asked with an exasperated yet resigned expression. "May I ask why?"

Reia shook her head.

No, if I tried to explain, you might talk me out of it.

"Trust me," Reia said, not quite keeping traces of pleading from her tone. "The most important thing now is that you live long enough to free Rela from the burden we just placed on her. Whatever happens, please free her."

Chapter 52:
One True Failing

Jira (March) 2, 1547
Wellum Home, City of Rammon

Kiata Wellum futilely wished she could access the anotechs like she had a few years back, but the first and second decommissioning ceremonies had severed her connection and left some disturbing blanks in her memory. Her third joining ceremony had restored some of her memories and occasionally allowed her to call upon the anotechs. Master Niklos assured her that such a thing was normal and that the full connection should return in a few years. The knowledge had set her mind at ease at the time, but she knew now that she could not wait a moment longer.

She wished Nils Clavon luck and speed on his quest to see Kayleen to the safety of the Riden Mountains. Kiata's grip on her banistick tightened painfully as her thoughts brushed against the hasty parting with her daughter. A large part of her wanted to leave Todd an encrypted message and chase after Nils and Kayleen.

Torn between waiting here and retreating to the palace, Kiata paced and took a few practice swipes with her banistick. Reia would need her. Kiata hated not being with her sister during this desperate time, but she knew Kezem would send someone to seek her and Todd. She dashed off another futile wish, urging Todd to hurry home from his mission. If Kezem's men did not find anyone in the Wellum home, they might search for Nils and Kayleen. Kiata would not let that happen.

While her thoughts still tumbled about in a flurry of wishes and partial plans, a simple knock sounded at the door. Kiata froze as trepidation and curiosity mingled in her gut. As she stepped close to the front door, she traded her banistick for a kerlak pistol and set it to high stun. She doubted the caller was friendly, but it would be terribly bad form to kill a neighbor, even in these stressful times.

A second knock sounded, and then came the terrifying sound of the locks clicking open. No sooner had the sound registered with Kiata, the door swung out and a flood of burgandy uniforms crashed into her front room. Three quick shots dropped a trio of eager soldiers before a fourth, fifth, and sixth tackled her to the floor.

As she fell backward, Kiata managed to smack one of her assailants aside. Landing on her back, she squeezed off another stun beam into one of the soldiers and jerked her head violently right to avoid a devastating blow. She lost her grip on the kerlak pistol and heard it clatter away.

The soldier's hand met the floor with an audible crack where her head had been a second before. His howl ripped at Kiata's nerves. Her shoulders hurt where the remaining soldier—the one she had temporarily knocked aside—used his weight to pin her to the floor. Kiata reached for the pressure points in his upper arms and squeezed hard. The young man recoiled, giving Kiata enough room to bring her knees up into his chest and heave him off balance.

Momentarily free, Kiata rolled to her right. Something heavy landed on her, forcing her back to the ground. It was a man. His left arm slipped around her neck. Pressing off the floor, Kiata brought her left elbow up and drove it back as hard as she could where she hoped the man's head might be. The blow connected with a satisfying impact, but she paid for it with sharp pain in her elbow. The man behind her went limp, but she lacked proper time to revel in the small triumph.

Two men reached for her arms. Kiata let them each get a grip before grasping their shirts and yanking them toward each other. They bumped heads but not with enough force to do any real damage. Kiata snapped to her feet, thrusting her arms forward to push the two men away. She drew her banistick and sent it hard into the two dazed men in front of her before whipping it downward and back to deal with the man who had tried to strangle her.

"Well done," said a mocking male voice from the threshold.

Kiata raised her banistick to a guard position and eyed the speaker warily. He stood calmly in the doorway flanked by four men, two kneeling and two standing. All held kerlak rifles pointed her way.

Her breath caught. Deflecting or dodging one energy beam at this range would be very difficult. The possibility of facing four at once filled her with icy fear. Her eyes darted about the room, making sure no more surprises waited to make her day worse.

"Have you no words of greeting for a former master?" Kolknir asked. His dark blue uniform was laden with pins and tiny ribbons. He took a small step into the room. "You should congratulate me on my new rank. I am now a sublord."

"Your men haven't exactly given me much time to talk," Kiata said, again scanning for further signs of trouble.

"You'll have to forgive them for being so eager. I promised a reward for the first to subdue you," said Kolknir.

"You always were an inspiring instructor," Kiata said dryly.

Kolknir tipped his head in a small bow.

"And you were one of my finest students. You have no idea how long I pleaded with Lord Kezem to let me spare your life. I told him I believed I could turn you to our cause." His voice tried too hard to sound refined.

"Really? What did he say?" Kiata quirked an eyebrow at Kolknir and carefully stepped over one of the fallen soldiers. If she was about to die, she wanted a lot of room to take as many of them with her as possible.

"Unfortunately, he did not believe me," said Kolknir. "I told him everything comes down to motivation." His slow words chilled Kiata. He chuckled at the alarm in her eyes. "I am certain your little girl would make fine motivation."

Kiata's whole body tensed, but she willed her muscles to uncoil.

Neelyak is safe. Nils got her away.

"You don't have her," she said, shaking her head and praying she was right. She longed to kiss her daughter one more time.

"What makes you believe that?" asked Kolknir, affecting innocent curiosity.

"Because you're twisted enough to flaunt her if you did have her," Kiata explained.

Kolknir's chuckle deepened into gentle, rolling laughter.

"You are correct, for now, though more of my men are seeking her than those I have here. It simply gives you more time to contemplate the moral dilemma."

As Kolknir spoke, he took another small step forward, giving his men enough room to file in. Some bent to tend their comrades, but most fanned out along the walls. Soon, Kiata would be surrounded.

"You would risk Lord Kezem's favor to prove a point? That's either brave or stupid, possibly both," said Kiata, trying to fight off the sinking despair that threatened to sap her energy.

After his soldiers completed the loose circle around her, Kolknir said, "I'm sure he would forgive me for the novelty of seeing the queen's own sister raise a weapon against her. What do you say, Kiata? Will you help me prove my point?" Kolknir's cold smile sucked warmth from the air.

Kiata fought the urge to speak, but her response slipped out anyway.

"No." Her voice sounded weak to her ears, and she could only imagine how pathetic it sounded to Kolknir and his men.

He gave her a puzzled, almost wounded, look.

"Not even to save your own daughter?"

"What would it gain to save her, only to leave her in your hands?" Kiata fired back.

"Not even to save her from pain?" Kolknir pressed.

Despite knowing Kolknir wielded the words as empty threats, Kiata felt the pain of them. She couldn't believe she was having such a conversation with this vile man. "Anyone who fashions such a threat against a child has tarnished honor," she said, blinking away tears. "Your promises are only true as far as they suit you." The declaration came out stronger than her first statement, thanks to the anger coursing freely through her. When it ebbed, she added, "Should my poor daughter ever find herself in such a position, she would already be beyond hope."

"Good logic, Kiata, but I wonder if your reasoning would hold during the real test. Could you listen and watch as—"

"Could your men?" Kiata interrupted. "Could they listen and watch you harm a child?" She glared at the soldiers surrounding her.

Most of them had the grace to look down.

"Ranner, shoot her. Stun only, please," said Kolknir.

The soldier to Kolknir's left jerked in surprise, giving Kiata enough time to move her banistick into line as he shot three blue stun beams in quick succession.

Kiata ducked under the first two and deflected the third into one of the men standing to her left. The soldier uttered a surprised cry as the beam plowed him into a wall.

"Stop!" Kolknir shouted.

Everybody froze.

Sighing, Kolknir said, "Wesley, Collins, Abrams, the backup plan. We have need of it."

Three men chorused, "It will be done," and hurried from the room.

Kiata felt relief at their parting, but it was followed by worry for whatever ills composed the backup plan. Tense moments passed in painful semi-silence. Only the sound of ragged breaths and a few moans from soldiers regaining consciousness stirred the tension. As Kiata decided not to wait for the backup plan to be implemented, Kolknir's voice seized her attention again.

"I am testing my theory, but if this goes poorly, I will kill them," Kolknir promised.

"Who?" Kiata asked, her banistick half-raised to take a swing at the nearest soldier.

She didn't have long to wait. Wesley, Collins, and Abrams returned with a small herd of terrified neighbors. They shuffled past Kolknir with lowered gazes. From their tight-lipped expressions, they had obviously been warned not to speak. Master Ullier's face boasted a puffy, black and blue left eye which leaked slow tears of blood and bore the marks of a rifle stock.

Groaning, Kiata fought the impulse to fling her banistick to the ground in frustration.

"That's your backup plan?" She poured contempt into the question. "It's a fine example of what Kezem's order offers the people." She tried to make eye contact with her neighbors, but they studiously considered the ground.

"Drop your weapon," Kolknir ordered. His voice held none of the levity it had possessed before.

Kiata hesitated.

Kolknir moved so fast he was a blur, snatching a small child out of the line and pressing a dagger to her throat. Kiata couldn't even be certain where he'd drawn the dagger from. The girl whimpered. Kiata's breath hitched. The child, Ishella Ullier, was only a few months older than Kayleen.

"No! Leave her!" shouted Adam Ullier, the girl's father. He took a step toward Kolknir only to be stopped by several rifles leveled at his chest and three pairs of hands grasping his arms. His frightened eyes roamed the room, settling on Kiata. "Do something, Ranger!"

"What do you really want of me?" Kiata demanded, glaring at

Kolknir. "Surely, it must be more than trying to prove to Kezem you can bend someone to your will. I will not harm my sister for anything." She prepared to attack Kolknir. It wouldn't save the child, but the one casualty was the best Kiata could hope for at this point.

Grabbing a handful of Ishella's golden hair, Kolknir pulled the child's head back, exposing her neck. The girl's jaw trembled and tears streamed freely down her face. Kolknir's right hand swept the dagger close enough to draw a thin line of blood. A whimper escaped the child before she remembered to keep silent. Her tears dropped onto Kolknir's hand.

"Look into her eyes, Ranger," Kolknir challenged. "Can you really make that move?"

She couldn't or she wouldn't. Kiata's mind flashed to a training exercise many years ago where Kolknir tried to teach her that sacrificing one life or even two might be necessary. She had hated the lesson and her inability to dispassionately fulfill her duties.

"Let them go," Kiata said. Her voice sounded hollow. She let her banistick drop to her side.

"They will be free as soon as I have your complete surrender," Kolknir promised.

Kiata's thoughts raced. Other than threatening her, Kolknir had no use for her neighbors. He probably wouldn't kill them out of spite. Kezem wanted to conquer Rammon, not kill its inhabitants. Too much bloodshed would force the people to choose a side. Heart thudding in her ears, Kiata concluded Kolknir would keep his word. She straightened out of her combat stance and let her banistick tumble from her fingers.

Kolknir's eyes lit with feral triumph, and he laughed again.

"Now kneel," he ordered.

"Release them," Kiata countered, standing her ground.

Kolknir nodded to his three hand-picked henchmen who hustled the prisoners out the door. He maintained his firm grip on Ishella.

"I will not repeat the order," he warned.

"She has suffered enough," Kiata said, slowly dropping to one knee and then the other. "Let her return to her father. You gain nothing by forcing her to watch what comes."

"As you wish," said Kolknir, releasing his hold on the girl.

She wisely scampered away.

Before Kiata could regain her feet, Kolknir tucked his dagger behind his back. When his hand returned, it held two flingers. He threw them with quick snaps of his wrist.

The first raked along Kiata's left cheek and the second struck her high in the right shoulder. She cried out at the sudden pain and found herself falling backward. Many hands caught her and forced her back to the kneeling position. One hand pressed against the back of her head, pushing downward. Instinctively, she tried to wrest her body free of the grasping hands. Her right shoulder protested every movement.

"Up," said Kolknir.

The hands pulled Kiata to her feet and bound her forearms and wrists together with rope. The man who had pushed her head down now reversed direction until she faced Kolknir again. Most of the hands let go, but two tall men each had firm grips on her upper arms.

Stepping close, Kolknir plucked his flinger from her right shoulder. Absently flipping the flinger with his left hand, Kolknir tenderly traced the tips of his right fingers over the wound on Kiata's face.

"You never learned that lesson about sacrificing others. I think it was your one true failing." He had said as much all those years ago.

Kiata's response from the past echoed in her mind and strengthened her heart.

If this is failure, Master, then I am glad to fail.

Kolknir let his hand drop and studied the damage done to her shoulder.

"Such a tiny wound," he said. The next instant, his dagger was back in his hand and then lodged in Kiata's shoulder.

She had braced for something like this, so only a groan and a stream of tears told him she felt the dagger.

As Kolknir slowly pulled the blade out, he tugged down, smiling when it earned a small cry from her.

"Better," he said, admiring his handiwork. He flicked his eyes at the soldier standing to her right.

The man tightened his left hand but released his right hand. A second later, his right hand found the wound on her shoulder and squeezed.

The increased pain darkened Kiata's vision. She thought she would welcome unconsciousness.

I'm sorry, Reia. I love you, Todd. Be safe, Kayleen.

Epilogue:

Retsi (May) 28, 1547
Priest's Quarters, Temple of Marishaz, City of Chara

A faint knock tore Father Morgivesh Niktol's concentration away from his half-finished sermon. He sighed.

If you wanted an uninterrupted life, you should have joined Tormi at sea.

A second, more insistent, knock prompted him to speak.

"Hold, friend. I hear you."

"Are you Father Niktol?" inquired a woman. Her words, despite being muffled by the door, possessed urgent energy.

The queen's cryptic message suddenly made sense. Niktol's heart lurched. He hurried to the door, flung it open, and hauled the startled woman inside.

The woman threw off his hands, spun away from him, and assumed a fighter's stance in the center of the small welcome room, fierceness and confusion equally present on her face. The cloak that had previously hidden her features hung from her shoulders.

Niktol shut the door then turned and spread his hands in a non-threatening manner.

How did you escape? How did you get here? How much do you remember? Those questions and a hundred like them crowded Niktol's head.

"Welcome, friend. You are safe here. I am Father Niktol."

The woman straightened slowly and stared down at her hands in confusion. Frustrated tears glittered in her eyes as she looked to Niktol.

"I can't remember who I am," she said in a hoarse whisper, "but I felt drawn here. Can you help me?"

I will do whatever it takes to keep those I love from harm.

Niktol remembered the queen's declaration. He had not exactly dismissed it, but he had never imagined Queen Reia possessing the power or the will to do what she had done.

Trust that time will restore all to right. Protect my treasures until the proper time.

"Can you help me?" repeated the woman. Her haunted eyes scanned his welcome room for signs of danger.

Niktol wondered what sort of burden he had agreed to bear, but he could see the prolonged silence weighing on the woman.

"Dear lady, I do not know how much I can help you, but I do know your name. You are called Kiata."

The End

(There's more to come in *Reshner's Royal Guard.*)

Thank You for Reading:

I hope you enjoyed this story, despite it's unsettling end. Please understand that it's the middle of a trilogy. The conclusion to this saga can be found in *Reshner's Royal Guard*. Honest reviews are always welcome as they help others find the books.

Please visit my website: **www.juliecgilbert.com** and get on the newsletter (**https://www.subscribepage.com/n7e818**) to keep up with new releases and bonus content. Check out the audiobooks. They have fantastic narrators.

Sincerely,

Julie C. Gilbert

Appendix I: Annotated Glossary

Adrik Bentanner – RT agent working under Gareth Restler
Akia Zelene – daughter of Resh's governor
Alden Tarpon – son of Vera and Tyko; RT agent
Arista Restler – mother of Gareth and Nera
Ariman Keldor – RT agent; Taly's father; Niktrod's son
Atien Belcross – former scientist; worked in the palace once upon a time
Brook Tarpon – eldest son of Vera and Tyko; Nera's husband
Cadrish – speech tutor for the Royal House Minstel
Covin – Elish male; twin of Zareb; Royal Guard; serves King Terosh
Dalonos – "dark ones"; anotechs who have a proclivity to pursue evil intent
Darmon Zelene – Governor of Resh; Akia's father
Deanna Koffrin Minstel – deceased scientist; wife of Crown Prince Taytron Minstel; mother of Elia
Dennel – one of Lady Mavis's trusted servants
Dillain – Royal Guard
Ectosh Laocer – Royal Guard captain; secretly loves the queen
Einer Akurin – RT agent working under Gareth Restler
Eldon Altran – eldest son of Mavis and Dravid Altran, Governor Lord and First Lord of Idonia; brother of Kezem; Calia's husband, father of Emry and Jaedin
Elia Minstel – daughter of Prince Taytron Minstel and Princess Deanna Koffrin Minstel; being raised at one of Lord Kezem's estates
Gareth Restler – eldest son of Arista, Merisia's husband
Hiram Alikron – former speaker for Ashatan Council; deceased; secretly served Lord Kezem
Jolinda Ekris – Ranger Master of Healing, Ashatan Council member
Kale Corida – Ranger Master of Tracking, Ashatan Council member
Kezem Altran – youngest son of Mavis and Dravid Altran; Governor General of Idonia; Third Lord of Idonia
Kia Meetcher – daughter of Meralla and Donovan Meetcher, deceased members of the RT Alliance; being raised by Lord Kezem
Kiata Antellio Wellum – Nareth Talis Ranger; Reia's older sister; wife of Todd
Kila Creston Minstel – deceased queen of Reshner; assassinated by Niktrod Keldor; mother of Terosh

Kira McNoughten – mother of Teven, who died of Heskrin during Terosh's Kireshana
Kolknir – Kezem's agent; mercenary; former Ranger master; serves the Lady as well; trains Lucas Telon
Liam Deliad – Ranger Master of Arms, Ashatan Council member
Lucas Telon – former Ranger master, serves the Lady; trains with Kolknir; in love with the queen
Maledek – part played by both Lord Kezem Altran when he doesn't wish to reveal his identity
Mavis Altran – mother of Eldon, Mitrek, and Kezem; former princess; disowned by her father when she married Dravid Altran to escape an arranged marriage to a Gardanian prince; Teorn's elder sister; also known as the Lady
Merisia Restler – daughter of Vera and Tyko; Gareth's wife; ran away from the RT Alliance to protect her unborn child
Mitrek Altran – middle son of Mavis and Dravid Altran; Governor Judge and Second Lord of Idonia; brother of Kezem; husband of Delia; father of Silvia, Arabeth, and Sullivan
Nera Tarpon – daughter of Arista and Tobias; Brook's wife; becomes an agent for the Lady
Niklos McGreven – Ranger Healer master; substitute father for Reia and Kiata
Niktrod Keldor – man who assassinated Queen Kila; father of Ariman; grandfather of Talyon
Reia Antellio Minstel – Ranger's new queen; Kiata's younger sister; adopted by Antellio family
Talyon Keldor – RT agent; Ariman's son; Merisia's friend; Niktrod's grandson
Taytron Minstel – deceased elder son of Kila and Teorn Minstel; Terosh's brother
Teorn Minstel – deceased father of Taytron and Terosh; Mavis's younger brother
Terosh Minstel – Reshner's new king, son of Kila and Teorn Minstel
Todd Wellum – Nareth Talis Ranger, often works with his wife, Kiata
Tyko Tarpon – father of Brook, Alden, and Merisia; works for the Lady; husband of Vera
Surd Antar – Aster Captain; head of the Royal Guard; works for Kezem
Vera Tarpon – mother of Brook, Alden, and Merisia; wife of Tyko
Zareb – Elish male; twin of Covin; messenger for Prince Taytron

Creatures

Cannafitch – Thin-boned mammals with semi-hollow chest cavities that have leathery wings and can glide across vast distances. Although color can vary slightly, the majority are brown. They feed on small woodland creatures, though on rare occasions they will attempt to take on a korver or a tretling.
Camrood – Skittish beasts can be found in the wild but are often raised for racing purposes and butchered for their hides.
Ferbel – Small, fluffy rodent often raised as pets. Eaten in some regions of the planet.
Korver – Until scientists began purposefully enhancing korvers, the average animal was about a meter tall and a meter and a half from nose to tail. Genetic alterations have resulted in several specimens that are about twice as big as normal korvers. Scrappy pack animals that live and hunt together, normal korvers do not usually pose a threat to human travelers. The new breed of korver can command much larger packs, which definitely poses a threat to travelers.
Rine bats – Small winged mammals that use echo location to hunt their prey.
Shiners – Small insects that prefer dark caves or tree hollows where their inner light can make a difference. They feed primarily upon marin moss. They in turn are a food source for many species of birds.
Tretlings – Prized for their abundant wool, tretlings are hearty, yet simple creatures.
Wallays – These small, thin creatures happily burrow by the hundreds under nice, flat farmland. They harden the walls of their tunnels with a mucous-like substance called cradul. Farmers spend a lot of time and effort combatting wallays. When a wallay colony moves to a new location, the tunnel walls eventually weaken. This can lead to graveground.
Zalok – Majestic creatures that can grow several meters tall. Before the discovery that their scales could have hallucinogenic properties when treated with crela dust and heated, zalok packs dominated the many cave systems in the Riden Mountains. Scale color can vary slightly, but the most coveted color is purple.

Notable Places on Reshner
(Each city has formed its own personality over time.)

Azhel – The unofficial spiritual capital of Reshner, Azhel features temples and holy places for nearly every religion practiced on the planet. The citizens who call Azhel home tend to be calm and deeply committed to exploring spiritual matters.

Calsola – All manner of racing provides the backbone of Calsolan commerce. Although hovs, hov bikes, and even footraces have a place in Calsola, the residents have always had a special fondness for horse racing. The citizens on a whole tend to be wildly free-spirited. Fittingly, this is the first city encountered by derringers on the Kireshana.

Chara – A refined southern city located southwest of Rammon and right along the Glass Coast, Chara has the perfect climate for growing things. As such, it has cultivated quite a reputation for its famous wines and performing arts.

Estra – This sparsely populated city is located south of Chara on the poorly named southern continent called the Frozen North. The citizens here are no strangers to harsh conditions, but they are also proud of their patch of frozen paradise.

Huz Mon – Probably as noteworthy for its infamous salt mines as it is for being the second major city encountered by Kireshana derringers, Huz Mon is located just north of the Riden Flats.

Idonia – Home to the Altran family, Idonia generates most of its income by processing ore from the Nedis Crystal Mines. Idonian glass swords are prized as collectibles by those rich enough to purchase them.

Kalmata – Located near but not quite on the western coast of Reshner's habitable continent, Kalmata is known for processing salt from the West Remon Sea as well as tosh from the Imberg Tosh Mines.

Kerimia – Although not technically a city, this large village has a thriving black market, especially for firfe spice.

Korch – Nestled along the top edge of the Talmeth Mountains on the southwest corner of Reshner's habitable continent, Korch had built a reputation for being hearty. This probably springs from the difficulties of pulling a living out of the inhospitable, volcanic mountains and the dangerous Talmeth Forest. Every few years, Korch hosts the Colored Crossblades Tournament.

Meritab and Meritel – Often called the Twin Cities, Meritab and Meritel, are located southeast of the Riden Mountains and northwest of the Clear Mountains. Naturally, the nearness has produced a healthy atmosphere of friendly competition in everything from dance performances to colored-crossblades tournaments to shooting contests and even cooking competitions.

Osem – This port city mainly draws its living out of the North Asrien Sea, but Osem is also notable for its large contingent of Rangers.

Rammon – The Capital city of Reshner boasts a bustling Merchant Quarter and an elegant Palace District. Nearly every important noble house maintains a residence in the North Quarter or the West Quarter of Rammon. The East Quarter and Merchant Quarter houses most of the middle-class families. Poor folks tend to stay in the South Quarter where they can easily get jobs working for farmers on the Kevil Plains.

Resh – The city that marks roughly the half-way point of the Kireshana lives up to its name, which means "rest" in Kalastan.

Ritand – The name is shared both by a city and a fiercely independent island province northwest of the main continent. The long history of hostility between Ritand and Rammon has its roots in a family feud between two brothers from House Minstel.

Ritten – Known mainly for its many factories, Ritten takes raw materials from the Riden Mountains and the Imberg Tosh Mines and produces many of the technological wonders enjoyed in the cities. Everything from the latest model of klipper fighter to the newest comm can be found in Ritten.

Terab – Separated from the rest of the habitable continent by the Felmon Desert, Terab has developed largely apart from the rest of Reshner. Its citizens tolerate the rule of House Minstel in name and submit to royal or Ranger rulings in most legal matters, but they also keep culturally isolated from the rest of the planet.

Planets, Moons, Regions of Space

Corid – One of Reshner's three moons.
Edge Planets – a thin ring of planets that form the perimeter of known space. GAPP strongholds near the galaxy's core would love to conquer the Edge planets and use them as outposts for taming and exploring the Wilds.
Gardan – This close neighboring planet to Reshner is ruled exclusively by the Creston family. Recent history has seen some progress but mostly setbacks in efforts to align Gardan and Reshner.
Gemuln – One of Reshner's three moons.
Kalast – The long-dead planet that both Jalna Seltan and the anotechs once called home. Few know much more than that Kalast has had a strong influence upon Reshner's culture and language.
Marishaz – Reshner's largest and most majestic moon. It is named after the goddess of secrecy.
Mitra – This neighboring planet is probably most known for the Blood Harvest which sweeps away the Royal House every thousand years so none can claim a longer reign.
Porit – An edge planet close to both Reshner and Gardan, known mainly for its famous crystals and deadly vipers.
Reshner – A small, Edge planet rich in wildlife and a wide variety of plants. Reshner is ruled jointly by House Minstel, the Senate, and the Governors Council.
Wilds – A region of space that is largely unexplored. As the Core planets experience overcrowding and depletion of resources, many minds think the Wilds may hold the solutions. Unfortunately for them, Edge planets hold the key to accessing the Wilds.

Plants

Alipo – The sap found inside the delicate stems of alipo plants has mild paralytic properties that can be strengthened in combination with cormea and radon.
Amtea – The leaves of this plant can be made into a reviving tea that will counter most mildly paralytic agents and sedatives.
Astera – Both the pointed leaves and velvety petals of this delicate plant have healing applications. Blue astera petals can be boiled down to make a bitter broth which is known to cure Kemloth Fever. Adding a few wuzle roots to the broth can neutralize much of the broth's bitterness.
Cal – A strong, durable tree that grows in abundance in the Calsol Forest but can also be found elsewhere on Reshner.
Clava – A species of hearty grass that can grow nearly everywhere on Reshner.
Colbies – Small, green flowers thrive in cool, high altitude environments such as the Talmeth Mountains.
Copalas – Orange and yellow wildflowers native to the Riden Flats but spread everywhere by windstorms.
Corlia – A common plant used to relieve pain.
Cormea – This plant's leaves can deaden pain quite effectively, but too much cormea can paralyze the patient. Cormea has long been combined with radon to make stun weapons more potent.
Crela – Although used sparingly in healing substances designed to treat physical wounds, dust made from powdered crela leaves should not be ingested. Combining crela dust with powdered zalok scales and heating to just the right temperature can create a strong hallucinogen. This fact was discovered by Channer Mazai.
Dandi – The sap of this tree can be used to stick toom leaves together as bandages.
Danesque – A type of deciduous tree with strong, hearty wood sought for furniture and wooden weapons.
Dayde – Native to dark forest locations such as the Felmon Forest, dayde flowers come in a variety of fluorescent colors.
Deklov – A bitter-tasting herb that promotes faster healing.
Fireblooms – These beautiful but dangerous plants can be found everywhere on Reshner, but the most brilliant displays are located on the Ash Plains. Fireblooms come in a variety of yellows and reds, so fields of fireblooms appear to be on fire.

Fossa – A plains tree that can survive without much water.
Ira – Dried ira petals can provide a convenient, lightweight food source for Rangers traveling long distances. If treated with bastrel, ira petals will also turn flames purple, which can be handy if one needs to signal distress. Ira petals are also used to treat fever. They have a sweet, tangy scent.
Kintral – A type of evergreen tree with soft wood good for carving. The root systems of these trees have evolved to be nearly twice the length of their height because of Reshner's infamous windstorms.
Krinton – A fast-growing grain.
Marin Moss – The major food source for shiners.
Mesta – Shoots of this plant are part of the basic requirements for curing Cornada.
Mintas – A very common plant that can be found across Reshner's habitable continent. Some people believe it only has uses as a flavoring agent for teas or candy, but just as many people believe the leaves contain a relaxing agent that can cure foul moods.
Neralas – Green or gold wildflowers found in most flat areas.
Porlas – Red wildflowers found on the Balor Plains and Riden Flats. They have a very strong scent if crushed.
Quemin – Small, scrappy bushes that grow in dense patches.
Radon – Nareth Talis Rangers will combine radon, alipo sap, and cormea to give their kamad daggers the ability to safely knockout foes. Shootav pellets typically contain both cormea and radon in various amounts, depending on the intended use.
Rineth – An evergreen tree found all over the Riden Mountains.
Ristal – The wedge-shaped leaves of this mountain weed can be used to answer for several known poisons, but only skilled healers should be sent to collect it as ristal leaves resemble several other leaf-types, including a few that are poisonous.
Sanda – A staple crop for most farmers who make their living on the Riden Flats.
Sannin – Used to treat both acute and long-term aches.
Sholcas – Brilliantly white wildflowers that grow well after acid storms.
Toom – Common plants with wide, thick leaves ideal for binding wounds or creating makeshift bowls for mixing healing pastes.
Wuzle – The roots of this scrappy little grasslands plant can be used to make strong teas and broths. Ironically, although capable of turning a substance bitter, wuzle roots can also effectively cancel out other bitter substances.

Weapons and Objects

Banisticks – These weapons can be as simple or complex as the maker desires. Starting in their third year, or sooner on rare occasions, Ranger apprentices spend as much time as needed designing his or her weapon. Although it is possible to make them of soft metals, most banisticks are fashioned of kintral or danesque wood. Reia chose to use the latter wood because its softer nature takes better to carving. The tiny, curved leaves linked together are shaped like mintas leaves. Through careful arrangement, Reia also placed the likeness of astera, ristal, corlia, and ira because each represents a different aspect of the healing profession.

Criessa Darts – Darts are the most common way to inject somebody with criessa, a powerful sedative that has an unpleasant side effect of intense cold.

Flingers – These pronged throwing weapons are popular both with Kireshana derringers and Coridian Assassins.

Kamad Dagger – Beautiful and deadly, kamad daggers are highly favored by the Coridian Assassins. The graceful, gently curving edges hide sharpened teeth along the full length of the blade. These invisible teeth provide a swift way to inflict deep wounds upon an enemy. Individual blade length may vary slightly, as they are designed for a specific assassin. However, in keeping with royal tradition, each kamad dagger must bear a zalok's likeness somewhere on its handle.

Kerlak Pistol/Rifle – Kerlak weapons are based on energy. Typically, they can fire either blue or red beams. Blue beams are for stunning opponents while red beams seek to destroy. Occasionally, kerlak weapons will be created with only a blue setting, but most of these are for competitions like the annual mock-war waged between Meritab and Meritel.

Kerlinblade (fire-light blade) – In the hands of a skilled fighter, a kerlinblade offers many options for both offense and defense. Quality and functionality differ as certain kerlinblades are crafted for military purposes while others see only action in dueling arenas. Weapons created for colored-crossblades combatants tend to have a limited range for width but, a wider range of colors. The handle decorations usually have more to do with personal preference, but those wielded during team events during tournaments are much more standardized. Prince Terosh's kerlinblade was commissioned by his father, King Teorn, as a Kireshana gift.

Klipper Fighter – a single person aircraft used mainly for defense of small installations. Occasionally, klipper fighters are also used in racing and practice battles waged among the few reckless, bored, and very rich young nobles.
Serlak Pistol/Rifle – Serlak weapons fire pieces of metal. They have fallen out of favor with the nobility, but still see plenty of use as they are generally cheaper to make than kerlak firearms.
Shootav – These are relatively small, cylindrical weapons that fire pellets capable of stunning most medium sized creatures that could threaten a traveling Ranger.

Appendix II: Kalastan Language Guide

Months (all months = 30 days)

Idela - January
Lanolin – February
Jira – March
Enis – April
Retsi – May
Zeri – June
Temen – July
Allei – August
Pirua – September
Kest – October
Lalri – November
Ferrim – December

Words and Phrases

Alosoolsusonana – to success on your journey
Ashasten – great storm
Dalest Nareth – Darkest Night
Ceme – it's me
Chalmd – calm down
Dimesunarethdrims – tell me your nightmares
Dulad – second
Ehcamemastas – it would cause me much trouble
Enlivetninliv – in life and in death
Essepetraesmeaproc – this house is mine to protect
Ichonasevpetraminstel – I choose to serve House Minstel
Isercuessecaiu – I will embrace this cause
Kireshana – renewing fire journey
Neskrimda – please don't scream
Sela – dear one, daughter
Seblaetdiscurtotevons – find and disable all enemies
Totmielstom – with all my heart
Tuisola – we are alone

Healing Song

Shelsuoresfet
Abriesepalasu
Sansemasuspira.
Peremscritonsuelstom.
Peremlevesusalua
Alieucongrasi.

Idesuon
Mekeroesus.
Prasuoramantomoa.

Difetesasehsuliese.
Cremploraidesicry.
Kerosimsus
Ninqwirmessecam.

Selvafel
Shelsupertosovali.
Efnonencorponamin.
Etoiknoivalirencresonta
Jusalevteparosu
Compleame.

Ehvikerohatotpuntier
Praetonsufietahiasu.

Idesuon
Mekeroesus.
Prasuoramantomoa.

Should your ears fail
To bear these words to you
Feel them with your spirit.
Let them write upon your heart.
Let them carry your soul
To a place of safety.

I told you once
My love is yours.
May you hear it many more.

Hard as it is to see you like this.
Please believe me when I say
A love like ours
Cannot be conquered this way.

Part of me feels
Should you perish so would I.
If not in body then in mind.
Yet I know I would go on living.
Just to carry the part of you
At one with me.

If ever love had any power
May it be enough to heal you.

I told you once
My love is yours.
May you hear it many more.

www.ingramcontent.com/pod-product-compliance
Lightning Source LLC
Chambersburg PA
CBHW050912250626
47155CB00001B/207

* 9 7 8 1 9 4 2 9 2 1 2 3 3 *